HARLEY MERLIN AND THE CULT OF ERIS

Harley Merlin 6

BELLA FORREST

ONE

Harley

I wanted to make Wade cry. A searing heat burned in the pit of my belly, my very being buzzing with the vibrations of Chaos.

"You okay?" He sat across from me on a tall stool inside the Luis Paoletti Room. This place was filled with so many good and terrible memories that we should've learned by now that only extreme things happened here: kisses and explosions and brushes with death and destruction.

I nodded. "Stop worrying about me and focus on what happened to the president. Think about it clearly and hold it in your mind, or this is never going to work."

"Whatever you say, boss." He smiled and closed his eyes. I pushed my newly honed reverse Empathy into Wade. Using my powers like this was dangerous—I felt like I might rip myself apart by accident if I took one wrong step. *Go bold or go home, right?* I'd been living by that mantra ever since my Light and Dark sides had decided not to tear each other to shreds.

Wade's smile fell away, his eyebrows knitting together in a somber expression. He opened his eyes slowly, the glitter of tears sparkling in their deep-green depths. A tear fell down the side of his face and stopped at the curve of his kissable lips. *Not now, Merlin.* I was trying to make him feel sad, not turned on.

"That's crazy," O'Halloran whispered from the other side of the room. I'd gotten scarier since my meeting with Echidna and the terrible debacle with the president, and even the likes of O'Halloran had become warier around me. I didn't like that so much, but I supposed it came with the territory of being way more powerful than my peers.

It had been weeks since the president of the United Covens of America had volunteered his life so we could escape Katherine, thus allowing her to complete the second ritual in her quest to challenge a Child of Chaos. A collective despair had spread across the nation, but magical society as we knew it hadn't fallen into the disarray we'd expected. There'd been initial riots and public outcry, but that had faded away once the first, knee-jerk shock subsided. In the wake of that, a new leader had stepped up to the plate and brought the nation back from the brink of collapse.

As with any situation like this, the vice president had taken over the running of the UCA—in this case, a woman named Helena Caldwell, who seemed to be as well-loved as President Price had been. She was the hero we'd all needed in the aftermath, even though she was just doing her job. We'd worried that people would join Katherine's cause out of fear of what she might do, but Vice President Caldwell had rallied everyone back to sanity with her no-nonsense attitude and obvious adoration for the nation she served. She'd reminded everyone of what President Price had wanted for America and what his vision had been, and that did not include bowing to terrorists and psychopaths. Heck, even I'd sat and watched a couple of her speeches over breakfast, and I wasn't usually a news girl.

"We will not bend to threats of terrorism, and we will not break. We will not tolerate this regime of fear and discord. Utilizing every military force we have, we will ensure that Katherine Shipton does not succeed, not only for our own peace but for the memory of President Price. I assure you that we are working day and night to prevent her from waging her war upon innocent people, and we will triumph over evil." That had been her last speech to the public, from this morning's newsreel. She had a way with words, I had to give her that. I just hoped she had the ability to put real action behind them.

Still, even with her guidance, this new terror of Katherine Shipton remained. It was all anyone could talk about. Katherine had instilled a sense of dread amongst the magical community, and it felt like everyone was holding their breath, waiting for her to pop up again and kill someone else. To many people, it was no longer a question of "if" Katherine succeeded in her mission, but more like "when." I shared that mentality.

Personally, this newly felt terror wasn't the worst part of the second ritual's aftermath. After everything that had happened, all eyes in the magical world were firmly on me. I could feel the heat of thousands of glares and whispers, stinging me every day since my Suppressor broke. I'd become notorious, and not in the oh-so-cool superstar kind of way. There'd already been countless letters to the SDC asking that I be put away in a high-security facility until it could be proven that I was safe to be amongst "good people." Levi had relished telling me about them, letting me know that he happened to agree. At the moment, we were existing in a fragile peace—as long as I did as he asked and didn't step over the line, I could remain. But those letters were his backup, a threat, to highlight just how serious he was about getting my abilities in order.

"How are you doing that?" O'Halloran's voice brought me back into the room. Right now, he served as a constant reminder of Levi's doubt in me, as Levi had assigned O'Halloran to watch over me during any and all training sessions. It was supposedly part of his new role as preceptor, with him having taken over Nomura's duties until a replacement could be found. Meanwhile, Nomura himself was rotting away in a basement prison cell, inconsolable over losing the chance to save his son. I really did feel bad for him, but remembering what he'd done to me took some of the sting out of my pity. Being forced into astral projection will do that to a girl.

"It's just Empathy reversed," I replied, as if it was that simple. Empathy came as naturally as breathing to me, but the reverse version required a lot of mental focus and a bucketload of Chaos energy.

Tears were streaming down Wade's face now, his shoulders heaving as he sobbed. I was turning the sadness right up to eleven, just to make sure I was doing it right. But it wasn't easy to watch the man I loved in pieces, sobbing his heart out in front of me... *because* of me. If nothing else, this newfound balance had made me understand the subtext in what Marie Laveau and Papa Legba had continuously told me: *Nothing comes for free.* Now, I was realizing that it meant something far simpler than I'd first understood; it simply meant that everything in this world had consequences. Right now, me using my souped-up skills meant my boyfriend was in tears. Cause and effect, action and consequence.

Feeling slightly guilty about leaving Wade in this state, I slowly drew my reverse Empathy away from him to give him the chance to recover. The sadness faded from his eyes, his body relaxing as the misery I'd caused ebbed out.

"Man, I hope they hurry up and find someone else for this job. I'm having a hard time wrapping my head around all this new stuff." O'Halloran folded his arms across his chest and heaved out a sigh. "And, to be honest, I'm not a big fan of being a glorified babysitter. No offense."

I chuckled. "None taken."

The SDC had become as notorious as its inhabitants, so finding a replacement for Nomura was proving to be difficult. Most magicals wouldn't touch us with a ten-foot barge pole, what with all the bad news stories surrounding us lately. We weren't a joke anymore; we were a jinx. Nevertheless, the SDC was known for being the scrappy underdog, and that hadn't changed a bit. We were still on a mission to stop Katherine. The National Council was giving us absolutely zilch where intel was concerned, choosing to work exclusively with the high and mighty LA Coven, while Levi kept me in the SDC, even when the others were out on field missions. But since when had I let that stop me?

At least that gave me time to think about how to get Finch out of

Purgatory and stop Katherine from completing ritual number three. He was the only one who could get me into the Cult of Eris without Katherine and her minions immediately evaporating me, though Wade and the others still weren't sure it was a good idea to trust him. I wasn't sure either, but he was our best bet. We couldn't afford to be cautious anymore, not with Katherine two rituals in and more powerful than ever.

"Well, that was an experience," Wade said, brushing the tears from his cheeks.

"You can say that again," O'Halloran muttered.

"You scared of me, O'Halloran?" I teased.

He snorted. "Not in the slightest."

"You sure about that? Everyone seems petrified of me these days." I took a deep breath and brought the magic back inside me. "Although, if it wasn't for me, you'd be out of a babysitting job."

He laughed. "Levi's just terrified of powerful magicals. He quakes when he's around his own kid. Tragic, really."

"I'm inclined to agree." Wade took a shaky breath, checking himself over as if to make sure he was all there.

"You really think that's all this is?" I was genuinely curious. O'Halloran knew more about Levi than any of us, except for Raffe.

"Of course it is." He waved his hand. "All of this nonsense with you is just a knee-jerk reaction to that power play you made after Echidna. He doesn't forget things easily, especially not being made to look tiny in front of people he thinks are beneath him. You embarrassed him, and he's punishing you. Simple."

"It's still annoying though, right?" I grinned at him.

"*Very* annoying, but also pretty interesting," he replied, glancing at Wade. "Makes you wonder what the hell the California Mage Council ever saw in him in the first place. He's like a spoiled kid. But, hey, I'm not part of the elite. What would I know? I've got no clue how those people make their decisions. It could be names in a hat for all I know."

Wade smiled. "That would explain a *lot* of things."

O'Halloran fixed his gaze on Wade. "That reverse Empathy stuff is pretty neat. I've never seen it done before. All my years as a trainer, and I'm still learning." He seemed pleased by the notion. "You think it would work on me?"

"Only one way to find out." I turned toward O'Halloran and pushed my Empathy into him, twisting the vibrations of Chaos so my target felt what I wanted him to feel. I had no idea whether this would work, with O'Halloran being a Shapeshifter, but I had to try. "What kind of bees make milk?"

"Harley..." Wade had a warning tone in his voice.

O'Halloran frowned. "I don't know, what kind of bees make milk?"

"Boobees." I surged a wave of amusement into him as I delivered the punchline of my favorite dad joke. Within seconds, he'd cracked up so hard that he'd collapsed on the floor in a fit of hysterics, clutching his stomach as he wheezed out laughter.

"Boobees!" Tears streamed down his face as he pounded his fist into the floor, barely able to breathe, he was howling so hard. Wade stared at him as if he'd just lost his mind, while I grinned with satisfaction. My reverse Empathy was definitely taking on some new flavors here, but I didn't mind using it to make people laugh instead of cry. Especially on a Shapeshifter, as normally I had no way of reading them. *Now to see how far I can push it.*

"What did you do that for?" Wade asked, smirking at the sight of O'Halloran in hysterics. The guy didn't laugh a whole lot. I figured he could use a chuckle.

"You'll see," I replied, keeping my attention on O'Halloran. "Do you know what progress the National Council has been making with Katherine?" He was psychologically weakened and ridiculously relaxed from all the laughing, which gave me the perfect gateway to ask something important. It had worked with Mallenberg, though I didn't like to remember that too much, and I hoped it would work with O'Halloran, too.

He held his chest as he spluttered out a few more chuckles. "Boobees, man. That slayed me." He looked up at me with dopey eyes. "Funny you should mention the National Council; there's been word from one of our agents that the Cult of Eris might have a mole. We're due to receive some important intel about the location of the Recruiter's favorite playground."

"Playground?" Wade chimed in, now intrigued. *See, nothing to worry about.*

"Yeah, it's where their Recruiter goes to meet potential new cult members." O'Halloran's expression suddenly changed to one of shock, as if he'd just realized what had come out of his mouth. Immediately, I loosened my hold on him and dragged the Chaos energy back into me, kicking and screaming.

"You okay?" I tried to put on an innocent smile, but I could sense he knew what I'd just done. I'd broken down his defenses and used my reverse Empathy as an interrogation technique. Even O'Halloran, for all his good humor, wasn't going to take kindly to that. *We can't be cautious.* The time for a softly-softly approach was over. And, with Levi keeping me from leaving the SDC, I had to take my shots where I could, even if that ended with me feeling a stab of guilt.

"Fine," he muttered, as he got up and dusted himself off. "I think that's enough training for today."

"But I was just—" I tried to protest, but he cut me off.

"I said that's enough for today." He shot me a look that was equal parts sullen and worried. "Don't breathe a word about what I've just said, do you understand? Otherwise, Levi will send you *and* me to Alaska."

"I won't say anything." I turned to Wade for reassurance, but he looked torn, as if he'd just witnessed something he didn't quite like. O'Halloran stormed toward the door. I really did feel bad about manipulating someone I respected, but we needed to get this show on the road, and I'd learned something *very* valuable from it.

So, you've got a mole in your midst, Katherine? There was a delicious irony to that.

TWO

Harley

"Did you just… interrogate *O'Halloran?*" Wade asked as we left the Luis Paoletti Room. "I thought the guy had a mind of steel. How did you manage that?"

He stared at me with surprise. Of all the people in the coven, the members of the Rag Team were the only ones who weren't frightened by me, and I didn't want that to change. Especially not with him, not after how far we'd come together.

"You know how people say that dad jokes are a form of torture?" I tried to suppress a smile.

"Tell me you aren't about to start a new career as a stand-up comic."

I grinned. "No, but you could say I dad-joked him into submission. Turns out the folks who say that aren't wrong. In the right circumstances, it gets the job done."

"I've never seen him so pissed off. You really shouldn't do that without people's permission."

"He *did* give me permission. He asked me to try it on him, remember?" I knew Wade was right, but I wanted to ease the uncomfortable knot in my stomach.

"He won't make that mistake again." Wade's expression turned thoughtful. "So, the National Council suspects there's a mole in the Cult of Eris..."

"And they'll be finding out where our favorite lion-woman likes to hang out. O'Halloran called it a 'playground,' but that better not be literal. If she's going after more kids, I'll wring her furry neck." I glowered at the thought of Naima.

"Hey, she still has an unfulfilled wish to snap mine, so you'd better get in there first."

I looked up at Wade shyly. "You can count on it."

He met my gaze and pulled me to a halt, leaning in to kiss me tenderly on the lips. The rest of the coven melted away as I looped my arms around that neck Naima wanted to snap and kissed him back with heartfelt desire. He was the one good thing to have come out of the wreckage. It felt weird to put a label on what we were, but we were officially a couple now, and that was just... amazing.

"So, where to now, since you've put O'Halloran in a foul mood and stunted your training for the day?" Wade smiled as he pulled away, interlacing his fingers with mine.

"Infirmary."

"Why, are you sick?" He jumped into Crowley protection mode, which made my heart swell with affection. He'd been obsessed with my wellbeing since the Suppressor break, which was both cute and sort of annoying. At every meal, I found more food being shoveled onto my plate and an endless supply of superfood smoothies, with a side dish of vitamin pills, being slid across the table toward me.

I shook my head. "No, I want to talk to Krieger about Ephemeras to see if he can make one to help me and Finch with the cult infiltration." Ephemeras were the one-use magical artifacts that could take the power of another and give it to someone else. I'd been thinking about them for a while, knowing having one in our possession might come in handy for infiltrating either Purgatory or the cult itself.

Wade froze beside me, his muscles tightening. "This again?"

"What do you mean, 'this again?' Of course it's 'this again.' Until we can get Finch out of there and get on with stopping the third ritual, it's always going to be 'this again.' You won't change my mind that this is our best shot."

"I'm not saying it's not our best shot, but I still don't think it's a good idea to get Finch involved. He's a loose cannon at best, a very clever double agent at worst."

I cast him a withering look. "Katherine tried to have him killed, Wade. He's not a double agent anymore. Loose cannon, maybe, but he's not still working for her. No way. You saw him yourself—he's done with her."

"She's his mother, Harley. He'll never be done with her."

"He'll never be able to forgive that kind of betrayal. I genuinely believe in his hatred of her, if nothing else. That's enough to put him on our side."

He shrugged. "You want to put all of our trust in a ball of hate?"

"Beats the alternative. I'd say putting all our eggs in one hateful basket is a pretty savvy thing to do. Hate is powerful. You just have to look at Katherine to know how true that is." I smiled at him and squeezed his hand, even though we were bickering. "Love is powerful, too. Katherine killed Adley, and Finch won't forgive that, either."

He turned toward me and lifted his hand to my face, brushing my cheek with his thumb. He looked torn, as if he wanted to really let loose with his thoughts, but he didn't know if he should. We were still trying to work out the kinks in our new dynamic, and learning to keep business and pleasure separate was proving to be the hardest part. I'd lost track of the times we'd been kissing or snuggled up with a movie, only to end up talking about Levi and the National Council. They weren't exactly mood-setting topics, that was for sure.

Regardless, my heart still pounded like a caged kangaroo every time I was near him, and the pure love and desire radiating out of him let me know he felt the same. We could bicker as much as we liked, and we'd still want to get all tangled up with each other afterward. That was the way we'd always been, aside from the tangling... but I liked that change very much, especially now that I knew the Suppressor had nothing to do with it. The desire to tear open Wade's very expensive shirts was all my own, no Suppressor leak necessary. *Starting to sound like a maniac now, Merlin.*

"I'm just worried, that's all," he said with a sigh.

"You're always worried."

He smirked. "Even so, this situation has me even more worried than normal."

"The breaking into Purgatory part?"

He shook his head. "That's risky, which is putting it mildly, but the bit that comes after that worries me the most. Finch's offer to help might just be a ploy to get himself out of Purgatory. What if he makes a run for it once he's free?"

"He wants revenge on Katherine as much as we do. He won't run. He won't have the chance to."

"You're infuriating, do you know that?" He took his hand from my face and dragged me along the corridor toward the infirmary. *Victory!*

I chuckled. "You do tend to tell me at any given opportunity."

"Okay, Ephemeras aside for now, considering how rare they are, how would we even begin to go about getting Finch out of Purgatory? Hypothetically speaking, of course."

I grinned. "Of course. Well, I've actually been thinking about using Santana and her—" My voice died on my lips as Levi came barreling around the corner, with Alton at his side. Like a guilty schoolboy, Wade dropped my hand and put his arms behind his back, which made me stifle a giggle.

"Oh. You two." Levi shot us both his customary glare, which I ignored.

"Good afternoon, Harley, Wade." Alton dipped his head in a little bow and flashed us a conspiratorial smile. He'd stayed on as Levi's assistant after everything that had happened, but it was still strange to see him in such a lowly position.

Levi eyed me curiously. "I hope you're not up to anything untoward. You're to keep to the coven and refrain from doing anything reckless. I realize that's a constant struggle for you, but I must insist upon it." His tone was cold and distant, though his eyes burned with the familiar contempt I'd gotten used to.

I gave him a saccharine smile. "Who, me? Wouldn't dream of it."

"After the mess you made with the president, I don't want you anywhere near the investigation against Katherine. Do I make myself clear?" He puffed out his chest like an overstuffed pigeon.

For the millionth time, geez. "You've made yourself very clear, Director Levi. I've just been training with O'Halloran, and now I'm off to… uh, attend to some business regarding my abilities. A bit of research. I trust that's okay with you?"

It was getting increasingly difficult to play the part of diligent magical, when all I wanted to do was scream at him that this was as much my fight as anyone else's, if not more. Then again, I wasn't about to give him the satisfaction of a slinging match. It was in my best interest to stay on his good side.

He arched an eyebrow. "Hmm. Well then, I suppose that's agreeable."

"Thank you, Director." I gave a small bow, similar to Alton's, and kept the sweet smile on my face.

You're getting good at this. I didn't know if it was the increase of Chaos inside me or what, but my ability to be calculated and deceitful was becoming particularly sharp. I wondered if that made me more like Katherine, but I quickly brushed the thought away. No, my manipulation was just a means of getting closer to Katherine and her cult so I could achieve my end goal of destroying them. The old rules didn't apply anymore.

"I must reiterate how dangerous you've become," Levi continued, just when I thought he'd stopped. "Your very presence here may endanger us all, given the loose grip you have over your supposed 'balance.' I, for one, do not believe you have achieved any balance at all."

"I take it that means I'm still not allowed to do any investigative work? Even outside of the Katherine Shipton issue?" I asked wryly.

"Not until you have truly mastered these abilities of yours. You're not permitted to join in the investigation against Katherine, nor will you leave the premises. We will leave the hunt for Katherine in the more capable hands of the National Council and their security teams. You are much too personally involved in this to think clearly and act rationally."

You mean, the security teams who failed to protect President Price? I held my tongue, but I thought it with every fiber of my being. "I'm aware of that, Director, which is why I'm spending so much time studying and training—so that I can master these abilities." I was surprised by the calm, even tone in my voice, and it seemed to shock Levi and Alton, too.

"Technically speaking, you're also a victim of Katherine's," Levi droned on. Behind him, Alton rolled his eyes, and I fought to push down a snort of laughter. It was good to see that Alton was still on our side, even though he'd buddied up with Levi.

"I remind myself of that every day, Director," I replied.

He scowled, clearly annoyed by my serene behavior. He wanted me to scream and howl at the injustice as much as I wanted to give that to him, but he wasn't getting any kind of rise out of me. No way, José. He'd have to deal with this new, obedient, pleasant me, whether he liked it or not.

"Well then, I'll let you continue on with your day." He turned to look at Wade, who'd been silent the whole time. "Keep a tight leash on Miss Merlin, if you would. We can't have her running off as she pleases."

What, am I not standing here anymore? I kept my face calm, but inside, I was seething. What was I, some kind of dog to be kept at heel? If he thought that way, I wondered why he didn't just throw me in one of the Bestiary boxes and get it over with. Then he could come and sneer at me from a safe distance, without fear of me biting back.

"Yes, Director Levi." Wade nodded, but I could sense he was seething too.

"Do not disappoint me again, Crowley," Levi hissed. He hadn't forgotten Wade's failed spying attempt and the betrayal of discovering that he had used that trust against him.

Levi walked away, joined by Alton, who cast an apologetic look back over his shoulder before the two of them disappeared around the corner. I wondered where they'd been headed, and why he'd doubled back on himself, but Levi was a mystery. He'd no doubt just wanted to save face by not having to walk past us.

"Speaking of wringing necks," Wade said through gritted teeth. "Who does he think he is, speaking to you like that? I swear to any god listening, if he speaks to my girlfriend like she's some kind of animal again, I'll put him on his ass."

My cheeks flushed with heat. Although we'd decided we were going to be official, we'd never actually used the words "boyfriend" and "girlfriend" in front of each other before. And I just couldn't resist the temptation to tease him a little bit. After all, what were girlfriends for?

"You just wanted to say 'girlfriend,' didn't you?" I flashed him a mischievous grin.

"Maybe, but that's beside the point. I mean it, if he speaks to you like that again, I don't care what it does to my reputation, I'll send him packing with his tail between his legs." He cast me a shy smile that turned my insides to jelly.

"He's just marking his territory. We should be grateful he isn't peeing in corners or squatting in the hallways."

Wade chuckled. "He's done one good thing by talking to you like that, though."

"Oh?"

"I wasn't sure about this whole Finch thing at first, but we're doing it. The only thing is, we'll need some serious help to pull it off."

THREE

Harley

"What did Tobe say?" I asked. We'd come to a halt in the hallway while Wade gave Tobe a call. We needed to get the gang together, fast, and hatch a plan. Tobe had asked that we keep him involved so he could cover for us if he needed to.

"He can't leave the Bestiary. If we want him to be part of this, we need to go to him."

I nodded. "I'll send out a text, get everyone to meet us there."

"Good idea. Do you want Krieger to be there?"

"We can't do this without him." I took out my phone and sent out a group text, to get everyone to join us in the Bestiary, with a note to Jacob to pick Krieger up on the way. I got the feeling he'd already be in the infirmary with the good doctor, trying to break ground on the magical detector.

Fifteen minutes later, we were all gathered together inside one of the emptier halls in the Bestiary, away from the prying eyes and ears of the security personnel. Tobe was his usual stoic self, finishing off the last of his rounds before he joined us. He was giving nothing away, though I sensed his anxiety. He didn't like being on the shadier side of the law. Isadora and Louella had joined us, too, though Garrett was away on LA business. Meanwhile, Krieger seemed clueless as to why he'd been brought along, but it would all become clear to him soon enough.

"So, what trouble are we getting ourselves into this time? We blowing the doors off Purgatory or what?" Santana asked, with a mischievous smile. We all understood the gravity of the situation we were in, but I could always rely on Santana to lighten our spirits. Right now, we needed a little morale boost.

"Easy there, Ocean's Eleven," I replied.

She tutted at me. "Wrong movie, but I'll let it slide."

"Well, we're not quite blowing the doors off, but we do need to get Finch out of there." I looked around the group and noted the dubious expressions. "I know you all think he's a psycho, and I mostly agree, but he's the best tool we've got against Katherine and the Cult of Eris."

"'Tool' is the right word," Santana muttered.

Wade stepped up beside me. "If we don't use Finch, then we have nothing else to go on. He knows all about the third ritual and what it requires, and he's the only one with insider knowledge of the Cult of Eris and how Katherine runs the place. If we try to infiltrate without him, we'll probably end up dead."

"Bright and breezy way to start the day. Is it doom and gloom o'clock already?" Raffe chimed in, checking an imaginary watch on his wrist. Clearly, spending so much time with Santana had rubbed off on him. A nervous chuckle rippled around the group, but I could see they understood: it was Finch or bust.

Tatyana folded her arms across her chest. "The third ritual—consume the spirit of thine greatest enemy, in the Land of Erebus, on All Hallows' Eve. That spirit is Hester, and Katherine has her spirit trapped somewhere, ready to use." She paused. "Are you absolutely sure Finch knows where Hester's spirit is, and he's not just feeding you this to buy his way out of Purgatory?"

I'd told them all about my last conversation with Finch, and they'd been just as unimpressed as they were right now. Finch was a total risk, and I wasn't pretending otherwise, but without him we were at a complete loss. Katherine's strength was already way beyond anything we'd encountered, and we couldn't risk her getting even more power-ful. Otherwise, we might as well start practicing our groveling now.

Krieger raised his hand. "I apologize, but I have absolutely no idea what's going on here."

"Katherine is moving toward completing the third ritual—the one Tatyana just mentioned, with all the 'thines' and stuff," Jacob replied. "We need to stop her before she can complete it, for obvious reasons. But the only way we can do that, apparently, is to break Finch Shipton out of prison. He knows where Hester's spirit is—or, he says he does—and he wants to help us infiltrate the Cult of Eris to track the spirit down and stop Katherine. That's pretty much it, in a nutshell."

I nodded. "Only, she's much stronger now. I can't face her alone, not if I have to go in completely blind, with no idea what I'm looking for."

"And Finch can't just *tell* you where the spirit is?" Krieger replied.

"That isn't part of his deal, unfortunately. He told me he'd have to show me where the spirit was—it isn't something he can just tell me." I realized how it sounded, but we didn't have any other options. The National Council had the same information about Hester's spirit as we did, and they'd had zero luck finding a way into the Cult of Eris. Last I'd heard, a few of their agents were already dead, after risking several attempts to go undercover. With their numbers and skills, that said something for our current scenario. We needed an edge, and that edge was Finch.

Isadora tapped the side of her jaw in thought. "Why hasn't the National Council tried to strike a deal with Finch?"

I shrugged. "He'll only work with me. He thinks the National Council members are puffed-up, smug bastards with snazzy magical tools that don't serve any real purpose. He doesn't want anything to do with them."

Tobe chuckled. "I do not like to say so, but it would appear Finch has a point. They really are all flashing gizmos and no substance."

"Gizmos?" I laughed at the word coming out of Tobe's mouth.

"I have picked up some useful lingo in my thousand-plus years on this earth. 'Gizmo' has a rather pleasant mouthfeel." He looked pleased with himself, though he likely shared the same fears as the rest of us. This was probably the biggest risk we'd taken so far, but that was just it... we *had* to take it.

"Mouthfeel and gizmos aside," Wade cut in, "Katherine is likely forging ahead with her plan to complete the third ritual as we speak. So, if Finch is willing to work with Harley, and Harley only, then we might as well do this. Believe me, I'm as worried as the rest of you, but there isn't another way." I felt a wave of concern bristle off him, directed at me.

Dylan grinned. "The way I see it, if we have a shot at taking this bitch down, then we have to grab it by the horns and run."

Louella shook her head. "I understand the need to get this done, but if Finch really was the reformed criminal that he claims to be, then surely he'd swallow his pride and work with the National Council on this to bring Katherine in. Instead, he's pushing Harley into committing an actual crime by busting him out of the magical world's most secure prison. Maybe I'm missing something, but it doesn't make sense to me."

From the mouths of babes...

I cast her a reassuring look. "I think this has turned into something deeply personal for Finch. It's not just about his views on the National Council; it's about Katherine and the things she's done to him... and, I guess, to me. He was brainwashed before, but when Katherine killed Adley, everything changed. Finch loved Adley, and Katherine had her murdered, before trying to have him wiped out, too. Her own son."

Raffe nodded. "That's got to sting a bit."

"Yep. Plus, she couldn't even do it herself. She sent minions to do her dirty work, and he resents the fact that she couldn't even face him," I went on. "Although, she probably wouldn't hesitate now, if she had the chance."

Astrid pulled a grim face. "And she sent Kenneth Willow, of all people. The wannabe son."

"Ah yes, the budding psychopath with mommy issues all his own."

Isadora gave a wry laugh. After all, she'd been locked up by Katherine; she'd seen Kenneth in action and been forced to watch as his violent streak was let loose on children.

"Basically, Finch is against the regular magical institutions because they haven't done him any favors, and they mean nothing to him." I fixed my gaze on every member of the Rag Team, willing them to come over to my way of thinking. "He doesn't trust the National Council not to simply throw him back in prison once all of this is over and never let him out again, and he sure as heck doesn't trust the California Mage Council to hold up their end of the bargain, either. *If* he were to make one with them, that is."

"So, his endgame *is* to stay out of Purgatory?" Dylan replied.

"That seems to be the deal, yeah." I hated the words as soon as they came out of my mouth, but they were the truth. "I'm the only one he trusts to keep my end of the deal."

"And you would do that?" Krieger asked. "I'm not judging, but I wish to be clear on the details."

"It's not a bad deal if it means we can stop Katherine. The only person he wants to hurt is Katherine, and I'm all for that." I couldn't help wondering what Garrett would think of all this Finch business if he were here. Fortunately, he wasn't, so that was one less thing to worry about. "And, hey, I'm not saying we don't send Finch straight back to Purgatory. I'm just saying that once this is done, we make a case for him, try to get him his freedom."

Wade nodded. "If this is the only way Finch will help, then we should accept it. We're in dire straits right now, and All Hallows' Eve is only a week away. Time is running out, and… well, if Katherine succeeds with the ritual, then we're even more screwed than we are now."

I knew he'd stopped himself from saying something else. I was pretty sure he'd wanted to say, "and we have to be prepared this time," but he'd stopped to spare my feelings. I was grateful he hadn't said it out loud, but it was something I wholeheartedly agreed with. I didn't want to do a botched, half-assed job this time. This time, I wanted to get it right and put an end to her, once and for all.

"And, since it looks like we're going down this route, we do have a plan for breaking into Purgatory, right?" Astrid asked.

"That's where you come in." I flashed a nervous smile at the Rag Team. "Santana, I was hoping I could borrow one of your Orisha duplicates, as a replacement for Finch. It has to be convincing, but I know you've got no problems with that. I just need it to work without you in Purgatory with it. Can that be done?"

Santana thought for a moment. "I'd need a sample of Finch's hair or blood to make a good copy, but the distance thing shouldn't be a problem. If I ask really nicely, the Orishas can sometimes take on a physical form that's much more alive and alert than the duplicates I've used in the past. Let's just hope they're feeling generous." She smiled at me, but I could see the trepidation lurking beneath the surface.

"You'll have to make one for Harley, too," Raffe interjected.

"I was getting to that," she chided playfully. "I have terms of my own before I give you the two Orishas—one for Finch, one for you, to cover your ass while you're out of the coven. I'll have to make a better one for you, too, since the last duplicate didn't work out so well. Something a bit more realistic."

I frowned. "What terms?"

"I'm still not convinced that Finch is as reformed as he's making out. Even if he is, people died because of him, and that can't just be swept under the rug. So, if you want the Orishas, you have to promise me that you'll take Finch straight back to Purgatory, where he can make an official case to be set free—you have to swear to me you won't waver and just let him go. I know you've already said you're aiming for a legal release, but I want you to promise. After we're done with Katherine, of course. I'm not an idiot." She grinned at the others, but it didn't reach her eyes.

"You can definitely make these souped-up duplicates?" I wanted to be sure before I made any more deals, even if I agreed with her and she was my friend.

She nodded. "For sure. If I'm smart, which I am, the magical world won't even know that Finch is out until it's all over. He can make his case once he's proven himself to be one of the good guys, from the comfort of his cell. And, if he screws us over, he'll have a horde of pissed security personnel after him. He might be a Shapeshifter, but I doubt he can outrun the authorities forever, and we can just pretend we had nothing to do with it. Once my Orisha evaporates back into its spiritual form, it will be untraceable. This way, it's a win-win for everyone, and Finch will have to make amends the proper way."

"As long as he gets to make a case for himself, with our support, I don't see why he'd argue. And we'll have no reason not to help him if he does this for us without screwing us over," I said, though doubts churned over in my stomach. Santana was right to be cautious—Finch had killed people with his gargoyle attack, and that couldn't be easily pardoned. I didn't know if he could use temporary insanity as a defense, but at least he'd have more chance of gaining permanent freedom if he played by the rules.

"So that's a promise? No wavering?" Santana pressed.

"Cross my heart."

"Then I'll do it. Two sentient duplicates, coming right up."

Raffe nodded. "I'll stay with Santana here, to make sure she's got all the energy, peace, and coffee she needs to be parted from two Orishas at once."

"It'll take its toll on me, but if it's not for too long then I should be okay. I've been getting better at it since Levi outed my last duplicates. Now I've got more accuracy, and I know how to build improved versions, mostly thanks to Louella. She really is a research demon." Santana smiled at our youngest member, who blushed.

"It was just a couple of books I thought you'd find helpful," she murmured, embarrassed.

"Wait... so is it just *you* going into the Cult of Eris with Finch?" Tatyana narrowed her eyes.

I grimaced. "Yep."

Wade stiffened at my side. I knew he hated that I'd have to go in alone, more or less.

Tobe frowned. "You should consider using an alternative method of deceit for when you infiltrate the cult, Harley—a believable excuse for you to be away, without arousing Levi's suspicions. I fear he is on to you, especially where duplicates are concerned, and I would hate for him to catch wind of this... although I am a neutral observer, as you know."

Krieger nodded. "Levi might suspect something if you were to use the duplicates long-term, and Santana might be drained of energy while you're away, or while Finch is supposed to be in his cell. It's a very real possibility."

"I agree. That's the last thing we need," Astrid added.

"I'd like to go with you and Finch while you're undercover in the Cult of Eris," Wade blurted out. "You shouldn't undertake this on your own, and I'd feel better if you had a member of the Rag Team with you."

As an impartial observer, naturally.

"As long as we can make enough Ephemeras, I'm happy to have you along for the ride." I glanced up at him, feeling glad I wasn't going to be so alone after all.

Krieger cleared his throat. "It might be best, then, if you come straight to the infirmary once your plans are set to free Finch. Jacob can assist you with portals on this mission, as you certainly won't be able to utilize the mirror to Purgatory, since Levi will notice."

I shook my head. "I'm not sure we can actually portal into the prison, Doctor. There are alarms rigged to go off at the slightest intrusion."

"I have something that will help with that," Astrid cut in. "I got Smartie to delve into some pretty top-secret stuff, with a little help from Alton, the moment this started to look like it might be a plan. He managed to pull up the blueprints of Purgatory in quite a lot of depth. With those blueprints, I'm sure I could find a place you could portal in, undetected. I can also make a gap in the security field around Finch's cell, to stop any alarms from going off when you portal in. It'll be tricky, but it should work, as long as Jacob hits the right mark."

Jacob paled. "I'll do my best." We had to rely on Jacob instead of Isadora, as Levi insisted on daily meetings with her. If she went missing for a while, he'd know about it, and we didn't know how long we'd need to break in and out of Purgatory. He knew about Jacob now, but Isadora had managed to persuade him that Jacob was a novice with extremely shaky skills, framing him as a risk we couldn't readily use. It made him the perfect choice, even though I still hated putting him in the line of fire.

"You'll have to focus precisely on the location I give you," Astrid said.

"Yeah… Yeah, I can do that."

Isadora shot me a worried look. "You will have to be quick about it, if this is what you've decided to do. And you must be careful. Any alert to what you're doing, and your neck will be on the line. I don't want to have to watch that happen. We'll do everything we can to prevent it."

Tatyana nodded. "Be careful. This is bigger than anything we've ever done. None of us want to see you in Purgatory for this."

"Thank you," was all I could say, though the words lodged behind a lump in my throat. There was so much at stake, and I didn't know if being careful would be enough. The fact remained: if I wanted to keep Wade and myself out of Purgatory, I'd have to use every weapon in my arsenal to keep our entire mission from crumbling.

No pressure, Merlin. Nope, none at all.

FOUR

Finch

A *nother day in paradise.*
I stood from my brick of a mattress and walked to the glass panel. Same view. Same guards on rotation. Same old Purgatory. I was sick of the sight of glass and chrome. If I never saw that architectural mix again, I'd die happy.

I banged on the glass until I got their attention. For folks who were supposed to be watching me, they had a nasty habit of ignoring me. Imbeciles.

"What is it, Shipton?" A gruff beast who'd downed too many steroids opened the grate.

"I'm starting to smell." I smiled sweetly, though I wanted to punch him in the nose. Officer Grimshaw was my chosen nemesis in this place. Grim by name, grim by nature. He hated me, I hated him. It was a veritable love story.

"And?"

"Human rights mean anything to you?" I shot back.

"You don't deserve 'em."

I narrowed my eyes. "I need a shower. Or I could just douse myself in the water from the toilet. You'd like that, wouldn't you?"

"As it happens, I would."

"I'll go quietly." My face twisted up in a smirk.

Officer Grimshaw sighed and turned to his boyfriend. "We got showers free? This one wants to make himself all pretty."

This one? I'd become a number in a cell. No name, just a box and a set of rules as long as my arm. But I was pretty sure I'd get the last laugh on this one.

Officer Chalmers, who was anything but charming, stepped up to the door and pulled back the hefty bolt. *That's it, boys.* They knew I wouldn't make a run for it. What would be the point? There was nowhere to run. Not that it stopped the thought from crossing my mind. Human instinct at its finest. Fight or flight.

"Wrists," Grimshaw ordered.

"Yes, sir." With a grin, I pushed my arms through the grate. A moment later, I was clapped in Atomic Cuffs. My favorite. I loved the way they just drained the life out of me and made me feel like a slug. The guards had allowed me to be in my cell without the Cuffs, after the whole you-almost-got-murdered-because-your-hands-were-tied thing, which was nice of them. *Small mercies.* Besides, no magic could breach the walls of this cell or bust open the door. I couldn't exactly stage a breakout.

At least I'd get a walk out of this experience. Apparently, a person can go mad if they're left locked up, pacing the floor. It was probably too late on that front. I had Shipton blood in me—madness was par for the course.

"Don't try anything funny, Shipton." Chalmers opened the door with a reluctant grimace. I wondered if it was a requirement to look like the back end of a garbage truck in order to work here. The guards all shared a grizzled, pumped-up quality that made me think they'd done time themselves or had been in a lumberyard for the past decade.

"What am I, a criminal?" The guards yanked me out of my cell and dragged me toward the showers.

"Shut your mouth, Shipton." Grimshaw shoved me in the back. Real nice.

Since my mother's failed attempt to murder me, these goons had been all over me like a rash. I'd almost been killed, yet *I* was the one under twenty-four seven watch. Ah, the logic of the judicial system. The stupid woman couldn't even be bothered to do it herself. But the solution was simple, really: watch the damned cameras and give a hoot if someone they didn't recognize waltzed in, or if someone they *did* recognize was acting shifty as heck. Why was I being punished for their idiotic mistake?

Walking along the ridiculous steel walkways, I contemplated jumping over the edge. Not seriously, of course, but it'd be five seconds of fun before I went splat at the bottom. Instead, I focused on the route ahead. So very familiar to me now. I'd lost track of the number of times I'd made this trip. Back and forth, always in chains. With no parole on my sentence, I was looking at a lifetime of this. *Yeah, not if I can help it.*

Soon enough, we arrived at the private shower block. Nobody else was allowed in while I was showering, aside from a bunch of burly guys in Kevlar. Any boy's dream, right? I stripped and stepped under the surprisingly hot water. There was something about showers that made me thoughtful. No idea why. The running water cascading over your face, blocking out the noise when it got in your ears. Only, I didn't like it when my brain took over. I had a problem with overthinking. Especially these days, when I had nothing to do but think.

Sliding down the wall, I sat under the hot torrent. It reminded me of being a kid at the Anker house. That really was a lifetime ago. I used to sit in the shower to forget about my day—the kids calling me "freak" and stuff. I didn't know, back then, that my mother had made me like this.

Why'd you do it, Katherine? Why'd you make me this way? "Nurture" definitely hadn't been in her vocabulary. I felt stupid, now, when I thought of how intently I'd hung on her every word. True abandoned-kid syndrome. I'd done so many things for her, and for what? To get a knife in the throat? I'd never been a son to her, just an object she could use. It had taken Adley to make me see that, but I hadn't been able to save her any more than I'd been able to save myself. I kept thinking,

Hey, at least I'm not dead. But maybe I'd have been better off six feet under.

Weirdly, Harley seemed to understand. She didn't forgive what I'd done with the gargoyles, but she saw that I didn't forgive myself, either. Even when Katherine had asked me to release those beasts, I'd had doubts about it. I'd wondered what Adley would think. If I had told her at the time, she'd probably have given me a pitying look and said something like, "That's not who you are, love. You don't have to prove anything to anybody." Something stupidly empathetic like that, because for some reason she never saw me as the monster I was. It didn't matter now, though. What was done was done, and any respect I'd had for my mother had died along with Adley.

"What are you doing in there?" Chalmers's voice split the calm sound of running water.

"Singing showtunes, what do you think?" I taunted.

"Well, pack it in and get yourself washed. We've got other things to attend to."

I got up and reached for the standard-issue shampoo-slash-body-wash-slash-paint-thinner. A nice bag of chemicals in a soap dispenser. It was no wonder my dye had washed out. This stuff was stronger than bleach. Grabbing a handful, I ran it through my hair until the suds stung my eyes. A little pain reminded me why I was here. Why I was still breathing. I wouldn't stop until Katherine was dead. I'd make her pay for what she'd done, with Harley's help. That was still strange for me to get my head around.

After so many years of lapping up everything my mother had told me and sipping her poison, Harley had appeared out of nowhere and thrown my entire world for a loop. She'd held a mirror up to me, and I didn't like what I saw. Typical family business. It amused me to picture us all around the table at Christmas—me, Harley, Katherine, Hester, Hiram. I doubted we'd even get through the entrees before someone wound up dead in their soup.

I glanced down at the dappled pattern of bruises across my skin. I'd healed well after the attempted assassination, but my ego would take a bit more work. Washing away the suds, I grabbed a towel and dried myself off. My sexy prison uniform lay on the bench opposite. I dressed quickly and headed out to the guards. They scowled at me like I'd smeared dog crap on the walls, before hauling me back to my cell.

"That's your last one for a week, Shipton," Grimshaw hissed.

I shrugged. "It's your funeral. You've got to smell me."

Heading back, I peered into the cells we were passing. I didn't do it very often. All around me, the cells were filled with serial killers, terrorists, every kind of "-phile," the worst types imaginable. And I was among them. Some looked like celebrities or ordinary people—femme fatales, good-looking jocks, and hunched retirees. Others looked exactly like you'd expect a killer to look, with missing teeth, weird tattoos, black eyes, jacked arms. Compared to them, what I'd done was nothing. *Yeah, but you got a lot of people killed. You did what they did. You just went about it a different way.*

I shuddered at the thought. I didn't want to spend my life here. I didn't want to be labeled the same way as these creeps. Katherine had been my general, and I'd been her soldier. I was only following orders.

The Nazis said the same thing. My brain had a habit of pulling me up like that. I called it my split personality, but there was more than one inside me. Anyway, after everything that had happened, my personalities were sort of blurring into one. A better me, I hoped. One that Adley would have kept loving, if she were still here. One that she could have forgiven.

I jolted as Grimshaw pushed me back into my cell, sending me sprawling to the floor. I shot him a dirty look over my shoulder, but he just laughed. Assholes, the lot of them. If it'd still been legal to beat us with batons, they would've. There were good officers, sure, but they hadn't been stationed to watch me. I'd gotten the barrel-scrapings.

"You want me to end up back in the ICU?" I snarled through the glass.

"Ideally," Chalmers replied. "Or the morgue, preferably with your mother."

My hackles rose, but I had to play nice if I wanted to get these

Atomic Cuffs off. They liked to taunt me by leaving them on after my shower, purely to piss me off. I'd be lucky if I wasn't still wearing them in the morning.

"How about you take these things off, and I stay nice and quiet for you?" I walked to the grate and put my arms through.

Grimshaw and Chalmers exchanged a weary look. "Saves me doing it in the morning," Grimshaw finally muttered as he took the Cuffs off.

As the grate closed and the two guards returned to ignoring me, I walked over to the bed and lay down, staring at the stupid chrome ceiling. Alone again, I wondered why it had taken me so freaking long to betray Katherine. I guessed it wasn't an easy bond to break, and I'd been in the land of the brainwashed. For years, she was all I'd known in terms of family. Even after they threw me in here, I'd still been a loyal dog to her. Waiting like a fool. Thinking she was coming to get me out. Thinking that she cared.

When Garrett had come to the prison and told me about Adley, I'd still been resolute. Even hearing with my own two ears that Katherine didn't give a crap about my feelings, I'd stayed loyal because I thought there'd been a good reason for everything she did. But then she'd tried to have me killed. It had been a blessing in disguise, turning my mindset 180. That was the deal-breaker. The no-go zone. Now I knew I meant nothing to her. And, if she kept going with her plans, she'd kill me and everyone else, too, as easily as tossing out the trash. Which, in her mind, was probably what she thought she was doing.

I was sick in the head, but at least I knew that. Katherine was oblivious to the disease festering inside her. She called it power and aspiration instead. All my life, I'd backed her because I'd hoped it would bring us closer. That I'd have a freaking mother one day. The fact that she chose weaselly little Kenneth to end me spoke volumes. I'd known him before he went into foster care, and I'd hated him then, though slightly less than I hated him now. Her picking him for the job was almost more insulting than her actually wanting me dead.

Katherine had used me, and then some.

I got back up and wandered to the glass wall of the cell I'd been moved to after the attempted murder incident. Sitting in front of it, I stared out at the mass of cells identical to my own. I missed trees. I missed green things. I missed rain. I missed the sun. I missed air that hadn't been recycled through a million magical pores. The view of guards and prisoners and chrome and glass was making me restless. I had books to read, but they didn't appeal to me right now. I couldn't focus. I was too worried about Katherine's plan to read trite fiction, although *Rita Hayworth and Shawshank Redemption* might have been inspiring.

I padded over to the small pile of books on my bolted-down table, just in case any Stephen King had slipped in. Unfortunately, there wasn't a single escape-action thriller in the stack. I plucked the first one up anyway and flipped absently through the pages. I didn't read a word. My mind was on Harley.

If she lets me help her, I know I can bring Katherine down. No one knew my mother better than me. She'd kept a ton of information from me, yeah, but I knew where she hid important things. I knew more secrets than she'd told me. I was clever like that. Plus, I knew the cult. I'd been there from the start, after all. I was even there when Katherine had Purged Naima. I had the knowhow; I just needed to get out of this box before it drove me nuts. I couldn't sit here while Katherine kept winning.

A rush of cold air made me turn away from my book. My mouth hung open as I stared at three figures standing in the blind spot of my toilet area. Harley was crouched on the edge of the toilet, while Wade was perched on the cistern. There was another guy with them, much younger, who'd ducked down beside them.

As coolly as possible, I set the book down and walked behind the partition. Ducking out of view of the guards, I sat beside Harley on the toilet seat. "What the hell?"

"And here I was, thinking you'd be glad to see us," Harley muttered.

"Are we going *now*?" I gaped at her. After so many letdowns, I hadn't actually expected her to come for me. I guessed desperation made people do crazy things. Like break into Purgatory.

Harley nodded. "Just shut up for a second, and I'll explain everything in a moment." She took a small device out of her jacket pocket and pressed a button.

"What's that?" I jabbed a finger at the device.

"It wipes the footage from your cameras and replaces it with a neutral loop of you, just before we showed up. It plays out as a projection on the glass, too."

I smirked. "I have to get me one of those. Let's get out of here."

Harley crossed her arms. "Not so fast, pal. We need to strike a deal first."

"Now?" I shot a look over my shoulder.

"This device will buy us plenty of time," she replied, with a cutting smile. "Here are the terms: once we're done getting my mom's spirit out of the cult and Katherine has been brought down, you'll be returned to Purgatory. From here, with the help of us and Alton, you'll make your case for freedom, following the proper avenues. We'll support your case and put forward some insanity defense, saying you were brainwashed or something. The Council knows what Katherine is capable of. We'll help you walk free, the right way."

Yeah, right. And I'll get a gift-wrapped present from my mom on my birthday. "And I can expect a pristine character witness testimony from you?"

Wade scowled. "If you don't screw us over, then yes. Or, rather, a terrible testimony about how unhinged you were when you did this stuff."

"Secondly," Harley continued, "Katherine can't be allowed to survive. If we do this, we have to destroy her. No hesitations. It's the only way we can end everything she's caused and disband the Cult of Eris, too. Cut the head off, and the body dies."

"I get the picture. Believe me, I'm good with it."

"Thirdly, if I get even so much as a whiff that you're trying to play us, then the whole deal is off. You'll lose any privileges you're getting out of this partnership, and my friend here will portal your ass straight back into this cell, with no hope of getting out again. Capiche?"

"Ah, so this is what it's like to have a sister, huh? I heard sisters were bossy. They were right."

Harley narrowed her eyes. "I mean it, Finch."

"Geez, is joking around banned, too?" I held her gaze. "Look, you've got to understand something. I want Katherine dead as much as you do. We're both looking to stop her. I've had a *lot* of time to think in this place, and it's made me question my loyalties. I want her taken down. The end."

Harley sighed. "All right. It'll be the three of us going to the Cult of Eris—you, me, and Wade."

"No, no, no. That won't work," I replied, waving a hand. "Two moles are already two moles too many. Any more than that and we'll be found out, for sure. Besides, I've already got two identities in mind for you and me, and they're perfect. Happy to toot my own horn on that. But I can't think of a third. If your big old manfriend up there comes with us, he'll get us killed."

Harley turned to Wade. "He might be right. We might be pushing it if the three of us go. You heard what happened to the National Council agents. Plus, we don't know how many… uh, *things* Krieger managed to get hold of."

I eyed them both curiously. I wasn't about to get killed just because my half-sister wanted to bring her bodyguard along. But it made me wonder what was going on between these two. A little fledgling romance, perhaps? From the way he was looking at her, it definitely seemed like it. My heart twisted unexpectedly. Adley used to look at me like that. And, if they didn't listen, Wade would have to deal with Harley's loss in the same way I'd dealt with Adley's.

Wade shook his head slowly. "Then… I guess I'm not coming with you to the cult. I'm not happy about it, though." He glared at me. "If anything happens to Harley, you can rest assured that I will come down on you so hard, you won't know what hit you. I won't show mercy."

I waggled my fingers. "Ooh, I'm trembling in my boots. Where'd you get that line? *Terminator? Braveheart? The Avengers?* I'm dying to know."

"You'll be dying, for sure, if you hurt her in any way," Wade shot back.

"Did the SDC give you guys a humor-ectomy or what?" I couldn't help myself. The sincerity coming out of Wade was hilarious. I felt like I'd waltzed into some cheesy drama. Besides, I'd never been one to walk away from pushing someone's buttons. It was one of the reasons Garrett and I had gotten along so well.

Speaking of which, there's a guy I'd really like to make amends with. Garrett hadn't deserved the betrayal. Even when he'd come to tell me about Adley, I could see how much I'd wounded him. And yet, he'd still come. He'd still thought it important that I knew what had happened. We'd talked about everything a little bit, when he'd come to see me, and I knew Garrett understood why I'd done what I'd done. Still, there had to be more I could do to fix things with the only friend I'd ever really had.

I looked to Harley. "Okay, I accept your terms. So what's next?"

FIVE

Harley

"I've got some tricks to pull before we can go anywhere," I said, keeping my eye on Finch. The portal had closed behind Jacob, but that didn't mean Finch wouldn't try something funny.

I pulled out the small, gilded box that Santana had given me, with the Orisha inside. She was working away on my duplicate back at the SDC, and I just hoped this worked. Carefully, I opened the box and released the bluish spirit. It buzzed and thrummed around my head, awaiting the instructions that Santana had told me to give it. But first, I had to get a lock of hair from Finch. Gathering a tiny, controlled ball of fire in my fingertips, I grabbed Finch and singed off a cluster of copper strands.

"Hey, what the—" He tried to protest, but I already had what I needed. Ignoring him, I turned to the skittish Orisha.

"Please, spirit, do as Santana has asked with this lock of hair." I handed it to the curious being and watched in surprise as it snatched the entire cluster out of my hand and vanished it into thin air. A few seconds later, the shimmering bluish light stretched out, growing limbs right before our very eyes. Finch gaped as it swiftly turned into a complete imitation of him. *Great, as if one Finch isn't bad enough.*

"Well, well, I didn't know they allowed turds in prison," the Orisha spoke, the voice still slightly too feminine. Clearly, it had no issue getting right into Finch's mindset.

Finch spluttered. "What did you say to me?"

"Ah, the turd speaks! Will wonders never cease!" The Orisha grinned, exactly the way Finch would've done. *Please don't get us into trouble, Orisha.* As if hearing me, the duplicate Finch turned to look at me. "Don't worry, I'll tone it down for the men in black out there."

Finch moved toward the duplicate and reached out to touch it. "You're... You're me."

"Sure am, genius. Now, hands off the merchandise." The Orisha slapped his hand away, her voice getting more and more like Finch's by the second.

Wade chuckled. "I'd say the duplicate is more like Finch than Finch."

I pulled a worried face. "Santana did say she might struggle with filters."

"Finch doesn't have one," Wade reminded me.

"At least you've given up that ridiculous hair color." The Orisha flashed a mischievous grin at Finch. "Copper suits us much better. Ooh, and this body—what've you been doing to yourself? I ache all over. Yeesh."

Finch pointed at the duplicate. "I'd never say 'yeesh.' Don't say that again."

"I'll say what I want, thanks," the Orisha shot back. "It's your ass I'm covering, after all."

"What are you?" Finch peered closely, evidently creeped out by the accuracy. I was, too.

"A divine being. I have to say, this is one hell of a demotion."

He looked at me. "You did this?"

"Nope, this is all Santana and this kind Orisha here. They've agreed to cover us while we're away at the cult," I replied.

"And don't you forget it," the Orisha chimed in. "*Yeesh,* this is going to take some getting used to." She tugged down on the crotch of her replica prison jumpsuit, adjusting it awkwardly, much to Finch's horror and my amusement.

Finch's cheeks had turned a faint shade of pink. "How about you take *your* hands off the merchandise!"

"Nope, all mine now, buddy. Until you get back, that is." The Orisha grinned, her voice now perfectly aligned with Finch's. "Just a word of warning—I don't trust you. But Santana has asked me to do this, and if she thinks it's a good idea, who am I to say no? Desperate times, eh?"

"This is insane," he mumbled. "I wasn't expecting this."

I shot him a withering look. "What were you expecting? That we would come in all guns blazing? The idea is to get in and out as quickly and quietly as possible. No muss, no fuss."

The Orisha beamed. "Ooh, I like that one. No muss, no fuss. I'll keep it."

"Hang on a sec, we can't leave here without my Esprit," Finch said, averting his eyes from the Orisha as she continued to readjust the jumpsuit. I was glad the guards couldn't see what we were up to; they'd be pressed to the glass, not knowing whether to arrest us or howl with laughter.

I shook my head. "We don't have time to get your Esprit, Finch. Plus, it'll only make you more dangerous, and I'm not chancing that."

Finch sneered at me. "I need my Esprit if we're going to pull off a good disguise, Sis. It'll help me fine-tune my Shapeshifting. You didn't think I was going in as myself, did you?"

"No... I guess not."

"Besides, if, by some twist of fate, we get trapped in the cult, we'll need all the mojo we can muster to get ourselves out." He folded his arms across his chest, and the Orisha copied him.

"Mojo is good, too," she murmured.

I realized I had to do as he'd asked, or we'd never get out of here without alerting the guards. The camera loop wouldn't work forever, and I didn't exactly know how much time we had before it failed. Annoyed that Finch was somehow getting his way, I turned over my shoulder to look at Jacob.

"Jacob, can you radio in to Astrid and Krieger?"

He peered up at me. "Me? Oh… right, sure." He pressed his ear like a newbie bouncer. "Krieger, Astrid, do you read? Harley wants to ask you something." He looked back at me. "I've got them on the line."

"Ask Astrid if there's any safe way to portal into the storage room that has the prisoners' possessions."

He did as I'd asked, the rest of us waiting for a reply. A few minutes later, he spoke. "She's given me the coordinates. There's another safe spot in the corner of the storage room, but we'll have to use the camera loop on the security there, too. If you give Astrid five minutes, she'll send a new loop to the device. You'll need to press the blue button to get it to work. She just needs a moment to hack the cameras."

"That woman is a miracle," I said.

"Harley says you're a miracle," Jacob repeated. I chuckled, but I didn't mind Astrid knowing what I thought of her. He glanced back at me. "She says, 'Thanks, you are too.'"

The minutes seemed to drag by, until a green light flashed on the device, letting me know the new loop had been received. Meanwhile, Finch kept trying to touch the duplicate, only to get his hand savagely smacked away.

"This had better not be some kind of trick," I warned as I prepared to cancel the loop on Finch's cell.

He grinned. "What do you take me for?"

"Everyone ready? Jacob?"

"Ready when you are," Jacob replied. Tendrils of bronze energy swirled around his fingertips as he gathered the strands of his portal ability and tore open a much smaller gap in space and time. In the weeks that had passed since the president's death, I wasn't the only one who'd been practicing. Jacob's skills had improved massively with Isadora's ongoing help.

After Finch had snatched up a bottle of something from a shelf in the bathroom area, Wade shoved him through first, with the rest of us moving to follow. *What are those? His pills?* I knew he had to take something for his psychosis, so at least he was being responsible about it.

Just before I stepped through, I pressed the red button on the device to stop the loop and the projection, returning the cell to its previous state.

"Will you be okay?" I asked the duplicate.

"Oh yes. I'll fit in just fine."

I didn't doubt her. Santana's magic was powerful stuff. Giving her an encouraging nod, I jumped into the gaping mouth of the portal. It snapped shut behind me, spitting me out into a dark, unfamiliar room.

The others were huddled in the blind corner, keeping out of sight of the cameras. I pushed down on the device's blue button, just as Astrid had instructed. It sparked for a moment before the light glowed in the gloomy light.

"The cameras should be on a new loop," I whispered.

"Should be?" Finch arched an eyebrow.

"Well, seeing as we can't actually check the camera footage, we have to hope for the best." I nudged him out of the way and took a step farther into the storage room. "Storage room" was a misnomer, as the space before us stretched out like a warehouse, with shelves upon shelves of belongings.

Finch whistled. "Imagine what we could find in here."

"Your Esprit. Nothing else. You're with me so I can keep an eye on you." I took him by the wrist and dragged him toward the right-hand side of the storage facility. "Wade, Jacob, you take the other wall. We're looking for a copper-colored, custom lighter, if memory serves." I was aware that there would likely be guards on the other side of the main door, and someone could easily step in at any moment. So we had to be quick and quiet—two things that didn't seem to fit with Finch's character.

Wade opened his mouth to protest, but he quickly shut it again. We needed to find this Esprit as quickly as possible, and splitting up was the best way to do that. As he walked toward the far shelves with Jacob beside him, I felt a wave of disappointment and concern flow away from him, finding its way to me. I didn't know if he was doing it deliberately, but it still made me sad. I didn't want to go on this dangerous mission without him, and it would hurt like heck to be separated, not knowing if I'd make it back from the cult in one piece.

"Aw, sweet of you to remember." Finch chuckled to himself, breaking my train of thought.

"Better the devil you know, right?"

"Devil?" he tutted. "I thought we were over that."

I frowned at him. "Old habits die hard."

"Any more sayings you want to throw at me? Beauty is in the eye of the beholder? Keep your enemies close? Don't eat yellow snow?"

A small smile crept onto my lips. "I'm still getting used to the fact that we're working together. It's a little weird right now, but I'm sure it'll get easier."

"Not where we're going," he replied. "But I get what you mean. I'm still pretty surprised you came for me. It's not like anyone else has bothered."

"Well, I'm not like her."

He turned his gaze away for a moment, his expression suddenly unreadable. "No, you aren't. It's probably one of the only likable things about you."

I laughed. "You don't get to choose your family, right?"

"Another excellent choice in the book of terrible sayings. Almost as bad as 'blood is thicker than water.' I'm glad you didn't go for that one, 'cause then I'd have had to reconsider."

I was surprised by how funny he could be, even if I was the butt of his jokes. "Come on, let's find this lighter before the loop runs out."

I began to scour the shelves for the familiar copper lighter I'd seen him with in the SDC, what felt like forever ago. There was so much stuff here that I was starting to worry we might never find it. Finch, on the other hand, seemed as cool as a cucumber.

"So, you ended up in the foster system, right?" he asked as he casually sifted through the endless belongings of every prisoner who'd ever been in here.

I shot him a warning look. "Yeah. Why do you ask?"

He shrugged. "Just curious about you. Making up for lost time... or something like that."

I supposed, given the circumstances, it couldn't hurt to get to know each other better. After all, we'd be spending a lot of time with each other in the near future.

"I was left at an orphanage when I was around three, and I stayed in foster care until I moved out on my own at eighteen. I moved from family to family, but I usually ended up back where I started. The last family was the exception, but I got to them too late." I smiled wryly at him. "The damage had been done, so to speak."

"Probably better than being raised by a stranger and getting snatched away by a psycho at sixteen, though," he replied.

"You definitely beat me on that one." I never thought I'd ever have a reason to count myself lucky for being in foster care, but at least I hadn't been brainwashed and tormented by the one person who was supposed to love me unconditionally. Even though I couldn't sense Finch's emotions, I didn't need my Empathy to know what he was feeling. It was written all over his face, in the pain that lingered behind his eyes and the last frosty-white tips of his old hair, reminding me of the person he'd been; it was the unresolved bitterness and anger that I also felt burning away inside me.

There might be hope for you yet, Finch. Not that I was ready to trust him completely. With or without Katherine's influence, he would always be a remarkably selfish person. He wasn't fooling anyone with his "I accept your terms" façade. Even before I'd told him the terms of the deal, I knew he wouldn't go back to Purgatory without a fight. However, if I was going to get him to do things the proper way, to make amends for the terrible things that he'd done, then I needed to win him over. I needed to make him realize that he still had penance to pay. I just didn't know how I was going to do that yet.

"Found it!" Finch grasped at a plain black box on one of the lowest shelves and shoved it in my face. His name was scrawled across a label in bright red ink, only it wasn't the name I'd gotten used to. "They used Anker instead of Shipton. Names are funny, aren't they? They hold a ton of power, even without us knowing."

I froze at his words. There was no way he could have known about the promise that I'd made to Echidna, about letting her name my firstborn child. To be honest, I hadn't given it much thought myself since I'd accepted her deal, but now everything came rushing back in a nauseating wave. I mean, it wasn't as if I was planning on having kids anytime soon. But what if I did want them, one day? What would Echidna's name do? Would it hold some kind of power, too?

I shrugged it off, knowing I had years before I had to worry about it. "Is your Esprit in there?"

Finch flipped the lid and took out the lighter, igniting it. "Yep. Good to go."

"Jacob, Wade, we have it!" I hissed across the warehouse, still conscious that there might be guards stationed outside the main door. The two of them reappeared shortly after, their faces streaked with dirt from the belongings that had been left to gather dust.

"You found it?" Wade asked.

I nodded. "We should probably skedaddle before someone comes in."

"Agreed. Jacob, can you portal us back to the infirmary?"

"On it. Although, we should probably get away from all this stuff." He hurried back toward the corner where we'd entered the room. With a rush of air, a portal burst into life, the edges of the gaping mouth thrumming with Chaos energy. I jumped through first, dragging Finch with me, while Wade and Jacob brought up the rear.

We staggered back out into the familiar surroundings of the SDC infirmary, and Jacob zapped the portal shut. Dr. Krieger was waiting for us in the middle of one of the empty wards and ushered us hurriedly into his office, before closing the door behind him. On the workbench in front of him, two strange objects caught my eye. They were orb-shaped and no bigger than a baseball, with bright colors swirling within an outer casing of gold and glass.

My mouth fell open. "You got them?"

"Yes, but I could only find two." Krieger glanced at Finch, who was observing the two orbs intently. "However, I'm not sure we should discuss this in front of *him*."

"He'll need to know how to use these things, so you might as well. No point hiding anything from him now." I sighed and set myself down on one of the stools around the workbench. Wade sat beside me, while Jacob and Finch took up the last two stools.

"Well then... There's one for you and one for our reformed criminal." Krieger's German accent held an edge of sass that made me smile. "They were procured at very great expense, I might add. I have been assured that they're the real deal—Ephemeras aren't easy to come by these days, as so few of them were made."

"Are they ready to use?" I reached out to touch one, but a warning look from Krieger made me withdraw my hand. "I thought they were supposed to be gemstones?"

"They'll be ready after you channel your magic into them, whenever you decide you're ready to proceed with that process. And you are quite right—the gemstones are inside the orbs, which provide a protective casing that should slip through any radar. It will also mean the size can be changed, to make them even less noticeable. I will need to know what your plans are so that I can fill each Ephemera with the power you require—provided we have a magical here at the SDC who possesses that ability," he explained.

"And the ability can only be used once, right?" I knew enough about them from Isadora, but I'd been doing some research of my own, ever since I'd decided that breaking Finch out was the right thing to do. Ephemeras were rare artifacts, as the art of making them had long been lost. They were highly sought after, but only a few people still knew where to find one. I guessed Krieger's success had something to do with Cabot's shop in Waterfront Park, but I didn't like to pry too much. Still, from what I knew, the ability that got poured into them could only be used one time, making the objects powerful but very temporary.

Krieger nodded. "That is correct, although they may react differently with you, Harley. You might get more time out of a single use. I've tried to tamper with them both, to give boosted abilities, but it will remain to be seen if that works out."

"Cool, we've got a few things to go over before we need these, but we'll give you plenty of time to get them up and running before we leave," I said.

"The more time, the better."

"Noted." I looked at Wade. "We should probably check in and see what the others are doing so I don't randomly end up crossing paths with my duplicate and get Levi's panties in a bunch."

"Good thinking." He took out his phone, dialed a number, and put it to his ear. "Astrid? Yeah, we're back. Do you know where Harley's duplicate is? Have them bring the duplicate over to the infirmary so we can avoid the real Harley bumping into the duplicate Harley. We won't need the duplicate of Harley to leave the infirmary, so it'll just be a one-way trip. Great, thanks, Astrid. See you soon."

I put my thumb up. "All good?"

"Astrid is going to get Dylan and Tatyana to bring the duplicate to the infirmary once she's finished checking the dark web for cult movements, and I'm about to phone Santana and get her and Raffe to come here, too."

"Why won't we need my duplicate anymore?" If this new, improved version was anything like Finch's duplicate, nobody would be able to tell the difference.

"We can't afford to have the duplicate slip up, not with Levi watching so closely. It can stay here, under Krieger's watch, until we need it again."

I nodded, knowing he was right. "I'm still working on a good excuse. We have to make this watertight." I looked around the room, noticing one figure was missing. "What about Isadora? Is she coming?"

"She's with Alton and Levi, keeping the old Grinch busy."

Finch snorted. "Isadora is here?"

"Where else would she be?" I shot back.

"I thought she'd be chained up in one of Katherine's cages by now. If she's really here, why isn't she running miles away from this place?"

I narrowed my eyes at him. "What do you mean?" Had Finch known about Isadora since day one? It sounded like it. I didn't know what to make of that. Then again, it wasn't as if he'd have just blurted it out when he'd been roaming around the SDC, masquerading as a coven member. Still, it irked me a little.

"She's a sitting duck for Katherine if she stays here. Katherine has been after her for ages."

"Katherine did manage to take her, but we got her back," Jacob interjected, a half-sheepish, half-proud look on his face.

I nodded. "Yeah, as it turns out, once you complete the first ritual, you don't need a Portal Opener anymore, so Katherine has no reason to come after Isadora."

"Aside from the Merlin connection, you mean?" Finch tapped his fingertips on the workbench, a knowing look on his face. "She doesn't want any of us alive, Harley. No Shiptons, no Merlins, nobody who has any connection to her whatsoever. Then again, I guess that makes us all sitting ducks."

"Well, these ducks aren't sitting for long, so stop with the scaremongering. Isadora is just fine here, for now, and so are we. We'll be leaving soon enough, and hopefully, when we come back, that'll be the end of it." I shook off the shiver that had run up my spine. "Now, what we're about to do is ridiculously dangerous, and I need to know what you've got planned. I'm not walking into the Cult of Eris blind, so you'd better start talking."

Finch smiled an eerie smile that made my stomach twist into knots. He seemed to be reveling in the idea of ending Katherine more than any of us, his eagerness casting a dark glint in the depths of his eyes. What lay ahead was one of the most terrifying things I'd ever have to do in my life, and the more I thought about it, the more I wanted to run in the opposite direction. Entering Katherine's cult wasn't just dangerous, it was completely insane, but it was our one shot at getting her.

We couldn't miss it, no matter how afraid I might be of what awaited us in the Cult of Eris. If we did, we might never get a chance like this again.

SIX

Harley

"Long time, no see," Santana muttered as she leveled her gaze at Finch. The entire Rag Team was now gathered in the infirmary, with my duplicate having turned back into an Orisha. The only one still missing was Garrett, and I could see that irked Finch a little. After all, they probably had a lot to talk about.

Finch smirked. "Yeah, it's weird, isn't it? You'd think Purgatory would just let us have days off, right?"

"Gotta say, I'm loving the frosted tips. You having a quarter-life crisis or something?" Santana was on a roll today.

"The hairstylist said it was back in fashion. Purgatory is a little behind, though." Finch ran an anxious hand through his new dark auburn hair. I'd caught him looking at his reflection a couple of times, and the reddish tone didn't seem to sit well with him. Too many Katherine memories, no doubt.

"Are you sure this is the right thing to do, Harley?" Tatyana looked at me uncertainly. Nobody was comfortable having Finch here. The tension and concern were like a tidal wave, crashing straight into me. I'd relearned how to put up a mental barrier to keep most of it out, but little barbs prickled every now and again.

I sighed. "You've all got to trust me on this one. We've taken big risks before, but this one might just have the payoff we've been looking for. It's the right thing to do, even though I know it feels weird." I glanced at Finch, eager to stop a spat from breaking out. "So, what do you know? Spill."

"At least I can count on you for a warm welcome, Sis. It's gotten pretty frosty in here." He looked around the room with a smug smile on his face. With him being a Shapeshifter, it annoyed me that I couldn't sense his true emotions, but I got the feeling he didn't really feel smug. He was just putting on his Finch façade for the curious, wary public. "The first person we need to gun for is Naima. From what you've told me, you've already met her a couple of times. And it sounds as though she likes you a hell of a lot, Wade. She doesn't get her claws out for just anyone."

Wade narrowed his eyes. "Just stick to the facts, Finch. We don't have time to mess around."

"This Krieger kid must've cut out all your funny bones." Finch chuckled to himself, while Krieger shot him a disapproving look.

"You had best watch who you're calling 'kid,' *kinder*."

"Of course he's a German!" Finch smirked at me but carried on before I could snap at him. "So, Naima was Purged by Katherine. She performed a really dark spell to break into the Reykjavik repositories, and Naima popped out after. Sweet, really. Anyway, she runs the cult's Bestiary out of the ruined Fort Jefferson in Dry Tortugas, where Katherine has her base of operations."

Santana frowned. "Dry Turtles? Where's that? I've never heard of it."

"Dry *Tortugas* is a cluster of islands off the coast of Key West, Florida. I had to talk her out of putting her base in North Brother Island, in New York. She was desperate to put it there, right in the faces of the New York Coven. She always talked about Typhoid Mary, and how she'd spent her last days there. It'd been her perfect site, but I told her it was too risky. People would look for her in New York. People would sense the interdimensional bubble. So, she moved to Florida."

Dylan whistled. "No wonder she's been flying under the radar. That isn't even California's jurisdiction."

"You don't say." Finch's words dripped sarcasm. It made me wonder whether Dylan reminded him of the kids who'd teased him when he was a kid. "She's been running her operation across the country. California is a tiny part of it."

Raffe waggled his hands. "Hold up a second, did you say *Bestiary?* Naima is running a Bestiary for Katherine?"

"Yep."

Everyone looked at each other in surprise. Evidently, they'd missed it the first time, given the idea of Katherine living in Florida.

"She needs a lot of power," he added with a shrug. "Fort Jefferson is remote. You can only get there by boat or seaplane, and it doesn't get a lot of visitors. Even if there are tourists, they can't see the base. It's tucked away, nice and safe. I used to know the routes in, but they've probably been changed since I've been in prison."

"You think Naima is your way in?" Astrid pressed.

Finch nodded. "She'll be our best shot. She's the Recruiter, after all." He paused. "Now, there's Kenneth Willow to deal with, once we're actually in the cult. He'll be loitering around, for sure. He hangs on Katherine's apron strings like a leech. Since he didn't manage to get hold of Giverny Le Fay, like you told me, he'll be doing his best groveling to get back in Katherine's good books."

"How did Kenneth get out of prison in the first place?" Tatyana asked. "I know they took him to a higher security prison in LA after he was in our cells for a while, so he could await his trial, but how did he escape?"

"He tricked the guards and killed them," Astrid replied. "I read it in some of Smartie's files, but they wanted to hush it up so people didn't get freaked out. He's been loose for a while."

"Would've been nice to know," Finch muttered.

"My question is, why did Kenneth want Giverny?" Astrid asked. "I have my guesses, but I'd like to be sure."

"She's got some special ability that Katherine really wanted for the last ritual," Finch said. "Her main goal has been to seek out rare magicals, at any cost, to get all her ducks in a row. You should see some of the abilities she has in her crew. It's insane. And, from what you've said about these kid-snatchings, she hasn't let up on getting the crème de la crème."

I remembered how it'd felt to be briefly under Giverny's control, when we'd gone to her for the Light blood. "Maybe she was after Giverny's Hypno power?"

"I'm not sure of the specifics," Finch replied. "There might've been something else she wanted."

Astrid nodded thoughtfully. "Makes sense, considering the nature of the last ritual. Katherine needs twelve powers, and I'm guessing they can't just be ordinary ones. Otherwise, it would be too easy."

"Yeah, that would explain why she's been hunting out all these magicals and killing off the ones who aren't powerful enough for her." I grimaced at the memory of those poor kids who'd been savagely murdered by Katherine and her minions. She likely needed the rarest of abilities, which were only gifted to a sparse number of magicals. I cast a nervous glance at Jacob and Louella, who seemed equally on edge. If that was the case, there was every chance they were still on Katherine's radar.

I toyed with the pendant around my neck as I remembered the danger that Jacob had been in at the Smiths', and how Katherine had used me as bait to get to him. Imogene's gift sat alongside the St. Christopher necklace that the Smiths had given me, both pieces of jewelry giving me strength. My mom's replica alongside the gift from the only kind parents I'd ever known—or could remember, at least. I realized they'd likely be back from Hawaii by now, and I should probably drop in on them at some point. *Be a good adopted daughter.*

"Bingo." Finch smiled. "She's gathering magicals to sacrifice so she can take their powers at the end of the game."

"Kenneth isn't all that powerful though, right?" I got my head back into gear. We had to focus on what we could control now, in the hopes that Katherine would never reach that endgame position.

"He can't even get murder right," Finch said.

Wade shook his head. "Not particularly, although he's good with hexes. He's needy, which is probably why Katherine keeps him around. She knows he'll do absolutely anything she asks him to. Like killing her son." He cast a glance at Finch. "Kenneth is a functioning psychopath, but that neediness toward Katherine will work in our favor. We just have to play him right."

"And what about Shinsuke Nomura?" I hadn't forgotten about him, though I'd tried to forget what his father had done to me, shutting me out of my body and locking me in astral projection. "Preceptor Nomura tried to broker a deal for his freedom, using me. Do you think he might be open to persuasion if we can get to him?"

Finch snorted. "A deal? Don't make me laugh. Handing you over would have been about as useful to the mighty Hiro as a chocolate teapot. Katherine would never have returned Shinsuke alive to his father. She hates weakness of any kind. Parental weakness, particularly. Sins of the father, and all that. I suppose I should have realized." His voice stuck again. "Shinsuke will know too much by now. No way she would've let him go."

"He'll be too useful to her, too, I imagine," Wade chimed in. "Even though he's a known Mediocre, he comes from a family renowned for breaking away from that label and putting in the hard work to be powerful. Plus, I bet she feels really smug about having the son of Hiro Nomura in her ranks."

"Yeah, I don't know too much about him. I was in prison before he joined her, I think. What's his deal? Any juicy powers I should know about? I'm guessing not, since he's a Mediocre by birth, but stranger things have happened." Finch looked at me with a knowing expression.

"I think he has a peculiar Earth ability," Krieger said, plucking a file from one of his shelves and flipping through it. "Yes, here. I made a note about it after an evening when Hiro had spoken about his son. His Earth ability seems to be blended with a Magneton ability, which is highly unusual."

"See, stranger things," Finch said triumphantly. "I knew there'd be another reason for Katherine keeping him around. I'd be interested to see how far he's come under Katherine's teachings."

"Anyone else we should worry about?" I was eager to know everything we were up against.

"There's one more," Finch replied. "Her name's Thessaly Crux. She's the one we really need to be careful about. She's a powerful Electro and mega loyal to Katherine. Naima might be her lieutenant, but Tess is like her second-in-command. She's a total savage, suspicious of everyone —even me."

I frowned. "We met an Electro when we went to see Marie Laveau. She was with Naima. Do you think this Thessaly girl might be the same one?"

"You went to see Marie Laveau?" Finch sounded stunned. "Why?"

I smirked. "To break my Suppressor. I went through a *lot* to do that. Marie Laveau was just the tip of the iceberg."

Finch blew out and shrugged. "Well, I guess that Electro you met could've been Tess. She was the only Electro in the cult when I was there, so it's pretty likely. Then again, she might have recruited more of them since I've been gone. It's a rare ability, but Katherine's been *very* busy hunting." He paused. "Tess had a twin with the same power, Larissa, but she wasn't as bright as Tess. She got killed in a mission to abduct more kids from LA. The kids were more powerful than Rissa had anticipated. Let's just say it didn't end well. Blood everywhere. Bits, too. You don't want to know about the bits."

I shuddered at the thought. "So, Naima is our way in, since she's the Recruiter. But *how* do we get in? Are we just going to waltz up to Fort Jefferson in disguise, knock on the door, and hope for the best?"

Finch shot me a withering look. "Oh yeah, because that'd work. We need to be *recruited* by her. See, it's in the name already. *Recruiter.* She's intelligent, yeah, but she's not as good with people as she is with Purge beasts. She'll be the one most easily fooled. I wouldn't know where to find her, though."

"You could always speak to Garrett," Dr. Krieger suggested, closing his file and replacing it. "He's working with the LA Coven these days, isn't he? They're likely to have more knowledge of Naima's whereabouts than we are."

I nodded. "Yeah, we got some intel that the National Council knows about one of Naima's playgrounds."

"Yes!" Jacob suddenly stepped back and forged a rapid tear in the fabric of the universe, disappearing through his portal. He returned a few minutes later, while the rest of us stared at the empty space in shock. Only, this time, he wasn't alone. Garrett stood beside him, looking very confused. His eyes drifted across the room and stopped short at Finch.

His mouth fell open. "What the—?"

This was going to be good.

SEVEN

Finch

"Jacob!" Harley looked like Jacob had just smacked her in the face with an octopus.

Wow, awkward much?

He shrugged. "Everyone keeps saying we're running out of time. I figured we need as much help as we can get."

I kind of liked this kid. He had guts. I just wished he hadn't dragged Garrett into this. Man, it felt like I was going on a date or something. My stomach was twisting up with nerves. I hadn't seen Garrett in weeks, and even when he'd visited, things had been tense. Not that I was going to spill my guts out now. Not in front of these people.

"Even so, you could've warned us first," Harley complained. She clearly didn't like surprises. *Killjoy.* "Someone in the LA Coven could've seen you! Not cool, Jacob."

To my surprise, Mr. Rule-Follower Wade Crowley was the one to defend the kid. "Hey, he's the captain of calculated recklessness. And he's right, we're running out of time."

"Yeah, and I wasn't seen. I made sure." Jacob smiled proudly. Anyone would have thought he'd just solved world peace.

She shot him a look that could melt steel. "Still, you could've said something first, Jake." Ah, so it was "Jake," was it? I didn't know too much about him, other than his rare ability. I knew he'd been on Katherine's list, and I was pleased she hadn't managed to get her paws on him. *You can't have everything, Mother dearest.*

"Does someone want to tell me what *he* is doing here?" Garrett pointed a shaky finger at me. The elephant in the room. "Tell me you weren't actually stupid enough to break him out of Purgatory."

"Surprise!" I gave him my best jazz hands, but he wasn't amused. The SDC really had lobotomized this bunch.

"It was a… calculated risk," Harley replied.

Garrett shook his head. "If anyone gets wind of this, and I mean *anyone*, you're screwed. If you get caught, that's a life sentence, no parole."

Well, hello to you, too.

"That won't happen, Garrett," Harley replied. Ever the optimist. "We covered ourselves. Astrid helped, and so did the rest of the Rag Team. Everything's in place, and nobody is any the wiser. Do you hear any alarm bells ringing?"

Garrett pinched the bridge of his nose in a way that made him look like a weary old man. "Not yet." He let out an equally ancient sigh. "So, what do you want from me? I've just left a briefing with the National Council, so I'm pretty beat. Don't give me the long version, because I don't think I want to hear it."

I stayed silent after that nice rebuffing. I might as well not have been in the room. It'd probably have made Garrett a whole lot happier. Whenever I looked at him, I was reminded of what I'd done. I'd put this distance between us, and I'd have done anything not to have dragged him into Katherine's plan. He'd said it was okay last time I saw him, but I didn't believe that. Out of everyone, I regretted betraying him the most. I was pretty much ambivalent to the rest of them.

All of this was surreal. I'd always been at Katherine's side, pretending to be part of the SDC. Now, I was truly at their mercy. Which was probably no less than I deserved. Part of me still wondered if I should be left to rot in Purgatory, yet I couldn't see myself ever going back there. I'd made my promises, but I didn't intend to keep them. My mind was already on the brink of insanity, reminding me that I needed to take one of the pills in my pocket to smooth out the edges. But these pills wouldn't work for much longer if they threw me back inside. Another stretch in Purgatory and they may as well have kept me in an asylum instead.

"We need you to tell us where Naima is, Garrett," Harley said. *Yes, Sis, right to the point.*

Garrett plopped himself down on a stool. "We've got our sights on her and one of her favorite haunts for recruiting. The National Council is in the middle of debating what to do about it. That's all they seem to do—talk about things and never actually *do* anything, but what do I know? I just sit and listen." Someone was feeling disenchanted with his new position.

"How do you know all of this?" Astrid asked. Her eyes had brightened the minute he'd come into the room. *Aw, bless her heart.* Even so, there was something weird about the human. Half the time, I wondered if the SDC was experimenting with androids. She definitely hadn't been like this before. Had something happened to her? I was so out of the loop. And I didn't think Garrett would stoop that low. A non-magical? No way.

He eyed her with an affection that made me curious and a bit nauseous. "There's someone inside the cult who's feeding us information: locations, identities, that sort of thing," Garrett said. "It's going to take us a while to verify everything we've received, to make sure it's not coming from some kind of double agent. And the National Council really loves spending a lot of time farting around."

Harley grinned. "If they'd been smarter, they would've come to us for help. Astrid would've verified everything in five minutes flat."

"I know she would've," he replied softly, "but they want to keep the SDC out of everything. Seriously, it's almost comical how they keep saying, 'But we have to make sure Levi doesn't know about any of this.' It's like a running joke."

Garrett, dude. There was definitely something going on between him and Astrid. He got all giddy whenever he looked at her. I supposed it was okay, as long as he was happy. Right? But he could've done so much better than a measly human. She was about as impressive as my right armpit. Not that I was in any position to give romantic advice. Adley had loved me unconditionally, and I'd treated her like a tool for my own benefit. She'd come to me, wanting to just do normal couple things, and I'd just keep talking about work or trying to persuade her into doing something for me. She never said she minded, but I could always see how disappointed she was that we weren't... well, ordinary.

I couldn't even remember taking her out to a movie or dinner. It had always been work, or digging up this info, or that info, or standing her up because Katherine had sent me an urgent message. I'd always tried to make it up to her, but I hadn't been the best boyfriend I could've been, even though I loved her so much. I really did. I'd look at her and want to do those normal things, but Katherine was so embedded in my brain that I couldn't properly *see* what I had in front of me. In the end, I'd used the woman I loved, and she'd died because of it. Adley's death weighed on my shoulders. It always would.

"You want to tell us this location?" Harley pressed. All business, all the time. I didn't know whether it was useful or irritating. Time would tell.

Garrett nodded. "Her favorite recruitment spot is a bar called Azarius. A dive, really, in Salem Coven's jurisdiction. Katherine is spreading her net wider than we thought. Anyway, it's in an interdimensional pocket like Waterfront Park. I can give Astrid the coordinates."

"That'd be good," Astrid replied. Her voice was oddly empty. *You picked a lame horse, buddy.*

Harley smiled. "Okay then, we have the location, and we have Ephemeras to sneak into the cult, although we still need to finish making those. The only other thing to do now is prepare an alibi. Wade was right about the Orisha duplicate—I don't want to put that sort of strain on Santana, and we can't have the duplicate fizzing out while I'm away. We learned that the hard way last time, and we want to keep Levi's nose out of this."

"Any thoughts?" Wade replied. He'd gone all gooey too. It was sickening. All of them were at it. Dylan had his steroidal arm around Tatyana's shoulders, the Mexican was leaning against Raffe's chest, and the rest were making goo-goo eyes at each other. *Ugh, pass me a bucket.*

"An idea came to me earlier, but I wanted to see what you thought of it." She beamed at Wade, just as nauseating. "I thought you could stay here with Finch in one of the storage rooms of the infirmary. Meanwhile, I'll go and speak with Imogene."

"Imogene?" Wade didn't sound convinced. I remembered her well enough. Nice lady. Killer legs. Sharp mind. Knew how to wear a dress. Totally wasted on the California Mage Council, of course. She was the only decent one among them. And I'd heard she could be a bit feisty when she needed to be. My sort of woman. *Although, she's not Adley.* My mind had pulled me up again. There'd never be another Adley as long as I lived. That woman would have done anything for me. She would've gotten me out of this mess, if I'd just asked her. She always told me I could be more, that I didn't need to do these things, and I'd refused to listen. Hindsight was a total kick in the nuts.

I remembered sitting with her over coffee, and her pleading with me to go to a therapist. My behavior had been erratic, to say the least, with bursts of anger and bouts of depression. She wanted me to see what I'd become, because she said it was miles away from the man she'd met and fallen in love with. I kept telling her she was being controlling. And now, all I wanted was to sit across from her again and look into those big eyes of hers and watch her red lips move as she spoke and laughed and teased me. I wanted to lean over and kiss those lips, the way I'd done a thousand times, taking it for granted that I'd get to again. Those were the moments where everything else fell away, when I kissed her and held her. I forgot what I was, then. Now, I just wanted to sit and listen to what she had to say about her own life. I'd never listened. And now, I'd never get to.

Harley nodded. "I was supposed to go and speak with her about my abilities, after the Suppressor break, anyway. She might be able to give me a solid alibi, and I'll just claim it's for an assignment or something. She hates Levi as much as the rest of us, but that doesn't mean she won't say anything. I'll come up with an excuse that makes her keep it a secret." Her gaze drifted across the rest of us. "The main thing we need to remember is, Levi has to stay in the dark about all of this."

Ugh, Levi... A scrotal paramecium that I hated more than anyone. He had the brain capacity of a toad. How he'd weaseled his way onto the Mage Council still remained a mystery. Money, probably. Had it not been for the Atomic Cuffs during my sentencing, I'd have used my Telekinesis to throw that arrogant ass like a rag doll, until every bone in his body was broken.

And then, I'd use that Telekinesis on my mother. I'd squeeze it around her throat and pull until her eyes bulged out and her face turned purple. If I could even get that close.

Katherine had become more powerful than anyone could've anticipated. Even me. But everyone had a weakness. Mine had been Adley. Harley's was evidently Wade. *Everyone* had something that made them vulnerable. I knew I wasn't Katherine's weakness, but she had to have one. I just needed to figure out what it was so I could get close enough to watch the life sputter out in her eyes. *Wouldn't that just be the happiest day of my life.*

EIGHT

Harley

With Levi's reluctant blessing, I went to meet Imogene the following afternoon in Moll Dyer's Bar. Waterfront Park was surprisingly empty for a weekday afternoon, but I hadn't been here in ages. I guessed things had changed; people were probably more hesitant to go out with Katherine rampaging around, slaughtering presidents and stuff.

"The world has become a rather strange and unusual place in recent weeks," Imogene said quietly. We were sitting outside at a patio table, with soft music drifting out from the bar and sunlight glancing down through the interdimensional bubble of Waterfront Park. I could see people wandering past—humans, oblivious to our existence. It made for good people-watching as we nursed two drinks, both glasses glinting with condensation. Imogene wasn't her normal self, that was for sure. She seemed withdrawn and tired, with dark crescents beneath her eyes. "It's hard to fathom that President Price isn't with us anymore. He did so much for us all, and now... he's gone. I still find it hard to say out loud." She dabbed a napkin to the side of her eye before taking a large gulp of her gin and tonic.

It was difficult to watch her like this, so vacant and un-Imogene-like. President Price's death had hit us all hard, but I guessed she'd known him better than any of us. Being on the California Mage Council, she had to have bumped into him a couple of times. I wanted to ask her more about their relationship, but I didn't know how to, or whether I even should. The poor woman seemed to be on the brink of tears most of the time.

"It was a huge blow," I agreed, feeling like I should be saying something more profound.

She sighed. "I just don't know how the nation is going to recover from this. The new president is an excellent stand-in, but she is just that—a stand-in. Without President Price, things will never be the same again. That gentleman was the last of his kind, a true leader, who only comes about once in a generation. My own mother always spoke about the assassination of JFK and the shockwaves his death sent through the nation—magical and human alike. I didn't understand until now."

My eyes nearly fell out of my head. "Whoa, hold up. JFK was a *magical?*"

She smiled sadly. "No, but that didn't mean the magicals didn't care."

"Did you know President Price well?" There, I'd spat it out.

"Not particularly, but I admired him greatly. He was a hero amongst men, able to unite even the most conflicted of covens." She paused, her gaze wistful. "'Thou know'st 'tis common; all that lives must die, passing through nature to eternity. He was a man, take him for all in all. I shall not look upon his like again.'"

"Did you just make that up? Because that was beautiful."

A soft chuckle escaped Imogene's lips. "It's Shakespeare, Harley. *Hamlet*, to be precise. A mixture of my favorite scenes."

"Ah, I never cared much for Shakespeare at school. Mostly went over my head."

"Anyway, if I continue to wallow, I'll drink this entire bar dry, and that would *not* be an entertaining sight," she said, visibly gathering herself. "How are things with Director Levi and the SDC? We ask for weekly reports, but Levi rarely delivers them on time. And, with everything going on, I'm sure you can understand how little time we have to chase him down on these matters."

I shrugged. "It's as good as can be expected, given the circumstances. He watches me constantly, or he has someone else do it. He doesn't trust that I've got my abilities and affinities in order. He barely lets me out of the coven unless he can reach me on my phone at all times." I lifted my cell phone and waved it at her. "He's got a GPS tracker installed in this thing, just to be sure."

"I'm sorry to hear that. I would've thought Alton could lessen Leonidas's more dictatorial edges. Is that not the case?"

I shook my head. "He pushes Alton around like a servant and forces the entire coven to adhere to his rules. Anything above a certain danger threshold is a big no-no, including eating breakfast after six a.m. It's like forcing soldiers to knit sweaters for puppies instead of protecting the unit or letting them serve on the front line."

"He's a ridiculous man, Harley. That may well be the G&T talking, but he really is." She laughed. "I still can't quite understand why Alton put himself in such a lowly position and left the SDC open to such exposure. I hope, in time, he'll be able to temper some of Levi's worst instincts."

"Your guess is as good as mine," I replied. Nobody outside of the Rag Team knew the real reason Alton had stepped down, and that wasn't about to change. I liked Imogene, but if she caught wind of what Alton had done, she wouldn't hesitate to see him punished. That was her job, at the end of the day—to maintain order amongst the covens in her jurisdiction.

"You see, Harley, the thing about Levi is he really loathes being around magicals who are more powerful than he is. When he was with me on the Council, I used to catch him sending dirty looks my way when he thought I wasn't looking. I regret not calling him out, but I don't like to stir the pot too much, not when it's not necessary to do so."

I nodded. "It's not the first time I've heard that. Even Raffe says the same thing. It's got to be pretty bad, if it's coming from his own flesh and blood. Still, it makes you wonder what made him like that."

"That poor boy," Imogene murmured. "I don't know the precise details of Director Levi's inferiority complex, but… someone told me it had something to do with a duel from his youth. He bit off more than he could chew, by the sounds of it, and almost got himself killed in the process. His wife was pregnant with Raffe at the time, and the residual terror of abandoning his wife to widowhood and leaving his child fatherless was too much for him to bear. Ever since, he has been exceedingly cautious around powerful magicals, for fear of it happening again."

I let her words soak in. It was weird to think of Levi as an ordinary guy, with fears and neuroses like everyone else. "I'd probably be more sympathetic if he weren't intent on making my life miserable."

She smiled and took another sip of her drink. "Speaking of powerful magicals, how are you doing, now that the Suppressor is gone? I've heard of your progress in Levi's rather flaky reports, but they're usually tinged with negativity. Now that you're here, I should like to hear of it in your own words. So, tell me, do you feel balanced yet?"

For some reason, her question reminded me of Clint Eastwood. *Do you feel lucky? Well, do you, punk?* I didn't exactly have an answer yet.

I toyed with my lime and seltzer. "It's been quite a journey so far. Pretty difficult, to be fair. I mean, there's all this magical energy loose inside me, and I'm still coming to grips with it." I shrugged, not wanting to get on a downer. "I'm handling it, though. It's easier now that I don't have to work at the Science Center, so I've got more time to focus on improving myself. And it's been cool to discover everything I can do now. I'm still learning, and I know there's a lot more for me to discover, but I'm working through it as best I can."

"You have the means to do so, Harley. You've always been exceptional, and now you're simply catching up on the years of education and guidance you've missed out on," she said. "I would suggest measured breathing techniques and some meditation. Either that, or you could utilize the Euphoria technique of thinking of something or someone dear to you to help ground you in the here and now. You could, in fact, focus on the pendant that I gave to you if you ever feel as if things are getting out of hand. I gave it to you to help tie you to your past and to your present. It will surely ground you if you're ever in trouble."

I instinctively reached for it and rubbed my thumb across the silver plating and the rough gemstones. Even that simple action brought me comfort, reminding me how grateful I was for the gift. "It already helps me, in a lot of ways. If nothing else, it reminds me why I have to keep going."

"Then it's doing what I intended." She smiled at me as she swept a droplet of condensation from her glass.

"Can I ask you something, Imogene? Purely hypothetical, of course."

She arched a refined eyebrow. "Color me intrigued."

"How would someone go about being in two places at once?"

"Goodness, if I knew how to do that, it would make my own life so much easier!" She chuckled. "It's impossible, I'm afraid. It's one of the few mysteries that Chaos magic has yet to uncover. Splitting a consciousness into two parts simply cannot be done. There are Morphs who can remain in one body while taking on the form of another—be it animal or human—but that's not technically being in two places at once. The body left behind is inanimate and vulnerable, and so it doesn't serve the true purpose of what you're asking."

I felt completely deflated. If it couldn't be done, then that left me with the same challenge I'd started with. How could I divert Levi's watchful eyes away from me? Should I just use the Orisha duplicate to cover for me and hope for the best, or would it be better to find a more believable excuse? Levi was already tracking my movements through this freaking GPS, so I'd have to leave that behind somehow. *Jerk.*

Imogene was examining me intently, an amused smile on her face. As she watched me, she toyed with the bracelet on her wrist—the one that kept her emotions guarded. That thing sucked. I wished I could have sensed how she was feeling right now, to gauge how suspicious she was about my question.

"Yes, meditation is a rather good method for controlling one's abilities during trying times," she said suddenly. "In fact, there's a meditation seminar for magicals coming up in Anchorage. It's where magicals with overly exuberant powers go to regain control and a sense of inner peace. A rehabilitation retreat of sorts. Of course, such magicals are exceedingly rare, so, in order to stay in business, I believe they also welcome troubled magicals: the kinds who are newly released from Avarice, and coven prisons, and at-risk magical youth, and so on and so forth. Those who have been magically injured, also."

I gaped at her. "Anchorage, *Alaska*?" The irony was too freaking sweet.

"I would imagine so. I don't know of any other Anchorage," she replied. "If you thought it could be beneficial to you to have some time away somewhere you could rest and regain control, then you could always apply to spend a week or two there."

"Levi would love to have me out from under his feet for a while…"

"I should warn you, magic is banned in such places, unless you're in the controlled rooms and within the given times." She gave me a knowing look. "What's more, contact with anyone outside the retreat is limited so that you can concentrate on meditation. I've heard it works wonders."

Do you know what I plan to do? Are you really on to me? If she knew something was up, she wasn't trying to dissuade me. Maybe things really had gotten dire in the National Council, and now she needed all the help she could get to take Katherine down. Help beyond what the National Council could offer, with all their red tape and bureaucracy. Garrett had said it himself—they were all talk and no action. Plus, we'd never let her down in the past, and even though the SDC members were persona-non-grata, Imogene had always had a soft spot for the scrappy little underdogs.

"Can I ask one thing?" Imogene's tone had a worried edge.

"Sure."

"You're not planning on going to Europe anytime soon, are you? For non-related purposes, of course." Her eyes held that same knowing glint. *Why would I be going to Europe?*

I frowned. "No, of course not."

"I just wanted to check. You see—and, again, this may be the G&T talking—the National Council has recently sent agents to follow Katherine's trail there, and I know you have a high stake in her capture. You have likely already heard about some of the recent robberies?"

I nodded. *So she thinks I'm going to try and follow Katherine to Europe?* I'd recently seen reports on the magical news channels that some of the central repositories across Europe had been broken into. Maybe Imogene thought I was going to try and apprehend Katherine on one of these robberies or capture one of her people to interrogate. It worked in my favor, as I didn't think Imogene would be too keen on the idea of me infiltrating Katherine's cult outright.

"I understand the personal nature of your vendetta against her, as it's one we all share in some small way. Global chaos is not something any of us want to see." She sighed. "I just feel I ought to warn you, though I'm certain you wouldn't entertain the idea of flying solo." She gave me a pointed look. "I know you're headstrong, but I would hate for you to get tangled up in any ensuing mess, or for anyone to misunderstand your intentions. It's hard, I know, but you must let the National Council do its work."

"Thank you, Imogene. And no, I don't have any plans to go to Europe. Anchorage sounds like exactly what I need right now. Peace and quiet. I'll definitely look into it."

Imogene downed the last of her drink like the elegant lady she was. "Well then, let me know how it goes if you do decide to go."

"For sure," I replied, my mind already racing with the undeniable hope she'd laid out for me. I wondered what I'd actually tell her when we met here again in a few weeks' time and she hadn't known my true intentions. *Oh, by the way, I didn't go to Anchorage or Europe. I killed Katherine Shipton instead, on her home turf. Hope you don't mind. Would you like another G&T?*

Yeah, I could live with that.

NINE

Finch

Being stuck in a storage room with the Muppet Babies wasn't exactly how I'd planned to spend my post-Purgatory days. I could have handled Wade on his own, but Raffe and Santana had decided to keep me company too. Nice of them. *Not*. Watching them fawn over each other was worse than being marched to the showers by Grimshaw and Chalmers. But I supposed they were growing on me. Like barnacles, or a nasty rash, or ticks.

I had to appreciate their abilities, at least. It took guts to control a djinn, and Santana had this one on a leash. Raffe probably thought I didn't know, but the flash of red in his eyes every so often—usually when I made one of my perfectly timed comments—was a dead give-away. I'd known since day one what he was. I had to give him props, though. Djinn tended to cling to stronger people.

"So, what's the cult like?" Santana asked. We'd all been silent for too long. Clearly, she didn't like the quiet. I happened to prefer it over trivial small talk, but I figured I'd humor her.

I shrugged. "A lot like a coven. Only, the risk of random death is higher. Then again, you all live here, so you're probably used to that by now."

"You used to live here, too. Or have you forgotten that?" Raffe replied.

"No, I remember." I smiled at him to save face. I remembered everything I did here. I remembered stealing down the hallways to get to Adley's office. The same office Krieger now had. I remembered laughing along with Garrett and the others: Rowena Sparks, Lincoln Mont-Noir, Poe Dexter, Ruby Presley, Niklas Jones. Those few moments in the day where I'd been able to forget my true purpose, the one on which Katherine had set me. I half wondered what those guys were up to these days. They didn't seem to have crossed over to the dark side of the Muppet Babies. Only Garrett had made that switch. Then again, he'd once been close with Wade. I supposed that had given him the leeway to change sides.

"You're going to keep our girl safe, right?" Santana pressed. "If not, I should warn you, I've already got a design in the works for turning your balls into earrings. I can add them to my collection."

I laughed. "Ah, so that's where Raffe's have gone, eh?"

"I mean it, Finch." Judging by her scowl, she wasn't messing around.

"Relax, I'll take real good care of her. It's my neck on the line, too, in case you'd all forgotten. If she dies or anything happens to her, I'm in trouble too. And I'm really not ready to die yet."

They don't trust you. They had no reason to. Even before my arrest, I'd been foul to the Muppet Babies. The Rag Team and my team of antagonists in endless competition. Well, more like Garrett's team, though I was the mastermind for the most part.

I didn't know whether it was the company of new people after so long with no one to talk to except burly officers, but I was starting to see them through slightly different eyes. Not too different, but there was a marked shift. *Harley, you've got a lot to answer for.* My half-sister's appearance in my life had changed so much, without me even realizing it. I didn't know if I liked it, but this was my reality now. I was a temporary member of Team Muppet, whether I wanted to be or not. After everything I'd done to them, it was no wonder they were glowering at me with obvious suspicion. Still, they could've cut me *some* slack. I was helping them take down Katherine Shipton, not running an errand to Waterfront Park.

"We've got to remember that he's one of us, now," Wade said suddenly. "His life and Harley's life are in his hands. He knows that. He's not going to screw up."

I eyed him curiously. "Uh... yeah, what he said." I hadn't expected support from Harley's uppity dreamboat. If anything, I'd have expected him to be the one preparing my balls for jewelry. I'd almost killed his girlfriend, once upon a time. Deep down, he was probably boiling with hatred, but the guy was an expert at keeping it off his face.

"How do we know this isn't all some ploy to hand Harley over like a prize turkey?" Santana replied. She had a point. I was smart... but likely not that smart. That would've taken months of planning, and I would've had to rely on Harley's desperate desire for family. Man, that would've been a good play if I were still on Katherine's side. But I wasn't. Katherine could rot in hell for all I cared. We were taking her down, whether Santana believed me or not.

"I guess you don't," I said, keeping my tone blasé. They didn't need to know how much I loathed my mother. That was my private hatred. It wasn't for them to share.

"Because he's on our side." Wade looked between us as if we were naughty schoolkids. "Harley trusts him, so we should, too. She's good at figuring people out."

"Harley has been wrong in the past. Even with her Empathy, she didn't see Nomura's betrayal until he'd locked her up in astral projection!" Santana was nearly shouting now.

I snorted. "Nomura did what?"

"None of us saw that coming," Wade replied.

"That's gutsy of Nomura, man. I bet she didn't like that." I chuckled at the idea of her trying to get back into her body. I'd have paid good money to see that play out.

"Yeah, but Harley broke out of it, despite the odds. She's getting a handle on her abilities, and she's getting more powerful by the day. She isn't going to let Katherine win this one." Wade sounded so confident I almost believed him. Almost. I knew I was taking a liability into the Cult of Eris, but her powers would come in handy.

"And what if she can't beat Katherine? What if it's a repeat of ritual two?" Santana sounded sad. It piqued my interest. I'd been given the gist of everything that had gone on with the president, but it looked like not everyone had been bluntly honest with Harley. She'd been sure of herself, but she'd floundered. And they'd been too nice to give it to her straight.

"She *will* take Katherine down this time. She's been working on her abilities. She's not going to let that happen again," Wade said. *Oh, you're good.* His face was a perfectly blank picture that revealed nothing of his true feelings. Beyond his façade, I wondered if he had his doubts about my sis, too.

I flashed them all a grin. "Hey, she's got me this time. I've got the knowledge; she's got the skills. We're going to end Katherine."

"You're what worries me," Santana shot back.

"And around and around we go, in an endless circle." I sighed and spun around in my chair. At the end of the day, it didn't matter if the others trusted me. Harley did. We were going to do this, and that was all there was to it. Still, it was curious to see the other side for once. A team who didn't threaten each other with violence and seemed to genuinely care about each other. There was no one-upmanship here, only concern and support. It was a shock to the system after the cult and the team of SDC personnel I'd been on. I was on a journey of rediscovery. *Oh God, remind me to put a bullet in my head if I ever think like that again.* I'd be drinking kale smoothies and doing yoga by the time I was done with these people.

"You don't take anything seriously, Finch. How are we supposed to take you seriously?" Santana demanded. "One moment, you're Queen Katherine's jester, the next, you're on our side? Give me a break. It reeks of trouble."

"That might just be you," I retorted.

"Shut your mouth!" Raffe growled, his eyes flashing.

I glowered at him. "Keep your guard dog down, Santeria girl, or I'll have to put him down."

"Touch him, and you'll have a horde of Orishas trying to pluck out your eyes," she hissed.

"Ooh, is that a promise? Is this how you guys flirt? See who can lash out with the emptiest threats?" I knew I was taunting them, but I didn't care. This storage room was driving me mad. I wanted to be out in the open. I wanted to see a freaking tree! I didn't want to go from one box to another.

"Everyone needs to calm down. It's hot and stuffy in here, and it's getting to your heads," Wade cut in. "Harley is pretty much the only family he has left. He's not going to betray her, not the way Katherine betrayed him. Yeah, he's still an ass, but right now, this ass is part of the Rag Team."

For the first time in a long while, I was speechless. He was right. He was freaking right. Harley was the only family I had left, unless you counted Isadora. I didn't know her, and she didn't seem to want to know me. At least Harley was making some kind of effort. My mother had made it very clear how she felt about me, and she was going to find out just what I felt about her. *Nothing but hatred.* By process of elimination, all I had left was Harley. Dammit, was *I* the one desperate for family? I supposed we both were, in our own tragic little ways. Pathetic.

What would Harley even be like, as a sister? If things had been different, would we have been close? Even with our parents scrapping with one another, would we have found a way to be real siblings? I'd never really thought about it like that before. Would I have made a good brother? Was there still time for me to be one? What did good brothers even do? Well, for starters, they probably didn't try to kill their sisters...

At that moment, Harley burst through the door with a grin on her face. *Speak of the devil.*

"I know what to do!" she yelped excitedly. "I know how to get away from Levi without making him suspicious."

Wade beamed at her. *Lovesick idiot.* It was definitely too late for me to get all brotherly about their "relationship," if that's what was going on. Not that I had a problem with it. Normally, I'd have just said something to annoy them and amuse myself. Surprisingly, I held my tongue.

"What have you figured out?" he asked.

"I was talking with Imogene, and she mentioned something about a retreat in Alaska for troubled magicals. One of your duplicates would be perfect there, Santana." She looked like she might explode with excitement. "They don't have to do magic, and they don't even have to speak for portions of the day. The duplicate can also keep hold of my phone, with Levi's annoying little GPS tracker, and I can grab a burner from Astrid. Levi won't be able to follow me there or check up on me, and the retreat folks will be so happy to see me compliant, they won't worry about me being a duplicate."

Wade grinned. "That's amazing news."

Harley nodded. "I'll need you to vouch for me, for this retreat thingy. Make Levi concerned enough to let me go."

"That won't be a problem, believe me." He chuckled, the two of them gravitating toward each other.

I was pretty impressed by Harley's deviant thinking. *This girl will go a long way... and God help us all if she ever decides to turn evil.*

TEN

Harley

I sat in the Persian palace of Leonidas Levi, shifting uncomfortably on his rattan furniture while watching him flip through the retreat brochure that Astrid had pulled from the depths of the magical web. He hadn't spoken in what felt like forever, which I took to be a bad sign. Wade sat beside me, casting me the occasional encouraging glance.

You finally get to send me to Alaska, Levi. And, heck, I'm going willingly. I tried to gauge his emotions, but there wasn't much coming off him. I sensed the usual waves of suspicion and contempt, but nothing notable, nothing that could tell me what he was thinking.

Returning my attention to Levi, I thought about the duel Imogene had told me about. Along with his reaction to the president's murder, Levi had been weirdly humanized for me. He'd gone back to being his usual, dictatorial self in the aftermath, but the memory of his reaction had remained. Now, I could better understand his perspective on powerful magicals, even if I didn't necessarily agree with it. Given what he'd almost lost, and how that had hit him, his fears were a little more rational.

At last, he closed the brochure and narrowed his eyes at me. "What are you up to, Merlin?"

I'd added a little purple eyeshadow beneath my eyes, to make me look even more haggard than usual, and I was sitting limply in the chair—visual cues to make him think I was exhausted and worn to the bone. "It's for the benefit of myself and the coven. I've been trying so hard to get a handle on my abilities, but it's getting harder to achieve on my own, and I really think this could help." I'd thought about using my reverse Empathy on him to make him a little more flexible, but I didn't want to risk making him more suspicious. This was going to have to be the best performance of my life, with no added juice.

"Go on..."

"I will do whatever it takes to prove to you that I'm serious about controlling my powers, and this retreat is the perfect opportunity. Once I come back from this place, you'll be able to sleep easier at night, knowing I have everything under much better control," I continued. "Imogene Whitehall recommended it. While I was out at lunch with her, I told her that I'd been researching ways to get better control, and she mentioned this place. I looked it up straight after, and, well, here it is."

"Imogene Whitehall recommended it, eh?" He pursed his lips in an approving manner. "And she thought it would be useful to you?"

I nodded. "She'd heard good things about it, and the results speak for themselves. Did you check the last page with all the testimonies?"

"I did." He smiled with a secret smugness. "And how long would you be thinking of leaving us for?"

"A week at most, and I can check in with you as often as you need me to. There are specific phone hours, but I'll make sure I have mine on me at all times so you can get in touch." I could feel him getting closer to saying yes. His whole body was emitting pulses of contentment, as if the idea of sending me away filled him with the same joy as petting a puppy.

He looked to Wade. "And what do you make of all this, Crowley?"

"I think it's a good idea. It's no secret that she's been having a hard time getting a grip on her abilities, and I know my mom and dad send their troubled magicals to the same retreat. They've never had any problems with the magicals afterward, as far as I know."

"I have also heard excellent things about this retreat, though I didn't think you would ever suggest it yourself, Harley," Levi said. "I had been looking at such places to send you to if things got out of hand. However, it would appear you've done my job for me, which is always a welcome state of affairs."

Why, because you're a lazy toad?

"I really think it will benefit me in the long run. It'll be easier if I have guidance." I added the cherry to the top of the sundae.

He nodded thoughtfully. "Well then, I suppose I have no choice but to sign off on this trip for you. If you make the necessary arrangements, I will add my signature and consent to the paperwork. And I hope that you don't squander this opportunity, because I will want to see some payoff for my generosity in letting you go. I trust that you will return an entirely different magical."

"I hope that I will, Director Levi." *A free one, no longer having to worry about Katherine Shipton.* Inside, I was dancing around like a maniac, feeling pleased to pull the wool over Levi's eyes once again. He'd fallen for it, just as I'd hoped he would.

Still, a cautious part of myself warned me to be careful. I'd jumped a hurdle, but I hadn't crossed any kind of finish line yet. *Remember, if you get found out, they'll toss you and Finch back into Purgatory.* There'd be no Avarice, no Alaska, no softer sentence. Not for this kind of betrayal.

"Thank you, Director Levi." I kept my reaction small but grateful as I took the brochure back.

"Don't let me down again, Merlin," he replied. "You may go."

As I got up to leave, one thought kept playing in my head: *This is going to work. This is really going to work.*

ELEVEN

Finch

"Woof, woof." I grinned at Raffe. The guy didn't like me one bit. I wished I could've said the feeling was mutual, but I didn't care enough about him to hold any judgment.

Plus, I didn't want to rile him up so much it brought out the djinn. If there was one thing that scared me, it was a pissed-off djinn. Katherine had made me face one when I was sixteen, and the memory hadn't gone away. The beast had been inside an old woman, and my mother had urged the djinn to come out as part of an experiment. That thing had come running at me, mouth opening wide, eyes flashing red, black smoke billowing out of it. I remembered its hot breath and its leering voice telling me how much it was going to enjoy peeling me like an orange. Impulse had made me throw a wave of Telekinesis at it, but it had been touch and go for a moment. It was a lesson in courage, apparently. Now, I realized it was probably to amuse Katherine.

"Quit it, Finch," Santana snapped.

"You don't like it? I thought you did." I'd shifted into Raffe's form just to mess with her. There wasn't much else to do in this storage room, and I was close to losing it. *PTSD, anyone?*

"You're an idiot." I got the feeling she wanted to call me far worse.

"How about this one?" I shifted into Harley's form and smiled at them.

Santana narrowed her eyes. "Seriously, pack it in!"

"No, I don't think I will." I needed to get out of his damned room before it tipped me over the edge. I hadn't breathed fresh air in months. Even if it was filtered through the interdimensional bubble, I wanted to taste it. The dragon garden, maybe? Or one of the outer balconies? Anywhere but here.

"Finch…" Her tone held a warning, and Raffe had moved to her side to back her up. The loyal lapdog.

"Can't a guy have a little fun?" I toyed with the cap of my lighter Esprit. I'd gone so long without it that it felt strange to have it back in my grasp. "You know what, I think I might take a little walk. This baby needs a refill." The lighter had probably run out of neurotoxin by now, and I'd need a refill before we headed into the cult. When it shifted into a blade, I always made sure it was laced with a neurotoxic chemical that would temporarily paralyze an enemy. We'd probably be doing a lot of that where we were going.

Santana stepped forward. "That won't be necessary. You shouldn't even be allowed to carry that thing on you to begin with. A foam sword, maybe, or something made of balloons, but not that. Maybe, if you're very good, Wade will give you a water gun."

"Who're you to lecture me on dangerous things? You've got a ticking time bomb for a boyfriend."

Raffe's hackles rose. "Don't push it."

"Push what? You? How do you think your friends would feel if they found out your djinn had done me in? I bet they'd find a nice little cage for you and lock you up for good." I flipped the cap of my lighter up and down. The clink of it was riling Santana and Raffe up. I could see it in their pinched expressions. "At least I wouldn't accidentally tear you to shreds in the night." I flashed a wink at Santana. She grabbed Raffe before he could lunge at me.

"You're out of line, asshole!" Raffe roared.

I simply chuckled. "Nice to see that leash is real tight. Who's a good boy?"

"Stop it, Finch. This won't do any of us any favors," Santana replied. Her hands tugged at Raffe.

"Why don't I just get out of your hair? You two lovebirds are probably dying to rip each other's clothes off. Raffe looks ready to rip something off, at any rate." He could flash his red eyes at me as much as he wanted to. I was immune while I had Harley's trust.

Santana crossed her arms. "You're not going anywhere."

"Is that so? See, I thought that door was unlocked." I walked toward it. Santana and Raffe darted toward me and got between me and the door. *Idiots.* My Esprit glowed as I forged two powerful blasts of Telekinesis and sent the two of them flying to opposite sides of the room. I thought about using my Air to trap them on the ceiling, but it wasn't my strong suit. Still, I guessed they'd forgotten what I could do.

I slipped out of the room and sprinted for the safety of the hallways, still wearing Harley's guise. In a populated area, they wouldn't be able to do a damn thing. Not unless they wanted to out Harley. *Deviousness runs in the family, Sis.* I kept running until I reached the main corridor. Students and inhabitants wandered about their daily business. A few offered nervous greetings, while others plain avoided me. *Oh Harley, look what you did.* They were scared of her—scared of what she was capable of. I almost felt proud of her. She was more infamous than me, by the looks of it.

I turned to the sound of footsteps approaching at a rapid pace. Santana and Raffe had caught up with me. But it didn't matter now. I offered them a sardonic smile and gestured to the other people who were walking about.

"Try and stop me, and it's all over," I whispered. "If you reveal me here, Harley will pay. Purgatory isn't fun. She won't survive life in there."

They backed off immediately. *"Pendejo!"* Santana hissed.

"I'm going to guess that wasn't a compliment." I smiled at her. "Now, if you'll behave, I'm going to the Bestiary." I set off before they could reply. Behind me, I could feel them seething with hatred. *Good.* I didn't want them to like me. I didn't want us to be friends. Close ties only got people killed. I'd learned that the hard way. *But what about Harley?* I pushed the thought away and pressed on. I could worry about her later.

Even the security personnel stationed at the Bestiary seemed to be terrified of me in Harley form. That made me happy. These people reminded me too much of the Purgatory officers. They could do with a little humbling now and again, to keep them on their toes. I lunged at one, just to make a point. They staggered back as if I'd just grown four heads. Moving away from them, I chuckled. I just wished they could have been Grimshaw or Chalmers. Now *that* would have been satisfying.

"Tobe, my man!" I hollered as I walked straight up to the Beast Master. He was feeding pellets to some tiny creatures through a tray in the glass of their box. They looked like half-armadillo, half-moth hybrids.

He looked up at me in surprise. "Harley? What may I do for you on this rather subdued afternoon?"

It's been a long time, Tobe. I still remembered how it had felt to inhabit his form. I'd almost gotten away with framing him for the gargoyle mess all those months ago. If he really knew who I was, I wondered how he'd react. Would he swipe my head off with those terrible claws of his? Probably not. Tobe was a pussycat. He'd be more likely to offer me some sage pearls of wisdom about reforming my character than decapitate me.

"I was hoping you could help me with a little plant problem," I replied. Santana and Raffe were flanking me like nervous bodyguards at a political rally.

"Santana, Raffe." Tobe dipped his head in greeting. "Is everything well with all of you? I hate to pry, but you seem rather agitated."

"Everything is A-OK. Right, guys?" I glanced at them. My warning was clear. I didn't know if news had reached the old furball about my breakout. Right now, it didn't seem worth it to ask. Not with so many blackcoats lurking about.

Santana nodded slowly. "We've just got a lot on our plates, that's all. Too much coffee, too."

"Caffeine is not good for the body or the soul," Tobe replied. "Stimulants rarely are."

"Speak for yourself." I laughed. "I bet you haven't needed a sip in all your life. You were probably born stimulated to the max."

Tobe eyed me strangely. "I suppose I was, in a manner of speaking. Now, back to the matter at hand. What's this plant problem you require assistance with?"

He held my gaze, his amber eyes reminding me how wise and serene he was. It was a stark contrast to Naima, who had never been calm a day in her short life. His intent stare made me feel suddenly guilty. A sharp jab to the gut. I'd put him through a massive ordeal, even though I'd known he'd eventually get cleared of all the accusations against him. That had been a tough day at the office. My divided mind sometimes liked to remind me of what I'd done to him. Tobe, who'd never harmed a fly, yet people had believed him capable of releasing those gargoyles. Maybe I wasn't the only one who should have felt guilty about what happened to him that day. Thinking about that, I felt the guilt retreat.

"I was hoping you could give us access to the Devil's Tongue Triffids," I replied, doing my best Harley impersonation.

He frowned, rumpling his furry forehead. "Devil's Tongue Triffids? Why on earth would you need access to those?"

Devil's Tongue Triffids were a rare species of Purge monster that manifested as gigantic, carnivorous flowers that spat streams of vicious neurotoxin to trap and kill prey. More of the substance drenched their petals to entice prey in and render them immobile so they could be devoured. The neurotoxin was stored in bulbous sacs at either side of their main stem and had to be squeezed out while they were dopey from sleeping gas.

"It's for a project that Preceptor Bellmore gave us," Santana interjected before I had time to answer. I was shocked at her willingness to be my accomplice. The fiery girl had hidden depths, especially when it came to protecting Harley. I contemplated the kind of rift I could put between them if I told Harley what I'd heard Santana say about the president catastrophe. *Another time, maybe.* It didn't seem like a good idea to divide and conquer right now.

Tobe nodded reluctantly. "Well, I suppose I could—" He stopped mid-sentence as two figures came running through the hallway of the Bestiary, veering off toward us. My heart lurched. What the hell was the real Harley doing here? The crap was about to hit the fan.

Tobe's eyes narrowed at me. His spidey-senses hadn't been wrong about something being up.

Harley skidded to a halt, with Wade behind her. "Why weren't you answering your phones?" she hissed at Santana and Raffe. We were out of sight of the security guards, but we needed to keep a low profile. Hard to do, with two of the same person standing in front of the Beast Master General.

Wade gaped at me, his eyes wide. He shook his head, as if he thought he was seeing double. His mouth only stretched wider as realization started to creep in. He glanced from the real Harley to me, and back again, then back to her again. It was like something out of an old comedy sketch, Wade doing the quadruple-take of comic disbelief. Tobe wasn't too far off, either.

"How can there be two of you?" The Beast Master ruffled his feathers. "Unless... no... I was hoping you would not go through with it." His gaze returned to Harley, who'd finally noticed me. Well, there was no use pretending anymore.

Shaking off Harley's form, I shifted reluctantly back into my old self. Tobe wasn't going to like this. The moment he saw me, his face morphed into a mask of pure resentment. His eyes darkened as he drew up to his full height. His bestial muscles bulged beneath his fur, his wings shooting out to either side, each feather flashing like a blade. His hands splayed out, revealing the savage claws at the ends of his paws, while his talons clicked on the marble floor like the raptor's from *Jurassic Park*. I got the feeling I might face the same end as Samuel L. Jackson in that movie.

He growled, flashing his fangs. *"You."*

"Ta-da!" I waggled nervous jazz hands at him. Humor could defuse most situations. This one? Maybe not.

"How dare you come here!" Tobe spat. I'd never seen him so angry. Actually, I'd never seen him angry, period.

"See, the thing is—"

He cut me off. "How dare you hide yourself in front of me? How dare you deceive me? You are arrogant, and make no mistake, you are lucky I do not disembowel you where you stand."

"So, there's a chance of that *not* happening?"

He stood even taller, dwarfing me completely. *Oh, crap.* This wasn't going to end well. Tobe was going to kill me before I even got my hands on Katherine. I wasn't sure which I was more annoyed about. And I was going to make a total mess of the nice marble floor.

Harley stepped between us and put her palms to Tobe's chest. "Tobe, you need to calm down. He's not supposed to be walking around like this. I'm sorry he came here, I really am. The security personnel can't know we're here, or I'll get thrown in Purgatory! We got lucky, since they didn't see me come in. We don't want to do anything that might make them suspicious."

He looked at her and instantly calmed. His body relaxed, and his wings folded in. "I apologize for my outburst, Harley. There are certain troubling memories that appear to have gotten the better of me. I didn't know you had gone through with the act of freeing him; otherwise, I would have been more alert to strange happenings."

"I know, Tobe. I'm sorry for not telling you. There hasn't been much time, but please be assured that we were going to," Harley replied. His paw covered her hand and held it gently.

"I believe you."

"We portaled into Purgatory and managed to get him out, and we've been extra careful to cover our tracks. He's not supposed to be out, but I guess he doesn't understand the gravity of the situation." Harley shot me a cold look. "It's the only way we can get Katherine before she completes the third ritual. I know it looks reckless, but it's our only choice."

Tobe sighed. "I understand, Harley. I just wish such a grave task did not have to fall upon such young shoulders, and I wish you did not have to put yourself in such danger to achieve it."

"Me, too." She smiled up at him. *Did she take conflict de-escalation classes or something?*

"I'll call Astrid, get her to fix the cameras," Santana said. She plucked out her phone and dialed a number, wandering off behind one of the glass boxes. I hadn't realized my little outing would cause this much hassle. Believe it or not, I hadn't intended it to.

Harley turned to me. "You need to shift into someone else, pronto."

I shrugged. "Fine by me." I gathered my Chaos energy into my center and shifted into the only person I could think of. He wasn't here, so I doubted he'd mind. Plus, being surrounded by the Muppet Babies had made me nostalgic for my younger days. A more teenage body would do just nicely.

"Seriously?" Harley arched a disapproving eyebrow at me.

"No good?" I'd picked Jacob, just for kicks.

She sighed. "It'll have to do."

"For what it's worth, Tobe, I'm sorry for getting you arrested. It sounds mega cliché, but I'm not that guy anymore. I don't expect you to believe me, but… let's let bygones be bygones, eh?" I flashed a grin. I was aiming for charming.

"I do not know that I can forgive what you did, but—" Before he could finish his sentence, the lights went out in the Bestiary. Emergency bulbs glowed dimly in the blackness, and I heard creatures throwing themselves against their glass enclosures. The thuds were ominous, like approaching footsteps in a dark alley.

"What the hell?" Harley muttered, her figure a silhouette.

"Something weird is going on for sure." I scanned our surroundings. Overhead, electricity crackled, and temporary flashes lit up the Bestiary for a second before plunging it back into darkness. It was as if someone were lighting matches and blowing them out again.

Every crackle was followed by the snap of charmed locks. The glass boxes were being opened. One by one. I realized I was holding my breath. I'd seen this happen before. This was the work of a very powerful Electro. And she was trying to take down the Bestiary.

I only knew of one such Electro: Thessaly Crux.

TWELVE

Harley

"W hat's going on?" I yelled, grabbing Finch's arm in the darkness. It seemed too coincidental that this had happened while Finch was out exploring. Panic bristled through my chest. This couldn't be happening.

"An Electro. It's got to be Tess," he replied.

"Did you say an Electro?" Tobe's voice echoed softly.

"Nothing else could cause this." Finch sounded certain, but I couldn't see enough of his face to be sure.

"If it's that one from Marie Laveau's garden, I'm going to wring her neck!" I snapped. This was happening too quickly. If the Bestiary fell... *The Bestiary can't fall. I won't let it.*

"Krieger and I installed a backup security panel after the unfortunate incident with Quetzi. Come with me." Tobe's paw grasped at my wrist and dragged me after him, with Finch following close behind, his hand around my other arm. Together, we sprinted through the gloom and headed toward one of the far walls. As he'd promised, a metal panel had been fixed into the façade. Tobe wrenched it open with his beast strength and pulled down hard on a big red lever.

"Guys, keep the beasts in their boxes!" I yelled to the others. Security personnel should have been fumbling around in the darkness, but I couldn't see them, and I definitely couldn't hear them. The Bestiary had fallen into an eerie silence. Something bad had already happened to them, I just knew it. All I could hear were the terrifying clinks of the charmed locks as they dropped off, failing thanks to the glitching atrium, and the creak of the glass doors as they swung open.

A second later, I saw a ball of fire light up as Wade went running to slam any of the opening boxes shut. The others were doing the same, with Santana's Orishas flying around her, casting a glow on what was going on. We couldn't have these beasts on the loose, not again. There was a horrible irony in the fact that this was happening while Finch was in the Bestiary.

"What can we do?" I asked as we reached a panel. I was breathless with fear. I'd seen enough when Jacob almost cracked the interdimensional bubble to know that this would be a freaking catastrophe if the Bestiary failed.

"Flip those switches as quickly as you can," Tobe replied.

Creating a tiny ball of fire in my palms, I lifted the light so Finch could maneuver the switches. Everything in this panel was magically connected to the central stem, the very core and battery of the Bestiary. If that stayed cut off, then we were all doomed.

"Finch, flip the switches!" My heart clenched with anxiety. If Thessaly Crux was in here, then she would likely be on the prowl for anyone who might stop her or try to arrest her.

"Yes, ma'am." Finch stepped up and pressed all the power switches, using the light from my fireball to see by. Meanwhile, Tobe was yanking down all ten levers on the massive panel as if there was no tomorrow, which there might not be if we didn't get everything up and running ASAP.

Nothing seemed to be working. The switches had been flipped, the levers had been yanked, and still the Bestiary was steeped in darkness.

"Is she in here with us?" I whispered, my hands shaking.

Finch shook his head. "I doubt it. She's a smart one. She won't get any closer than she needs to. She's nearby, maybe just outside the coven. My guess is, she's touching the central stem with a Gemini device."

"A who-said-what-now?"

He sighed. "They really don't teach you anything here, do they? Magical contraption. Two devices, actually. They're rare and illegal, naturally. One must be connected to the central stem; the other will be in her hands. I've seen them used before."

"How did someone find their way into the Bestiary to fit the counterpart device?" Tobe asked, yanking down his last lever.

Finch shrugged. "She must've found a way to sneak it into the coven to attach it. Robotics, maybe? I know she has a tech guy. Trouble is, there are no cameras directly pointing at the stem, right?"

Tobe shook his head. "The radiation is much too powerful. It distorts and corrupts any image that anyone attempts to capture. Although, I did not see anything out of the ordinary via the mirrors angled toward it."

I looked toward the beautiful central stem of the Bestiary that ran from the ceiling to the floor in the dead center of the room. It contained batteries forged from crystal cylinders and held thousands of wires in neatly wound patterns, running through the entire stem like veins and capillaries, each one sending power across the globe. On that stem, somewhere, was one half of the Gemini device.

"There's one way we can stop the device," Finch said.

I glanced at him. "How?"

"We need to flip these switches again, in a certain order. I've used a Gemini device before—I know how to overcharge it so it breaks." He looked panicked, but that nagging doubt in the back of my head wouldn't shut up. This was all too weird, and way too convenient.

"You want us to power down the Bestiary?" I couldn't believe I was saying it.

He shook his head. "Not exactly. Look, I know you don't trust me completely, but if you do as I say, you'll get autonomy back. Not only that, but you'll send a pulse back through the other end of the Gemini device that's powerful enough to fry Tess's hands. Hopefully it'll knock her out, but first things first."

"If you've got any part in this, Finch, I swear to God I'll—"

He grabbed my hands and stared into my eyes. "I know how this looks. Believe me, I do. But if the Bestiary stays down, the whole magical world will collapse into the real world. The interdimensional pockets will spill out."

I glanced back at the room and saw Wade, Santana, and Raffe sprinting across the Bestiary floor, slamming doors to keep the beasts at bay. Raffe had gone full djinn, rounding up any escapees and hurling them back into their boxes. There was terror on their faces as they came face-to-face with a huge serpent. Between the three of them—Santana, Raffe, and Wade—they wrangled it into submission and slung it back into confinement.

Tobe stepped up behind me. "I do not know why the backups aren't working. I can only assume there is a device attached to the stem, as Finch has said. I only hope he's as trustworthy as he attests to being."

"Come on, Harley." Finch gripped my hands tighter. *Why do I have to make the choice?*

"You really think this will work?"

He nodded. "I really do."

"Then… we have to do it."

"Finally!" He looked back at Tobe. "Now, there is no room for error. None. So you'll have to do exactly what I tell you. To the letter, got it?"

Tobe and I nodded.

"Tobe, you get back on the levers. Harley, you're on switches."

I forged a small ball of fire in my right hand and held it close to the panel. "Which ones?"

"Tobe, pull the second lever. As soon as he's done that, Harley, you need to push the fourth switch in."

That nagging doubt was getting louder. "How do you know all of this?"

"I've seen the panel before. I saw Tobe's sketches when I was plotting to let the gargoyles go. Katherine wanted me to get them for her, but I was arrested before I could. I've still got the memories, though. So I know which switch and lever does what, and I've always been good with electronics. This will work."

My suspicions softened. Maybe his checkered past had finally become useful. After all, he'd had free rein of the coven before he was suspected of being Katherine's associate.

"Tobe, pull it. Harley, get ready." Finch cast me a hard look. "It's now or never."

I gritted my teeth. "Fine. Tobe, do it."

I made a vow, there and then—if Finch was playing us, then I would see him punished for foxing us again. He wouldn't even make it back to Purgatory once I was done with him.

Tobe pulled down hard on the lever, and I flipped the fourth switch. As fast as possible, we made our way through the pattern that Finch gave us until, at last, there was only one switch left. The main switch, the one that would hopefully bring life back to the deadened Bestiary. It was my job to press it, and I'd never been so scared to flip a switch before. To my right, Tobe pulled down the last lever, leaving the rest up to me. Praying that I was right about Finch, I lifted the plastic casing of the last switch and pushed on the yellow bar. It clicked down, and now we had nothing to do but wait.

A moment later, sparks of bronzed electricity gathered around the Bestiary cages, spiraling up in mystical tendrils. As if a gust of wind had swept them away, they surged toward the central stem and got sucked into the inner workings. The wires and fiber-optics lit up like it was the Fourth of July, electricity bristling through every vein, as if someone had just defibrillated the entire thing. It popped and crackled with a thousand tiny explosions, bronzed particles dissipating into the atmosphere, until, finally, the Bestiary lights flickered to life and the central stem began to thrum. The power had come back.

I sank down against the wall, able to breathe again. Holding my head in my hands, I looked up at the lights. I'd never been so grateful to see lit-up bulbs before. It also made me realize just how quiet the Bestiary had been without the whirr of the central stem constantly pulsing away in the background. It was nice to hear it again and feel the vibrations running through the floor beneath me.

"Do you realize what we have just done?" Tobe stared at the central stem. "We have just prevented a devastating attack upon, not only the coven, but the rest of the magical world. I cannot even begin to imagine what would have happened if we had not. I shall be able to think of little else for the foreseeable future."

I looked to Wade, who seemed to be putting the last of the runaways in its box, with Santana and Raffe backing him up. They'd done just as much as we had to prevent this from taking a downward spiral real fast. And they looked exhausted.

Finch smiled. "I knew it would work."

"Looks like some of that underhanded stuff you did here came to some good," I replied, my body drenched in a cold sweat.

"You should be glad that Katherine didn't get her hands on it first. I'm not saying getting arrested was a good thing, but at least she didn't get those sketches." He folded his arms across his chest and looked up at the towering central atrium.

Not far from where we'd left him, Raffe darted across the room and stooped to pick something up beside the base of the stem. A second later, he came running toward us with something clutched in his hands. It looked like nothing more than a smoking jumble of plastic, all mixed up with a few still-glowing crystals and a tangle of molten wires, but I sensed it was far more than that. Finch confirmed my suspicions as he took the smoldering item out of Raffe's hands and held it up to the light.

"Yep, just what I thought. This is one half of the Gemini device."

Raffe gaped at it. "It fell off the atrium."

Behind him, Santana walked toward us, her phone pressed to her ear. She ended the call shortly afterward, her face set in a grim expression. "I like fireworks as much as the next girl, but I needed my brown pants for that one." She shook it off in true Santana style. "I've just been on the phone with Astrid. She's sending security magicals to do an in-house and outside perimeter sweep for Thessaly Crux. She's sending medical staff to come and look at the personnel in here, who got electrocuted by those initial blasts. She's already pulled up Thessaly's file, and she's looking through it now. She'll phone back when she's got more info."

"What would we do without you?" I flashed her a smile.

"Flap about, probably," she replied. "So, who got the lights back on?"

I nodded toward Finch. "That was all Finch's doing, believe it or not. He knew what to do to destroy that heap of junk over there. It was messing with the atrium, but he knew a way to get it to overload and break off."

Despite everything, Finch had somehow managed to prove himself. He'd asked me to trust him, and I had. And he hadn't let me down. It surprised me, but I was also secretly pleased. That nagging doubt in the back of my head had gotten so loud, to the point where I was certain he'd somehow twist everything and turn on us, letting the Bestiary collapse for old time's sake. I'd been very wrong, and that was a tricky pill to swallow. Even Tobe seemed a little sheepish about the whole thing.

"Thanks, Finch," I said. "We'd be totally screwed if you hadn't stepped in like that." I got up from my spot on the floor and moved toward him. I didn't know whether to go in for a handshake or a hug, so I settled for standing there awkwardly, just looking at him, instead.

He shrugged. "I only did it so I could get this lighter filled. Tobe, can you help a guy out? I need that neurotoxin for what we've got coming up."

Wade came hurtling around the corner, his cheeks red. "Is everyone okay?"

"All fine. Finch fixed the power problem." I filled him in on the rest of it as quickly as I could, rendering him speechless. "Where have you been?"

"Slamming all the doors shut and putting the locks back on so none of the beasts could escape," he wheezed, catching his breath.

"My gratitude, Wade." Tobe bowed slightly, his amber eyes brimming with concern. "I ought to conduct my own checks of the Bestiary, to ensure that none of my beasts have managed to break free. Although, I'm certain you have done an exemplary job."

"I did my best."

Finch shook his head. "Not so fast there, Beast Master. I need the neurotoxin, and I need it now."

Wade shot him a dark look. "Neurotoxin? No way."

"Yeah, that doesn't sound like a great idea," Santana added.

"Worst possible idea," Raffe chimed in.

"Wait... is that why you were out here prancing around, almost blowing our cover?" Wade's eyes widened in disbelief.

"Hang on, now. Neurotoxin might not be a bad thing, where we're going. It's highly effective stuff. I remember from my own experience with that blade of yours, Finch," I grumbled. "Tobe, if you've got a safe way of getting us some, it might actually be really useful. It'd be one more string to our bow, and we need all the strings we can get."

Tobe sighed with exasperation. "I have such a hard time denying any of you. I will assist you, but I must reiterate that I'm not aiding you for *his* benefit. I just do not wish to see you end up in Purgatory." He turned his attention to Finch. "You may collect the neurotoxin you require, but at your own risk. As I am sure you know, Devil's Tongue Triffids are notoriously dangerous. You seem to know a great deal of things that you should not."

Finch grinned. "You're right there, Beast Master. But what's a guy to do if people leave things lying around?"

Tobe growled. "Do not push your luck. I have a great deal of patience, but it appears to wear thin when it comes to you."

"Even when I saved your Bestiary?"

"You are still standing, are you not?"

Finch frowned. "Yeah."

"And you are still in possession of both your head and your bowels, are you not?"

"Yeah." He looked so confused. I stifled a laugh.

"Then you have received the extent of my gratitude." Tobe's amber eyes flashed with a warning. For a split second, all of Finch's cocky arrogance fell away, leaving an alarmed kid who didn't know what to do. It was all the more poignant as he was still in Jacob's form.

"You won't say anything to anyone, will you, Tobe?" I interrupted, wanting to relieve Finch from his paralysis.

Tobe shook his head. "I will not breathe a word of it."

I walked right up to him and put my arms around him. The Beast Master embraced me in a tight bear hug. This was the hug I'd thought about giving Finch, but Tobe made a great substitute. He was warmer and furrier and less likely to turn on me. Finch had definitely proven himself today, but that didn't mean I trusted him completely. It was safer to keep a buffer of caution up when it came to him. That way, if I made it out of this mission alive, and he hadn't done anything to betray us, I'd be pleasantly surprised. *Gotta keep the bar low.*

"Thank you, Tobe," I murmured into his fluff.

"For what?"

"For being on our side."

He chuckled, the sound rumbling in his throat. "I always endeavor to be on the side of good, Harley. It just so happens that the pendulum is swinging in your direction."

I hoped with all my heart that he was right—that I was doing the right thing, for the right reasons.

THIRTEEN

Harley

After discreetly making our way out of the Bestiary, leaving Tobe to tie up any loose ends and explain how he'd jumped into action to fix the glitch, we reconvened in the infirmary, well out of sight of any cameras. We stood around the central table in Krieger's office to draw up our plan of action. The Ephemeras glowed on their fancy golden stands, off to the right of the tabletop. It was hard to take my eyes off them, given the swirling, almost liquid tendrils that churned inside.

Garrett had gone back to LA to give them the results of his "research," but the rest of the Rag Team was present, Louella and the real Jacob included. Nobody had told Jake that Finch had temporarily used his face to sneak back through the coven. It had been creepy enough to see Finch all gussied up in my form; I wasn't going to put Jacob through the same thing.

"So, after the duplicate has safely been sent to Alaska, we'll portal to Salem, where we'll meet Naima in Azarius," I said, pointing to a picture of the dive bar that Astrid had brought. She'd made a whole folder on what we were going to do, though she'd promised to shred the evidence as soon as we were gone. There couldn't be a single trace left for Levi to find.

"That's right," Astrid replied, with a satisfied nod.

"That means we need to get our disguises on the go. Finch?" I looked at him. He'd been way less catty since coming back from the Bestiary, even though everyone had relaxed around him. After the miracle he'd pulled back there, there was more gratitude than suspicion between the Rag Team and my half-brother. Apart from Wade, that is, but he was always concerned when it came to me.

"I've got them all in order and ready to go. It didn't take long. I had a lot of time to think in my cell. Child's play, really," Finch replied, his arms folded defensively across his chest. "I've picked two siblings, presumed dead after a mission that went wrong in the Arctic Circle. I remember the story on the news, so it sort of stuck. There were polar bears involved—not pretty. But no bodies were found, just blood. It's an easy cover. And they're definitely dead. A hunter out there said there's no way they could have survived. So there won't be any surprises."

"Do these siblings have names?" I prompted.

"Yeah, Volla and Pieter Mazinov. Volla was renowned for her abilities with Water and Earth, and Pieter was known for his skill with Fire. I thought they'd come in handy, since you've got the Elementals down, and I can just borrow the Fire from you, thanks to these babies." He tipped his head at the Ephemeras. "I didn't know we'd have these, so I was just going to BS my way through it and get you a Kaleido mask. But this works even better. I can give my Shifter skill to you, to make a better impersonation of Volla, and I can use your Fire in case anyone asks me to show what I've got. So to speak."

I was beyond glad that Krieger had managed to get hold of a couple of the Ephemeras. The last person I'd heard of who had one was Jacob's mother. His father had gifted her one with his Portal power inside, so she could make a quick getaway if she needed to. It had saved Jacob's life. I hoped it could do a similar thing for us, keeping us from getting skewered by Katherine.

"And these siblings—what else can you tell us?" Tatyana asked. "I'm not too familiar with them, though the surname rings a bell."

"It should. They were wanted criminals, until recently. They were trying to steal a cache of ancient weaponry when they were mauled to death. We can use their identities to get into the cult, no problem. Their rap sheet will come up, and Naima will be thrilled to have us. We'll be just her kind of people."

I nodded. "That's good to hear. Dr. Krieger, can you help us out?"

"I most certainly can. So, if I have this correct, Finch's Shapeshifter ability is going into one and your Fire ability is going into the other?"

"You got it," I replied.

"Very well, then. If both of you could come over here, we'll begin." He gestured to the Ephemeras, and we walked over to the table. "If you give me a moment, I'll program the first Ephemera to receive your Fire, Harley." He tinkered with the first orb, pressing tiny buttons in a sequence I didn't understand. A moment later, the whole thing lit up red. "Please place your hand here." He pointed to a flat golden panel on the side of the orb, which seemed to form the shape of a hand. Tiny needles had risen from inside the metal, and I got the feeling I knew what they were for.

"It's going to hurt, isn't it?" I asked.

Krieger smiled. "No more than an injection."

Great, I hate needles. With a grimace, I placed my hand against the designated area and felt the tiny needles sink into my skin with a sharp bite. A pulse of energy shot down my arm and entered the orb, filling the swirling mist with bright scarlet light that throbbed with power. The needles retracted, and I pulled my hand away.

"Did it do it?"

Krieger nodded. "I believe so." He fiddled with a few more buttons, which reduced the baseball-sized orb down to the size of a marble. The glow inside slowly faded to a dull pulsation, which could easily be hidden beneath our clothes or worn as a piece of jewelry around our necks. "I've provided a small cloaking shield around the orb so that it won't be detected by any magical machines. This will not affect its use." He handed the small orb over to Finch, who slid it into his pocket.

"My turn, I guess?" Finch smiled sardonically.

"If you would," Krieger replied as he prepared the orb. Meanwhile, I stared down at my hand and saw the tiny pinpricks—eleven in total. They'd heal up pretty quickly, by the looks of it. Already, they were starting to fade.

Finch followed the same procedure, placing his hand on the orb and letting the tiny needles do their work, his arm spasming as a bolt of his Shapeshifter ability poured into the orb. The glass ball inside lit up with a silvery light that looked like the beginning of a thunderstorm, then Finch took his hand away and let Krieger shrink the orb down. Once the cloaking shield had been implemented, Krieger handed the small golden orb to me. I took it gratefully and unhooked the chain of Imogene's gift, slipping the orb onto it via a small hole in the top, then reattaching it around my neck. It fit neatly beside my pendant, which Krieger had altered with a complex morphing spell to look like a simple silver disc at the end of a silver chain, identical to one that Volla Mazinov had worn in many pictures. The two things brought me comfort for the trials to come. The St. Christopher medallion was helping, too, and it already matched a similar item Volla had worn.

"Now, while Ephemeras can normally only be used once, I have managed to tweak these to give longer endurance to the abilities inside," Krieger said. "Keep an eye on the gems inside. Once they start to dim, it means the power is ebbing, and they will cease to work once the light goes out. So, we will just have to hope they work as they should."

I'd almost forgotten that part. "How long will a Shift last, if I use it?"

"Given your heightened skill with all that Chaos energy, and my alterations, I would imagine it can continue for a week, if you remain in your Volla form for as long as possible and shift back and forth only once or twice. It may even last longer than that, but it isn't an exact science." Krieger's tone was anxious, which only made me more nervous.

"I'll wait a bit, then, until I shift. We don't want to use up time we might need later. Plus, I could do with knowing who we're impersonating a little better." I glanced at Astrid. "What can you tell us about the Mazinovs?"

She took out Smartie and placed it on the table. Her hands moved quickly over the screen, drawing up files and photos that would help us blend in. From one of the images, a young man and a young woman stared back, both dressed in thick hunting gear with rifles slung over their shoulders. They were good looking, the woman with short white-blonde hair that had been styled up in textured spikes, while the young man had a mane of golden curls. Their eyes were the same shade of cobalt blue, and they both stood tall, with lean muscles and broad shoulders. A video clip played shortly afterward, showing them walking toward the camera with a definite swagger. *Ah crap, this is going to be tough.*

"They spoke with faint Russian accents, which Tatyana can help you with," Astrid said. "They'd traveled a lot, so their accents weren't thick. They were known to be very charming and flirtatious, and an instant hit with any men or women they encountered. There were a lot of broken hearts when it was declared that they were MIA."

Finch grinned. "Not hard for me. I can do charm."

"That won't get you far if you don't speak like them," Tatyana interjected. "Russian accents aren't as easy as you might think. This isn't James Bond."

Finch shrugged. "I've always been good with accents."

"If you're still struggling, I can come up with a voice bug to alter your speech," Astrid said, noting my discomfort. This was all getting a bit too real. "I already had some prepared, just in case. Smartie will need a few minutes to collect data on the voices of these siblings, then I can download it to the bugs. They'll have to be injected into your necks, and you won't be able to turn them off unless I do so remotely."

Finch and I exchanged a glance. "We'll go with the bugs," he said. I cast him a grateful look for taking one for the team. "I've got to say, I'm looking forward to using a bit of Fire."

"You can only do so once or twice," Krieger repeated, his brow furrowed.

"Yeah, yeah, I know the score. I'm just saying."

I smiled at him. "You some kind of pyromaniac? Should I be worried?"

"I used to like to burn things when I was a kid. Does that make me a pyromaniac?"

"We'll have to wait and see." He was looking at me in a strange way, as if he was trying to figure me out. "Hopefully, we won't need to use it."

"Way to burst my bubble, Sis." A chuckle bubbled out of his throat. A real, genuine laugh that took me by surprise. I knew we'd have to get to know each other better on this mission, but I'd been nervous about it up until now. For some reason, that laugh dispersed some of my fears. At the end of the day, we'd both always wanted the same thing—a family. Now, we had the mutual desire to take down Katherine Shipton to add to the mix.

Maybe we aren't so different, after all...

"So, once you've met with Naima, what happens next?" Wade chimed in, his eyes fixed on me. He was worried, and rightly so. I was already going out of my mind, and we hadn't even left the SDC yet.

"We go with her to the Cult of Eris and let Finch lead the way to Hester's spirit." The name stuck in my throat, lodged behind a big ball of sadness. I was both dreading and looking forward to seeing my mom's spirit. Seeing her again, even in spirit form... I couldn't even begin to imagine how it would feel. I just hoped my emotions didn't get the better of me when it finally came down to it.

"And then what?" Raffe replied.

I took a breath. "Jacob, Astrid, and Dylan are going to portal to Key West while we're in Salem, and Astrid is going to take a boat to the islands, where she'll plant an emergency device in case you have no other way out. It has to be Astrid because she's human, so she won't alert any magical sensors. We get ourselves out of Fort Jefferson once we have the spirit by causing a commotion in the Bestiary if we have to.

We press these other buttons you've given us, if we can, and Isadora will come to get us out." I tapped the pendants around my neck, which Krieger had altered to create emergency get-out buttons that would signal our location to Isadora. There was no way Jacob was coming to get us from the cult itself. Having to portal to the opposite dock in Key West was close enough.

"And, in the meantime, I'll be controlling the two duplicates," Santana added. "With Raffe for support. Keeping two duplicates running, when they're so far away, is going to be a tough egg to crack, but Louella is going to keep researching to help me get through it."

Isadora nodded. "Meanwhile, Tatyana, Wade, and I will run interference and make sure nobody knows about any of this. Wade and I will be waiting for your signal to come and get you." Her eyes hadn't left me throughout all of this, and I could feel her anxiety coming at me in waves. I was going right into the belly of the beast, with no assurances that I'd make it out alive.

"Perfect," I said, though I could feel how tenuous it all was. It relied on everything going right, and experience had taught me that not everything worked out quite as well as we planned.

"We should make sure your duplicate has everything she needs, Harley, when I conjure her again." Santana came over to where I was standing and offered me an encouraging smile. Just the kind I needed.

I picked up my duffel bag and handed it to her. It was stuffed full of my clothes, my ID, and everything else the duplicate might need to be a convincing version of me.

"It's all here, except my phone. That's in my room, but the keys are in here to get in there. You'll have to take it just before my duplicate is set to leave for Anchorage. I didn't want to bring it in here in case Levi came looking, using the GPS."

"No problem, *mi hermosa*. I'll make sure I have everything before the duplicate takes the mirrors to Anchorage. The usual idiot check." Santana grinned, then closed her eyes and drew out the chosen Orisha. It flitted in the air before me, giving off a faint bluish hue and a vibrant energy of excitement. Santana mumbled something in a rich and ancient language, and the ball of light sprouted limbs, lengthening out to resemble me. A minute later, I was staring right into my own eyes, face-to-face with my duplicate.

"What are you all staring at?" she said. "Anyone would think you'd never seen me before. Not very convincing, is it, if you go around gawking at me."

I laughed. "She's good, Santana. She's very good."

"Hey, this is mostly me here," my duplicate replied. "Isn't that right, Santana?"

"It sure is, *mi hermosa.*"

"Hey!" I protested.

Santana chuckled. "I've got to keep it believable."

"Shame I won't be spending more time here, huh, Wade?" My duplicate flashed him a mischievous grin that made his cheeks turn a deep shade of beet red. "You'll be begging Santana to keep me on once Harley gets back. A little treat to yourself."

Finch was howling with laughter, and the rest of the Rag Team members were stifling giggles. My duplicate certainly knew how to hold the attention of a room, even if it was at Wade's expense.

"Hands off, okay," I warned, half teasing. Poor Wade looked like he wanted the earth to open up and swallow him whole. Still, it was pretty funny. This version of me was going to give a lot of people a run for their money—the perfect duplicate to go on a retreat for troubled magicals.

"I'm just getting it all out before I end up in the monastery." My duplicate flashed me a grin.

"So, does this mean we're ready to go?" I glanced around the room, feeling the collective apprehension.

"Looks like it," Wade replied, his expression sad. It wasn't going to be easy for him to watch me leave, not knowing what might happen to me. It wasn't going to be easy for me, either. In that moment, I wished everyone else could disappear, just for a short time, so we could properly say goodbye to each other. This was all happening too fast, and I felt a desperate need to pump the brakes, if only to kiss him and hold him for what might be the last time. But I couldn't let myself think like that. If I got all doom and gloom, I'd have a harder time keeping up the confidence act when we met Naima.

"How about you try that Shifter goodness on for size?" Finch broke the tension, his eyebrow arched.

I shook my head. "Not yet. Not until we're in Salem. There's something I might need to do first, and I don't want to waste my one shot at shifting, if I only get the one shot." I held Wade's gaze to try and let him know what I meant. A small, sad smile crept onto his lips. He understood why I couldn't just yet. I wasn't going to say my goodbyes while in the body of Volla Mazinov, no matter how funny it would be to see him try and kiss me.

"Makes sense," Santana said, before anyone else could protest.

Tatyana nodded. "You probably should wait until the last moment."

"Agreed," Astrid said. "From a purely logical standpoint, of course."

I love you girls. They all got it, even if the boys were stumped.

"Well then, I guess we should get going." I let out a shaky breath. "Santana, you take duplicate-Harley up to my room and then on to the mirrors to Alaska. Isadora, Finch, and I will head to Salem, while Alton covers for her for the time we'll be gone."

Wade raised his hand. "I'll be coming too, but just to Salem. There's a, uh… last-minute briefing we need to have before you go." I waited for Finch to chime in with some crude remark, but he didn't. Instead, he wore a sad smile and kept his mouth shut. Though I tried to push away any affectionate thoughts toward Finch, I couldn't help but feel the tug of the sorrow written on his face. He knew all about the gift of being able to say goodbye. He and Adley hadn't been given that chance.

"Okay, so while we portal to Salem, the rest of you will be coordinating from the SDC. Everyone know what they're doing?" I pressed on, feeling a confused flurry of emotions.

Astrid nodded. "The emergency protocol device should be in place within the next few hours. Until we come for you, it'll be radio silence. You'll be on your own."

"Remind me why we can't have earpieces again?" I said, grazing my teeth across my lower lip.

"They'll find any earpieces or bugs on us when they do the initial check at the cult," Finch replied. "These Ephemeras should fly under the radar, even without the cloaking device. Nobody is looking for them. But they do look for earpieces and bugs."

"Right." My heart sank. Being cut off from the Rag Team was going to be tough, and that was an understatement. I'd gone on dangerous missions before, but never without the help of my friends. Going forward, I'd have to rely entirely on Finch.

"Your speech devices are ready," Astrid said, bringing me rapidly out of my funk. She took two minuscule items, which looked like grains of rice, out of her pocket and placed them on the table. "Krieger, could you prepare two syringes?"

"Certainly." He turned around and plucked up two gigantic syringes, complete with needles that looked needlessly huge. "Ready when you are, Astrid." My stomach churned as I remembered the huge needle they'd used on me for my Reading. *Ugh.*

As if I wasn't already freaking out enough. Why did it have to be needles?

FOURTEEN

Harley

"I really do need to have a last-minute briefing with you, but I'm glad we've got a bit more time," Wade whispered as we walked along, the two of us behind Finch and Isadora. We'd arrived in Salem a few minutes ago and were making our way down Bridge Street to reach Azarius. There was a coffee shop and a parking lot to our right, with a kiosk at the opposite side of the empty lot. That was our way into the interdimensional pocket, where we'd find Azarius. Not wanting to be caught out in the open without my new face, we ducked into a side street while we went over the final details of the mission.

"Me, too." I'd managed to convince Astrid not to activate the speech devices until Wade gave the all-clear so we wouldn't have to have an awkward, Russian-tinged goodbye. My farewells to the rest of the Rag Team had been hard enough, but this was going to be a killer. A week or so without hearing his voice… I didn't want to imagine it, but it would soon be my reality.

"So, just a last check to make sure everyone knows what's going on." Wade addressed the other two, the four of us gathered together in a tight huddle. "As agreed, as soon as you have Hester's spirit, you'll get out of there and signal us with either the tech Krieger has put into your pendants, or the emergency device on the dock. Isadora will be able to trace your location through either and come to get you."

Everyone had agreed that the job was too dangerous for Jacob, since he was both a Portal Opener and a Sensate. Katherine would've drooled at the prospect of such a tasty morsel for her collection. Even though he'd have portaled Astrid and Dylan to Key West by now, he was under strict instructions to portal back to the SDC until Astrid and Dylan called for him again. Dylan was staying on the mainland, while Astrid ventured with the tourists to Dry Tortugas to drop off the emergency device.

"Got it." I squeezed his hand.

"As for getting around the island itself, I've got these memorized." Finch whipped a scroll of blueprints out of his jacket pocket and handed it to Wade.

"How did you get these?" Wade sounded shocked.

"I had an old hiding spot in Krieger's office, when it used to be Adley's. I snatched them before we left." It didn't really surprise me that Finch had hidden stuff like this in the coven, though I wished we could've found them before breaking him out. There might have been a way to do this without him, if we had. Although, I supposed, in a strange way, I was starting to warm to him.

"Obviously, we can't take them in with us, but they might be of some use to you," Finch explained. "These black lines are the outlines of Fort Jefferson itself, and the white lines are the interdimensional pocket."

"That doesn't answer my question," Wade replied. "*How* did you get these?"

Finch smiled. "Dry Tortugas used to be a busy shipping lane. My great-grandfather, Drake Shipton, bought the island with Fort Jefferson on it after the military abandoned it. He left it to Katherine in his personal will, but it was never disclosed in any official documents. Nobody even knows it's owned by him, as far as I know." He paused. "Although, the bubble does change location sometimes, when there's a threat. I've seen it move to the Indian Ocean after a suspected breach, to one of my great-grandfather's other islands. He liked property on formerly busy shipping lanes, what can I say?"

"So our great-grandfather was Jack Sparrow? Is that what you're saying?" I smiled nervously.

He smiled back. "Only much, much cleverer."

"Well, I'll take these and see what Astrid can make of them when she gets back," Wade said. The clock was ticking toward our goodbye, and I wanted it to stop altogether. I knew I was stronger than ever, but I didn't want to have to do this alone. The Cult of Eris hadn't given me much choice.

"Be careful out there," Isadora said, moving forward to hug me.

"I will." I hugged her back tightly, not knowing how long it might be until I saw her again.

"We'll be there as soon as you need us. I'll be waiting for your signal," she added, as she released me. She cast an uncertain look at Finch, as if she wasn't sure if she should bid him farewell, too. He was her nephew, after all.

"We should be going, then." Finch covered the awkward pause, as he shifted into the guise of Pieter Mazinov, complete with his mane of curly golden hair and his cobalt-blue eyes. He already had the necessary swagger, and the speech device would soon kick in. I just hoped I could pull it off the same way. Being a different person was totally new territory, and I'd have to call on every ounce of tomboy in me to make it work as Volla.

"Can we have a minute?" I kept my gaze on Wade, ignoring the eyeroll from Finch.

"Sure, it's not like we've got a schedule to keep to," Finch replied.

I turned to Wade and looped my arms around his neck, feeling his hands smooth around my waist as he pulled me flush to his body. I really hoped this wasn't going to be the last time I got to hold him like this. Otherwise, I'd have made the most of last night, instead of falling asleep watching a dumb movie. Now that the moment had come, I didn't want to leave him.

What if I don't see you again? The prospect was too terrible to even contemplate, yet here it was, weighing on my mind. I had to fight to shove it down, knowing it would only make things harder. I had a mission to complete. I clung to him even tighter, never wanting to let go. Tears were already brimming in my eyes, my eyelids fluttering wildly to try and keep them at bay.

"It's going to be okay, Harley," he murmured.

"I know," I lied. "It's just going to be weird without you."

"If you need me, use your pendant to call for backup. We'll be there before you know it." He brushed a strand of hair behind my ear. "And just know that, whatever happens, I... I love you, Harley."

My heart stopped, my mouth struggling to form the words. I wanted to say them, I really did, but they didn't come easily to me. I couldn't remember the last time I'd told anyone I loved them. Wade was waiting, looking flustered, but I was having a hard time finding the words, even though I felt it. I really, really felt it.

"I shouldn't have—" Wade started to speak, but I cut him off.

"No, no, I... I feel the same way," I blurted out. "I love you, Wade."

His face broke out into a giddy grin, and I knew my expression mirrored his. "Come back to me, okay?" he murmured.

"I will. I promise."

Slowly, he leaned in toward me, his lips grazing mine in a soft, tender kiss that made my knees tremble. I pulled him closer, pressing my lips harder against his, my mouth moving with passionate intensity. It was desperate and sad and remarkable, and I didn't want it to end. Once it did, I'd have to step into the unknown.

"Geez, anyone would think you were going off to war," Finch muttered, breaking our moment. "The plan is to get in and get out... alive. I've got no intention of dying at the hands of those cult fanatics. Harley isn't going to, either."

"Hey, weren't you one of those fanatics until they tried to have you killed?" Wade shot back.

Finch shot him a deadly look. "Touché, pal. Touché."

With Wade and Isadora gone, I clasped my hands around the Ephemera. Energy radiated from inside the ball, which would soon explode inside me. *What could possibly go wrong?*

I winced as the entire ball shot out the tiny spikes, each one burrowing into my flesh as I gripped it tighter. The Shapeshifter energy pulsed through me in a sudden jolt, my body going into an automatic response. Looking down, I watched as my hands and arms and clothes shifted into those of Volla Mazinov, my mind holding onto the picture of her so I got it right.

Finch whistled. "Nice job, Merlin." His voice had already been altered to sound like Pieter, after Wade had radioed in to Astrid to get the devices going.

"Do I look like her?" My own voice sounded weird and echoey, and definitely not my own. I ran a hand through my hair and felt how short and strange it was.

He nodded. "Spitting image. That Chaos inside you must be incredible if you can do such a good shift the first time. Usually, they're a complete disaster. Limbs in all the wrong places. That kind of stuff."

I gaped at him. "You didn't think about telling me that *before* we came here?"

"What would be the point? You'd freak out and lose your nerve. You did good, Sis. Adrenaline works for you."

"We got lucky," I muttered.

"Hey, luck is nothing to sniff at. If it works."

I looked toward the street. "Should we get on with this?"

"Thought you'd never ask." He grinned as he led the rest of the way to Azarius. He was enjoying this. Either that, or he was teasing me to cover his own fear. I didn't know which I preferred.

We stepped through the kiosk and headed down a set of dingy steps, emerging into another world entirely. Cobblestone streets stretched out before us. It was medieval, almost, with Tudor-style façades to the buildings that made me feel like I'd entered a time warp.

Overhead, an endless night swirled through the bubble's roof, lighting everything up with a silvery glow from the constant moon. Hooded figures wandered the streets, some already drunk, others brawling on the cobbles. There were shops of all kinds and a bevy of bars and pubs along the main route.

"There." Finch pointed up ahead to a wooden sign, which was swinging even though there was no breeze. *Azarius.* We approached it with the attitudes of the Mazinovs, adding a little swagger.

Stepping into the gloom of the dive bar, we headed straight toward the bar itself. It smelled of stale booze and sweat, combined with the acrid tinge of smoke. There weren't too many people inside, but the whole place had a creepy 1700s vibe to it, complete with nooses dangling from the walls, ancient torture devices, and old witch trial announcements taking pride of place in rusty frames. There were paintings, too, of witches being burned at the stake. A stark reminder of a very dark time in magical history. From what Finch had told me, this was where a lot of criminal magicals were known to come and go about their evil business, so it was no surprise that Naima had chosen this spot to do her recruiting.

"Is she here?" I whispered as we sat up on rickety bar stools.

Finch smiled. "Do you see a tigress lurking anywhere?"

"No, I guess not."

"Looks like we'll have to wait." He flagged down the bartender and ordered a drink. "Do you want anything? A Witch's Brew, perhaps?" He scanned the list of drinks.

"There isn't one called that."

He smirked. "There is. Or a Hangman's Delight, maybe?"

I eyed the dirty counters and moldering fridges. "Nah, I'm good."

"Suit yourself." A strange green-tinged drink arrived in front of him a few moments later, in a filthy glass that turned my stomach. He didn't seem to care, taking a deep sip and leaning back in satisfaction. "It's been so long, my old friend."

"I keep forgetting," I said. "I guess you can't get these where you've come from."

"They don't exactly have a bar in Purgatory, no."

We sat in awkward silence for a while as he contentedly sipped his drink and subtly tried to bob along to the heavy metal music blaring out of the speakers. "Does Mrs. Anker know what happened to you?" I figured it was a decent question to break the tension.

"I don't know, to be honest. She sort of ended her duties with me when I turned sixteen."

"Did you get along with her?"

Finch shrugged. "I guess. I've had a lot of time to think about this. My suspicion is, Katherine never wanted me getting too close to her, so she'd been told to punish me randomly, probably to stop me from getting too attached. The outbursts were always unexpected. She was nice enough, for the most part. Heavy drinker. Had a bunch of stories about some guy she used to love. Never married, even though she was a 'Mrs.' I think she wished she'd married that dude, so she conjured up a fantasy. She was odd, but never really cruel. She punished me, the way she'd likely been asked to, but she never went too hard on me."

"How did you end up with her?"

"Random selection. Mrs. Anker didn't know Katherine all too well. She was more scared of her than anything, for obvious reasons."

"Would she be worried, if she knew where you'd ended up?"

He chuckled bitterly. "Worried? I doubt it. She probably doesn't remember me leaving."

"Still, that can't have been an easy childhood, ferried between Mrs. Anker and Katherine."

"Ease up, Dr. Phil. Both our childhoods sucked. End of story. But at least you weren't indoctrinated from an early age."

I smiled. "No, I guess not." I paused, steeling myself. "There's something I've been wondering about."

"And I bet you're going to ask me."

"What was the point of you releasing those gargoyles? What did you want to achieve?"

He looked at me in surprise. "It was a power play, to show what Katherine could do—how easily she could bring down a coven and reveal the magical world to the human world. It was supposed to be a hefty warning, and the start of her world domination. She wanted the humans to discover a small fragment of our world so that the magicals would have to take drastic action to cover the mess. Action that needed Katherine, I guess. She wanted to rise from blood and destruction and chaos and be a savior."

"Sounds like her," I murmured.

"You know, her influence over those monsters has always creeped me out. She used to talk to Purge beasts all the time in her Bestiary and get me to watch. The gargoyles were always her favorite. The rest didn't really listen to her so much."

"I wonder why."

"Your guess is as good as mine. Maybe they sense something in her that they like."

I glanced over my shoulder at the sound of the door opening. A figure walked in, but he wasn't anyone special—a gruff-looking dude in need of a drink. He came to the bar and ordered, taking his drink and striding over to a secluded spot in the shadows. Through the foggy haze of bluish smoke, I noticed another figure I hadn't seen before. They were sitting in the farthest corner, tucked away behind the leather arm of a booth. They wore a hood low over their face and were drinking alone. I watched a waitress approach to ask if they wanted another drink, but the terror drifting off her was overwhelming. The waitress was scared of the hooded figure, whoever they were.

I opened out my Empathy and sent it toward the hooded figure in the hopes of gauging their emotions. The feelings that came back were vague and diluted, but they were definitely there—insecurity and humiliation, but also a whiff of affection and a strong current of deter-mination. I hadn't expected those kinds of emotions from someone who had the waitress running scared. There was something else, too—a distinct sense of toxicity. It was a familiar sensation, and one that I'd experienced before, in the Bestiary. The figure felt like a weird version of a Purge monster. It reminded me of Tobe, in terms of intensity.

Naima.

"She's over there," I whispered. "At least, I think it's her."

Finch smirked and set down his drink. "Well, there's only one way to find out. Just be ready to back me up if this goes south. We might need to make a run for it."

"What?" I tried to protest, but he'd already gotten up from his stool. To my surprise, he wasn't headed for the hooded figure. Instead, he made a beeline for two men sitting at a nearby table, minding their own business.

"Hey, we don't want your kind in here!" Finch barked, and he launched two blasts of Fire at the two men, forcing them to jump from their chairs to the floor. I gaped at Finch. I had no idea why he'd targeted those guys.

"Are you out of your mind?" one of the men wheezed up at Finch, who held a burning ball in his hands.

"Security magicals have no place here." Finch launched another attack. One burst of Fire hit the bar floor, scorching a hole in it.

"We don't want trouble. We're just here to drink," the second guy shouted.

"Find somewhere else!" Finch sent out another fireball, while I sent out a vibration through the floor that shot up in a tree. It knocked aside the table as it exploded through the hole I'd already made. *If Finch is trying to get all eyes on us, it's working.*

"Stop before you do something you'll regret!" the first guy warned.

Finch grinned through Pieter's face. "When the end of the world comes, those who follow the system will be the first to fall. When Katherine rises, you will suffer. She will soon reign supreme, and I'd rather be on the winning side than end up dead in the dirt with you losers."

I cast a subtle glance at the corner and found that Naima was watching us, though she remained in her seat. Her amber eyes flashed with curiosity.

"Don't say we didn't warn you," the first guy hissed as he ducked out of the way of the Water tornado. He held his phone to his ear, evidently calling for backup from any security magicals in the area.

Finch turned to me. "Run," he whispered.

Turning tail, we sprinted for the door, down the cobbled street, and up the stairs through the kiosk, with Finch sending a couple of magical smoke bombs over his shoulder for good measure.

Yeah, if that didn't get her attention, nothing will.

FIFTEEN

Finch

Harley and I ducked down a side alley between two buildings. Up the street, our followers pounded the sidewalk and missed us completely. They looked pissed. And they'd be calling for their pals to come help.

We pressed up against the wall. The shade from an oak tree cast its darkness on us and kept us out of sight. It had been a bold move, but it'd definitely caught Naima's attention. As I peered up the alley to see if anyone was doubling back, laughter burst from my throat. I couldn't help it. It hit me like a punch in the stomach. I sank down onto the ground, howling.

"Ah man, I haven't had this much fun in a long time." I wrapped my arms around my chest as I collapsed in hysterics.

Harley stared at me as if I'd lost my mind, a faint hint of a smile on her lips. She was dying to laugh. I could tell. She had to see the funny side of this. We'd just smoke-bombed two off-duty security magicals for the sake of getting into the Cult of Eris. It was insane. And hilarious.

"Oh come on, you're allowed to laugh." I jabbed her playfully in the leg. "Stop being such a coven drone."

She snorted. "A coven what?"

"A try-hard. Someone who takes covens too seriously. Wade's the perfect example. He was born a drone, poor sucker." I grinned at her. *Let's push some buttons.* My favorite pastime.

"Hey, Wade isn't a drone!" she protested. "He's broken his fair share of rules and done plenty of things you'd probably go crazy over. He helped break you out of prison, remember?"

My laughter subsided to a wheeze. "You got me there. He did good."

"Yeah, well, don't call him that again," she said, catching her breath. The smile remained on her lips. She was amused, she just didn't want to show it. Hell, she probably agreed with me. Wade was the epitome of the upper-class elite. He'd been as indoctrinated as me, learning how to stand in line and obey. Maybe Harley was good for both of us. *You're getting soft, Finch.*

"Fine. I won't call your boy a drone."

"Much appreciated." She looked down at me, and her smile widened.

I laughed. "You totally agree with me."

"I mean, he's getting better at bending the rules…"

"Must be your good influence."

She rolled her eyes. "Now I know you're mocking me."

"Only a little."

"How's your Ephemera?" She nodded to my pocket.

I took out the small orb. The gem inside was still glowing brightly. "All good. Looks like Krieger did a good job ramping up their power. I reckon I've got a couple more uses."

"Well, don't go overboard."

I grinned. "Yes, Mom."

We both turned as footsteps approached, and a dark figure cast a shadow down the alleyway. For a second, I worried the security magicals had come back. They hadn't. It was the same hooded figure from the bar. Naima, for sure. I'd have known that face anywhere. For a moment, I forgot I'd shifted into Pieter Mazinov and wondered why she didn't look shocked to see me. And then I remembered she had no recognition of this face at all. *Good.*

During my time in the cult, nobody had messed with Naima. Her temper was short and always leapt toward violence before anything else. Right now, she stood as imposing and fearsome as ever. Terror gripped me unexpectedly, in case she had somehow figured out what I was doing here. She'd finish the job that Kenneth Willow hadn't been able to, in an instant, if she sensed who I really was. The only thing keeping me from making a run for it was Harley. She'd told me that they'd overpowered Naima twice before. With her pumped-up powers, I hoped she could again, if she had to.

It changed my view of Naima completely. As I looked at her with fresh eyes, I realized she didn't frighten me anymore. Instead, I felt sorry for her. Katherine was her world, and Katherine didn't give a damn about anyone but herself. Naima was trailing after the impossible. If she kept on trying to seek validation and affection, it'd destroy her, too. Katherine wasn't capable of returning such feelings. I doubted she ever had been.

"Who are you?" Naima cut straight to the point.

I got up and dusted myself off. "Pieter Mazinov, and this is my sister, Volla." I stuck out my hand for her to shake. She eyed it but didn't take my hand. All people, aside from Katherine, were beneath her.

"I know of you. I thought you were mauled to death by polar bears."

"That was the story. The heat on us was too much; it was the best thing we could do to get the bounty hunters off our tail." I didn't miss a beat. "We've been keeping a low profile, to keep up appearances. But then we heard about Katherine and her cult, and we had to come out of hiding. We want to join."

Naima flashed her fangs. "Why?"

Harley stepped up beside me. "Because of Katherine's success so far. I don't see anyone else actually doing something about the state of the system. She's a total badass. She's actually getting stuff done. She killed the freaking president of the UCA!" She wore a twisted smile on her new face. *Attagirl.* "If there's a reckoning coming, we want to be on the right side. We'd be idiots to stay on the sidelines when she could bring people like us to glory."

"I was rather impressed with the way you handled yourselves in there," Naima said after a short pause. "But that is not enough to gain access to the Cult of Eris. We have had a great deal of trouble regarding moles sent from the magical authorities, and it is very tiresome to have to execute them. We will not be making similar mistakes again."

"So you won't let us join?" I narrowed my eyes at her.

She shrugged. "You are not on my list of potential candidates, who have been personally headhunted by Katherine herself. So, no, you will not be permitted to join her ranks. I imagine you have no way to prove that you are not spies, and so you are not worthy of our time."

Well, that didn't turn out the way I thought it would. I'd seen plenty of people brought into Katherine's ranks who were way less useful than the Mazinov siblings. I was totally stumped. How were we supposed to convince Naima to let us in now? I'd had one route, and she'd blocked it. Not that I was giving up. I was itching to see Katherine again, and not in a good way. Nothing would stop me from succeeding in my mission. I guessed that grim determination still ran deep in both of our veins.

SIXTEEN

Harley

N*o way, beastie.*

I hadn't come all this way just to fall at the first hurdle. The National Council hadn't done us any favors, pushing their agents into the cult and getting themselves found out and killed. Naima's suspicion of us was palpable, disguises or no disguises. I realized pretty quickly that we'd have to do something drastic to win her trust.

"I guess all of those spies said the same thing, but we aren't traitors." I sucked in a breath. "In fact, we've got intel you might want. See, there's already a mole inside the cult. That's why we've come to you. The authorities are getting too close to Katherine, and we want to stop them from worming their way in."

Naima flashed her fangs in annoyance, while Finch shot me a what-the-hell-are-you-doing kind of look. I ignored him, keeping my focus on Naima. She was our only safe way into the cult, and if we didn't make this one shot, we might as well have gone home right then.

"I've got contacts in the National Council—rebels who hate the system just as much as we do. Someone is giving them information from inside the cult. We just don't know who. My brother and I hoped we could help." I kept up the play, more determined than ever. It felt a little strange to call him my brother out loud. Even with the disguises on and our fresh identities, it was pretty much the truth. *Half-brother,* I had to remind myself, to keep some distance between us.

Finch nodded. "The authorities have never done us any favors. If they've got someone inside the cult, we want to expose them. For Katherine's sake. If she's going to create a new world order, we can't have anyone getting close enough to take her down."

"Our source inside the National Council kept us under the radar for a year after that 'accident' with the polar bears," I continued, bouncing off Finch. "They created the story to keep the do-gooders off our tail. He's trustworthy, our guy. We've got no reason to doubt him or the intel he's given us."

"Yeah, and if Katherine's game, we can provide her with the National Council's intel directly. If that's what it takes to prove we're here solely to serve her, then we're more than willing to give up what we've got," Finch added.

Naima said nothing for an age. "What intel, exactly?" she purred at last.

"Our source told us that the Librarian had been taken by Katherine but had managed to escape. They discovered where the Librarian went after she escaped Katherine, at our request. We were planning to go to the Paris Coven ourselves to finish the job, but then we heard someone had beaten us to it and killed her in the infirmary," I said, not missing a beat.

Naima smirked. "Apologies for that. Time was of the essence. I had to complete the task before she could recover from the addling that had jumbled her mind into nonsense."

"You did it?" I kept my expression amazed, not wanting her to see the anger that bubbled beneath.

"Naturally." She flashed a proud grin, baring her fangs. "Katherine gave me the mission personally, and I could not disappoint her. It was so easy, in the end—like cutting through butter. I confess, I left a bit of a mess, but at least the job got done."

"I doubt we'd have made a cleaner job of it. My sister here can get a little volatile when she wants to. I've seen a man explode after she filled his veins full of water. Not pretty, but totally cool." Finch gave a wry laugh. I forced a twisted smile onto my face, even though I wanted to make a mess of Naima right there in the alleyway. *You killed her, you heartless bitch.* I vowed to remember that so I could take my revenge when Katherine was out of the picture. I'd made a promise to Odette, to protect and save her, and Naima had made me break it. I'd break *her* for that.

Naima stared at us for several minutes, leaving us hanging. I hated her with every fiber of my being, but that didn't change the fact that we needed her. Vengeance could wait, and I had it in buckets. Heck, the list was getting longer by the day: *Katherine, Naima, Kenneth Willow, Levi...*

"Follow me." She turned without another word and headed off down the alleyway, prompting us to scurry after her like eager rats. Still, I couldn't help breathing a sigh of relief as we trailed after her. This could be it—the entry point we'd been waiting for. I just hoped the risk paid off, as I realized I might have just gotten the National Council's mole in a big old pot of hot water.

Nevertheless, I wasn't about to let my guard drop, and I knew it would be stupid of me to think we were just going to waltz through what was to come. Naima was not the kind of woman—or rather, Purge beast—to be underestimated. Yeah, she was Katherine's lackey, but she was also a creature of Chaos, with a sharper mind than she cared to reveal. Pretending to be a simple, brutish follower of the cult seemed to be part of her act. Plus, I'd have to be very careful about what intel I chose to give up going forward.

We followed Naima down a labyrinth of quaint streets, drawing a few looks from the neighborhoods we went through. A hooded figure wasn't exactly a comforting sight. Then again, I figured they'd just think we were part of some reenactment group. Salem tended to be rife with that kind of thing, the town reliving its dark past with a macabre sense of enthusiasm.

Before long, we reached an eight-story building on the corner of some unknown road. An American flag was flying from the central balcony. The building was painted a pretty shade of jade green, the trimmings washed with crisp white. It looked like it had just come out of *Hocus Pocus*, and I expected the Sanderson sisters to come rushing out, singing at the top of their lungs and charming innocent kids across the neighborhood.

The real-estate dream I'll never have. I followed Naima up the wooden steps as she pushed through the front door. Judging by the reception desk, it was a hotel of some kind. An enormous gold-and-crystal chandelier hung from the ornate ceiling overhead, casting shards of light across the plush crimson carpet. Service staff in scarlet uniforms crossed the foyer, while guests lounged on velvet sofas, and soft piano music drifted out from one of the adjoining rooms.

This didn't seem like Naima's bag, but then I supposed that was a little judgmental. Yeah, she was a Purge beast, but who was I to say that meant she didn't like the finer things in life? The staff seemed to know her very well, all of them greeting her with bright smiles and elegant bows. I guessed the fact that she had a furry face and a mean set of fangs didn't mean a whole lot to them. *Clients are clients, right, as long as they've got the dollar to pay?*

Glancing back at the other people in the foyer, I noticed one of the clients wearing a long, striking necklace, the ruby in the center glowing slightly. Bronze tendrils rippled across her fingers as she spoke to the guy beside her, like someone trying to flip a coin between their knuckles. The understanding clicked into place: this wasn't an ordinary hotel.

"Ah, Miss Naima, a pleasure to see you back among us," the receptionist—a middle-aged man in a sharp suit—said, as she approached the desk. "Your usual suite is ready." He took a key from one of the hooks and slid it across the counter, a polite smile fixed on his thin lips.

Weird...

Naima didn't say a word to us as she crossed the foyer toward the elevators and pressed the call button. Finch and I exchanged a look as we waited behind her, feeling very out of place. The Mazinovs weren't exactly dressed for this kind of fancy place, and my short, spiky blonde hair was definitely drawing some looks.

The doors pinged open, and we entered the elevator. There was a uniformed man inside who smiled at Naima and pressed the button for the penthouse, folding his arms behind his back as the doors closed again. *There's a freaking elevator bellboy! Is this the Ritz-Carlton or what?* I moved to the back of the elevator and pressed myself against the wall. Glancing to the right, I caught sight of myself for the first time, in the full-length mirror that covered the sides of the elevator, and had to stop a gasp from bursting out of my throat. I looked exactly like Volla Mazinov, which was sort of the point. But it was still eerie to see.

I had spiky, platinum-blonde hair that was buzzed at the sides, and skin as pale as snow. *No way this chick could've been eaten by polar bears—this is snow-camouflage 101.* Cobalt-blue eyes stared back at me from a strikingly pretty face with angular cheeks and a strong jaw and lips that could've put Angelina Jolie out of business. My frame was slender but lean with muscle, dressed up in highly impractical black leather trousers and a simple gray T-shirt, with a black shearling coat over the top. This was the closest to cool I was ever going to get.

I realized I'd been staring at myself a little too long and fixed my gaze on the ceiling instead. I had the temptation to whistle, but I resisted it. Meanwhile, classical music filtered in through hidden speakers, making the experience all the more awkward. It was a truth, universally acknowledged, that speaking in an elevator was tantamount to insanity.

I tried to focus on the mission ahead, which only resulted in my mind racing a mile a minute, thinking about all the worst-case scenarios. Katherine could murder us. Naima could slit my throat open with her fangs. A cult member could discover our disguises. We could ruin the National Council's investigation. I could sneeze and accidentally phase out of Volla Mazinov's form. *Yep, we could definitely be murdered about a million different ways.*

I almost jumped out of my skin when Finch squeezed my forearm. He was looking at me, his gaze encouraging. There was a protectiveness about him that kept taking me by surprise. It reminded me of those training sessions we'd shared at the SDC, before he was revealed as a traitor.

Maybe this is the real him. Bad mouth, terrible temper, but... well, good. Deep down. But I couldn't turn weak around Finch. I couldn't let him see me vulnerable, in case he used it against me. I shook off his hand and folded my arms across my chest. He'd tried to kill me not too long ago, and nobody changed overnight. Nobody.

Just when I thought we'd found our way onto Willy Wonka's magic freaking elevator, on a ride that would never end, it jolted to a halt and the doors opened out onto the swankiest suite I'd ever seen. The penthouse sprawled across the top floor of the hotel, with more rooms than my old apartment and a sofa the size of a bus. Smaller versions of the downstairs chandelier hung from the ceiling in every room. The view from the windows looked out on the water, where storm clouds were rolling in.

"Katherine is paying you way too much," I blurted out.

Naima chuckled. "We do not receive recompense for being part of the Cult of Eris, Volla. If it is wealth you seek, then you have come to the wrong organization."

"I think she means you've got nice digs here." Finch flashed a grin.

I nodded. "Yeah... it's beautiful."

Naima cast her paw around the suite. "This entire hotel is a front for the cult, and is a respite for magicals only. If a human were to walk in, they would simply be told that the rooms were fully booked," she explained. "All revenues collected go toward serving the cult, financially speaking. While the members are not paid, an organization such as Katherine's cannot evolve without investment."

"Makes sense," Finch said casually, looking unimpressed by the suite. He'd probably seen plenty like it during his time with Katherine.

"We have hotels such as this all across the United States," she said proudly. "Even Alaska."

Poor Alaska.

"Is that so?" I was genuinely impressed, and equally horrified.

"Yes, we have been operational for more than five years, and we have amassed an incredible fortune from such enterprises."

"Looks like it." Finch plopped himself down on the huge sofa and put his feet on a strange, furry footrest that resembled a dead creature. I headed down the small set of steps to the living room where Finch had made himself at home, but I paused as I noticed something unsettling. The Persian rug had been rolled to one side, and a salt pentagram, complete with ancient symbols, had been drawn directly onto the marble floor. Small copper bowls at each corner were filled with various herbs and chunks of colorful crystal.

"Having a party?" I joked, though my heart was thundering.

Naima smirked. "In a manner of speaking. You are about to join the Cult of Eris. If you wish to back out now, I am afraid you will not be permitted to leave the premises alive."

"Nope, no backing out," Finch said, jumping up. "We're good to go."

I nodded. "What he said."

"Very well then. If you would care to step into the center of the pentagram, we will begin." Naima ushered us into the middle, arranging us so we were standing in a triangle. With her hands on both our shoulders, she began to chant something in Latin, the sound rumbling out of her throat and sending a shiver through my body. *"Ex terra ligare Munera tua potestate ut educeres nos iter est."*

The pentagram lit up like I'd just stepped in front of headlights, the glare searing into my retinas. Fiery white light surged across the salt-drawn edges of the pentagram, and violent puffs of hot black smoke nearly scorched my skin. At every corner, an explosion of white light burst upward, lifting the copper bowls into the air before sending them crashing back down and spilling their contents into the middle of the symbol. I looked down at my feet, only to see that there wasn't a floor anymore. Instead, there was a gaping black void.

I screamed as the light of the pentagram swallowed us whole, and my body began to disintegrate. My arms evaporated like ash. Finch was already mostly gone, his head the last thing remaining. Every part of us was being sucked through the ground, into an insanely narrow wormhole, with an almost comical slurp.

I could've handled the disintegration if it weren't for the pain that came with it. I could literally feel my body being strung out like spaghetti, my entire being stretching and straining. Worse still, I couldn't cry out in pain, because I had no idea where my mouth was anymore.

And then, we landed. Well, more like fell onto the ground, splattering with all the elegance of tomato sauce. Threads of white light spiraled all around, piecing us back together. Naima, who was clearly used to this horrible way of traveling, had her back to us, patting herself down.

I patted my whole body, too, making sure nothing was missing— only to find that I had patches of shearling jacket and patches of leather jacket, and similar blotches of skin along my arms: snow-white and my own, slightly darker tone, combined in a terrifying patchwork. The worst thing that I could see was my fingers. Half belonged to me, half belonged to someone else, differing in size. I shot a look at Finch and almost screamed.

He was a mishmash of himself and Pieter Mazinov, put back together like gruesome blobs of Play-Doh. It looked like Shapeshifters had a bit of trouble with this mode of transportation, and I could only imagine what I must look like. Panic hit me with the force of a freight train. What if I'd used up my one Ephemera shot at Shapeshifting? What if I couldn't fully get Volla back again? Even like this, if Naima saw us, it'd be game, set, and match.

Finch lurched forward and grabbed my shoulders. "Breathe, Volla. Breathe."

I looked into his eyes and nodded, trying to slow my hyperventilating. He was already slipping back into his full Pieter Mazinov persona, the Frankenstein's monster parts of him retracting into a full disguise. I had to focus; otherwise, this had all been for nothing. Closing my eyes, I sucked in as many deep breaths as humanly possible and felt myself slowly coming back together as Volla. The Shapeshifter energy was still inside me. I could sense it pulsating wildly, mingling with the rest of my overactive Chaos.

Opposite us, Naima retched, bending double before standing upright again. "Apologies for that," she said, recovering. "The Strainer, as I like to call it, always makes me feel somewhat strange." She turned, at last, and I prayed I'd managed to put myself together again in time. A laugh rasped from her throat as she looked at me. "My goodness, and I thought I had issues with the Strainer."

"What? What is it?" I lifted my hand to my face, feeling the edge of a droopy eye.

"You appear to be melting, Volla." Naima chuckled.

Finch moved closer and gently massaged my eye socket, urging the skin to go back to where it was supposed to be. I felt sick. This was beyond weird and creepy, with my eyes falling out all over the place. Looking down, everything else seemed to be in working order. My fingers were all the same length. Still, I was grateful that Finch was actually watching my back, pushing my skin about like it was the most normal thing in the world.

Naima flicked her wrist at me. "There is nothing to worry about, Volla. It happens to everybody. When going through the Strainer for the first time, they all fall apart and have some difficulty putting themselves back together again afterward."

Humpty Dumpty, eat your heart out. Although, I wondered if she realized the poignancy of her statement. A lot of the people who came here were lost souls with nowhere else to turn. And the rest? Well, once they went in, they'd never be the same again.

"Welcome to Eris Island," Naima said. We'd landed in an empty, plain room, with one enormous floor-to-ceiling window at the far end. It looked out upon the island and the Gulf of Mexico beyond. Only, it didn't look the way I'd expected. I'd seen images of Dry Tortugas online, before we'd left for the mission, and it hadn't looked like this. Rainforests stretched as far as the eye could see, covering an area much bigger than the solid, human island beneath it, while giant stone statues protruded from the canopy like titanic guardians overlooking the water. A sandy beach curved along the nearside edge of the island, a sun-faded pier jutting out into an azure inlet.

Another beach lay beyond the first one, hazy behind a wall of interdimensional bubble. Pasty tourists lolled on the white sand, stretched out on sun loungers, oblivious. But I couldn't see Fort Jefferson anywhere. I wondered if Finch had lied about the location of this place, but a small smile played upon his lips.

"Who are those folks?" he asked, casting me a conspiratorial look.

Naima grimaced. "Pay them no heed. They are mere humans. They do not know that Eris Island exists upon what they prefer to call 'Dry Tortugas.' A bizarre name, if you ask me. Here, you will refer to it as Eris Island, and nothing else."

It must have taken Katherine a long time to conjure up this sort of lush greenery to go with the rest of it. Above us stretched clear blue sky, and colorful birds flapped from tree to tree. All throughout, curious structures were hidden within the canopy—like treehouses, almost, though shaped like metal orbs, reflecting the color and camouflage of the trees around them. I realized that we must be in a similar structure, though it stuck out from the top of the rainforest.

"This way." Naima led us through a door to the right and ushered us down a sloping metal bridge, which disappeared into the canopy. I held my breath as the shade surrounded us, the world filled with the chatter of birds and unseen creatures. From the nearby orbs, figures emerged, edging closer to get a good look at us.

I spotted Kenneth Willow immediately and had to dig my nails into my palms to stop myself from powering a fireball at him. Another familiar figure emerged from the left-hand side, though I'd never actually seen him before. The resemblance to Nomura was uncanny. It had to be Shinsuke—they had the same features, only he was much younger.

Before long, a big cluster of people had come out to check on the new arrivals. They eyed us suspiciously, muttering to one another. *No pressure, Volla.* It was unnerving to be among the cultists like this. I felt sure they could see right through me, but nobody had launched an attack yet. That had to be a good sign, right?

"Your journey begins now," Naima said ominously.

"Pardon?" I replied.

She smiled. "You must submit yourselves to the Three Trials of Eris. If you succeed, you will be marked with the Apple of Discord and welcomed into the cult."

I tried not to shudder at the thought of molten metal being poured onto my skin. That was going to hurt, and then some. And I was pretty sure that kind of thing was going to be permanent. I'd always wanted a tattoo, but that wasn't what I had in mind.

"If you fail, however, you will suffer the Death by a Thousand Cuts and be fed to the sharks that gather in the island's cove," Naima went on. "The Gulf of Mexico is full of them, and we often have the occasional orca to join in the feast."

My blood boiled at the memory of the Thousand Cuts. They'd tried to kill Mrs. Smith that way, but they wouldn't get the chance to do it to me. Still, the repercussions of failing made my stomach sink. I'd expected to have to do some kind of craziness to get in, but death hadn't exactly been on the table.

Naima shot me a cold grin, probably spotting the uncertainty on my face. "And you should know that no one ever quits the Cult of Eris. No one. If you pass the trials, you are one of us for life."

I glanced at Finch, a creeping doubt slithering into my head. Did the same thing apply to Finch? If nobody ever quit, then was he here because he was still part of the cult? Or was he here to help destroy it?

SEVENTEEN

Harley

"How do you know they aren't spies?" Kenneth Willow stepped forward. *Of course you'd be the one to ask.*

Naima scowled at him. "That is my business."

"Have you scanned them for bugs?"

"What do you take me for? Yes, they are clean," she returned. "No bugs, no devices, nothing."

Evidently, things were anything but rosy between Katherine's lieutenant and the kid who wanted the position so desperately. I wanted to ask when she'd scanned us, exactly, but I held my tongue. It would look way too suspicious. I was just glad we hadn't been stupid enough to wear earpieces into this place, though it seemed as though Astrid's speech device and the used Ephemeras had flown under the radar, thanks to Krieger's cloaking shields.

Kenneth narrowed his eyes at Finch. "Hey, I know you."

"You do?" Finch's tone was casual, while I was on the verge of a nervous breakdown.

"Pieter Mazinov, right?" *Oh, thank God for that.*

Finch nodded. "What's it to you?"

"I've seen you on wanted posters. Aren't you supposed to be dead?"

Finch laughed. "Supposed to be, yeah. We had to take the heat off for a bit. Faking your death by polar bear attack is a pretty easy way to make the authorities forget about you. If you leave enough blood, they don't even want to check it out. We got a bit woozy after that, though, didn't we, Volla?"

"Two pints from each person is two pints too much. Looked impressive, though," I replied, finding my voice at last. Well, Volla's voice.

Kenneth seemed satisfied with Finch's response, pushing his nose into the air like he'd smelled something rancid. I had to hand it to Finch: he was doing an incredible job of keeping his cool, considering he probably wanted to knock seven shades of crap out of Kenneth. He was already making a good impression, which would work in our favor. A few of the cultists had even laughed with Finch about the polar bear situation.

However, I got a mixed vibe from the rest of the group that had gathered. Shinsuke, in particular. He had a shifty wariness about him that set me on edge, my Empath senses feeling concern and fear brimming through him. *Bit off more than you could chew?* I sort of felt sorry for him. He looked like a lost kid who'd gotten in with the wrong crowd and didn't know how to get out again. Plus, if what Naima said was true, there *was* no way out. I wondered if he would be ready to renounce the cult, if given the opportunity.

While Finch entertained the masses with a fantastical tale of polar bears and hiding out in a snow cave, I took a moment to really look at the people surrounding us. In all the chaos of arriving and being bombarded with grim news, they'd all become a bit of a blur. I spotted a young woman at the back of the crowd, her hands bandaged. Finch followed my gaze while giving a dramatic pause, halfway through a story about the Northern Lights and an over-amorous penguin. He cast me a knowing look and suddenly said, "The sky was electrifying." A hidden signal to me, letting me know that this was Thessaly Crux—the one who'd tried to disable the Bestiary with that Gemini device.

"Enough of the welcome brigade. It is time you began your first trial," Naima announced, surveying the crowd with her amber eyes. It was strange how much she resembled Tobe, and yet the two of them were worlds apart.

"Which is?" I replied, giving it my best Volla Mazinov blasé attitude.

"An aspiring member must face the cult's current members. It is Thessaly Crux and Shinsuke Nomura's turn." She flashed me a grin. "Although, since Tess is indisposed with an injury, the duty shall fall to Kenneth Willow instead."

Kenneth smirked. "Even without the injury, I'd beat her anytime. How you getting on there, mummy-hands?"

Tess snickered. "Listen, you've got enough of an Oedipus complex without bringing me into it."

"You best be careful, or it'll be more than your hands giving you trouble," Kenneth replied, his eyes narrowing. I watched him shoot dark looks at those who dared to laugh, and I was struggling to stifle a laugh myself.

"Oh yeah? I'd like to see you try it, suck-up."

"You want to go, Crux?" Kenneth snapped, though he made no move to attack her. It was all for show, as far as I could tell. He clearly hated Tess, but I sensed he was also afraid of her. To be honest, I'd have liked to see them duke it out, and my money was firmly on Tess—bandages or no bandages.

"Ha, in your dreams." She cast him a butter-wouldn't-melt smile. Judging by the unsurprised reactions of the other folks who'd gathered on the bridge, this confrontation wasn't a rare occurrence.

"The trial, Naima?" I tried to get the focus back on us. The sooner we finished these stupid trials, the sooner we could finish the mission at hand: rescuing my mother's spirit before All Hallows' Eve.

Naima nodded. "We shall depart to the battle arena, where you will face your opponent. Cult members, prepare yourselves for the ceremony." She led the way, her black cloak swishing like a movie villain's as we followed her along a network of suspended metal bridges. I looked back just in time to see Tess, even with her bandages, strike a sharp jolt of Electro energy into Kenneth as she passed him. It looked like it caused her pain, but that had to be worth it. Kenneth juddered violently, his body going into spasms, while his eyes rolled back into his head. I could see him fighting to say something, but the jolt made it impossible. By the time he stopped shaking, Tess had already stalked off in the opposite direction.

After ten minutes of walking, we arrived at a clearing with a raised platform in the center. It was crafted from a single block of volcanic stone so smooth and shiny it almost looked like a disc of black glass. A band of tiered seats ran around the edge, where spectators could watch, but there was a significant, sheer drop between the arena lip and the seating. I guessed that was where the cult members would take up their positions whenever they came back from their "preparations."

As if reading my mind, they appeared from the trees, sweeping out of the shadows. This seemed to be the cult uniform—a long, silken robe of deep red, with golden patterns sewn into the fabric. They wore their hoods low, as any good cultist should, their heads dipped. They took their seats around the stone arena, using a different walkway than the one Naima had led us up.

"Aspiring members, you may take your places," Naima said, gesturing to Finch and me. We looked at each other. Since Shinsuke and Kenneth hadn't come back, we figured we were supposed to stand at the end nearest Naima—anything to put distance between us and them when they appeared.

In one swift display of athleticism, Naima leapt from the black disc and landed on a smaller, square platform opposite. It had two seats on it, but the other remained empty as she sat down. *Katherine's throne, perhaps?* We'd yet to see the woman herself, but I guessed we'd only get the chance if we made it through these trials.

"The trials have changed," Finch whispered to me as we moved closer to one another.

"Huh?"

"The trials. They've changed. This never used to be part of it."

"Is that a good thing or a bad thing?"

Finch shrugged. "Depends on what nasties Kenneth is getting ready to use. Remember to dodge the puffs of colored smoke—they're hexes, and he's probably been working on some pretty gross ones."

"Oh yeah, I remember those," I muttered. Flashbacks of Purgatory and Giverny Le Fay bombarded my brain, making me remember Wade's blindness and the flurry of smoke bombs that had gone off all around me.

"I don't know how strong Shinsuke's abilities are going to be, but he's a Nomura, so—go figure. Just keep watching for Kenneth. He's probably got the least skill but the most tricks up his sleeve. Literally."

I smiled. "Watch my back, I'll watch yours."

"Deal." He shot me a grin. Not for the first time, I wished I could sense him with my Empathy. I wanted to know what was going on in that head of his. Was this all an act, or had he really changed? It would make things so much easier if he had. Maybe I could relax into this newfound warmth toward him, if I only knew whether he was genuine or not.

Five minutes later, Shinsuke and Kenneth made their way up the walkway to the stone disc and came to a halt at the far end. They kept some distance between them, unlike Finch and me, who were pretty much glued to each other's sides. Had they discussed tactics during their brief absence? I doubted it. Kenneth was acting as if Shinsuke wasn't even there, showboating around the edge of the arena as if he were putting on a matinee. Shinsuke, on the other hand, looked focused and very Nomura-like.

"I will begin my countdown," Naima roared, silencing the crowd. "When I reach one, you may begin. And remember, new recruits are not allowed to kill cult members."

I stared at her. How was that a fair fight? So our enemies could skewer us if they wanted, but we couldn't unleash our full powers in case we accidentally killed their guys? *Biased, much?*

Shinsuke bowed to her, while Kenneth merely shrugged.

"Ten," she began.

Shinsuke shed his robe where he stood, revealing a muscular physique that I hadn't expected. *The man works out!* It brought thoughts of Wade and his own muscular arms. Shinsuke wore a black sleeveless shirt that seemed to be made of some type of rubber, revealing the Apple of Discord at the top of his right arm. On his back, he carried the same double Esprit as his father—two Samurai swords, the elegant, ivory handles sticking up above his broad shoulders.

"Hey, wait a minute, they're allowed weapons?" I hissed at Finch.

He shrugged. "An Esprit's an Esprit. His just happens to be two massive, killer katanas."

I missed my own Esprit, which I'd had to leave behind for obvious reasons. Facing Kenneth without one wasn't exactly my idea of a good time. Still, I had good control over my abilities these days, Esprit or no Esprit. It just felt weird not to have it. It had become such a huge part of my identity as a magical.

Kenneth's Esprit was mounted on his bow tie, as usual, the red ruby glowing in the shade of the trees. I hated the sight of that thing. I thought of the kids he'd killed back at the abandoned port and let my hatred strengthen my Chaos. I'd been gagging for a chance to wipe the smirk off his face, and now I had one.

This is going to be good.

"Let's hope you can use your Fire one more time," I told Finch.

He nodded and slipped his hand into his pocket. His grimace let me know the spikes of the Ephemera were doing their work. I only hoped the ability would last long enough to make an impact. If it didn't, everyone was going to wonder why the famed Firestarter wasn't using his most prized skill on the battlefield. *Krieger, you better have made this work.*

"You deal with Kenneth, I'll handle Shinsuke," Finch said, as Naima reached "six" on her doomsday countdown.

I gave him an uncertain side-eye. "Why do you get Shinsuke? Colored puffs of evil smoke, remember?"

He laughed. "Because if I take on Kenneth, I will beat him, and I will kill him, and no one will be able to stop me," he said.

"Well, when you put it like that…"

"ONE!" Naima roared.

I thought you'd never get there.

EIGHTEEN

Finch

———

I sprinted toward the center of the arena and skidded to a halt. New energy brimmed in my veins. It was stronger than I'd expected this time. I guessed I had Harley to thank for that. Supercharged Fire power, coming right up. *Just keep it going.* I didn't want it to sputter out mid-fight. That'd draw some attention, for sure.

I lifted my hands and let the new ability surge down my arms. It was weird and unnatural. And it left a tingling that I kinda liked. A stream of violent Fire shot out of my palms and hurtled toward Shinsuke. His eyes widened, but he was a pro. He dodged out of the way and pulled out his katanas. *Bastard.* I had to blink as he ran at me. I didn't know whether it was just my imagination, but it looked like the blades had gotten longer.

Meanwhile, I let Harley get on with it. She didn't need my help on this. She'd faced Katherine and survived before, and Kenneth would be nothing compared to that. I kept an eye out for errant puffs of smoke. I loathed those suckers, the lowest of the low. A real magical would never rely on dirty tricks.

I picked up the pace and slid between Shinsuke's legs. The glass was perfect for that. He looked back in surprise as I stood up and shot a fireball at his face. It singed his cheek on the way past. I needed to work on my accuracy. His blades shortened. *Yep, definitely not imagining things.* This had to be the Earth-slash-Magneton hybrid Krieger had yapped on about. It was insanely cool, but pants-crappingly scary.

He slashed the blade at my face, but I ducked back. I heard the whisper of it as it sliced the air right in front of my nose. I'd been unlucky enough to get my dad's schnozz, but I didn't want it getting chopped off. A fireball surged from my palm in retaliation. Shinsuke swiped at the air with his blades, dispersing the crackling ball into ashes. *Close one.*

"How do you prefer yourself? Medium or well-done?" I grinned at him as a jet of near-liquid Fire shot out of my hands. He flipped his swords backward and arched over, the razor-sharp tips digging into the glass as he propped himself up. The stream sailed right over his torso. *This guy is good.* Nomura by name, Nomura by nature. I'd have to get a little crazy to beat him. Fortunately, craziness was in *my* nature.

I sprinted at him full-pelt as he stood back up, waiting until the last moment before I slid to my knees. I surged another jet of Fire at him. It hit him full in the stomach, knocking him back. He jumped up a second later, seemingly unharmed. The rubber top he was wearing had somehow absorbed the blast. That neat little addition was going to make my job a whole lot harder.

I ran for the edge of the arena and jumped off. A gasp went up from the crowd. *Always breaking the rules, Finch.* I clung to the side and shimmied my way around the lip. Tucking my body right under the glass, I waited. Through the shiny stone, I saw a shadow approach. Shinsuke had taken the bait. I waited until he came to the very edge before swinging myself up and launching a volley of fireballs at him. He was quick. A few swift slashes of his blades, and the fireballs shifted trajectory. They powered toward the crowd, who dove out of the way.

"Nice try," he said. A sheen of sweat glistened on his forehead. Things were getting a little hot in the kitchen.

I backed away from the edge. With every step I took, I fired another blast at him. The swish of his swords was all I could hear. Curious, I glanced over my shoulder to see how Harley was doing. She seemed to be holding her own, dodging hex puffs left, right, and center. And Kenneth was already soaking wet from her Water power. *Ah, the drowned rat look. Perfect.*

I jumped back in surprise as a katana blade narrowly missed my chest. It had grown longer again.

"I need to learn how to do that," I said, brushing off how close he'd come to snagging me. I could think of a thousand uses, not all of them safe for work. Still, it was going to be hard to take this guy down. I was desperate to mix it up and use my Telekinesis, but I couldn't. Pieter Mazinov didn't have Telekinesis—it was Fire or nothing. I just hoped it held out. Krieger had said it would last a fair while, but he'd also said it wasn't an exact science.

"Even if you could, you wouldn't have the patience," he replied.

"Bit sure of yourself, aren't you?"

He smiled. "I've trained to be."

I looked at him and knew I needed to get more creative. Thinking fast, I lunged at him and jumped into the air, using the flat top edge of his katanas to balance on as I sprang over his head. I somersaulted, landing with his back to me. Using the split second of surprise, I powered two palms' worth of Fire into his shoulder blades. He staggered forward under the pressure, smoke rising from his rubber suit.

A moment after, he was up again. *Stay down, geez!* I launched another jet at him, this time hitting him square in the chest. He staggered back once more, but he wouldn't go down. Instead, he crossed his blades in front of his face, widening the metal to form a shield. The fire bounced back, heading right for me. I dove to the floor, feeling the heat of the flames as they whizzed over me.

Suddenly, he was on me. His knee pushed into my chest as he shortened his blades to tantos. With a smile of triumph, he rested the blade against my neck. If I was going to get out of this alive, I needed to come up with something fast. A thought hit me. *Keep him talking.*

"Wouldn't you call that cheating?"

He frowned. "What?"

"Using weapons. Hardly fair, right?" Discreetly, I put my hand in my pocket and felt around for my Esprit. I'd morphed it into a dagger identical to the one Pieter Mazinov used.

"Sore loser?"

"Who says I've lost?" I brought the knife up and slashed it across Shinsuke's arm, just below that stupid apple. Nobody would question me using it. An Esprit was an Esprit, after all. Shinsuke stared at the wound. It was only a small nick, really, but the neurotoxin would soon get to work. I didn't want to kill him, just slow him down a bit.

"Hey..." His eyes turned foggy as he slumped forward. The neurotoxin had worked. Pushing him off me, I stood over him. He tried to crawl away, but by now his limbs would feel like lead, and his motor senses would go next. They'd all come back, but he'd have one hell of a hangover.

Urging Fire into my hands, I pummeled it into his back until he stopped crawling. Only then did I stop. I wanted to make sure I hadn't killed him. As I reached forward to check for a pulse, he lifted his hand in surrender.

"Pieter Mazinov is the winner!" Naima bellowed.

You bet your furry ass I am.

Now that my part was over, I sat down beside Shinsuke's limp body and watched the rest of Harley's fight. I patted him on the rump. "Good fight, Nomura. You did good."

He groaned in reply.

"Yeah, you'll feel better in the morning." I used his body as a backrest, folding my arms across my chest as I got settled in for Harley's victory. I'd thought about helping her, but this wasn't really a two-on-one sort of game. If Harley wanted her place in the cult, she'd have to win on her own. Honestly, I was still trying to wrap my head around being back here. It was home, but also not. It was kind of like a dream and a nightmare colliding.

Harley was giving as good as she got, sticking to the abilities of Volla Mazinov. Volla was known to spurn Esprits, thankfully, so we didn't have to manufacture a fake one or make up a story about her losing it. Harley was skilled in her own right, using her powers without one. But that had to be making it ten times harder to control her superstrength Chaos.

I laughed as a tornado of Water came down on Kenneth's head. He slipped and slid on the wet glass, falling on his ass like a circus clown. A howl of laughter went up from the crowd. Kenneth glared at them, but there wasn't much he could do. He dragged himself up and tossed a flurry of hexes at Harley. His powers weren't all that impressive. Pretty, yes. Fear-inducing, no. Then again, I knew what that smoke could do. And so did Harley. She was avoiding it like the plague.

My laughter died as I watched my sister in action. She was fearless and intimidating, even when wearing someone else's face. Every move Kenneth made, she countered it. Every time he lunged at her, she was already prepared to dodge out of the way. It was like watching a dance. *Soppy, much?* I couldn't help but admire her. All of her focus was on the fight. It never slipped, not once. And she was owning it. Even the crowd had fallen silent as they observed her. I bet even the real Volla Mazinov wasn't half as good as this. *God rest her soul. Polar bears—what a way to go.*

It had only just occurred to me that this had to be deeply personal for Harley. She hated Kenneth Willow almost as much as I did. I'd done my fair share of bad, but I drew the line at killing kids. Kenneth had no line. She must have been seething. And she was definitely showing him what she was made of.

Before long, I noticed Kenneth begin to tire. Nothing obvious had happened, but that was the point. Harley had to be using her reverse Empathy on him. He kept looking around as if he thought someone was behind him. She had him running scared. He was weakening before my very eyes. If I'd thought Shinsuke's blades were cool, this was cooler. Evidently, she was implanting terror in him, the kind that was sapping his will to fight and draining him of his energy. His eyes widened, and he ducked, even though Harley hadn't done anything. Shaking, he looked back up at her.

"I won't be defeated by a girl!" Kenneth searched his pockets for more hexes.

Harley smiled and lifted her hands. Water surged up from the nearby ocean and powered through the trees, taking out a few branches on the way. It gathered in a swirling vortex over Kenneth's head. He was still searching frantically. Finally, he realized something was happening. Everything had gone way too quiet. The moment he looked up, Harley dunked the whole swirling pool onto his head. It hit him like an anvil, drowning him in a powerful deluge. The crowd gasped, their mouths hanging open.

Ah, poor Weeping Willow. I grinned with satisfaction. That little punk had gotten what was coming to him. I still wanted to murder him in his sleep, sure, but I could ease off on my vendetta for now. The time would come for all that. Kenneth wouldn't escape me forever.

On her plinth, Naima clapped. She looked thoroughly amused. "Volla Mazinov is the winner!"

Kenneth lay on his back, coughing up water. His eyes rolled back into his head as he lolled there on the black glass. Harley had smashed this fight. And there wasn't a neurotoxin in sight. *Good job, Sis.*

Somehow, we'd managed to pass the first trial without giving ourselves away. I glanced at the crowd to gauge their reactions. Immediately, my eye was drawn to Tess. Anyone's eye would've been. She had smooth, ebony skin, hair buzzed right to the scalp, eyes like two pools of rich, rich caramel. Pools I wouldn't have minded drowning in. More than that, she was sharp as all hell. Right now, she was smirking at the sight of an utterly humiliated Kenneth. *My kind of girl.*

I loathed Kenneth. Words couldn't describe how much. I'd known him before he got taken in by the foster family where the Ryders recruited him. He'd kissed my ass, too. He'd wanted to join me and Katherine back then, but I'd said nothing to my mom. Until the Ryders found out about him, that is. Even then, I'd warned Katherine that he'd end up a gigantic liability. The little brownnose was unstable and spiteful at best, savage and downright dangerous at worst. He couldn't think straight in any pressurized situations, especially if humiliated. He'd hold on to this particular grudge for a *long* time.

I've got my eye on you, twerp. I got the creeping feeling he'd try to come after Harley, once he'd coughed all the ocean water out of his lungs. I hoped he had a few decent chunks of seaweed in his throat, for good measure.

"You have gained the right to stay upon Eris Island, but only for the night," Naima announced. "Your next trial begins at midnight. If you survive that, you may live until morning, when the third trial will take place."

"You want to cast a bit more light on these trials, Naima?" I shot back, getting a giggle from the crowd.

She smirked. "Now where would be the fun in that?" She turned her attention to said crowd. "Tess, as you were unable to perform your duties, I must ask that you escort the Mazinovs to their *temporary* quarters."

We get it, we're only staying if we finish the trials. No need to keep hammering it home. I got up and gave Shinsuke another pat. He was out cold. Dusting myself off, I headed for the metal walkway off this glass disc and waited for Harley. She caught up with me a moment later, the two of us walking toward Tess. She'd made her way out of the crowd and come to fulfil her task, like a good little cultist.

"If you'd like to follow me," she said in those sultry, honeyed tones that could get my head torn off. I was all for the praying mantis vibes.

"Lead the way." I had to remember not to act like Finch. Otherwise, we'd never make it out of here alive.

NINETEEN

Harley

"All good?" Finch asked as we followed Tess along a labyrinth of treetop walkways. We passed a bunch of those weird, orb-like treehouses, but apparently none of them were for us.

I nodded, panting. "Tired but good."

"You were awesome out there," he said, surprising me for the millionth time. Coming from him, I wasn't sure whether to take it seriously.

I shrugged. "I did what I had to." In all honesty, I was absolutely freaking ecstatic that I'd not only managed to maintain Volla's persona, but I'd also successfully handed Kenneth's ass to him on a silver, watery platter. I wished I could have hurt him a little more, but knocking him flat was the best I could do to punish him for everything he'd done, at least for now. "You weren't too shabby yourself."

"Ah, you know, couldn't let us down."

"No, really, you handled yourself well, considering... well, you know." I didn't want to say too much in front of Tess, in case she over-heard us. This woman was definitely the one from Marie Laveau's garden. I was glad her hands were burned. *Serves her right.*

A concerning realization hit me: there was no way we wouldn't end up meeting Katherine at some point. *What would I even say to her?* I'd have to keep it cool and try my very hardest not to let my hatred show.

Walking in silence behind Tess, I took a moment to take in my surroundings. The settlement was basically a network of orbs in the trees, with all the amenities housed in larger structures shaped more like beehives. *Ironic, with her being Queen Bee and all.* Smoke billowed out of the beehives, and the heady smell of grilled food filled the air. My stomach rumbled involuntarily, reminding me that it had been a long time since I'd eaten.

I realized Katherine must have designed Eris Island to be a self-sustaining world, with oxygen pumped in from the trees and animals running around. There was fresh water from streams and pools and enough firewood to last for years. If they had to move quickly, there'd be no time to gather supplies from the outside world, and they didn't need to. It was all here, carefully created by Katherine's hand. Plus, the interdimensional pocket itself was run from the secret Bestiary that Finch had told me about, giving it the power to move if necessary. With that at her disposal, Katherine didn't need to worry about anything. She'd covered every possible base.

"So, this is where you'll find the kitchens and the communal dining area. If you want anything to eat, just come up here and the chefs will make something for you. Mealtimes are more or less set, since we've got a lot of mouths to feed, but the chefs don't mind rustling up an impromptu snack or two. Just don't ask for a five-course, gourmet experience." Tess led us toward one of the beehives and opened the door to let us in. Wooden tables were neatly arranged to one side, while a huge kitchen had been set up on the opposite side.

People were sitting at the tables, playing cards and eating cake. Evidently, they'd been excused from battle arena duties. They were dressed in ordinary clothes, not a red robe in sight, and, weirdest of all, they were laughing and chatting, as if they were at some twisted summer camp. They looked up as we entered, a few lifting a hand in greeting. Everywhere I looked, I saw smiling, happy faces.

This wasn't the institutional, militant vision I'd seen in my head.

These were seemingly ordinary people hanging out and enjoying themselves. And why wouldn't they? They had everything they needed here. A place to live, food in their bellies, like-minded company.

"If you make it through the next two trials, you can make yourselves at home," Tess said. "We can pretty much do *whatever* we want, as long as we continue to serve the cult faithfully."

I frowned at her. "What does 'whatever we want' mean?"

She smiled. "Whatever makes you happy. For some, it's cake. For others, it's… well, whatever floats their boat, whatever stirs their coffee." That didn't exactly make it any clearer, but I sensed it wasn't all peaches and cream in this place. It couldn't be.

"Can I grab something before we go?" Finch asked Tess. His eyes were wide as saucers, fixed on the hot buffet.

"Sure, but be quick."

"You want anything, Volla?" Finch asked, but it took me a moment to realize he was talking to me.

"Oh… uh, yeah. Whatever you're having."

He hurried over and started scooping ladleful after ladleful of unknown food into two boxes, stabbing a wooden fork through each one and running back with a big grin on his face. The food really did smell good, and my mouth was salivating. With that, Tess led us out of the canteen and down another endless stretch of walkways, until we reached a small stone hut at ground level. I guessed we weren't good enough to warrant one of the fancy orbs. Not yet, anyway.

"This is where you'll be staying until Naima requests your presence for the second trial," Tess explained, opening the door. The interior was actually pretty nice, with two freshly made beds and a small seating area around a fireplace.

"Nice. I like it." Finch set the boxes of food down on the table and made to take his boots off, but Tess stopped him.

"You can leave your food here for now. There's more I need to show you before you can get settled in."

He pulled a face. "After what we've just been through? Don't we get a break?"

"Do you want to be one of us or not?" Her tone cut through the room like a machete.

"I was just saying." He got back up and headed out. I had to try hard not to let my fear get the better of me—his Finch personality was seeping through, and that could spell disaster.

Trudging along, we followed Tess. I had no idea where she was taking us. I just hoped we weren't in for a nasty, unexpected surprise. I envisioned Naima suddenly launching the second trial at us before we'd even had time to rest. Fighting Kenneth had taken a lot out of me, and trying to keep up this persona was even tougher. The Shapeshifter energy was sapping more of my energy than I'd anticipated, but I had to make sure it didn't slip. If it did, I'd never get it back, and I'd be stuck on Eris Island as myself, surrounded by the enemy.

"If you succeed in your trials, you'll enter a world unlike any you've experienced before. Not just a world, but a community beyond your imagination," Tess said as we walked. She sounded like she was advertising a resort vacation. *Good old-fashioned brainwashing.* "Here, we devote ourselves to Eris—to Katherine."

"What do you get out of it?" I asked, feeding some Empathy into Tess. I wanted to feel what she was feeling. All I got back was an undercurrent of anxiety and a smattering of suspicion. It seemed as if she was trying to guard her emotions and was doing a pretty good job of it. Usually, when people guarded their emotions, I felt them even more. Not with Tess, though. She was a pro, apparently. I wondered if Katherine taught them how to suppress emotions, or if that just came with being a member of the cult—a blind, emotionless zombie.

"We give ourselves to her because she will forge a new world in which we are the ones to make the rules. She will become a goddess among mortals, and we'll be the avenging angels at her side." A smile turned up the corners of her lips. "With Eris, we will all take our rightful place as superior beings. And those who don't follow will fall with the weak humans who would see us dead. They will discover what it's like to be powerless. Either you're for us or against us, and when the time comes, only those on our side will win."

Someone's been guzzling the Kool-Aid. Finch and I exchanged a look. Then again, he was probably used to this kind of talk. He'd spent long enough around it. Not too long ago, he'd been the one lapping up the propaganda.

"Sounds good," I replied.

Finch nodded. "Yeah, world domination is right up our alley."

Tess gave us a thin smile, and we kept on through the island. It seemed like a good moment to find out more about Electro-girl, since it was just the three of us. There had to be more to her than being a simple cultist, especially given how high she'd risen through the ranks.

"Where are you from, originally?" I asked.

"Atlanta," she replied.

"Did you like it there?"

"It was okay." She kept her gaze forward, giving nothing away. Her emotions were still guarded.

"Any brothers or sisters?"

She cleared her throat. "One. A twin, but she's gone now."

"Gone where?" I figured dumbing myself down might get her to open up more.

"She died." Her voice sounded somewhat strained, as if she was struggling with the words.

"Sorry to hear that. Were you close?"

She sneered at me. "She was my twin. Of course we were close."

"Oh, yeah. I suppose so." I paused. "I've heard that when one twin is in pain, the other twin can feel it."

"Yeah, I never used to believe that, but I do now."

Finch cast me a concerned look, but I continued anyway. "Why's that?"

"Because I felt it when she died. Right here." Tess covered her heart with her bandaged hand. "I've never known pain like it." She shook her head, as if she knew she'd said too much.

"Was she part of the cult, too?"

Tess whirled around. "What's with all the questions, huh?"

I shrugged. "Just interested. I like getting to know people."

"Well, stop. Until you've passed these trials, I don't want to hear another question out of you, do you understand?" I'd clearly touched a nerve, one which made me see Tess in a slightly more human light. Already, she was staring at me with a glint of tears in her caramel eyes, pain etched on her face. She must have loved her sister a lot, and I doubted a scar like that went away quickly.

"I didn't mean to cause any offense." I put up my hands.

She sighed. "It's fine. I just… I don't like to talk about it, that's all. Now, come on, I've still got a lot to show you."

Half an hour later, we broke through the tree-line and found ourselves on a lookout. I didn't recall walking up this high, but interdimensional bubbles could be manipulated to do just about anything the architect wanted. Looking at the ancient walls that stretched out below us, I realized where we were. We were standing on the wall of Fort Jefferson, looking down into the empty center.

In the vast, hexagonal expanse below, I saw people. Some were chained to posts, left to bake in the hot sun. Others were slumped on the ground, battered and bleeding. A group in the corner were missing limbs, while one man was covered in runes that had been carved into his skin. He was crouched in the very center of the hexagon, his face turned to the sky, his arms raised.

Another cluster were covered in blisters, boils, and burns. One had plants growing out of him, the vines wrapping around his arms. Opposite sat a furtive group of people in various states of becoming animals, complete with tails, patches of fur, feline ears, and limbs shortened to become bestial legs.

"What is this place?" I could barely get the words out, praying Astrid had avoided capture.

"It's our play arena," Tess replied. "We bring in humans from the outside world—foolish tourists who want to visit Dry Tortugas. We bring them from elsewhere, too, so as not to arouse suspicion. Big cities, mostly, so they won't be missed. So many humans go missing every day. What's one more?"

"What do you do to them?" I tried to get Finch to look at me, but he'd dropped his gaze. Had he known about this?

Tess shrugged. "Whatever we want."

I shuddered as discreetly as possible. There it was, the hidden meaning behind those words. Katherine had incorporated a mass arena of torture into her world, where the cult members could come and torment these humans in whatever way they pleased.

"Like spells and stuff?" Finch said, though he still couldn't look at me.

"Yes, like spells and stuff, if that catches your fancy. Cult members come here to do all kinds of things: try out new hexes, learn more about the effects of magic on the human body. We toy with them as we see fit, and then we kill them, using spells we'd never normally dare to use. Weapons, too, to hone our physical skills. Sometimes, we get them to fight back, to make it more of a challenge. There's nothing more invigorating than watching a human fight for their life, knowing they'll never win. No harm, no foul. Everyone goes home happy."

Except the freaking humans, you mad cow! It was taking every ounce of strength I had not to shove Tess over the edge of the lookout and watch her tumble into the hexagon. The humans would have ripped her apart, and I wouldn't have stopped them.

"Fascinating. Right, Volla?" Finch leveled his gaze at me, his tone carrying a note of reassurance to keep me grounded. He needed me to stay focused, and my resolve was slipping. I kept my eyes on him. If I looked back at those poor humans, I'd lose it. By coming here, we'd truly stepped through the gates of hell, and I had no clue which circle we were currently in.

One thing was for sure: we couldn't do anything to wage war against the cult right now, not with just the two of us. I had to pull myself together or risk blowing this entire operation. We had a job to do, to stop Katherine in her tracks. It was bigger than this, even though my heart was breaking for those humans. If we tried to do anything now, we'd end up in this hexagonal pit with the very people we wanted to save.

Get it together, Merlin. Add every one of these cult bastards to your list if you have to, but get it together.

———————

My head hung over the edge of the toilet seat at our temporary hut. Tess had brought us back not too long ago, and after what I'd just witnessed, I was in very real danger of hurling my stomach into the bowl. Finch had devoured his box of food as soon as we got in—how he'd managed to eat anything was beyond me. Right now, food was the farthest thing from my mind. All I could think about were those poor humans—and what would happen if we were found out.

Finch knocked on the bathroom door. "How you doing in there?"

"Bad."

"Mind if I open the door?"

"Go ahead."

He peered inside. "Just wanted to let you know I found some spying hexes, but I burned them. They always use them on the newbies. There aren't any in here, though."

I looked up at him, feeling green around the gills. "Spying hexes?"

"Yeah, they tuck them around these huts when they bring new recruits in."

"Are they watching us?"

"Fortunately, no. Spying hexes work like tape recorders. They can't listen in live. Not that they'd want to, with you retching like a dog." He chuckled. "They'll be pretty miffed when they can't find a recording to listen to. Guess they'll just have to live with it."

"How are you doing this?" I groaned, wiping sweat from my forehead. I couldn't believe how easily he was dealing with everything.

He frowned. "Finding the spying hexes? It's simple when you know what you're looking for."

I shook my head and sat back against the bathroom wall. "Not that. All of *this*—the humans, the trials, everything."

He perched on the edge of the bathtub opposite. "It's nothing personal. I'm just mission-oriented. Always have been. I guess it's the one good thing that Katherine taught me. I can separate myself from anything that might be a distraction. And I mean anything." He paused, kicking his feet against the tub. "Right now, my mission is to get into the cult, find Hester's spirit, and screw Katherine over as much as possible before I get the heck out again. Nothing else matters. You should follow suit."

"I'm not wired like that."

"Then rewire yourself," he said simply. "The way I see it, the only way we can save those humans, and the ones who'll keep coming after they're dead, is to destroy the cult. You need to compartmentalize."

"How do I do that?" I swept a hand through my spiky blonde hair.

"Well, we need to think about how we're going to get Hester's spirit. Sure, I know where it is, but we can't get close to the cult's operational compound until we pass these trials. So, that's step one—pass the trials. Simple. Step two, retrieve Hester's spirit. Step three, get out of here. Step four, stop Katherine and bring about the demise of the cult. Think about it like that, in bite-size chunks."

I knew it would take more than words to change my way of thinking, but I saw his point. I needed to focus on the bigger picture. Yes, what was happening to those humans was terrible and gut-wrenching and nauseating, but if we didn't stop Katherine, that could be the fate of the rest of the human world.

"We're in this together. If you fail, I fail. If you die, I die." He smiled. "Not to be dramatic."

"I'll do better," I said, surprisingly energized by his unexpected pep talk. "I know what we need to do. I'll stay focused. It was just a shock, seeing that back there."

He nodded. "Unfortunately, it's not new. I've seen it before."

"Only seen it?" I had to know just how far down the rabbit hole Finch had gone when he was Katherine's lackey.

"Yeah, only seen it. I had limits to what I'd do for Katherine, even back then." He sounded hurt that I'd suggest otherwise.

"What were your limits?"

He shrugged. "I never got involved with any of the human stuff. I did what Katherine asked, and she didn't force me to do anything to them. I organized missions for her and tried to reduce collateral damage where I could. I ran missions of my own. I suppose you wouldn't believe me if I said I never wanted to get anyone hurt, huh?"

"Gargoyles, Finch. Gargoyles."

He nodded solemnly. "Fair point. But that was the first time I knew people were going to get hurt. I wasn't even sure I wanted to go through with it, but I knew I couldn't let Katherine down. I was so deep under her spell that disappointing her was the worst thing that could've happened to me. It would've felt like my world had crumbled."

"So, what was your guilty pleasure then, if it wasn't torturing humans?" I wanted to break the sad tension in the room.

He dropped his gaze. "It's stupid."

"Go on."

"You'll laugh."

I grinned at him. "So?"

"Ugh… I used to ask for the newest comic books from the outside world. That was my vice." He glanced at me with shy eyes. "What can I say, I'm a sucker for a superhero."

"Well, you were following a supervillain around for long enough. It was bound to have an effect." I wanted to tell him that it wasn't stupid at all, that it was actually sort of sweet, but I didn't want to offer that big of an olive branch just yet. He'd probably watched other cultists torture humans without much trouble. He wasn't *that* innocent. Even so, it made me look at him in a different way, seeing the lost boy instead of the broken man. He'd had his childhood stolen from him, so it was almost natural that he'd have wanted the things he'd never had as a kid.

He chuckled sadly. "I guess I never thought of it like that."

"So what you're saying is, Katherine keeps her subjects happy by giving them everything they want, within the limits of the island. In return, they do whatever she wants. That right?"

"Hit the nail on the head."

"I guess that's one way to get a job done." I laid my head against the bathroom wall and tried to ignore just how creepy all of this was. But Finch was right. If I kept myself focused on the endgame, I'd be able to get past everything else, at least for long enough to do what I needed to. I'd never forget that there were innocent people being tormented on the other side of the island, but that was a good thing. I wasn't supposed to forget. I was just supposed to get the bigger obstacle out of the way first—if I could cut off the snake's head, the rest would collapse. And they'd be free.

I didn't remember falling asleep, but I blinked open my eyes to find Finch shaking me roughly by the shoulders. I was still in the bathroom, a blanket covering my body. Frantically, I jumped up and pushed past him, hurrying to the mirror. I hadn't meant to drift off, and I feared the worst might have happened. But even though I'd fallen asleep, Volla had stayed with me. There were her cobalt-blue eyes, staring right back.

"Oh, thank God." I heaved out a sigh of relief, just as Finch lifted a finger to his lips and shook his head. "What? What is it?"

"Naima's here," he said. "It's time for the second trial."

TWENTY

Harley

S till yawning from my unexpected sleep, I followed Naima and
Finch out of the hut. Tess was waiting for us in the glade beyond
the hut, that same strange smile on her lips. It was pitch black outside,
aside from the glow of the treetop orbs and the silvery light of a cres-
cent moon glancing in through the interdimensional pocket. Everything looked creepier in the darkness, the stone statues looming out of
the canopy like hulking titans. This place had seemed like paradise in
the daylight, but night had transformed it into a *Lord of the Flies*
nightmare.

My boots thudded on the metal walkways, leaving an echoing clang
as we made our way to our next destination. If Naima was taking us
back to that horrific hexagon, I didn't know if I'd have the stomach to
make it through the second stage of our induction. *Bigger picture,
Merlin. Focus.*

"What's with the stone giants?" I needed to break the silence
between the four of us.

"They're the guardians of Eris Island," Tess replied. "They're depic-
tions of the Children of Chaos, the very beings that allow us to be here,
and where Eris will soon take her place as a goddess among mortals."

"She's planning on turning to stone?" I flashed a forced smile, but nobody laughed.

"Nice one, Volla." Finch's tone held a warning. This wasn't the time for jokes.

Tess pointed to a nearby titan as we crossed a walkway that came close to its towering height. I looked up toward its sculpted face, and it set my nerves on edge. It had the horns and face of a goat, the torso of a man, and two enormous stone wings folded behind its back, with cloven hooves instead of feet. *Ah, so Satan is watching over this place.*

"Baphomet, right?" Finch said.

Tess smiled. "It was designed with his image in mind, yes. In our case, it's supposed to represent the might of Erebus. Katherine deemed it the most fitting example, as it stands for the tradition of a perfect social order. The kind she hopes to bring to our world."

It sent a chill through me. "Is that really what Erebus looks like?"

"As I said, it's a representation, meant to encompass more than just Erebus himself." Tess shot me a withering look that silenced me. Somehow, I'd managed to become the class idiot without meaning to.

"I must pause here for a moment," Naima said, leading us down a sloping walkway toward the eerie titan. We lingered on the damp grass, watched by Tess. In the darkness ahead, I heard rustling and the screech of an unseen bird.

Naima went right up to the stone giant, pressing her hand to a carved star embedded between Erebus's hooves. She mumbled something in Latin, and the stone slid away, revealing a secret doorway in the statue itself. She disappeared inside, then returned a few minutes later with two charmed jars in her hands. I recognized the glass and the symbols etched along it; these were jars that held Purge beasts. Taking a closer look at the stone titan, I realized this must be where Naima hid her own version of the Bestiary—the powerhouse that made this entire operation work.

"The second trial is as follows," Naima said, brandishing the two large jars. "You must tame a Purge monster each. I have specifically selected these rather charming creatures, as I have had some trouble taming them myself. Not all Purge beasts are created equal—I am a testament to that—and, despite my skill in this field, some creatures simply cannot, and will not, be controlled. These are two such monsters."

So how do you expect us to tame them, if you can't? I didn't say it out loud, but I wanted to. It was almost as if these trials had been designed with failure in mind.

"What are they?" I asked instead.

She smirked. "That is for you to discover." She set the jars on the ground and disappeared back inside her Bestiary. When she returned, she held a large box in her arms.

"These trials aren't supposed to be easy," Tess snarked.

I frowned at the box. "Is that another creature?"

"No, this is merely the raw meat you may use to entice the beasts into behaving, though it will not be as simple as bringing a stray dog to heel. They are as likely to eat *you*." She chuckled darkly and set the box down between the jars. "You have half an hour, beginning now. If you fail, you will die. Katherine will only accept the best and most powerful into the cult. The rest are merely feed for my monsters. And, while your performances in the arena were exceptional, it is not enough to secure your place among us."

"Why kill so many good soldiers if you need an army?" I couldn't hold the question back.

Naima nodded thoughtfully. "An excellent question. Had you arrived with exceptional ability—a rare power, perhaps—these trials would have been tailored differently. Knowing of your reputations, we are aware that you lack any such abilities. You are Elementals only, and while your abilities are very strong indeed, they are nothing that Katherine needs, per se. As such, you must endure much more difficult trials to ensure you are worthy of your place."

"Quality over quantity, right?" I smiled, keeping up the ruse of Volla's sharp attitude.

"Precisely."

Tess nodded. "A lot of ordinary magicals die in these trials, but it's all for the greater good. That is how Eris weeds out the weak, to have only the most skilled at her side. Why have an army riddled with Mediocrity?"

It made a twisted sort of sense, not that I agreed with any of it. I could only imagine the kill rate in this place, and that wasn't including the human experiments on the far side of the island.

"Good luck." Tess grinned at us, lifting her hands. A white light shot out, forming a time-lapse bubble around us. The last time I'd seen one of these was in New Orleans, when Papa Legba's townhouse had started to crumble. I didn't exactly have good memories linked to these things, and I doubted that was about to change.

"We must go, Tess." Naima stepped toward the edge of the bubble and beckoned for Tess to join her. Together, they disappeared through the membrane to safety, leaving Finch and me alone with whatever was lurking in those jars.

"Okay, then. Beast time," Finch said, carefully approaching the nearest jar. I walked toward the second jar and tried to catch a glimpse of the creature inside. Black smoke swirled and twisted, but I couldn't make out a distinct shape.

"Can they see us in the time-lapse bubble?" I asked tensely.

Finch shook his head. "Definitely not in this one. It'll be extra sturdy."

I exhaled, unsure of whether that made me feel relieved or more nervous. At least it meant we could use all of our abilities to get these beasties tamed.

I reached for the jar and unscrewed the lid. For a moment, nothing happened. And then, a stream of black smoke poured out of the glass, growing limbs and a body, its ugly head appearing as the mist faded away. A gargoyle—my favorite. Only this one looked way nastier than any I'd encountered before, foam frothing at its wet lips, its eyes black and wild, its knotted muscles pulsating beneath its scaly skin.

To my right, another creature was forming after being released by Finch. It was way bigger than the gargoyle, with a huge body that seemed to be made from rock, its torso and arms covered in moss and lichen, while weeds sprouted from its face. A golem.

"Looks like you've made a friend," Finch said, nodding at the gargoyle. It had set its sights on me before I could even ask to switch. It sniffed the air and grimaced, something dark and slimy dripping from its sharp teeth as it spread out its wings and howled.

"Yeah, they've got a thing for me." I flashed him a grin before launching myself at the gargoyle.

"Must run in the blood!" Finch ducked a savage blow from the golem.

I laughed bitterly. "Why couldn't we have been normal? Like, imagine if our parents had been lawyers and accountants." I grappled with the gargoyle's throat, wrapping a lasso of Telekinesis around it and yanking it halfway across the expansive bubble.

"Accountants are way worse than what we ended up with, believe me!" Finch shot back, as he sent his own lasso of Telekinesis toward the golem, swiping it off its feet. It crashed to the ground, sending a shudder through the earth that almost knocked me down, too.

I rounded on the gargoyle and drove a fireball into the back of its head. It yelped in pain and scurried away from me, breaking loose from the Telekinesis. It didn't get far, as I shot a judder of Earth through the ground, a circle of small trees shooting up around the creature, penning it in. At least, for a moment. I'd forgotten about the wings. It howled again and burst out of the wall of trees, powering through the air toward me.

"You made it mad, Sis!" Finch chuckled as he tackled the golem, his legs dangling over the creature's shoulders as he rode around and tried to tug its head off with his Telekinesis.

"We're supposed to tame them, not kill them," I reminded him as I dove out of the way of the incoming gargoyle. It screamed at me and flapped its way up into the air again, its leathery wings vibrating.

Finch pulled a face. "Killing them would be way easier."

"But that isn't always the answer, remember?" I feinted out of the way of another aerial attack and sent up a spiral of powerful Air. With all the work I'd been putting into controlling my abilities, my success rate with Air and Earth had gotten a lot better. The gargoyle got caught in the maelstrom, spinning around and around like a lone sock in a washing machine. It was almost comical to watch, though I was aware this thing would devour me if it had half the chance.

With my focus fixed on the gargoyle, I'd forgotten about Finch's golem. I didn't see it until it was right on me, pinning me to the ground with its hefty stone foot. The breath rushed out of my lungs as I fought to break free, but it had me trapped. Turning over my shoulder, I watched Finch try to wrestle with the creature and push it away from me, but he was having some trouble. Meanwhile, I'd lost my hold on the maelstrom, and the gargoyle was about to make a dart for freedom.

"A little help?" I wheezed.

"I'm trying!" he shouted back. "It's not easy moving a million-ton golem off your back."

"Well, it's going to squish me if you don't!" I felt a rush of air close to my face and turned to find the gargoyle crouched on the ground, staring at me with hungry eyes. I could have sworn it even licked its lips. Here I was, stuck under the golem's foot with no way out, with a ravenous, wild gargoyle about ready to eat me.

Suddenly, the golem lurched forward, taking its foot off me. It staggered clumsily, kicking out at the nearest thing, which just so happened to be the gargoyle. The winged beast went flying, tumbling backward. Its sharp claws shot out, raking across the earth to slow itself down, while the golem lumbered off in the opposite direction. Finch still sat on its shoulders, tugging harder at the invisible reins of his Telekinesis in an attempt to wrangle the creature.

"Use your neurotoxin!" I shouted, dragging myself to my feet. The gargoyle was on its way back.

"What?"

"Use. Your. Toxin!"

"This rock stuff will break my Esprit!"

I rolled my eyes. "Then put it directly in its freaking mouth!"

"Nice to see your dark side peeking out." Finch laughed, but I saw him pull his Esprit from his pocket. He reached for the golem's mouth and pulled back as hard as he could, the monster arching and stumbling around. A moment later, Finch jabbed the tip of the blade right into the golem's tongue.

The golem collapsed forward, unleashing a wounded groan. It hit the deck with an enormous thud that made everything shake, cracks appearing all around its fallen body as it lay still.

"Is it breathing?" I returned my focus to the gargoyle, narrowly avoiding its sharp claws as it slashed at my head.

Finch gave the monster a sharp kick. It groaned in response. "Yep, looks like it. I took the fight right out of it."

"Good for you. You want to give me a hand here?" I whirled away from a second set of claws in my face. The gargoyle was pissed now. As it divebombed me from the very top of the bubble, I staggered back. Not seeing the hunk of rock that protruded from the ground, I sprawled backward, grimacing as a jolt of pain shot through my nerves.

"Give me a minute. I need to make sure this thing is properly down." Finch turned his back on me, leaning in to open the eye of the golem. It didn't move, but my opponent was a different story.

The gargoyle seized its opportunity, landing nearby and scuttling toward me like a grounded bat. Before I had the chance to get back up, it crawled on top of me, its sharp teeth dripping as it sniffed at my face. I stared up at it, paralyzed with fear, my gaze fixed on the black pools of its eyes. It wanted to swallow me whole. It wanted to taste my flesh and savor every morsel. It reeled back and opened its mouth wide, preparing to devour me.

Panic flooded my senses. "Don't! Don't hurt me!" I screamed. Only, the voice that came out didn't sound anything like my own. It wasn't Volla's Russian accent, it wasn't my San Diego lilt—it belonged to someone else entirely.

The gargoyle reared back, baring its fangs at me. But it made no move to attack.

I stared at it, wondering what I'd done. I kept expecting it to lean forward again, but it didn't. Why wasn't it moving? What did I do? I propped myself up cautiously on my elbows, holding the beast's gaze. It looked confused but still made no move to attack me. Instead, it closed its mouth and sat there on my legs, as if it were waiting for something.

"Did you do that?" Finch asked, surprised.

I nodded in complete confusion. "I think so."

"How? Did you use your reverse Empathy thing?"

"I... I don't know."

"Glad I didn't have to compete with you in school. Here I am, using neurotoxin to subdue my monster, and you go and get yours to behave by shouting at it." He folded his arms across his chest, sulking a little.

To be honest, I had no idea what I'd just done. I didn't think I'd used any reverse Empathy, but then, it was hard to tell when I was panicked. My emotions and energies got all jumbled up, doing their own thing. Still, I had to test the theory, before this gargoyle snapped out of it and smelled the coffee. Gathering the same sensation of panic inside me, I pushed the emotions into my voice and stared at the monster.

"Sit, over there!" I pointed to an empty patch of grass beside me. My voice sounded different again—there was a deep, echoey resonance to it that seemed to erupt from way down inside my lungs. It was such a strange sound, and it kind of hurt to speak like that, my ribs burning with the strain.

To my shock, the gargoyle scuttled off my legs and sat down in the place I'd pointed to. Curious, I got to my feet and walked to the meat box, reaching in and taking out a chunk. The gargoyle licked its lips as it stared at the meat, but it didn't move a muscle to snatch it from me.

"Roll over," I instructed, in that same tone of voice. It did as I asked, rolling over on the grass and sitting back up. I threw it the chunk of meat, watching in disgust as it gulped the flesh down in one go. "Now, play dead." It collapsed on the floor with its wings spread out, unmoving. I threw it another chunk of meat, which it furtively swiped into its mouth with a long, slithering tongue. "And, sit." It did so, receiving a third chunk of meat. The gargoyle was catching on—if it did something I wanted, it got food. A fair exchange.

"You going to name it and take it on walks?" Finch asked, distracting me. "It's like watching Katherine play with her gargoyles…"

I glowered at him. "Don't say that."

"I can't help it. I feel like I'm having déjà vu."

"I mean it, don't say that."

"I don't mean any offense by it. It's just… well, I've seen Katherine do the same thing. And she wasn't the only one."

I frowned. "What do you mean?"

"Maybe there's more Shipton blood in you than you think."

"Yeah, my mother's."

He shook his head. "It's all the same stuff, Sis. You can't pick and choose. See, Drake Shipton could do the same thing. He could control gargoyles. He had a fleet of them that watched his trade ships, making sure nobody tried to steal his goods. A little-known fact. If a pirate ship or a competitor's ship went down, he blamed it on bad weather. And, well, there were no survivors left to tell the truth."

"Could Hester do this, too?" I wanted the answer to be yes. Somehow, I felt that, if my mom had this ability, I wasn't riddled with all the bad blood from her side of the family.

"Not that I know of, but Katherine didn't talk about her much."

I didn't know whether to be worried or thrilled by this development in my ability armory. In the end, it didn't really matter right now. We'd both completed our tasks and tamed these monsters.

"That gargoyle on a leash?" Finch eyed it hesitantly.

"I think so." I chucked another hunk of meat at it for good measure.

"Naima and Tess don't need to know the gory details. If they ask, we tell them I used Fire and you used Water and Earth, and a bit of Purge beast know-how. That's all there is to it, okay?"

I nodded. "Got it."

"When this time-lapse expires, they're going to expect to find a whole mess of Mazinov all over the place." He smirked. "Man, are they going to be in for a big surprise."

TWENTY-ONE

Finch

The time-lapse was set to expire at any moment. Harley and I were perched on the meat box, waiting. The gargoyle sat at her side like a freaking lapdog. A second later, the bubble evaporated around us. A nice, dramatic reveal for Naima and Tess. They stood on the other side with wry smiles on their faces. Those smiles faded as soon as they saw us. *Ha, things didn't go your way, huh?*

"You are… alive?" Naima sounded stunned. She looked at the gargoyle and the semi-conscious golem. She was no doubt boiling that she hadn't been able to get them under control herself.

"You didn't think we would be?" I replied.

Naima floundered. "Not many Mediocre magicals make it past this stage."

"Well, here we are." I gestured to the wiped-out golem. Harley seemed dazed, but I knew she had to be thrilled about this. Deep down. Really deep down, past all the Shipton worries. Controlling a Chaos monster was a rare ability, one more to add to her collection. Seemed like the adrenaline rush was the best part. I remembered Katherine telling me it was unlike anything else, the biggest high a person could get. Maybe that was all this dazed look was—Harley, high as a kite from controlling the gargoyle.

"I must congratulate you," Naima said. "How did you achieve it?" A hint of annoyance lurked in her voice.

Harley snapped out of it. "What can I say? That meat is really good."

"You only used the meat?" Naima wasn't buying it, and neither was Tess. She kept eyeing the creatures and looking back at us. "Confused" didn't even begin to cover it. *Bet you wish you'd let down that time-lapse bubble to get a closer look.*

"Does it matter?" I cut in. I didn't want them reading too much into it. "We completed your trial, so what's next?"

Naima sneered. "You will have to wait until morning. In the meantime, if you have anyone you wish to say goodbye to back in the real world, now would be the time to make those calls. There are phones that may be used, just outside the room where you came in through the Strainer."

"Thanks." I cast her a saccharine smile. As if I'd go anywhere near those phones. They were tapped for security, and I wasn't about to have anyone listening in to what we had to say. Besides, there was no need for goodbyes. We weren't staying here long.

———

Back at the stone hut, Harley and I sat in the bathroom. It'd become our sanctuary, in a way. She sat on the floor opposite, with me perched on the tub. She was still worried about spying hexes, and this put an extra wall between us and anyone listening. Plus, I'd checked the place again and found no new additions to the eavesdropping party. Not that she was convinced. We were both exhausted from what had just happened, and she was reeling. Gaining an ability like that wasn't an everyday sort of jam. I could almost see her head spinning as she tried to come to terms with it.

"You want to play a card game? Take your mind off stuff?" She hadn't spoken in about twenty minutes, and I hated silence.

She shook her head. "I'm not in the mood."

"Well, we've got until morning. So, we can either wait here like saps or do something."

"I guess we could take a look around the compound?"

I frowned. "Not sure about that. I might be bored, but I haven't lost my mind. People are wary enough of us as it is."

She smiled. "I didn't mean as the Mazinovs. Krieger said I should be all right to shift as long as I don't shift back into myself, and this gem is still going strong. Plus, I managed to shift back after the Strainer incident, and it didn't seem to affect this thing." She glanced down at the shrunken orb at the end of the chain. Sure enough, it was glowing steadily.

"It'd technically still be using the same burst of energy, so he's probably right. And, hey, if you want to head out there gussied up as some cultist, you be my guest. I'm not going to stop you, but I'm also not going to come with you. If I go, there's more chance we'll bump into the people we've shifted into." I glanced at her. "Why do you want to look around the compound, anyway?"

She hesitated, running her tongue over her lower lip. "Curiosity."

Yeah, right. "No, the real reason." I arched an eyebrow at her.

She sighed. "Fine, I want to go and look for my mother's spirit."

"I thought as much," I muttered. Of course she wanted to go and look for her mom's spirit. I knew the urge had to be overwhelming for her, just on a personal level, let alone a mission-related one. But I didn't think it was a good idea right now. I understood the urgency of the situation. All Hallows' Eve was a week away. That gigantic clock over our heads was booming. But we had so many eyes on us already, and that spirit was locked up tight.

"You going to give up the goods, then?" she asked. "Shed some light on where she is? If these trials don't go the way we want them to, we need to make sure we've got the location of her spirit. We've only got a week, remember? It'd be extremely useful to get some insider intel, like making sure that Hester's spirit actually is where you think it is and gauging the types of security. It's been a while since you were last here, Finch. Things might've changed."

I released a slow breath. "I know. But it would be better to wait it out, Harley. It'll be easier for us to get to Hester's spirit once we're official cult members. If we start sneaking around in those areas now, people are going to get suspicious." I held Harley's firm gaze. "Seriously, don't go looking for Hester's spirit. You won't be able to find it. It's already in the safest place it can be."

She frowned. "Why? Where is it?"

"It's locked away in Katherine's office."

"Where's that?"

I sighed again. "I'll tell you when we've passed these trials. We need to do that before we start snooping. One thing at a time."

"We don't have time to waste, Finch!" she said. She hated not knowing. But I wasn't doing this to be malicious. Holding on to this information until we passed the trials was the safest way to go. I knew how this place worked. If we got caught wandering into secure zones after we'd been initiated, we were more likely to get a slap on the wrist than get murdered. Until then, neither of us could go near Katherine's office.

"My way involves taking the least risk for the best gains. Trust me on this."

She folded her arms across her chest. "Well... I need to do *something*. We're on a seriously tight deadline here—emphasis on the 'dead.' A week is going to trickle away before we know it."

"Hey, I understand the time constraints as well as you do, Sis," I shot back. "I'm not saying you shouldn't head out and try and get some intel and scope out the security in this place. Just... if you're going to head out, stay in the compound. If we start wandering around the outskirts of this place, they'll get suspicious. That's the last thing we need right now."

"What about the Hexagon?" she asked.

"To do what? Play with the humans?" I had to put her off the idea of going there. "Just avoid that place and stay in the compound. All I'm asking is that you wait until after the last trial, and then I'll tell you everything."

She shot me a dubious look, but seemed to relent. "Maybe I'll just go and see what the guard details are like in the main compound, then," she said after a moment. "Clear my head and do a bit of recon on those hive buildings I saw through the trees. Get a feel for the local area, see what sort of security and weaponry they've got going on, ask some questions about security on the Hexagon... Maybe see if anyone's talking about the upcoming ritual, too."

I smiled. "Don't do anything I wouldn't do."

"So I can do whatever I want, then?" She got up and walked to the door.

I snickered. "Just be careful. Don't take any unnecessary risks. And *don't* go outside the main compound, I mean it. If you get caught sneaking around the woods, you'll ruin this. Oh, and don't use the phones by the Strainer. They're tapped."

"Like I said, I'm just going to have a little look inside the main area, see what the nightlife is like."

"And stretch your Shifter muscles while you're at it?"

She paused. "It might come in handy later. I can still feel the Shifter energy pulsing away, and the gems are still glowing."

"Plus, that extra juice you've got isn't doing any harm in super-charging that thing." I arched an amused eyebrow. If she got stuck without her Shifter ability, we were doomed. Not that I thought she would. "For Shifters, phasing from one new person into another is still classed as the same Shift, so to speak. You should be fine."

She nodded. "Krieger said I should be able to phase back and forth a couple times without it affecting the energy of the Ephemera. I can still feel the new ability in my veins, and it feels strong. Really strong. It doesn't feel like it's fading at all, and the gem is still glowing away, like I said."

I smirked. "That's all peachy with a side of keen. But, if you can't shift back, I'll have to come up with one hell of an excuse."

She closed her eyes, and a ripple of grayish light swept across her skin. Where Volla Mazinov had been, Tess Crux now stood in the bathroom doorway. I gaped at her. Shifting shouldn't have been this easy for a newbie. She was hammering through every obstacle like a pro.

"Am I in one piece?" she asked.

I nodded. "Yep, no droopy eyes in sight. How's the Shifter energy feeling?"

"It's weird. It's still here. I can feel it, alongside the rest of my abilities."

"Then it's not weird, it's a freaking miracle. I'm not using my Fire again unless I really have to. Preservation is key for mere two-bit magicals like me." I wasn't a special edition magical like my sister, who had all this extra mojo zipping about inside her. Growing up with her would have been a complete nightmare. If I'd thought I'd had to prove myself as an only child, having a sibling like Harley would've been a total ego killer.

"Oh, before I forget. You should take this, just in case." She reached for her St. Christopher medallion and handed it over to me. Reluctance was written all over her face.

I snorted. "We giving each other gifts now?"

"It's not a gift. I want it back," she replied firmly.

"Then why are you giving it to me?"

She smiled in that sick way that let me know she was thinking about Wonderboy. "These are the pendants Wade and Krieger charmed, for when we need to get out of here. But he also charmed them in case we got into trouble here and we needed to warn each other. Three presses for emergency exit, one for a warning. Don't get it mixed up. Krieger cloaked them so they'd pass under any of the cult's scanners. All you do is press down hard on it, *once*, if you need to warn me, or if you spot anyone approaching the hut and need me to get my ass back ASAP. It'll trigger my end and let me know something's up."

"Bit convenient." I frowned. "How come nobody told me about this earlier?"

"Krieger wanted me to be sure I could trust you before I gave you one."

I rolled my eyes. "He thought I'd hand it over to Katherine or something? Give her a one-way ticket to Isadora? Real nice."

Harley sighed. "You can't blame them for being suspicious."

A small smile crept onto my lips. "So this means you trust me, huh? I'm touched. And not just in the head, before you make some snappy joke."

She chuckled. "Just don't make me regret it, okay? If you have to call me back, I'll just pretend I was around the corner getting some fresh air. I'm sure they'll understand, given what we've just been through. Just remember to press the medallion *once* if you need me to get back here, okay?" She smiled with Tess's face, and I had to remind myself that this was Harley.

"I'm not an idiot, Harley."

She grinned. "You sure about that?"

"Make sure you avoid the real Tess, or you'll be in trouble."

"I'm not an idiot, Finch," she mimicked.

"And make sure you keep your questions vague if you ask anyone about your mom's spirit or the Hexagon. Your Empathy voodoo might be good, but we don't want any lingering memories of Tess asking a bunch of weird questions, you hear me?"

"I know what I'm doing, Finch," she said. "It'll just be some casual recon to see if my mom's spirit is still where you think it is. People are bound to be talking about it, and I'm not wasting any time, if there's even the slightest chance that you're wrong. And don't worry, I'll keep a low profile."

"Then you don't know Tess at all. She isn't a low-profile kind of gal."

"Well, she is tonight." Harley left the bathroom and disappeared through the front door.

Please don't screw this up...

It wasn't like me to be cautious, but I knew the stakes in this place. Asking questions and being discreet was fine, but there was a fine line to tread. I had faith in Harley's abilities, but the danger of Katherine finding out about us was a terrifying undercurrent that I was having a hard time ignoring. It was making any risk seem huge.

I looked down at the medallion in my hand and turned it over. I'd never been a religious sort of person, so I didn't really know what it was supposed to do. Bring comfort, I guessed. I slipped it around my neck and headed out into the main space of the hut. I really was bored out of my brain.

As I kicked back on one of the beds, my mind drifted toward Harley again. She was impressing me more and more. Not only with her skills, but with her resilience, too. It wasn't every person who could see humans being tortured and carry on. She was made of tougher stuff than I'd thought. It kept surprising me, to the point where I was starting to look forward to what she'd do next.

Thinking about Harley immediately led to my mind turning to the Muppet Babies waiting patiently back at the SDC. I wondered how they'd be feeling right about now. They were probably going out of their minds. Wade, especially. I wished I had some way of contacting them, just to rile Wonderboy up a little. Coven drones needed to be put in their place from time to time. And he'd be worrying more than the rest of them, having left his precious Harley in my care. He didn't think much of me, that was for sure. But then, he didn't know that I was starting to give a damn. It'd surprised me, too. I even knew what I might say: "Your girlfriend is quite the firecracker. She's definitely a Shipton. By morning, we either die or join the cult. Stand by for details once it's safe to talk. Sleep tight, buttercup. F." Wade would've loved that. Shame I didn't have a way to send him the message. He'd just have to keep on worrying.

I had to distract myself. Reaching over to my bedside table, I opened the top drawer and pulled out a book. It was a history of Eris. I almost detached my retinas looking at the cover. This Eris thing was getting way too literal.

As I flicked to the first page, figuring I had a little time to see what tale Katherine wanted her cultists to believe, my eyes flitted up to the door. Harley was right about us running out of time. And who was I to stop her from running some recon? She was right, I might have been wrong about the location of Hester's spirit.

And yet, I couldn't shake my nerves.

I toyed with the idea of shifting into someone else and trying to follow Harley out into the compound, just to see if she'd listened to my warning about the Hexagon. Something held me back. The risk of both of us getting caught, mostly. On her own, she was less exposed. She knew how to hide. I just hoped that'd be enough to keep her out of trouble here.

Steeling my nerves, I turned back to the book. I only got through a few sentences before what I wanted to say to Wade came back to bite me in the ass. The prospect of Harley possibly dying here would be driving him nuts, even without a message.

But the truth of the matter was, she really could die tomorrow morning. And, I realized with a sinking feeling, the idea wasn't sitting too well with me, either.

TWENTY-TWO

Harley

———

Disguised as Thessaly Crux, complete with bandaged hands, and praying my Shifter ability didn't let me down, I snuck along the network of walkways in search of people.

I wanted to see what these cultists really did in their spare time, and I wanted to put together a lay of the land so I had my bearings. Finch's warning about the Hexagon had made me want to go there even more, as that was likely where Katherine's office was. That had to be the reason he'd been so intent on me avoiding the place. If I was careful and kept to the shadows, I felt I could pull it off.

Besides, all I wanted to do was get an idea of the security there and, most importantly, try to find out what people knew about this upcoming ritual, and whether they had any idea where my mom's spirit was being kept. As I'd told Finch, I couldn't risk him being wrong about that.

Still, I decided to take a detour first to check out the nightlife in the cult and see what these people did with their evenings. It was more to decipher how much security I might come across than anything else. It didn't take long before I found myself back in front of the beehive that

Tess had shown us on her whistle-stop tour of the cult, my eyes drawn like a moth to the glowing lights coming from within.

I peered in through one of the windows and saw that most of the tables were full now. Drinks were flowing, and the people inside looked happy. They were all talking and laughing, the sound floating out into the night, as if what they were doing was the most natural and wonderful thing in the world. If it weren't for the human experimentation on the opposite end of this island, an onlooker would think that the Cult of Eris was just some in-touch-with-nature, grassroots sanctuary for magical misfits.

I turned away from the beehive and headed down another set of walkways, toward the path that Tess had led us across to reach the Hexagon on the other side of the island. Twenty minutes later, I found myself in the shadows of the jungle, looking at the hulking great building, with its rusty exterior and looming walls. Katherine seemed to have styled all of the other buildings on the island in this design, sticking with the hexagon. It was interesting that she'd chosen to implement this shape in the making of her interdimensional realm. I'd read that bees did the same, using hexagons because they required the least amount of material to hold the most weight in their hives. And Katherine clearly thought of herself as the queen bee.

Up ahead, I saw lights flickering and people moving around, crossing a slanting bridge between the walkways above and chattering amongst themselves. They were coming in and out of a central doorway in the center of the Hexagon, which seemed to be the only way to get inside. I knew I had to be careful if I wanted to check it out. The real Tess could be around here somewhere, and us encountering each other would be nothing short of a disaster.

I sank back into the shadows cast by the overhanging trees and wondered what Wade was doing right now. I missed him so badly that it was actually starting to hurt. What I wouldn't have given to have him here with me, right now, taking away all my worries and fears. We'd only been apart for less than twenty-four hours, and I was acting like we'd been separated for a lifetime. Then again, it had been a heck of a long day, and it wasn't even over yet.

"Are you on detail tonight?" My ears pricked up as I heard voices up ahead, two figures walking together on the lower walkway beside where I stood. It led up to the bridge into the Hexagon.

"Yeah, I'm covering Georgia and Arlo on guard duty," a second voice replied.

"Until when?"

"Until I get told I can leave."

The first voice snickered. "Hey, at least it's a promotion. I'm watching the labs until six. Might as well be in a pigsty."

"Same thing, isn't it?"

"Funny what happens when you take away their humanity, isn't it? It's like they really are animals underneath." The first speaker sighed. "I envy you, man. I'd give anything to guard the ingredient instead."

The second voice snorted. "Ingredient? Is that what we're calling it now? This isn't *Masterchef*, dude."

Their voices drifted out of range, leaving my mind racing. Was the ingredient my mother's spirit? It seemed pretty likely, given where we were, but then, I didn't know the ins and outs of the rituals. There might've been more than one thing Katherine needed to make it work.

Determined, I crept along the walkway in an attempt to follow them, keeping my distance. Nobody would bat an eyelid if Tess went inside the Hexagon, but I was still worried she might already be in there.

Glancing behind me to make sure nobody was following, my mind turned toward Finch. Would he be okay at the hut on his own? He had the medallion if anything went wrong, and I couldn't feel him calling for help. I didn't know what it would feel like, exactly, but Krieger and Wade had charmed my pendant to pulsate against my chest if either of us was in trouble. If I had to run back, the hut wasn't that far.

I kept to the lower walkway for as long as I could, trying to get a better look at what was going on, spotting the two guards a little way ahead. Even in my Tess disguise, I had to be wary. There were more guards stationed in front of the main entrance, and pretty much every cultist would be looking out for suspicious behavior. I'd have to play it cool to get past them and act like Tess would—no nonsense, no drama, all ferocity. The National Council and their agents had set them all on edge, which wasn't exactly useful for us. But, surely, they wouldn't say a word to me, looking like this?

The flow of people was almost like a hive, with them coming and going to different parts of the island in an endless flurry of activity, meandering across the interlinking walkways to either head back to the main compound or go into the Hexagon for their nightly duties. I could see the lights of the beehive clusters I'd left, in the distance, but I couldn't go back now. Those two guards were headed into the Hexagon, and I needed to follow them, in case they led me right to my mom's spirit.

"What are you doing out here, sneaking around like a thief in the night?" A voice hissed from behind me, making me jump. I whirled around and came face-to-face with Kenneth Willow.

Panic ricocheted through me like a gunshot, making my heart beat so hard I thought it might fall out of my chest. *Crap, crap, crap, crap, crap!* And then, I remembered who I was masquerading as. In my fright, I'd forgotten. Tess wouldn't take any trash from this guy, and I wasn't going to, either.

"None of your business, Willow," I shot back. "Shouldn't you be in the infirmary, licking your wounds?" I assumed they had an infirmary. If they had a torture playground, they had to have some kind of hospital. Priorities, right?

He scowled. "I wasn't even hurt. I have no wounds to lick, thank you very much."

"Could've fooled me. The way you were flat on your ass, I thought you'd never get up." I smirked at him. "Oh, wait, no, I *wished* you'd never get up."

"I only stepped in because *you* were too weak to do the job."

"Ah, so you admit it, you were second choice?"

He glared at me. "I wasn't second choice! Eris knows how powerful

I am, so she makes sure I don't have to do all the trivial stuff—she needs me to put my energy elsewhere, where it's actually needed. You're just lucky I covered your ass, instead of making you do the trial with your sad little hands."

"You forgetting the reason I burned my hands, momma's boy? I was on a real mission for Eris, not some stupid distraction to get you out from under her feet."

"Well, I've never been injured in the field." He stuck his nose in the air.

"Then you haven't been working hard enough."

He looked about ready to explode. I was tugging at all his little insecurities, knowing exactly how to get him riled up. The kid tried to act so damn tough, yet he couldn't even spring Le Fay or kill Finch. He probably had the lowest success rate of any member here. It was a miracle Katherine hadn't offed him yet, and I had no idea how he'd managed to weasel his way through the trials. Maybe, thanks to the Ryders, he hadn't had to endure them.

"Anyway, the field missions don't matter to me. They're trivial labor, too, as far as I'm concerned." He leaned back on the walkway fence. "I'm sure I don't need to remind you that *I* am integral to the rituals. You aren't. You're nobody, as much as you'd like to think otherwise. I don't recall Eris assigning you to an important position." He tutted smugly. "Green isn't a good color on you, Tess."

"Oh yeah?" I balled my hands into fists. This conversation was about to get violent. Kenneth seemed to be itching for a fight, and I was more than ready to give him a second round. I'd knock him flat on his ass again, same as before. *Although, you don't have any Electro ability, remember?* I kept forgetting I had rules to conform to.

"You want me to prove just how easily I can beat you?" Kenneth's eyes narrowed.

I was about to reply when I felt a warm, burning sensation at the top of my chest, right where the pendant lay. It was too bizarre not to be the warning trigger that Krieger had set up. Finch had pressed the medallion, and he was calling me back. *He's in trouble.*

"I wouldn't want to embarrass you for a second time today," I retorted. "Anyway, I'm busy. I don't have time for stupid games or you peacocking around the place. Go and do your rounds, or whatever it is you're supposed to be doing." I pushed my reverse Empathy onto him, just to make sure he did as I asked. I filled him with a sudden feeling of anxiety and a desperate need to go and check on his duties. His face changed immediately, his gaze veering over my shoulder toward those distant lights.

"Same goes for you, Crux."

I let him have the final word as he shoved past me, heading into the gloom. As soon as he was gone, I took off down the walkways at break-neck speed, sprinting for the stone hut. I just hoped that, wherever the twerp was headed, he didn't end up running into the real Tess. If he did, they'd have a very confused exchange. I mean, nobody could point a finger at me or Finch as the Mazinovs, but there'd definitely be word of a Shapeshifter messing around with Kenneth.

Then again, I wondered how many people here would *love* the chance to mess with Kenneth's head. There'd probably be a line-up as long as my arm if anyone suspected any foul play.

Safe in that thought, I ran through the darkness, praying I wasn't too late to help Finch.

TWENTY-THREE

Harley

I burst through the door of the stone hut to find Finch lounging on one of the beds. He was reading a book called *The Art of the Demon Deal*, his foot jiggling as his eyes moved from left to right. I didn't know where he'd gotten the book, and I didn't really care. I swept my eyes around the room to check there were no hidden assailants. The medallion lay on his chest, innocent enough. Nothing seemed to be wrong at all. In fact, he seemed to be having the time of his life.

"Why did you call me back?" I snapped.

He shrugged and set down the book. "I was getting bored. And this book was bumming me out."

"Are you serious?" Just when I'd been starting to warm to him, he went and did something like this. Something so ridiculously Finch-like.

"What?"

"I was about to infiltrate the compound! I was following some guards who were talking about an 'ingredient.' I was right there, looking at these beehive thingies, and then you call me back because you're freaking bored? Why didn't you take a nap or something, like an ordinary person?"

He sat up, frowning. "Then you were looking in the wrong place, and you'd have ended up following those idiots to nowhere. That 'ingredient' could have been anything. We might as well finish these trials, get full-member status, and *then* go crazy on the snooping afterward. We can't get into the place where Hester's spirit is being kept until we're full members."

"Which means losing time we don't have—we discussed this already!"

"I know, but I chickened out. There's no use risking our necks now. I didn't want you going there and getting us outed. It'll just get us killed quicker. You should be thanking me, not sniping at me."

I ran a hand through my hair, only to find I had little, and gave myself a mental kick. *I'm still Tess, idiot.* I'd been in such a panic over Finch that I'd forgotten to shift right before entering. That would have backfired if Tess had been in the room.

Then it hit me. Finch was worried about me. He'd called me back because he didn't like me being out there on my own.

Saying nothing, I closed my eyes and shifted back into the form of Volla Mazinov. The new energy still thrummed inside me, powered up by my extra Chaos and clinging on for dear life... I knew I couldn't risk doing this again, in spite of my urge to look around. Until all of this was over, I'd have to stick with Volla, now, for both of our sakes. If I failed, he failed.

In the tense silence that followed, I took a moment to think about my odd new relationship with my half-brother. Was Finch's concern for me purely about not compromising the mission, or was it something more than that? Was it some fledgling brotherly streak in him, some urge to protect me? *Is your heart growing a couple sizes, Grinch?*

I wasn't going to let him see me softening up toward him, even if I was. I still didn't trust him completely. Not yet. And maybe not ever. He'd yet to fully prove himself, to the point where I could forget all the bad things he'd done, and I didn't honestly know if he'd ever be able to.

"What's the time?" I changed the subject. Delving too deep into emotions wasn't the kind of thing I needed at the minute, with so much going on.

He rolled over to check the clock on the bedside table. "Two a.m."

"So we've got a couple hours until morning." I walked to the other bed and lay down on the covers. There was no use changing out of my clothes, since they were pretty much stuck to me. "We should get some sleep before dawn. I've got a nasty feeling this third trial is going to kick our asses."

I turned over before he could answer and tried very hard not to think of what was to come.

Darkness surrounded me on all sides, with a thin sliver of anemic light casting a sickly pool down onto me. Around the edges of the faint light, creatures snapped and drooled, jaws and glittering eyes flashing in the shadows. Howls pierced the air, sending a shiver of dread up my spine. Claws raked at my legs and leathery wings flapped out of sight, all these beasts desperate for a taste of me. And I was struggling to hold them off.

A flicker of movement caught my eye. Someone was coming toward me in the dim light. *Finch...* The monsters didn't touch him. Instead, they parted like water to let him through, bowing on their paws as he passed by to reach me. I opened my mouth to speak, but the words faded on my lips as another figure appeared behind Finch.

Katherine Shipton breezed through the monsters as if they weren't even there. I didn't know if it was the darkness or something else, but she looked different, like she was actually bringing light with her. As she got closer, I realized that was precisely what she was doing. The ethereal glow was coming from inside her, illuminating her skin with a pulsing, bronze light. The way she moved, she resembled some goddess, bright and beautiful and serene, unfazed by anything happening around her.

Finch smiled at me as he neared. "It's going to be okay."

I wanted to scream, to tell him to watch out for the figure behind him, but the words wouldn't come. My mouth opened and closed, but no sound came out. I was mute... and Katherine was getting nearer by the second. Finch seemed totally oblivious to her presence, and I didn't know what to do to get him to see her. I tried to move forward, but a claw swiped at my ankle, and I stumbled. He was so close, but I couldn't reach him.

Katherine entered the pool of light. If she got her hands on us, we'd never make it out of this monster pit alive. I wasn't fooled for a second by her godlike appearance. Even Lucifer had been an angel once, and Katherine was far worse in my books.

She came up behind him and leaned toward his ear. Her mouth moved in a whisper, and I couldn't hear what she was saying. A moment later, Finch smiled back at me and took a knife from his pocket. His eyes were fixed on mine, his smile turning sour and strange. The blade flashed in the glow of Katherine's ethereal light, and realization dawned. He was going to kill me. She'd given the order, and he was going to execute me on the spot.

Finch stepped toward me, but I couldn't move. My limbs were completely frozen. I couldn't do anything to stop him or defend myself. This was it. After everything I'd been through, and everything I'd done to try and stop Katherine, I was about to die. Finch was under her spell again, and my death was the only thing in his mind.

He put his hand on my shoulder and rested the tip of the blade against my chest, between two ribs. I tried to cry out as he leaned in, the full weight of his body pushing pressure against the blade as he moved to embrace me, but I couldn't breathe a word.

"It's going to be okay," he whispered in my ear, the blade lodged in my chest. "This will all be over soon."

I woke up with a start, blinking up at the ceiling overhead. My body was drenched in sweat, my lungs clawing for breath as I looked around. I didn't recognize anything, prompting panic to make my heart race even faster. Why wasn't I in my room at the SDC? Where was I? What was going on?

You're in the Cult of Eris. Relax. I sat up sharply and noticed that multiple objects were hovering in the room: a lampshade, a clock, a potted plant, and a couple of cushions. I glanced at the bed opposite and saw Finch sitting on the edge of his bed, staring at me as if I'd just grown snakes for hair. He wasn't saying anything, which was even more unnerving. It wasn't like him to be silent.

"It's my Telekinesis," I said sheepishly, as I brought the objects back down. "It acts up sometimes when I'm sleeping."

He arched an eyebrow. "You're lucky I got rid of those spying hexes."

"I know." I shook off the last of the tension in my muscles and tried to relax. "It usually happens if I'm having a nightmare. I can't stop it."

He nodded. "When did it start?"

"After my Suppressor broke."

"Figures. All that power inside you needs a way to manifest, balance or not." He smiled. "You've got a doozy of a heritage from Hester and Hiram. No wonder you're having… floating issues." A note of bitterness lingered in his voice.

"I could say the same about you, with Hiram and Katherine, but I don't see you making things hover in your sleep." I cast him a wry smile, but he didn't seem to be in the mood for jokes.

"I was destined to go down a dark path. It's in my blood to be bad. You got lucky with your goody-two-shoes parents. Seriously, you've got no idea what it's like, trying to fight your own nature."

I thought about the pills that he had to take for his psychosis and wondered if that was part of what he meant. He thought those issues had stemmed from a hex, after all. Katherine had used his mental health struggles against him, just adding to the vast list of terrible things she'd done. I wanted to reassure him that his psychosis didn't mean he was bad, by any means, because it was as much a part of him as the blood in his veins. It wasn't put there. It had always been in him, which wasn't easy to live with, or to come to terms with.

I held his saddened gaze. "Goody-two-shoes? Come on, Hiram and Hester weren't perfect at all. You know that as well as I do," I said. "At the end of the day, it's got nothing to do with how good or evil your family is. If you check the family tree close enough, you'll see there's a bunch of both—good, bad, and everything in between. It's not about blood; it's about what you do with your abilities, when you're called upon to use them. It's your choice, not your bloodline's. You make your fate, not them."

"Nice after-school special there, Harley," he replied, with a cold laugh.

"I mean it."

"You can say that because you know our dad was hexed, so he wasn't really that bad, and your mother was a saint. They were like a celebrity couple, your parents." He paused. "Do you remember anything about our father?"

I nodded slowly. "Sort of."

"What does that mean?"

"Well… I've got a couple of memories of him, but I've only ever remembered them in weird, dream-like situations. I was little in both of them, probably around two or three. He was throwing me up into the air in one of them, and he was smiling. In the other, he was watching me sleep and talking about how he was going to protect me." I dropped my chin to my chest. "He sacrificed himself for me. And, someday, I'll clear his name."

Finch gave a wry smile. "Nice guy, huh?"

"Yeah. I was trying to catch these silver fish in this stream, and he was helping me. He kept laughing each time I missed, and it was infectious." I closed my eyes to try and remember my Euphoria dream more clearly. I'd clung to it ever since it had come to me, and I'd vowed never to let it go. It was all I had of him, other than the first dream, where he'd stood with Isadora, discussing how they could save me.

"And… he loved you?" The desperate tone of his voice made my heart break.

"He really did. At least, I think he did. From what Isadora has told me, he didn't want to let go of me, but he knew he had to. I think he would've been happy to run with me for the rest of my life, but he couldn't risk Katherine catching up and killing us both. Even if it was just to make amends for what he did to my mother. I suppose, in a way, he gave everything so that I could live." Sudden tears filled my eyes, and I tried to wipe them away as discreetly as possible. My feelings surrounding Hiram were always in conflict. I'd seen him with me on that riverbank, and I'd had his note with me for as long as I could remember, before I gave it to Marie Laveau, both of those things reminding me that he'd loved me. But that could never fully blot out the knowledge that he'd killed my mother—curse or no curse.

"What did he look like?"

I glanced at him. "His hair was black, but we've got his eyes. You have his nose, and if you turn in a certain light, you've got the same jawline. He was tall, too. I guess that might've been my perspective as a kid, but he seemed like a giant to me."

"I wonder what he'd think of the way we turned out," he said quietly.

"I think he'd be impressed we're in the same room together. I think he'd be grateful that you're watching out for me. And I think he'd be happy that I was watching out for you, too. He abandoned us both, in a way, but I don't know if he would have done that if he hadn't been cursed, or if he'd thought he could fight Katherine. I suppose I'll never know for sure, but I always try and convince myself that he wouldn't." I paused, not knowing whether to continue. "He'd probably have fought for you, too, if he thought he could win."

"You think?" His tone brightened slightly.

I nodded. "I'm pretty sure that was the kind of guy he was. He made mistakes, sure, but he also understood that there were consequences for his actions. He'd have been in your life if Katherine had let him."

"I wish I'd known him." He sighed heavily. "Even just an hour alone in a room with him. It's weird not to know what your father even sounds like."

"He had a deep, comforting voice. I'd play it to you if I had a recording." If I could've reached into my head and plucked out the memory for him, I would've. "Did Katherine ever tell you anything about him?"

He snorted. "She told me everything she wanted me to hear. She definitely never described him the way you just did."

"What did she tell you?"

He shrugged. "That he was a selfish, cruel, cold man who didn't give a damn about me or her. She told me he'd demanded she get rid of me when he found out she was pregnant. I believed every word. All my life, I thought he was this evil figure in Katherine's past who'd destroyed her life in every way he could. It made things easier to handle, I suppose, when I found out he'd been killed."

I thought of all the things he'd said about Hiram after the gargoyle attack and during my visits to Purgatory. His hatred of Hiram had been palpable, as if he loathed our dad with every fiber of his being. Now, it sort of made sense. He'd been fed poison by his mother to make her own evil seem less horrifying.

"He wasn't like that," I said, shocked. "He'd never have asked Katherine to do that. He'd have cared, if he'd been given the chance."

"I'm starting to think you might be right."

A knock at the door made us both jump out of our skin. I was already in Volla's form, and Finch quickly shifted into Pieter Mazinov as the door handle turned. It opened a moment later, revealing Naima and Tess. They didn't need to speak; we knew why they were here.

Dawn had arrived, and the third trial awaited us.

TWENTY-FOUR

Finch

The trials had changed since I was last here. I had no idea what we were heading into. But, judging by what we'd already gone through, it wasn't going to be a slice of pie. Potential death, imminent death, and more death were pretty much the options.

Dawn streaked across the interdimensional bubble, bolts of pink and red shooting through wisps of cloud, turning the purplish haze to a clear blue. Aside from the occasional storm, this place could be mistaken for paradise. Katherine had chosen well. And so had my great-grandfather, all those years ago. Drake Shipton had more islands to his name than the East India Trading Company used to have. All the places that the National Council had no clue about. I'd have liked to have met the guy, just to test the mettle of his gigantic balls.

As soon as we headed down the main walkway, I realized where we were going—the same disc of black glass where I'd put Shinsuke on his ass. The Red Robes were already sitting in wait. *Bunch of sheep.* I noticed a few hungover faces in the crowd and smirked. Not that much had changed since I left this place. The cult worked hard and played hard. And while some got their kicks turning humans into mutants, others were a bit more traditional. Booze and music and long nights.

My guts almost erupted from my throat when I noticed the figure sitting in one of the stone thrones. In the gloomy half-dawn, I'd almost missed her.

Ah, Mother... there you are.

I'd been wondering when we might meet again. She didn't like to fraternize too much with the underlings, but she showed up every now and again to light a fire under everyone's backside.

I glanced at Harley. She was staring dead ahead, her eyes narrowing. *Easy, tiger. Don't give the game away.* I rested a hand on her forearm to remind her we had to keep it cool. She gave a subtle nod and dropped her gaze. This wasn't going to be a walk in the park for either of us. It'd take every ounce of strength we had, combined, not to try anything stupid.

"This is the third trial," Naima said, prompting us to halt in the center of the black disc. "No fighting, no taming, merely an interview with our divine leader. If she takes kindly to one or both of you, then you will live, and you will take your place among us. If she does not, then you will die by Death by a Thousand Cuts."

There it is, the death clause.

"Relax," I whispered to Harley. She was shaking now. Most likely with rage rather than fear, but it could've been a mix of both.

"Easy for you to say." She kept her gaze down.

This was going to be an awkward conversation. And that was putting it mildly. I'd have taken a golem and another round with Shinsuke over this, any day of the week. Why had Katherine picked this as the third trial? She was a blood and gore kind of woman, and this had none of the above. This was creepily intimate and deeply unsettling. Maybe it had something to do with how I got caught, and how the Ryder twins were outed. We'd been her prize soldiers, and we'd failed. Maybe now she wanted to select members personally, to make sure she got the right people. To avoid those kinds of failures again. Failures like me.

Or Kenneth Willow. I smirked at the thought. Harley had mumbled something about that sad sack in her sleep. Something about him being part of the rituals. I couldn't, for the life of me, think of any reason why Kenneth would be part of any of them. Where did he fit in? A jumped-up hex-thrower with a ridiculous bowtie and a puffed-up ego?

The dweeb himself was currently swooning over the sight of his beloved leader. He almost had anime eyes, he was gazing at her so lovingly. Harley and I weren't even on his radar, not with Katherine in the vicinity.

Still, I was dying to know what Katherine thought of me now. But I guessed I'd never find out. This wasn't the time for a mother-son heart-to-heart.

Pushed forward by Naima, Harley and I made our way to the edge of the black disc and bowed before Katherine. An amused smile turned up the corners of her lips. She was dressed in an emerald-green gown that made her look like a Celtic queen, her red hair in a braid over her shoulder. A gold circlet sat on her head, finishing the I'm-an-almighty-goddess look.

"Remember who you are, okay?" I glanced at Harley, in case she needed reminding.

She nodded. "Nothing else matters."

Naima and Tess had already stepped away from us, making the encounter all the more intimate. Yeah, there were a bunch of people watching, but it was really just us and her, her and us. She tapped her fingers impatiently on the arm of her throne and looked over us both, her eyes drawing in a first impression. Her face was hard to read. It always had been. She constantly wore this dark, amused expression. I'd only seen her lose her cool a handful of times, and the memories weren't something I wanted to repeat.

Steeling myself, I held her gaze. My muscles were wound so tight I felt like I was dangling off a cliff, holding on for dear life. Which, in a way, I sort of was. This was Katherine Shipton. My mother. The woman who wanted me dead. The woman who gave birth to me. The woman who wanted to destroy her own creation because she hated it so much. The only person on this planet who knew and understood my whole life. She'd shaped it with her own hands, after all. She'd manipulated everything. She'd shown me what she wanted me to see, whether it was about my dad, or the world, or the limits of my own power.

My only advantage here was that I also knew Katherine better than anyone. Nobody had seen every facet to her personality, except me. I'd been there at the beginning of all of this, and I was sure as hell going to be there when it crumbled. *How do you like me now, Ma?* But what could I do with that knowledge, gussied up as Pieter Mazinov? How far was I willing to go? Right now, I wasn't sure. My mind was still racing.

"Pieter Mazinov, yes?" Katherine spoke. You could've heard a pin drop.

I nodded. "Yes, Ms. Shipton."

"Eris will do. We should start as we mean to go on," she replied with a smirk. "I've got to say, you look pretty good for someone who had a nasty mauling. I thought your face would be hanging off or something. Or there'd at least be a rugged scar. Chicks dig scars, apparently."

"A ruse, Eris. A ruse to keep the authorities off our case."

"I've always thought faking your own death to be a little trashy. It shows a lack of resolve, to be quite frank. But I guess it worked out for you and your sister, since the authorities think you're in the belly of some half-starved polar bear."

I smiled at Harley-slash-Volla. "I wanted to protect my sister."

"How sweet." The words dripped sarcastically from her lips. I knew she was checking for lies or deceit. Her face didn't say much, but it didn't have to. I knew her style.

"Family is everything, Eris. Where we're from, it comes first above all things. In a way, this place is like a family, full of all the people that the magical world has cast aside—the black sheep that nobody cares about. And once we're part of this cult, our family values will extend to the rest of the members here. The cult will be prioritized above everything else."

Katherine chuckled. "I thought I kept the nature of the third trial a secret."

"That's true. We didn't know anything about it, Eris."

"Then why does your reply sound rehearsed? Or do you just practice that in the mirror every morning while you're brushing your teeth? A little ego-stroke to start the day?"

I felt heat rise to my face. "Something like that. It's been on my mind a lot since we decided to come to you and devote ourselves to your supreme mission."

"Goodness, my behind must be starved of affection."

I frowned. "I don't follow."

"You seem intent on kissing it."

"I'm a little nervous, that's all. It's not every day that I get to meet someone as inspiring as you."

"You should really put on some Chapstick if you're going to keep doing it, Pieter," she replied with an amused laugh. Despite what she was saying, I was winning her over. She loved an ass-kisser. That's why Kenneth Willow still had a position here. Ass-kissers were useful—they'd do anything she asked, without hesitation.

I bowed my head. "I'm sorry, Eris."

"Tell me, where is it you're actually from? Where do all these 'family values' come from?"

"We come from St. Petersburg, but we've moved around a lot."

She nodded slowly. "That must be where the strange accents come from. Not quite Russian, not quite Eastern European, not quite Transatlantic. A bit of a mishmash. Do you enjoy the ballet? I hear it's exceptional in St. Petersburg."

I shook my head. "I've never liked it. My sister got the artistic gene; I got the practical one." She was testing me with simple questions. If I faltered, she'd know I was lying. This was where things got scary. It sounded innocent enough, but it was anything but. There was logic in everything Katherine did and said, and this was my polygraph test.

"So what do you like?"

"I like to hunt. And I enjoy winter sports. Skiing, snowboarding, skating, anything like that."

"How very Russian of you." She eyed me curiously. "I imagine you put those polar bear pelts to good use?"

I smiled. "No polar bears were harmed in the making of our fake deaths, Eris."

"Tell me of your parents. Are they proud of you? Do you stay in touch?"

Oh, the irony.

"To keep up the ruse, we had to convince our parents we were dead. Otherwise, the authorities would have gone after them. We haven't spoken to them since we were in the Arctic. It hasn't been easy, but it had to play out like that. Like I said, protecting family is our priority."

Her eyes didn't stay on my face as I spoke. Instead, they drifted across me, scouring for any telling body language. "Do you get along with your sister?"

I chuckled. "Most of the time. We squabble like any siblings do, but we care about each other. And hey, we've stayed together this long without killing each other. Why break the habit, right?"

I had to sell every word, like my life depended on it. Because, at the end of the day, it did.

Katherine turned to look at Harley. "Now then, how about you?"

TWENTY-FIVE

Harley

My blood felt like it had frozen solid in my veins. I couldn't even look at Katherine without wanting to vomit or throw something sharp at her. Finch had dealt with his interview like a pro, keeping it casual but reverent, with a touch of nerves thrown in for good measure. After all, this was Katherine Shipton we were talking about here—there were very few people who could stand in front of her without losing their nerve. I thought I was one of them, but apparently not. I put it down to being Volla Mazinov. She was definitely crapping her pants.

"What Pieter said was very interesting, if a little saccharine. Let's see what you've got to say for yourself, shall we?" Katherine smiled back at him, but her verdict remained unclear. He was still standing, which I guessed was a good thing. No Death by a Thousand Cuts just yet.

Finally, the moment I'd been dreading had come. She was staring right at me. My hands were already shaking, but not with fear. Anger bubbled through every cell, threatening to spill over. I just hoped it came across as nerves instead, or else she'd figure me out right away. I tried to send out a slither of Empathy, to feel out what emotions were coming off her, but I hit the same wall I always hit. Every time I came face-to-face with her, I became more convinced that she had Shapeshifter abilities. Finch had likely inherited his own ability from her. Thinking back to O'Halloran's reaction in the Luis Paoletti Room, I wondered if I should try some reverse Empathy on her, to see if that would break through the wall. But that was a risk that didn't seem worth it right now. If she sensed it, in any way, I'd be screwed. No, I'd have to win her over the non-Empathy-assisted way.

"Cat got your tongue? Maybe you think I don't even need to ask who you are, since your brother has gushed enough about you." Katherine chuckled, the sound filling the eerie silence of the arena. Nobody in the stands was moving a muscle; they weren't even whispering to one another.

I dipped my head in a bow. "Not at all, it's only polite to make an introduction. Volla Mazinov, at your service."

"What, no salute?" she teased.

"Should I?" I made myself sound suitably dumbfounded and anxious.

She laughed raucously. "No need to just yet, Volla. I don't really go in for the whole saluting-your-superiors thing. It's a little too 'National Council' for my tastes."

"Good to know."

"You're feistier than your brother, huh?"

I shrugged. "He can get a little nervous around beautiful women. That's why I'm always his wing-woman. He'd be hopeless without me."

"Don't tell me you need the Chapstick, too?"

"Not just yet, Eris. I don't really go in for the ass-kissing thing." I mimicked her, hoping she'd be amused. I remembered just how much she loved a bit of banter. It was mostly to hear the sound of her own voice, I was pretty sure, but I figured it could work in my favor. She liked strong women—women who weren't afraid to stand up and speak their minds. That was why she surrounded herself with them. Well, that, and the fact that she detested men at their base level, thanks to my dad and his life choices.

To my relief, she howled with laughter. "How very refreshing."

"Really? Apparently, my personality is an acquired taste."

"Good thing I enjoy unusual flavors," she parried. "I hear Russian food is quite unusual. What's your favorite dish?"

"On a good day?" I racked my brain for knowledge of the Mazinovs, trying to remember what had been written in their file. There'd been a picture of Volla and her brother in a grand restaurant, clinking shot glasses with a plate of caviar on the table in front of them. I figured it was a good enough guess. "Beluga caviar with a side of decent Russian vodka. I miss that the most. I haven't tasted it in so long."

"I've always found caviar to be a little barbaric, but I wouldn't want to insult your heritage," she said.

"Have you tried it, Eris?"

"I confess, I haven't." She laughed again, which I hoped was a good sign. "And why have you come to this place with your brother? My lieutenant tells me you made quite the scene with a couple of unruly security magicals. You must have been desperate to get her attention."

"I don't believe security magicals have any place in a bar like that, Eris. It only ever ends in round-ups and false accusations," I replied. "We did what we thought was right. As for why we're here, we're eager to find our place among like-minded individuals—people who are tired of the status quo and want to make an actual change. Why should humans have the monopoly on this planet, when they're so much weaker than we are? And why should those who pander to them have any right to bear Chaos? Some call it far-right thinking; I call it the right *way* of thinking."

"You speak well, Volla. I've got to say, I'm enjoying your attitude."

"What can I say? I was born with it." I flashed her a grin.

"And what do you think you can bring to our organization?"

What is this, a job interview? I supposed it was, in a way. "Loyalty and strength. My Water abilities are renowned, and I figure they might as well be used for something important. Plus, I'm always game for a bit of patriarchy-smashing."

I quickly realized that these weren't simple questions. They were intended to gauge my body language, my hesitation, and any deceit that might be lingering in my words. I figured I'd done well so far, but it wouldn't be enough to win Katherine over. She didn't like the ordinary. She didn't like the same old people, with the same old answers.

"And what would you say are your greatest strengths and weaknesses, aside from your abilities?" Katherine continued. I was about to make a very risky move, and I prayed it paid off.

I smiled. "I get why you're doing this, Eris—asking all the simple, businesslike questions to try and gauge my body language and read between the lines. Also, I'm pretty sure you've got people at the hut right now, checking for the surveillance hexes. I should warn you, you won't find any. We aren't stupid. That was the first thing we looked for. If you want to know our deepest, darkest secrets, then ask us outright. You don't need to bother with all this fluff. We've got nothing to hide."

Dangerous silence drifted across the arena, peppered by a hissing gasp that rose up from the crowd. I doubted anyone had ever spoken this boldly to Katherine before, but I was certain I was doing the right thing. Either that, or it would get us killed. The thing was, she admired strength and ferocity above all other things; that was why she had a freaking tigress as her lieutenant.

Beside me, Finch had turned pale, gawking at me in disbelief. But the truth was, I wasn't willing to play Katherine's game. If I did, I got the feeling it would get us both rejected. She wanted exceptional soldiers, not your everyday, run-of-the-mill sheeple.

I fixed my gaze on Katherine. Her expression hadn't changed. It still carried that hint of dark amusement that always rested on her face.

"I'm curious, Volla. Why are you choosing to do this, in the middle of your last trial? You know it could get you killed, right?"

I smiled brazenly. "I'm aware of the consequences, Eris, but you need people who think outside the box. You need people who have minds of their own, not coven drones and hapless rejects with nowhere else to go. Pieter and I have stayed alive, and under the radar, for this long precisely because we're neither of those things." I put my hand on Finch's shoulder and squeezed it. "Pieter might come across as compliant, but that's because you made him nervous. Beneath all that, he's just like me. We've answered all the simple questions we're going to. If you want the truth, the really good stuff, then it's time to lay it all out in the open. Just say the word."

For the longest time, Katherine said nothing, and I began to think I'd made the wrong move in calling her out like that. Finch's shoulder was as tense as a rock under my hand, letting me know he was thinking the exact same thing. *Well, go big or go home, right?* Although, here, the option was live or die.

And then, she laughed. A bright, wild laugh that shattered the tension in the arena. "I have to say, I'm impressed by you, Volla. You remind me a little of myself at your age. Fearless. I like fearless."

I'm not a Shipton, Katherine. I'm a Merlin. And Merlins don't bow down to people like you.

"Good, because I'm not in the market for a skin-slashing. Do you know how many moisturizers it takes to get skin this smooth?" I shot back, grinning through sheer relief.

She held her stomach as she collapsed in hysterics. "You know, others bend over backward to try and win me over, but you—you seem to have gone for a different approach. And it's so very refreshing. Really, it's like a breath of fresh air." She paused. "Although, naturally, it doesn't mean you *have* won me over. That remains to be seen. Yes, this should be interesting. Very interesting."

"Ask whatever you want."

She stopped laughing and smiled strangely. "Very well, then I have my question. If you get it right, you get to live. If your reply doesn't satisfy me, you die. Sound fair?"

"I've got no complaints."

Her eyes darkened. "Who is your intelligence source on the National Council?"

"You heard about that, huh?"

"Naima tells me everything. I want to verify your source with my own, to make sure we're all on the same page here." She chuckled wryly. "You see, you aren't the only ones with information. I've got my own mole in the National Council, and I'd hate to get any wires crossed."

Bullcrap!

"You don't have a mole in the National Council, Eris. If you did, you'd know who the traitor within this organization is." The words poured out of me before I could stop them, impulse and adrenaline driving me to call her bluff. "You'd have had them strung up like a Christmas ham and let them dangle from one of your titans like an ornament. You'd have made an example out of them so everyone would know what happens to snitches. They don't get stitches, they get a noose around their neck."

Katherine smirked but said nothing, while another gasp went up from the crowd. Nobody spoke to Katherine like this and got away with it.

"I won't reveal our source to you, Eris, because it's the only way to keep our source safe. A secret isn't a secret once more than one person knows about it, Pieter being the obvious exception," I continued, spurred on by pure energy. "And, no offense, but I don't trust anyone. You'd be foolish not to feel the same way, and I know you aren't a fool."

The tension around the arena was at an all-time high, everyone's gazes flitting between me and Katherine like they were spectators at a tennis match. They were clearly shocked by this exchange. Beside me, Finch looked like he was about to keel over.

"Oh, I like you, Volla Mazinov," Katherine purred, at last. "Here I was, thinking I'd get the usual bowing and scraping, and then you come along like a blonde bulldozer and make my day that little bit more interesting."

"You'll have to spell it out for me, Eris. Are we dying today?"

She chuckled. "You could set cities on fire with that fighting spirit. I'd love to let you loose amongst some of my more stubborn enemies. As for whether or not you're going to die today?" She tapped a finger on her chin. "Let's just say, I'm content with the answers you've given. Well, I can't do anything if you suddenly get bitten by a poisonous snake the moment you leave this arena and end up with jelly for blood. But you won't be dying by my hand or anyone else's here."

"So we're in?" I asked. Finch visibly relaxed.

"Welcome to the Cult of Eris, my children," she replied with a nod.

I thought I might unravel with relief, but I had to keep up the act. I dipped my head in a casual bow and kept my gaze fixed on the devil herself. "Thank you, Eris. We won't disappoint you. You won't find more loyal soldiers than my brother and me."

"Don't ruin it now, Volla. My ass has been kissed enough for one day," she retorted, grinning. "But your day is not yet done. Now that you've been welcomed into the cult, it's time for the pledge. The last step before you can call yourselves true followers of Eris. Naima, if you would care to do the honors?"

I turned over my shoulder to find Naima prowling toward us with a small iron pot in her hands. I could see a surface of solid gold inside, and my heart lurched at the sight of it. Behind her, Tess carried the rest of the tools needed to make the Apple of Discord tattoo. Although, "tattoo" didn't really cover it. This wasn't a simple tattoo—this was going to be a freaking pot of molten gold poured right into the skin, branding me forever.

This is going to hurt.

TWENTY-SIX

Harley

"Kneel," Naima growled. Finch and I didn't wait to be told twice, even though I wanted to run across the black disc of the arena and dive over the edge, just to avoid this. Molten metal combined with skin could only mean a world of pain.

"This is going to tickle, right?" I tried to keep up the devil-may-care attitude of Volla, but it was proving difficult.

Naima cast me a stern look. "The pain is part of your rite of passage."

Right, of course it is.

She came to me first, with Tess following close behind. I thought about passing Naima off to Finch first, but watching the process was probably no better. I flinched as her strong paws shot out and gripped my wrist, her claws digging into my skin as she pulled my arm taut and flat. I guessed I didn't have a say about where my brand was going.

"For the pain," Tess said, shoving a piece of wood into my mouth for me to bite down on.

"Thanks," I muttered, my voice muffled by the twig. I wasn't really sure how they were going to get the gold inside the pot all molten, but Katherine answered my question a moment later.

She stepped forward to the edge of her throne plinth, and a metal walkway slid out to join it to the main disc of the arena. Walking across it, she stopped right in front of where Finch and I were kneeling. With a half-smile on her face, she pushed down the neckline of her dress to reveal her own Apple of Discord, fixed in the exact spot where her heart should have been. *Since we all know you don't have one of those.*

The Apple on her heart lit up with intense golden light as she turned her gaze toward the pot of solid gold and raised her hands. Fire coursed out of her palms in a powerful torrent, melting the gold until it started to bubble and spit over the edges. For the first time since coming to this place, I wasn't sure if I could actually go through with it. This brand was going to be with me forever, even after I escaped the cult.

"It'll be fine, don't sweat it," Finch breathed, giving me a reassuring look.

Easy for you to say. I wondered if he knew this from personal experience, which meant he must already have one of these things on him, somewhere. But where? I'd never seen it.

Before my resolve crumbled altogether, Naima extended a sharp, nasty-looking claw. I bit down hard on the wood as she dug her claw into my skin, dragging it around in the shape of the Apple of Discord, the blood pouring down my arm and dripping onto the glass below. The lines were deep, ready to take on a bunch of molten gold. *So that's how they do it?* It was even more grim than I'd anticipated, and I'd seen the Apple before.

I struggled to keep hold of Volla's form as I closed my eyes. Naima's claws would be child's play compared to what was on its way. Her claws clinked against the outside of the pot as she snatched it up, and I grimaced in agony as I felt the first singeing touch of the liquid metal. I bit down so hard on the wooden stick that I thought I might break my teeth. The pain was unbearable, my entire arm on fire as the gold filled the channels that Naima had created with her claw. Sweat trickled down my face as I fought to keep hold of my disguise, while trying not to pass out from the pain.

"It is done," Naima said.

I blinked open my tear-blurred eyes and stared at the golden mark just below the crook of my elbow. The metal cooled almost immediately, leaving the hard shell of the Apple of Discord, while faint veins of gold spider-webbed outward. My skin had curled and burned around the brand, purple and livid. I spat out the wooden stick and tried not to touch the new mark. It would only hurt more if I did. I already hated the sight of it, feeling sick to my stomach that I had to wear it for the rest of my life. This encompassed everything I despised, and it was lodged in my skin forever. I wanted to scream in anger. The pain, I could handle. The shame of having this thing on my arm? Not so much.

"So, your Apple of Discord is your Esprit? How does that work?" I asked Katherine, fighting for breath, desperate to distract myself. I didn't really know what to call the mark—it wasn't a tattoo, per se, and it wasn't a brand. It was something worse. A permanent melding of flesh and metal. Was there even a word for that? If there was, I didn't know it.

Katherine smiled. "Not all Esprits are found, Volla. Some, on rare occasions, are personally forged. Like mine." It was yet another testament to her insane power, that she'd managed to forge her own Esprit from gold and embed it right into her skin. "Madness" didn't even begin to cover it. I mean, who the heck did that to themselves? Although, it sort of made sense now, why she'd demanded everyone else get the same brand, to intrinsically link themselves to her. A sure sign of their loyalty.

I sank back onto my haunches as Naima turned her attention on Finch. She grasped for his left arm, the same one she'd placed my brand on, and clawed the Apple of Discord into his skin. I watched in horror as she lifted the pot and poured the molten gold into the channels she'd created, the skin blistering and burning as it sank into the lines. The fur of her paws seemed to protect her from the pot's intense heat, her features showing no pain whatsoever. As Finch bit down on his own wooden stick, I realized I'd been right—watching was no better than experiencing it first-hand.

"Now that you're members of this organization, you will adhere to my rules," Katherine said, as the two of us were left reeling. "The work will be hard, and there's a great deal to do, but if you are loyal and fierce, then you will find yourselves lifted beyond your current states. You will tower above your former Mediocrity and find yourselves charged with glory. When I have ascended to my immortal body, becoming a Child of Chaos in my own right, you will be the soldiers of my divine army. You will be rewarded for your loyalty, not only in this life, but in the next."

I tried to keep my expression neutral, even as my anger flared. *You think you have a say in our afterlives, too?*

"The world is long overdue a change. We've been in the shadows too long, and I'm tired of seeing the weak prosper and the mighty fall," she went on, in full cult leader mode. "Once I have achieved true greatness, we'll never bow and scrape to human fragility again. We'll show them what true power looks like and give them reason to fear us. They will be the ones bowing and scraping, and I am *so* looking forward to that. We will finally have a say in whom we deem worthy of this gift called Chaos. Magicals have forgotten how to treasure what they've been given, and my new world order will give them cause to remember. And if they defy me, they'll see the true might of a Child of Chaos."

Any more from you, Shipton, and your head won't fit inside this bubble. And yet, the crowd around us was hanging on every word. They were drinking it in, like the sheep they were. I almost felt sorry for them. They didn't seem to realize that they were following a wolf in sheep's clothing who'd just as easily have them murdered as anyone else. Katherine cared only for herself and her own mission. All this talk about everyone who followed her receiving due glory was a load of fluff, spoken to keep their spirits up and their hearts loyal to her cause.

However, there were a couple of strange emotions leaking into me. I spied Shinsuke in the stands and felt a subtle wave of terror coming off him, spiraling toward me in shivering tendrils. There was an unexpected flurry of concern coming off Thessaly Crux, too, as she tossed aside the wooden stick that had fallen out of Finch's limp mouth.

Raw, unfiltered energy buzzed from Naima while she finished off Finch's tattoo and removed the pot of molten gold. This kind of thing seemed to excite her a lot. She really was a creature of Katherine's making, getting a high from all the twisted acts that pleased her mistress.

Meanwhile, from off in the stands, I sensed jealousy pouring out of Kenneth Willow. He was staring right at me, hating my guts. He could probably tell how much I'd impressed Katherine and loathed the idea of being shoved out in favor of a newbie. Especially as Katherine had directly said how much she hated ass-kissers—a label he'd previously worn with pride. *What a douchebag.* The more I encountered Kenneth, the more I detested the very sight of him.

As the last droplets of gold cooled, permanently ingrained in our skin, Finch and I exchanged a look. We were both full members of the cult now. There was no going back after these brands. Now, we could get on with finding Hester's spirit before All Hallows' Eve came hurtling toward us and get off this freaking island. That was all that mattered.

"You will be taken to the compound in two hours to eat breakfast with the rest of the cult," Katherine said, smiling down at me. I guessed she really liked to see her new members down on their knees before her. "Until then, Naima and Tess will return you to your hut, so you can sleep off the pain of these brands. I apologize if it's in a bit of a state when you get there. My people won't have been too neat in searching for those surveillance hexes." She chuckled to herself as she turned and walked away, dropping gracefully down the gap between the disc and the stands and disappearing from sight.

We'd taken a terrifying step into the underworld of Katherine's cult. And our new lives here were only just beginning.

Back at the stone hut, after doing another search for any new surveillance hexes, Finch and I sat on our beds in total silence. We should've been celebrating how far we'd come, but I didn't have an ounce of happiness left in me. Even pretending to be a member of this crapstorm made me feel dirty and wrong, like I was somehow betraying everything I'd worked so hard to become. Like I'd become a traitor to the SDC, the Rag Team, and everyone I'd left behind, outside the walls of this interdimensional pocket.

"Did you have to do that the last time, or did you get some special treatment because of who you are?" I asked, finding my voice.

Finch frowned. "The tattoo?"

"Yeah."

He put out his forearm and let a ripple of Shapeshifter energy pulsate over his skin, Pieter's arm fading to reveal the original brand on Finch's real skin, right by the new one. The skin around his new brand was still raw, with blood coagulating into black clumps from the burnt flesh.

"I always kept it hidden, but I had to do it, same as everyone else. No special treatment, not even for me. I should've realized back then that Katherine didn't see me as her son. I was just a tool, like the rest of them. And now I've got two of the bastards." His voice was tight with pain and bitterness, and I knew it wasn't coming from the residual agony of the brand. He was genuinely hurt by Katherine's actions toward him, and I had a feeling the scars ran deeper than even he knew.

"Will I be stuck with this, then?" I muttered, touching the golden brand tentatively. Pain shot up my arm, making me wince.

He nodded sadly. "The Shifting can't protect you from it. You'll just have to remember to keep it hidden when we get back to the SDC. I can cover mine up by Shifting parts of my arm into someone else, but once your Ephemera is out of gas, that brand will stay. Maybe Wade can get you a bracelet or something."

"Great." I stared at the hideous mark, feeling sick to my stomach that I was going to have to bear this Apple for the rest of my life. A cuff or a bandage or a sleeve might cover it, but it would never go away. It would always be there, lurking beneath—a perpetual reminder of being here, and of the woman I hated more than anyone in this world. But, right now, there was no use crying over spilt gold. "You know, I wasn't sure if Katherine would actually show up to any of these trials." I needed to take my mind off this freaking gold disfiguration, channeling my anger into the person who'd caused it.

"She's never done that before. I guess, with this mole on the loose, she feels like she has to vet everyone who comes in."

I nodded. "You're probably right."

"You nearly gave me a heart attack, doing what you did. I know Volla Mazinov was supposed to be ballsy, but that was... well, panic-inducing."

"I took a risk and it paid off."

He smiled. "You were born under a lucky star, Sis."

"Hardly." I toyed with the pendant from Imogene around my neck. Finch was still wearing my St. Christopher, but I didn't mind too much. I figured he could use the spiritual guidance more than me, for now. "So, who do you think the mole might be? Any clues?"

"Not sure. I've got some thoughts. You?"

"I was trying to put out some Empath feelers while you were getting that brand. Shinsuke's running scared—like, all I ever feel from him is terror and uncertainty. He might be the weak link, and that could very well indicate he's the mole we're looking for."

Finch nodded. "I was thinking the same thing."

"I wish I could talk to the others, get their perspective on things."

Finch smirked. "You missing Golden Boy?"

"I miss them all." My cheeks reddened. Was I that obvious?

"He'd probably be like, 'It's getting too risky in there, I want you out.' He'd ruin the whole thing. See, that's the trouble with personal relationships—they make everything messy. What should be simple and clear gets clouded, when emotions are involved. It's better that you can't speak to him. Trust me. You'd get a bunch of doubts and stop focusing on the task at hand."

I chuckled. "You really don't think much of him, huh?"

"I never do when it comes to coven drones."

"He's *not* a coven drone!"

Finch grinned. "Whatever you say, Sis."

"Are you saying you don't have an emotional investment in this? I'd say having a bit of a heart has done you some good, even though it took you a while to get to this point. You wouldn't be here if it weren't for Adley."

"Don't."

I frowned. "Don't what?"

"Don't talk about her. If you think I'm going to whip out a guitar and get all my kumbayas out, you'll be waiting forever. I'm not a sharer. You can talk about Wade all you like, but I'm not going to talk about... about her." The pain in his voice as he said "her" threw me completely. It sounded like he had razorblades in his throat, his face twisting in physical agony at the mention of her. I supposed I didn't really know the depth of his feelings for her, and I probably never would.

"I didn't mean to drag up any bad memories."

He sighed. "I know, but it's not something I can talk about. With anyone. Not even myself, most of the time."

"Do you miss her?" I knew I was poking the bear, but I was genuinely curious.

"What did I just say?"

I lifted my hands in mock surrender. "Okay, no talking about Adley." I glanced at him. "Well, maybe one last thing. I'm glad you loved her. I'm glad she reminded you that you have a heart, even though that came at a terrible price. She didn't deserve that, and neither did you. That's all I have to say on the matter. My two cents, done."

Finch slithered off the edge of the bed, still noticeably sad. "I need some fresh air."

"Finch, wait..."

"I won't be long. I'll just go and do some recon on Hester's spirit, clear my head while I'm at it. And don't worry, I've still got this if I get into any trouble." He took the medallion out of his shirt to show me, before stuffing it back beneath the fabric.

"I didn't mean to upset you."

He snorted. "You couldn't if you tried. I'm just sick of these four walls. I need to go for a walk before I lose my mind."

I eyed him curiously. "Okay. Whatever you need. I'll be here when you get back."

"Sure… thanks," he muttered, as he made for the door. He might have been acting blasé, but his body language told a different story. His shoulders were slumped, his chin to his chest, his eyes glinting with sadness.

Even though I didn't like the idea of Finch wandering around in a state of depression, I was sort of glad to have a moment alone to think about Wade and the rest of the Rag Team. I was desperate to hear his voice again, to give me a bit of strength going forward. Being in this place, it was easy to forget why we were doing this, and I needed that bridge to the real world to remind me. Since I wasn't going to get that, the thought of him would have to do. However, as I lay down on my stomach, it was Finch's sad face that popped into my head. I couldn't help it. Glancing out of the window, I watched him walking away toward the distant beach. That meeting with Katherine had really struck a nerve with him, and being reminded of Adley had only added fuel to that fire. He looked so defeated that I felt sorry for him. I mean, at least my mom had never tried to have me killed, and she'd never had my partner murdered out of spite and cruelty.

As soon as Finch had disappeared from view, I replayed the day's challenges in my head. The Rag Team would be worried sick by now, all of them desperate for some sign that we were okay and that we were getting the job done. It had been a long day. A really long day. Between the three trials, my run-in with Kenneth, my encounter with Katherine, and the knowledge of all the terrible things that were going on at Eris Island, combined with the understanding that I would always have this stupid, awful thing on my arm, for the rest of my life, I was starting to wonder if we were in over our heads.

I tried to picture Wade telling me that I was doing a good job, but his face was hard to hold on to. The edges were fuzzy, and his voice wasn't right—it was just my voice, saying the words I wanted to hear from him. When the truth was, I wanted him to be here, with me, where I could see his face and put my arms around him and get that comfort that I needed. Still, it brought me some relief to know that, as soon as we had Hester's spirit and I pressed the pendant three times, he would come and get me. Isadora would be waiting to extract us, the moment the message came through. I was already looking forward to that day, not only because of the reunion, but because it would mean we'd succeeded in stopping Katherine from fulfilling the third ritual.

We were fully initiated now, with the brands to prove it. Now, we could move about more freely, and Finch would finally lead me to my mom's spirit. That moment was getting closer, and the anticipation was overwhelming.

"I love you, Wade." The words poured out of me, even though he wasn't here to hear them. "I'll come back to you, safe and sound. I swear it."

If only that was a promise I could definitely keep.

TWENTY-SEVEN

Finch

I wasn't hungry, but rules were rules.

Two hours after our interview with Katherine, Harley and I were sitting in the beehive canteen. We were tucked at the end of a long table in the center of the room, the newbies stuck where everyone could see. And everyone *did* seem to be here. The noise was deafening, with people chattering on about the third trial. *We're right here, kiddos.* They seemed eager enough to talk about us, but not so keen to actually talk to us.

"Eris should've decapitated them on the spot," hissed a girl with long blue hair.

"Where'd she get off, talking to Eris like that?" added a beanpole of a guy. "I bet Eris is just planning something better. There's no way they'll fit in around here."

Katherine sat at the high table, surveying her insipid subjects. It still amused me that she was a vegetarian, given her penchant for killing things. *All the good psychos are, though, right?* Naima stood guard behind her. She didn't eat with the rest of the sheep. As a Purge beast, that'd put everyone off their food. Tess sat to Katherine's right, while Kenneth sat on her left. It pleased me. Nobody wanted to be someone's left-hand guy. The right hand was where it was at.

At our table, Shinsuke sat to Harley's left, with a bunch of other cultists filling the proverbial pews. I didn't know the guy sitting beside me, and I didn't want to. What was the point? As soon as we had Hester's spirit, we were out of here. No use making pals.

"People don't seem too chatty around here, huh?" I said, making a sly dig at my neighbor. He was a shy-looking kid with a wispy mop of mousy hair. About as ordinary looking as it was possible to be. He shrank further into himself at the sound of my voice.

Still, it was awkward as ass for me. I knew a lot of these faces, but they didn't know me. Some of them had even been in my main unit on missions: Ifrit Laghari, a towering, six-foot-five Indian guy with biceps the size of my torso and a penchant for watching things burn. He was an Inferno, which meant he was a rare variation of a Fire Elemental. He could literally turn his body into flames and lose his physical form for a while.

Coral Falkland, who was barbed wire in human form—all spiky and no-nonsense, with a slight frame and striking face, complete with silver hair in a braid down her back. She was what was known as a Blade, though I'd always called her "Porcupine," which she'd hated. A Blade had the ability to forge knives through any part of their skin, manipulating the heavy metals in their body, which turned them into a ball of slashing, menacing fury that nobody could get close to.

Then, there was Bakir Khan, the son of a Russian bureaucrat and a former Miss Pakistan, who was always the brains of the outfit. He always looked impeccable, as if he was about to speak at some important meeting, his brown hair slicked back, his almond-shaped eyes taking in his surroundings at all times. He didn't have any especially impressive powers, unless money and IQ could be classed as rare abilities.

And, last but not least, we had Delphine Basquiat—the scariest woman I'd ever met, barring Katherine. Despite her name, she had close-cropped green hair right now, though it changed from week to week, and eyes that were blacker than onyx. She was almost as tall as Ifrit, with bulging muscles and a punch that could kill a man in one swipe. She reveled in killing more than anyone I'd ever seen. No hesitation. Blood, guts, gore—the messier, the better. And the fact that she was a Cellular made her all the more terrifying. She had the ability to manipulate people on a cellular level, making them bend to her will. It was a temperamental ability, and it didn't always work, but when it did... man, she went to town. I'd seen her explode people in a fountain of blood and viscera, only for her to lick the splashes from her face and move on without a word.

The nihilistic part of me wanted to shed my Pieter skin and show them who I really was. In my head, I hoped my last act would make Katherine choke on her food and die. But what was the likelihood of that? Anyway, I was learning to suppress the impulsive side of my personality. All I had to do was get through breakfast. Simple, right? Then, I could get away from Katherine, and all these idiots, in one piece.

It'd taken that last interview to make me realize how much I hated her. I could barely stand to be in the same room as my mother. I could never forgive what she'd done to Adley, and to me, no matter how hard I'd tried to give her a good excuse for both. I was done making excuses for her. She'd done it because she wanted to, because it served her interests. And that was all there was to it. That was the way the evil cookie crumbled. So why wasn't the ache in my heart healing?

I noticed Shinsuke staring at me, as if he wanted to say something. Instead, he looked back down into his breakfast.

"Sorry about that fight, Shinsuke. No hard feelings? A guy's got to do what a guy's got to do to survive, right?" I broke the silence between us, drawing his gaze back up from his plate.

Shinsuke nodded slowly. "It was a good fight. You're very skilled."

"How's your head today?"

"Sore, but I will endure." He even sounded like his dad.

Harley smiled at him. "You're not too shabby yourself. I guess you've got good genes though, with your dad being Hiro Nomura."

Easy, Harley.

Shinsuke paled. "I've worked hard to be successful by myself, without my father's help. You can't raise yourself up beyond the label of Mediocre without intensive training and dedication. Genes play no part in it. If anything, my father's genes did me a disservice."

"Not a fan? It must suck, having everyone mention him whenever they meet you, huh?" I shared his pain. I'd been through enough of it myself.

"It does grate sometimes, yes," he replied.

"Sorry," Harley said. "I didn't mean anything by it."

"I don't waste energy on bearing grudges or feeling wounded by others' comments. Besides, I've gotten used to it over the years." Shinsuke scooped up a forkful of omelette and put it delicately into his mouth. Everything he did was methodic. Even eating breakfast.

I glanced up to find Katherine eyeing us. Since we were the newbies, she had to. Meanwhile, her right-hand and left-hand lackeys were scowling at each other. They were arguing over something likely petty, and I couldn't see a clear winner. Tess tended to brush him off when he got like this, like a nasty bug. Kenneth was the one with the permanent grudge. *I'd love to tear out your spine and feed you to Naima's beasts.* I wondered if they'd prefer him thick-cut or crispy. They stopped a moment later, as Katherine turned away from us to shoot them both a warning look.

"How long have you been here?" Harley asked our tablemate.

Shinsuke shrugged. "A few months."

He cast a wary glance around. It was like he was pretending to be part of the crowd, but his body language said otherwise. His actions suggested he'd prefer to leave this place and never come back. *Biggest mistake of your life, huh? Same.*

"You don't like it here, do you?" Harley lowered her voice to a whisper. Clearly, she was sensing the same vibes. Only she had her Empath abilities to clarify.

Shinsuke's eyes widened. "I'm quite content." The words came out almost robotic. Not hard for Shinsuke, but this was even more automated than normal.

Glancing around the table, I got the impression Shinsuke might not be the only one dissatisfied by the cult. Despite the apparent happiness and tranquility, I could sense an undercurrent of tension. It hadn't been here before, when this place was my home. Something had definitely changed. I couldn't tell what, exactly, but I knew one thing: the core of the Apple was rotting.

After breakfast, Naima stepped down from her pedestal and took us to one side.

"Don't tell me, there's a secret fourth trial to get through?" I was only half joking.

She smiled. "No, there is not. In fact, it is quite the opposite. You and Volla are to have the rest of the day off to recuperate and gather your strength. Katherine is of the mindset that you have had quite enough excitement for one day and have done more than enough work to get into the cult. As such, you have been gifted with a brief respite."

Good. I sure as hell need it.

Since we were going out of our minds in the stone hut, Harley and I took a walk around the island. I hadn't mentioned where we were going, but she seemed willing to follow me. Keeping away from the walkways, I led her back to the opposite side of the island, to the Hexagon she hated so much. Only, this time, we weren't going to the lookout overhead. Instead, I took her to a shadowed entrance on the ground. It was hidden behind one of Katherine's stone titans.

The layout of this place hadn't changed since I'd last been here, and not many people knew about this entrance. This doorway was only for those in the know, Katherine's most trusted—namely, only me and her. For that reason, it was never guarded.

"And Katherine's office is definitely inside here?" Harley hissed.

I smirked. "Good guess. Why else would I be bringing you here?"

"You could've told me there was a secret entrance."

"Why? So you could go wandering around and get yourself caught?" I gave her a knowing smile. "This is where the good stuff happens. See, Drake Shipton had a lot of hidden tunnels and basements built into the island, and this compound. He was a paranoid bastard, but it paid off. This way, if the island is ever under attack, and there's no time to move it elsewhere, Katherine and her minions have a safe and undetected way out. The tunnels lead right under the ocean to the mainland."

I pushed open the heavy, rusted iron door and ushered Harley inside. Judging by the squeal of the hinges, this entrance hadn't been used in a long time. *Suits me.* The doorway opened out onto a long, dark tunnel made of concrete and steel. All of the corridors in this place looked the same. It was part institution, part nuclear bunker, part military base.

We made our way through a network of dimly lit corridors, ducking into doorways at the sound of oncoming footsteps. Nobody would pay us much mind, but it served to be cautious. Drake Shipton had had a point about that.

"Holy crap," Harley muttered as we made our way through one final corridor and came out into a wider, brighter hallway, with doors branching off at steady intervals. Cult members were walking about, some standing guard at certain doors while others hurried this way and that. Everyone looked stressed. And they had reason to be. Any slip-ups and it'd be certain death. This was the true cult.

I grabbed Harley and yanked her back into the smaller corridor as a figure emerged from the only door to my left. *Hello, Mother.* The room she'd just come out of was her private study. I'd seen enough people die in these hallways as a result of disappointing her.

I nodded to Katherine as she breezed past with Naima at her side. They strode down the hallway, people bowing as they passed.

As soon as they disappeared at the bottom end of the hallway, I slipped around the corner with Harley in tow and headed for the single door. Katherine's study was never guarded because it'd be a waste of manpower. No one was stupid enough, or suicidal enough, to enter without her say-so. *So, what does that make me?* Besides, it needed a password, and only two people knew that password. Me and Mother dearest.

I held the handle and whispered, *"Sit turpium cogitationem in chao."* Meaning, "In Chaos there is rebirth." I'd always thought it was a weird choice, but Katherine loved a statement.

The door clicked open.

Katherine's study had always left me in awe. Despite being underground, she'd fashioned a smaller bubble within the interdimensional pocket, crafting this place into an otherworldly room. It resembled an observatory, with a domed ceiling that looked out into a perpetual cosmos. The walls were made of gold and wood, giving off major steampunk vibes. Circular bookcases wrapped around the entire room, full to the brim with leather-bound tomes. Meanwhile, the floor was glass, with water running beneath it. There were glass panels in the walls too, poking out from between bookcases. Behind the panes, mournful Selkies, fanged water-serpents, and miniature krakens twisted and turned. Now and again, a fight would break out, but Katherine had trained them to behave. It was her very own version of the SDC's Aquarium.

"What if they come back?" Harley whispered, as I closed the door behind us and whispered the locking spell that would keep it that way. Katherine wouldn't be back for ages, which meant nobody was getting in.

I smiled. "They won't. It's eleven o'clock, which means Katherine and Naima are having their mid-morning meeting in the war room."

"The war what?"

"Big room, opposite side of the Hexagon. It's where they have all their who-should-we-kill-today chats. All of her most trusted soldiers will be there, which gives us a good hour to do some searching."

Harley frowned. "So... Hester's spirit is in here?"

"Why else would I have brought you here?"

"Well... where is it?"

I peered at the shelves on the far wall, where an empty glass panel sat. There was no water behind this one, only a gilded room. "Her spirit used to be in that cage there." I pointed at the panel. "But... not anymore. Katherine might have moved her to one of these charmed boxes for easy transport." The study was littered with them. Big wooden boxes of every size. I moved to the first one and flipped the lid but found nothing but sheets upon sheets of papers and files.

Together, we searched through every single box in the place. And when that turned up nothing, we started on the shelves, and under the massive oak-and-gold desk, and in every nook and cranny we could find. After twenty minutes of searching, I realized it was hopeless.

"It's not here!" I snapped.

Harley glanced at me. "We can go back to the hut and rethink this. Run through all the places you know about and brainstorm where else she might have put Hester's spirit. Somewhere closer to the spot she might need to do the ritual, maybe?"

"I hate this place." I kicked a box for good measure.

"Do you have any other ideas?"

My mind was racing. "I've got one other idea, yeah. The next logical place she'd hide Hester's spirit would be—"

Both of our heads snapped toward the study door as it opened. Nobody should have been able to get in—except Katherine.

Tess walked through, her expression equally surprised before it transformed into one of suspicion.

"And what the hell are you two doing here?" she asked, her tone cold. I almost said, "Katherine gave the password to *you*?" but I reeled it in real quick. It looked like I'd been well and truly replaced, not that I cared. Right now, I was just bothered that Tess had caught us.

This wasn't going to end well, and I really didn't want to have to kill Katherine's most valued cultist. All the lies in the world wouldn't be enough to cover *that* up.

TWENTY-EIGHT

Harley

Finch and I exchanged a look as Tess waited for our answer. There was nothing we could do—we'd have to play dumb. After all, we were the newbies here. Maybe we'd be able to convince her that we'd just stumbled upon this place—this hidden, high-security, critically important place. *Yeah, right.*

"We were trying to get a feel for the island layout," I said, finding my voice. "You showed us this place before, and we wanted to take a closer look at the human labs. Only, we made a wrong turn and ended up inside the Hexagon instead of on top of it." My heart was pounding so hard I was sure she could hear it from the other side of the room.

Finch nodded. "And then we saw Katherine heading along one of these hallways, and we wanted to talk to her about our place in the cult. You know, like, what are we going to do, when do we start fieldwork, that sort of stuff. But we lost her, so we had to ask for directions. Anyway, someone said this was her office, so we figured we'd wait, instead of wandering through the Hexagon and getting lost again. You know, seeing as she isn't here."

Tess eyed us both, saying nothing. Judging from the waves of suspicion coming off of her, she didn't buy our story, and I had no idea how this would turn out. It was all I could do not to sprint past her and make a run for freedom. Not that trying to escape would do us any favors, either. She continued to examine us, making me wonder what the heck she was thinking. We'd turned into rambling idiots, instead of the poised, composed siblings we'd been during the trials.

I braced myself for a fight. I'd out myself with the full extent of my abilities if it meant we got out of here alive.

"Well, you shouldn't be here. This door has a password—there's no way you should be in here," Tess said, at last.

Finch shrugged. "The door was open, so we figured it was okay to come in and wait."

"And you think that means you can just go waltzing into wherever you like?" Tess barked. "If Katherine finds you in her office, she'll kill you on sight. Nobody comes in here without her say-so, not even to wait. Do you understand?"

I nodded effusively. "Absolutely. Won't happen again. We didn't know."

"Yeah, major crossed wires, that's all." Finch cleared his throat.

Tess pursed her lips. "Follow me."

"Huh?" I didn't like the sound of that.

"You want to see Katherine, right? That's literally what you just said."

"Uh… yeah, of course," I replied, flashing a look at Finch.

"Right, well, follow me, then." Tess walked toward the door and opened it, gesturing for us to go on ahead. We hurried past her without hesitating, trying really hard to downplay the comedy duo act we seemed to have taken on. She closed the office door behind her and set off down the hallway, with us in hot pursuit.

Looks like we're seeing our favorite person again today. My stomach sank. Once was bad enough. Plus, I didn't actually have a good reason to want to speak with Katherine. I'd have to come up with one pretty quick, or Tess would never let us get away with what had just happened. It'd just shine a big, glaring here-are-your-spies spotlight on the fact that we'd been snooping in Katherine's private study.

We headed through more of the same clinical, concrete-and-steel corridors, until we reached a massive metal blast door that stood at the far end of one of the branching hallways. It looked ominous, and if Katherine was lurking behind it, then it would only serve to prove my point.

"What's this place?" I asked, continuing to play dumb. I knew exactly what it was. Finch had already told me.

"It's the war room," Tess replied, as if it was the most normal thing in the world. I envisioned a massive circular table inside, all lit up in low science-fiction lighting, with world leaders sitting around in sharp suits, debating what to do about the latest nuclear missile crisis. *Note to self: Ask Wade to change up our movie choices. Seriously.* Next time I saw him, I was picking the film.

Tess stood in front of a retinal scanner on the right-hand side of the blast door. A moment later, it slid open with a screech of metal on metal, a red light spinning wildly over the top of it. It definitely had a comforting end-of-the-world vibe to it, so at least I could give Katherine points for consistency.

Inside, the setup wasn't all that far from what I'd imagined. There was indeed a massive round table, with garish strip-lights framing everyone in a cold, blue glow, and a cube of screens in the center. Embedded into the table itself were touchscreen panels, though nobody seemed to be using them right now. In fact, the cube of screens was blank. *No war today, huh?*

Ten magicals sat in the sleek leather chairs nestled around Queen Katherine's Round Table. Her proverbial knights, hanging on her every evil word. I spotted Naima and Kenneth immediately, but I didn't recognize the other eight. There was one skinny woman with a long, silver braid down her back. Next to her sat a woman with short, sea-green hair and black eyes that didn't seem real. In fact, out of the ten magicals, there were only two guys. One was Kenneth, and one was a handsome Korean guy, who shot me a smile as I stood there. I quickly looked away, staring at the ground. Judging by the way they were all nodding and agreeing, they'd come to the end of whatever they were discussing.

"You all know what is required of you, and you know what will happen if you fail," Katherine said. "You are dismissed. Don't disappoint me. You've got no idea how hard it is to get bloodstains out of these dresses."

It looked like we'd arrived a few minutes too late to the party, but it wasn't hard to figure out what they'd been talking about. Clearly, Katherine's minions had been entrusted with some mission in the magical world, and they were about to set off to do her bidding. After a rumble of assent had made its way around the group, the cultists got up to leave, brushing past Finch, Tess, and me on the way out.

"Sorry you weren't invited, Tess." Kenneth stalked toward her, spying his prey. He really couldn't resist an opportunity to stick it in Tess's face. "Looks like you're benched until those delicate little hands of yours heal. You must be so embarrassed. You almost blow your hands right off, and for what? To fail your mission and have to come back with your tail between your legs? Shameful, really." He tutted like the smug idiot that he was. I glanced at Finch to make sure he wasn't having any sudden urges to swipe the smirk off Kenneth's face. He seemed to be fine. Either that, or he was covering his anger well.

"So, does that make you the substitute?" Tess shot back. "The best player is off the field, so they have to put an inferior player on?"

"You wish. Even if your hands *were* healed, you wouldn't get a look in on this mission. You failed Eris—you can't be trusted with the big stuff anymore."

"I can speak for myself, Kenneth, if it's all the same to you." Katherine walked up behind Kenneth, the guy's face morphing into a mask of horror. "Nice of you to really go in on the hypocrisy, though. I can admire that. I mean, let's not forget who spent three days cleaning the men's toilets because he came back empty-handed. That'd be a *real* shame."

Kenneth's cheeks had turned beet red. It was the ultimate they're-behind-me-aren't-they? moment, and Tess was relishing every second.

He turned around very slowly, looking up into Katherine's unimpressed eyes.

"Now, run along and complete your task, before I decide to put one of the Mazinovs on the mission instead and send you back to the men's latrines." She smirked. "It can definitely be arranged, if you need to relearn the value of humility. Plus, I'm sure I can just get someone else to take your place in the rituals, if you can't behave like a team player. It shouldn't be too hard."

Kenneth shook his head desperately. "No, Eris, I'll do as you've asked. I'll leave right away." He bowed so low I thought he might snap himself in half, before scuttling off out of the door, clearly terrified that Katherine might actually change her mind.

With the war room now empty, Katherine turned her attention to us. "Yes? I presume you're here to tell me something. Otherwise, this is a colossal waste of all of our time. And you know how much I love that."

Tess dipped her head in a bow. "I discovered the Mazinovs in your office, Eris."

"Whoa, whoa, whoa there! Hold up a minute, Crux." I put my hands up in defense. "You're making it sound like we didn't *intend* to be discovered. Geez, do you always give the newbies such a hard time?" I looked Katherine dead in the eye. "Look, we were bored out of our skulls back at the hut, so we went on a little adventure to try and get a good look at the human experimentation stuff. Pieter was curious about the hybrid aspect, while Earth manipulation is a little more my flavor. Anyway, this island is confusing as all hell, and we ended up in some corridor. Pieter spotted you, but then we lost you, since all of these freaking hallways look the same! I asked some dude with a buzzcut where we could find you, and he pointed us to your office. We were waiting for you to come back. No discovery necessary."

My heart was pounding in my chest. It wasn't easy to lie to Katherine, not when she was glaring right into my soul. I wouldn't have been surprised if she could hear how hard my heart was beating. I thought about using my reverse Empathy to soften her up, but I didn't know if she'd be as pliable as O'Halloran had been. That experiment had proven that Shapeshifters could be affected by my reverse ability, but I didn't want to risk her sensing me if I tried it out on her.

Katherine smiled. "And what did you want to talk to me about?"

"We wanted to know when we could get started with the field missions. Like I said, we were getting bored out of our minds. We've been in hiding for a year, so we're pretty eager to stretch our legs, you know?"

Tess looked pissed, but I didn't care. There was no way I was getting handed in to Katherine by any of these punks, not while I still had breath in my lungs to ramble off a big ol' excuse. I glanced at Finch, who hadn't said anything. If he didn't start chatting soon, it was going to look pretty suspicious.

He nodded, catching my glance. "Yeah, we hoped we could convince you to let us do some actual work. We want to be useful to you, Eris."

That's better.

"Even when you Purge minions from your own Chaos, it's impossible to get good help." Katherine sighed, but she didn't look like she was going to murder us. "I'm guessing Naima didn't tell you about this place when she returned you to your hut?"

I shook my head. "Tess showed us the top part of it yesterday, and we saw a bunch of humans all huddled up. So we just thought this was where all the cool stuff happened. That's why we ended up here—we had nothing else to do, so we fancied a look at what the cult does for fun. We didn't know it was out of bounds; otherwise, we'd have stayed at the hut and played our millionth game of *Go Fish.*"

"The Hexagon itself isn't out of bounds, but my private study and the Drake Shipton Library are off limits to all members, no exceptions." She still sounded faintly amused, which I took to be a good sign of our survival. "Although, I'm curious to know how you entered my study. You shouldn't have been able to."

It pained me not to point out the irony in calling this place *the* Hexagon. As if an extra side somehow made her military base better than the one belonging to the US forces.

"The door was open when we arrived, so we thought it'd be okay," I replied. "You know, a drop-in sort of thing if we needed to talk to you. Sorry if we got things confused, but an open door usually means someone's welcome, right?"

Katherine sighed. "I've thought about adding hexes to keep people out, but it's so inconvenient. I'd rather just disembowel anyone I catch trying to enter without my permission. Keeps things spicy, you know?"

"Uh, right," Finch muttered. "Not us, though? You ought to disembowel whoever left the door open."

She chuckled. "You're quite right. Would make things pretty interesting if it turned out *I* left the door open, wouldn't it?"

I was eager to move the subject away from disembowelment. "The Drake Shipton Library? What's that? I don't think we saw it on the way in."

She chuckled. "It's a library, what do you think?"

"It can't be just any kind of library if it's off limits."

"Don't test my patience, Volla. You're funny, but you're not *that* funny. These places are off limits to you, and that's all I have to say about that. Beyond those areas, you've got free rein to wander around as you please. Just don't piss anyone off and try not to get yourselves killed on your first day." She smiled coldly. "So, now that I've lost ten minutes of my very packed day, will you be all right by yourselves? Or do you need me to hold your hands and drop you off at the sandpit?" Sarcasm dripped from her words.

"Sorry about that, I've got no filter between my mouth and my head." I tried my best to give her a Volla-style apology. "And sorry for waiting in your office like that. It won't happen again. We're still getting used to being around other people again, so our social cues are a little off."

"Your lack of filter is very apparent, Volla, but it happens to be one of the things I like about you." Katherine brushed off my apology and tapped her chin in thought. "Actually, there was something I wanted to talk to the two of you about, too. I had it on my to-do list for one o'clock, but hey, let's go a little wild with the schedule. It's already a mess."

"What did you want to talk to us about?" Finch chimed in. He'd been relatively quiet throughout this whole exchange, no doubt swallowing his desire to punch his mother in the head or smash her face into one of the high-tech touchscreen panels.

Katherine grinned. "Ah, he speaks! I thought you'd gone mute for a minute there." She turned back to me, evidently preferring to talk with a woman. "Now, you mentioned that there was a mole in the cult. I know I said you could keep your secret, given the stakes involved, but I've changed my mind in light of this misdemeanor. I want to know who it is. Preferably now. Or I might get a little disembowelly after all."

I pulled an apologetic grimace, hoping she was bluffing. "Thing is, we don't actually know *who* they are. We just know they're here, and they've been cooperating with the National Council. If we did know who they were, I'd have ratted them out before we went through those trials, on the off chance you'd go easier on us."

"Well, well, aren't you the sneaky snake, Volla Mazinov? You got yourselves in here with that intel, but you don't *actually* have anything. If it weren't so annoying, I'd applaud you for your ingenuity. Reminds me of something I'd do, not that it makes it any better." She shot me a frosty look. "So, you're really saying you don't know who this mole is?"

"We don't, Eris. But we know there *is* one."

"Well whoop-de-fricking-do. What am I supposed to do with that, huh? If I never hear the word 'mole' again, I'll be a happy woman," she bit out, clearly peeved. "Oh well, I'll find a way to smoke out the traitor soon enough."

I was about to give a fake laugh when a cold wave of dread hit me from behind, punching me right in the gut. The kind of dread that only came from someone who felt their life was in danger. The kind of dread that might come from a mole who was in over their head, and who'd just figured out they were on borrowed time. The sensation was so intense and unexpected that I couldn't keep it out. I resisted the urge to glance over my shoulder as realization dawned. There was only one person in this room who could be sending out a flood of emotion. It wasn't coming from me, and it wasn't coming from Finch, and it definitely wasn't coming from Katherine.

Tess was the mole. Her emotional guard had dropped, and I was feeling everything. The panic must have set her off.

Son of a—! I forced a smile onto my face. "So, when can we get out in the field?"

"When I decide you're ready," Katherine replied.

"Ballpark?"

She laughed. "Maybe when I get tired of that motormouth of yours. Although, if you annoy me too much, I might just find another use for you. See if any of my members have a silencing spell they want to try out."

"Got it. Shut up, Volla. No problem." I lifted my hands in surrender. "We'll get out of your hair and leave you to the rest of your very busy day." I was desperate to talk to Tess about what I'd just felt, but I needed to catch her on her own, when she didn't have her guard up. If we'd just discovered the mole in the cult, then we'd just found our ally, too.

"If you would," Katherine murmured. "You're currently eating into my personal time, and I've got somewhere I need to be. Tess, a word before I go, though I'll need you to walk and talk if I'm going to get anything done today."

We shuffled out of the war room like overenthusiastic worshipers, and Katherine breezed past us. She beckoned for Tess to follow her. The two of them disappeared down one of the nearby corridors, leaving Finch and me alone again. My chance to speak with Tess would have to wait a while, until I could corner her somewhere safe.

"Why the weird face?" Finch whispered.

My throat felt tight. "The mole, Finch."

Finch arched an eyebrow. "You know something I don't?"

"I'm suspicious about something, yeah."

"Like what?"

"Tess. I think Tess might be the mole."

He snorted. "Tess? No way. She's about as brainwashed as it gets.

Have you seen how gooey-eyed she gets over Katherine?" He paused, a flicker of doubt moving over his face. "What makes you think she might be the mole?"

"Call it an informed guess."

"Nah, you must be getting your little Empath wires crossed. Tess is the last person it'd be. Honestly, I'd wager twenty dollars on it." *Which is precisely why she's the perfect mole, dumbass.* If I was right, then she had Katherine fooled—hook, line, and sinker.

In all honesty, I'd known he'd react like this. He thought he knew these people better than I did, which was true on the surface, but emotions rarely lied. I'd felt the cold flood of pure dread and terror coming out of Tess, and I knew what it meant. It wasn't a coincidence.

TWENTY-NINE

Harley

"So, what's the deal with this Drake Shipton Library?" Finch and I were pretending to look at a couple of the stone titans, and I kept my voice low in case anyone was listening in.

I was trying to fight off the disappointment of not finding Hester's spirit in Katherine's study, reminding myself that we still had five days until All Hallows' Eve. There were only so many places she could be, and we *would* find her, one way or another.

"It's where she keeps all the scrolls and manuscripts that the Librarian had collected. The Librarian destroyed a bunch of them when Katherine came to snatch her, but the cult got away with some of the greatest hits. The juicy stuff, you know? Like, the rituals, a couple of seriously nasty spells, a bit of Voodoo, and some pretty dangerous magic, too. Among other things. Sacred artifacts, famed Esprits from dead magicals, that sort of jam."

"Do you know where it is, inside the Hexagon?"

Finch shot me a withering look. "Seriously?"

"What?"

"What do you take me for? Of course I know where it is. I used to know how to get inside, too. She's probably changed the proverbial locks on me, but you never know. We could get lucky. In fact, that's the place I was going to suggest when Tess came in."

I frowned. "So we need to find a way in there without getting ourselves killed."

"Yep, there are guards stationed there all the time. Should be fun." He grinned, but I could tell he was still trying to shake off our last encounter with his mother. It didn't get any easier for me, so I could only imagine what it was like for him.

"What did Katherine mean about her 'personal time,' anyway? You'd think she'd be run off her feet, trying to bring about her new world order. What would she even do with personal time?" I envisaged scented baths and a half hour of restorative yoga, but that didn't seem like her style. "Is she skinning puppies or something?" That seemed more likely.

Finch chuckled. "I know exactly where she's gone."

"You do?"

"Seriously, Sis, you're starting to give me a complex. I'm not some class dunce you know. I used to run this joint, right at Katherine's side, back in the day," he replied. "Everything she knows, I know. And everything she does, I know about."

I raised my hands in mock surrender. "No offense intended. So where is she?"

"You really want to know?"

"I *really* want to know. Is she a hardcore chess player or something?" I smirked. "Oh, please say it's knitting or pottery."

He grinned. "It's something a bit more… Katherine. We might need to go there, actually. There's a key that she used to have, which might help us get into the library without having to deal with the guards."

"Well, then, what are we waiting for?"

"Don't say I didn't warn you." With a mysterious smirk on his face, he led me away from the titans and headed toward the beach in the distance. There was no clear path to wherever we were going, forcing us to push through dense undergrowth and slithering creepers to reach our destination. I shuddered as glowing eyes peered at us through the canopy, making me wonder if Naima kept some of her beasties a little more free range.

"Isn't there an easier way to get there?" I muttered, as a branch swiped me in the face.

Finch laughed. "You want to get spotted by the cameras?"

"No, obviously."

"So quit your whining."

I wished we still had Astrid's camera-tampering device, but trying to sneak in with what we already had was risky enough. And that device wasn't exactly small. Still, at least we wouldn't have had to go traipsing through creature-infested rainforest. I was admittedly glad to have Finch's sharp sense of direction and his knowledge of the cult's intricate layout.

We stumbled out of the rainforest about fifteen minutes later, finding ourselves in a secluded inlet of the island's beautiful beach. Ahead sat a huge beach house, with white-washed walls and balconies stretching out from every window. A porch wrapped around the entire ground floor, with swinging loveseats and wicker armchairs. It didn't exactly fit with what I'd imagined Katherine's private residence to look like, given how... well, nice it was.

"This way," Finch whispered. I followed him along a seashell path toward the back of the house, where he ducked down to unearth the doors of a storm shelter. It was hidden behind some huge potted palm trees, which he quickly shoved out of the way. Working his magic on the lock, he opened the right-hand door and slipped inside, with me hurrying after him.

It turned out that the storm shelter had been made into some kind of wine cellar, with rows upon rows of dusty, expensive-looking bottles lining the walls. There were wooden boxes, too, which seemed to whisper to me as I went past. *Grimoires?* Whatever they were, I wasn't going to get the chance to take a closer look, since Finch was already heading for the door out of there.

He opened it and peered into the hallway beyond before beckoning for me to follow him. We tiptoed down the darkened corridor, eventually reaching a narrow set of wooden stairs and heading up them. With every step I made, paranoia gripped me. One misplaced foot, one creak, and we'd be done for. Finch didn't seem nearly as bothered. He pushed open the door at the top and took another look around.

In silence, we escaped the subterranean depths of Katherine's house and entered the main body of it. I gasped at the beautiful kitchen spread out before me, with a granite-topped breakfast island and walls that had been tiled with sea glass and mother-of-pearl. Everything looked way too quaint and pretty to be Katherine's, but then, what was I expecting? Dungeons, chains, fire, and brimstone?

Key? I mouthed to Finch.

He frowned and shook his head, pointing farther up the hallway. I rolled my eyes and followed him.

Finch led me out into the main hall, where calming seascapes adorned the bird-egg blue walls. A wide staircase led up to the first floor, the steps seemingly carved from reclaimed driftwood, but it didn't look as though we were headed that way. Instead, Finch ushered me down the main hall toward a room at the very back of the house. As we edged along, I peered into the other rooms we passed. There was an elegant lounge behind one, with huge sofas and an endless array of books, and a bathroom with a tub the size of a pool and a rainforest shower that I would've given anything to stand under.

We stopped beside the last door in the hallway, which was partially closed. I ducked down beside Finch, the two of us crouched low. From inside, I could hear the rumble of a familiar voice. Katherine's voice. And, while I couldn't quite see her, I could make out the bedroom through the gap in the doorway. It was dimly lit, the windows shrouded in gauzy curtains. And, instead of a bed, there was a casket of some kind, set in the center of the room. *What the heck? Is she a vampire or something?*

The casket had glass walls instead of the usual wood—and there was a man inside. He looked ancient, his skin purplish and wrinkled like a raisin, his body unmoving.

I glanced at Finch and opened my mouth, but he lifted a finger to his lips. If I said a word, Katherine would hear us, even though she seemed pretty intent on enjoying her "personal time" with whoever this dead guy was.

"I thought of you today, Grandfather," she said softly. "It has been a good day—one you'd be proud of."

Oh my God, that's Drake Shipton! The realization smacked me in the face, making me feel sick. How long had that guy been dead? And why did Katherine have him in her bedroom? This was all getting a bit too *Psycho* for me.

"We had two new members join today. You'd like them, particularly the girl. That goes without saying, huh? She's got fire in her belly, that's for sure, but I'll have to keep my eye on both of them. Bold is good, but I can't have it getting us in trouble." She paused. "The rest are out collecting artifacts and rare magicals to add to our ranks. Everything is going as planned, and each day I take a step closer to fulfilling your dream, on your behalf. You might not be able to become a Child of Chaos, but I will... for you. I've only managed to get this far because of you, Grandfather. I won't disappoint you now."

This was beyond creepy, even for Katherine. She had her grandfather's body in a glass case and was telling him about her day, insisting this was all for him and not for her own self-gratification. I had to be partially thankful that he *was* behind a glass case, and she wasn't snuggling up to him or sitting in his lap to tell him everything. I shuddered and realized we should probably get out of here before Katherine finished up her game of show-and-tell.

Where's the key? I mouthed.

Not here, Finch replied.

Terrified we'd get caught, I pointed to the kitchen, at the top of the hallway, and Finch nodded. If there was no key, then we were going to have to get into the library the old-fashioned way—through the front door. Guards or no guards. Moving stealthily away from the door, we made a quick exit, running back through the wine cellar and the storm doors, and back into the relative safety of the rainforest.

Pausing to catch my breath, I stared up at Finch. "What in the name of everything that is ordinary and normal was that?"

He laughed. "I did warn you."

"Yeah, but you didn't warn me I was going to see Katherine yakking to a freaking corpse!"

"Not technically a corpse."

"I saw it with my own eyes, Finch. That was a dead guy! And, since she was calling him 'Grandfather,' I can only assume it was Drake Shipton. Geez, man, you could have prepared me, at least." I sank down on the ground as a wave of nausea crashed over me.

"Oh, it's so much more messed up than that. He's not dead, he's just half dead. Katherine had him resurrected a while back, for 'emotional comfort.' That purple color to his skin is where the Necromancy went wrong. When he died, he ordered her to lock his spirit to the earth, same way Hester's is, so she'd be able to bring him back in the future. But the Necromancer botched it, when the time came, and that shriveled prune up there is the result," he explained. "Katherine was so mad at the Necromancer that she killed him. So, now there are only four left. One of them being Alton. Not that she'll ever get her hands on him."

I realized that Finch didn't know just how close Katherine had come to pulling Alton's strings, but it didn't seem like the time to mention it. Instead, I focused on Finch's story and tried not to hurl at the idea of a botched Necromancy. Not to mention Katherine dragging her grandpa back from the dead for some "emotional comfort." How messed up could this woman get?

If what Finch said was correct, then Katherine had killed the only Necromancer she had in her ranks. *Poor guy.* That was a lose-lose situation if ever I'd seen one. Anyway, it meant she was likely on the lookout for another. *That was why she wanted Micah.* It made sense now. Although, she'd agreed to let Micah go, so maybe she wasn't that desperate after all. She probably figured she could get Micah back when she became a Child of Chaos. Either that, or she already had a different Necromancer in her sights, whom she could persuade into joining the cult.

"How long had Drake been dead when she resurrected him?" I asked, standing up again. I doubted I'd ever forget what I'd just seen, but at least I didn't want to throw up anymore.

"At least fifteen years. Nobody has ever been brought back after being dead for so long, even with their spirit locked to the earth. His body was kept on ice, per his request, but it was still a little… ripe. It's one of the stupider things Katherine has done," Finch replied bitterly. "What did she think was going to happen? Of course it got botched and she ended up with a raisin. It was never going to work. I told her that. Then again, she can get a little irrational when it comes to personal stuff."

"What do you mean?"

He shrugged. "Well, anything related to the Shiptons and the Merlins just sends her over the edge. Big time. Like, the kind of explosion you want to run the hell away from."

"Are we talking about the same Katherine here? Calm, calculated, cool-as-a-cucumber Katherine?" Up until our last encounter, when Katherine had tried to kill me, she'd always been eerily serene and collected whenever we'd happened across one another, and I was both Shipton *and* Merlin. "I figured she just viewed me as the human equivalent of a stone in her shoe. Annoying, but nothing to lose your mind over."

Finch snorted. "She hates you most of all, Sis. All of that cool-as-a-cucumber stuff is just a façade. Whenever anyone mentions your name, even in passing, she bottles it all up until she's gathered up so much anger that she bursts. You wouldn't want to be around when that happens. That's when the death rate in this place spikes." He smiled. "So, yeah, she's got an irrational streak when it comes to family. She just doesn't show it often, least of all to you—the one who pisses her off the most."

I supposed that made sense. Why would she show me just how much she hated me, when I could use that against her? Katherine didn't want anyone to know she had a weakness, but it looked as if I'd just discovered hers.

THIRTY

Harley

I kept looking for a chance to catch Tess on her own, but she seemed to have disappeared off the face of the earth—or at least Eris Island. Three days had passed with no sign of her, but our last encounter had served as a warning: we needed to be more careful about where we went and how stealthy we were while looking for Hester's spirit. However, time was running out. Stealth was starting to get pushed to the bottom of the priority list, and my stress levels were rocketing through the roof. I felt useless. And, what was worse, I kept having all-consuming panic attacks about what would happen if we failed. It had happened twice before; it could happen again.

Since we weren't yet being trusted to go on field missions, not much had happened in the last few days. The major players, so to speak, were out in the real world, working on Katherine's behalf, giving us the opportunity to explore the island a little more, in the hopes of finding a way into that library. The giant clock loomed over our heads, ticking down to All Hallows' Eve. But we still hadn't managed to come up with a way to divert the guards at the library door, and I was starting to wonder if we'd actually be able to do this.

The only good thing was that Finch knew his way around,

including which areas to avoid if we didn't want to get spotted by the cameras that were fixed, seemingly at random, around the metal walkways. So that was one less thing to worry about, as we tried to eavesdrop on the passing guards to find out who might be on duty, and at what times. We figured that, if we could somehow slip in while there was a changing of the guard, we might stand a chance. Unfortunately, that window of opportunity hadn't arisen yet, and that hefty clock was ticking toward the eleventh hour.

Each morning, we discussed our plan of action and separated for a couple of hours, coming back together at lunchtime. Our sole purpose was to get into the Drake Shipton Library and pray Hester's spirit was there, and, so far, we'd come up with nothing useful. I'd spent most of my solo time feeding reverse Empathy into some of the cult members who looked important, trying to coax out some information about whether or not they'd been in the Drake Shipton Library and what they might have seen there. Unfortunately, nobody could say, with any real certainty, that my mom's spirit was actually in there.

I had managed to find out that the "ingredient" that had been mentioned before, by those guards, was actually the raw materials to make a weapon, which stuck in my gut like a blade. But we could only deal with one thing at a time, as much as that pained me.

"You get anything from anyone today?" Finch asked, as I met him on the way back from the cluster of beehives.

I shrugged. "Nothing to do with the spirit. But I did manage to find out from one of the senior members that Kenneth's team was sent to the Smithsonian to steal some rare artifacts from the Egyptian collection, and Naima's team was sent to a spell repository in Berlin to steal a bunch of famous Grimoires. Apparently, Katherine is working with a German splinter cell and a Belgian unit to infiltrate the European Council, and has people working for her in most of the major European cities. She's like a big, fat spider sitting at the center of a web —I mean, this thing stretches even farther than we thought. Plus, I'm guessing that's how they knew where the Librarian ended up." The thought made my blood boil. "Anyway, they're expected back any day. No word on where Tess has gotten to, though, which is annoying."

"You still want to confront her about being the mole?"

"Yeah, she might be able to help us out. But she seems to have vanished into thin air. I've asked around, but none of the seniors have seen her, and nobody's heard anything about her being sent on a last-minute mission. So, either she's avoiding us, or something has happened to her."

"We'd only be wasting time trying to pry anything out of her. Besides, you can't be entirely sure it's her. Maybe you got it wrong." Finch suddenly pointed to a figure walking along one of the walkways above our heads. "See, that's probably your real mole, right there! I'd stake my pants on it. If nothing else, he might know where Tess is."

Shinsuke walked alone, his head down, moving quickly along the suspended path. I tried to send my Empathy toward him to get a feel for his emotions, but he was too far away.

"Why your pants?" I pulled a face.

He shrugged. "I don't know. It was the first thing I thought of. Let's just stick with the twenty dollars. No pants necessary. If Shinsuke's our man, you owe me. If Tess is our woman, I owe you. Now, come on, he's getting away, and I've got some questions for our little friend."

"He's hardly little, Finch. He's got arms bigger than your head, which is no easy task."

"Pfft, let's not forget who floored whom in the arena."

I smirked. "*He* didn't have an Esprit full of neurotoxin."

"Hey, a win's a win. Now, hurry your ass up before we lose him." He set off up one of the sloping walkways, half running to catch up to Shinsuke. My gut told me I was right about Tess, but I figured talking to Shinsuke wouldn't be such a bad idea. After all, him not being the mole didn't mean he wasn't still eager to get out of this place, and we could use all the allies we could get.

We followed him all the way to one of the distant clusters of the beehive structures. I hadn't been this far into the rainforest, but Tess had informed us that the training halls were around here. I guessed Shinsuke needed to blow off some steam.

Together, Finch and I entered the nearest beehive and found that it was separated into two floors, with two training pods on either side. They reminded me of squash courts, with glass panels offering some seclusion to solo trainers, while others could watch from the sidelines. However, right now, nobody was in here except Shinsuke. He'd taken the farthest pod on the bottom floor and was in the middle of a warm-up with his impressive swords.

Finch rapped on the glass. "Hey, you want some company?"

Shinsuke tilted his head. "If you need someone to spar with."

"Sure. I want to see those swords in action again." Finch grinned, but Shinsuke could barely muster a smile. Now that I was closer to him, I sensed the perpetual undercurrent of fear and concern within him, and it had nothing to do with Finch. He hated this place, I could tell.

"Do you mind if I join in?" I asked. "I didn't get the chance to fight you last time, and I'd be interested to see you work."

Shinsuke nodded. "The more the merrier, I suppose."

We gathered in a triangle and started small. I let Finch go first. He began by using small bursts of Fire, in an attempt to preserve whatever he had left in his Ephemera. Mine was going strong, but I'd noticed Finch's gem fading slightly. Shinsuke didn't seem to notice that the world-renowned Firestarter was being overly cautious, as he started to twirl his swords through the air, swiping in a blur of steel. I pushed my reverse Empathy toward him. I wanted him to feel remorse and nostalgia, and I sent through my own sad feelings about Hiro Nomura, to get the right emotions flowing.

A moment later, a tear trickled down Shinsuke's cheek. He brushed it away as quickly as he could, but not before I'd spotted it. My reverse Empathy was working great. All those sessions with Wade were paying off, even though I'd hated making my boyfriend cry. It wasn't any easier with Shinsuke. He was tough and stoic by nature, and seeing him tear up was difficult to stomach, even if it opened him up to giving us the answers we wanted.

"Your dad doesn't have that cool Magneton-Earth ability, does he?" I started off the questions, knowing how to get right to Shinsuke's core. His father was a sore spot, but also one that was easy to manipulate.

Shinsuke shook his head. "No, it was a surprise to both of us when it became apparent that I possessed it. Even in the early days, when it wasn't very powerful, we were both shocked."

"What about your mom? She a Mediocre too?" It was an act, considering that I already knew about Shinsuke's mom, but I had a feeling this would open him up even more.

"No, she was a powerful magical. And she was a strong person," he replied sadly, his voice thick with emotion.

"Was?" I prompted.

"She died a long time ago. She was an explorer and a collector of rare artifacts. She died of exposure on a mission to find an ancient cache of magical objects in Antarctica."

"I'm sorry to hear that. Sounds like you were close."

Shinsuke nodded. "Very."

"I take it she belonged in the cult, too, at one point. Seems to be a family type of place," I continued. Finch watched me closely. He seemed impressed.

"No, she didn't care much for Katherine—for Eris—although she didn't know her very well. They'd encountered each other a few times, trying to get their hands on the same artifacts, which annoyed her." Bitterness enveloped Shinsuke's words.

"How come you ended up here, then?"

He shrugged. "For me, Mediocrity wasn't an option, and I knew my father would be disappointed if I gave up my studies. But I was struggling—until Eris appeared and offered to train me. I went behind my father's back to come here, even though he disapproved..." He unleashed a ragged sigh, then frowned, seeming to realize he was saying too much, despite my reverse Empathy at work.

I nodded sympathetically. "It must sting even more, now that your dad is in prison."

Shinsuke whirled around and stared at me. "What did you say?"

"Your dad's in prison. Didn't Eris tell you?"

"No… no, she didn't."

"Yeah, he got locked up after trying to help her. We heard it through one of our sources before we came here. They brokered some sort of deal where, if he managed to catch and send Harley Merlin to her, she'd release you in exchange. He got caught and ended up in prison. He's awaiting trial, last I heard, but it doesn't look good. He'll probably be in Purgatory for the rest of his life."

Shinsuke let out a choked sound. "No… no, that can't be right. My father would never make such a sacrifice."

"Well, he did. I guess Eris is even more persuasive than you thought."

Finch snorted. "Foolish, really. Eris would never have held up her end of the bargain. Once you're in the cult, you're in the cult, right? Nobody gets to leave, not unless they get carried out of here in a coffin."

His words served as a stark, unwelcome reminder to me. Finch had been a massive part of this organization. If he wasn't dead, then it stood to reason that he'd always be a member of this thing. I just had to keep hoping that he was an exception, that he wouldn't suddenly turn on me and change his mind. There was still a huge risk that all of this was an elaborate ploy. But he'd had plenty of opportunity to reveal me to Katherine since we'd arrived, and I was still standing.

Shinsuke hung his head. "So my father was going to make an exchange?"

I nodded. "That's what I heard down the grapevine."

"I see." Frustration and pain were etched on his face. He knew Katherine had played him, in the worst way possible. And now, his father was in prison, his reputation in tatters. I could feel the shock and misery bristling off him in spiky jolts, though he was struggling to stop it from showing in his body language.

Don't worry, this isn't over for you. I didn't say it out loud, but I felt it. With a little bit of luck, I'd get him out of here, too… eventually. Once we had Hester's spirit, and had stopped Katherine from completing the next ritual, we'd stand a chance of getting anyone out who didn't want to be here anymore. And, judging from the vibe around the island, there'd be plenty of takers.

"Do you know much about these rituals that everyone keeps talking about?" I prompted. "Pieter and I don't know too much about them, but they seem pretty important to this whole Child of Chaos thing she's trying to do."

Shinsuke grimaced. "Eris is eager to complete the next one, though she has already fulfilled two of the necessary rituals. It has made her far more powerful than anyone anticipated. In a few more days, she will have achieved the third, and her power will grow again." He sounded nervous, and he had every right to be.

"Something about a ghost, right?" Finch said, keeping it vague.

"A spirit, not a ghost," Shinsuke replied.

Finch shrugged. "What's the difference?"

"A ghost is the echo of a tragedy—a hologram, almost, left over from a traumatic death. A spirit is the very essence of who we are, without our earthly bodies. It is the part that crosses over when we die. It is not supposed to linger on earth, though there are ways of ensuring it does. Eris seems to have bound the spirit of her worst enemy to earth, and she plans to destroy it, in order to complete the third ritual."

Nice one, Finch. He was asking the right questions in the right way, making it seem as if we were more or less clueless. Thanks to my reverse Empathy, Shinsuke was getting trusting vibes from us. Plus, we were official members of the cult now, and it seemed like this was common knowledge around here.

"I imagine she's got a bunch of worst enemies," Finch said. "Do you know whose spirit she's bound?"

Shinsuke shook his head. "I don't know who, but the spirit is being kept under lock and key in the Drake Shipton Library beside a statue of Eris until midnight on All Hallows' Eve, when the ritual must be performed. Katherine will take the spirit to the Land of Erebus and do whatever needs to be done."

Finch whistled. "These rituals seem like a lot of hassle."

"It is why she's so eager to stay organized. I believe she's already taking steps to complete the fourth, as soon as she has finished the third. From what I have heard, she's already looking for a way into the Bestiary."

I put on a frown. "Where's that again? I can never remember where they moved it to."

"The San Diego Coven."

Finch smirked. "Now it makes sense. I'm guessing that's how Tess got her hands fried, huh?"

Shinsuke grinned, confirming what we already knew. "That's true, but it was only a test run, to uncover the defenses there. They're preparing for another hit, very soon."

My heart sank. The first attack on the Bestiary had been a ploy to test our defenses and see how we'd react. Yeah, we'd stopped it, but it had only left us more exposed. Now that they knew what we'd do, it'd be easier for them to infiltrate it the second time around. But how soon was very soon? At least, if we prevented Katherine from performing the third ritual, we might not have to face another blow to the Bestiary. I just hoped we could do it in time.

And we knew precisely where Katherine was hiding Hester's spirit now, and that we wouldn't be wasting our time breaking in there. That was one solitary consolation in all of this.

THIRTY-ONE

Harley

"Now do you believe me about Tess?" I asked, as we made our way through the island, toward the Hexagon.

We'd trained with Shinsuke for a couple of hours, to keep up the ruse, and we were both exhausted. Finch's Ephemera had visibly dimmed, which was pretty worrying. If this came to a head, I knew he might have to use his non-Pieter abilities to fight. Then again, if we were fighting people, the disguises probably wouldn't matter anymore.

He shrugged. "Just because Tess felt uncomfortable doesn't mean she's 100 percent the mole. Most people feel uncomfortable around Katherine. It's how she likes it." He paused. "I really thought Shinsuke was our guy."

"What do you think now?"

He pulled a sour face. "Well, Shinsuke didn't know anything about his father. Like, he genuinely didn't. The mole would already have known about it."

"Hold up a sec. Does this mean the great Finch is admitting he was wrong, and I was right?"

"I seem to be doing that a lot lately," he replied, with a wry smile.

"Unfortunately for you, all my money is back in that storage room in Purgatory. It'll have to be an IOU."

"You do owe me. If it wasn't for my Empathy, we wouldn't have a clue who the mole was."

"Yeah, yeah, stop parading your skills around. It's impressing nobody."

"I don't know, you seemed pretty impressed back there in the training room."

"Nah, that was just gas."

"Well, now that we know my mom's spirit is definitely in the library, we should head there. I've got an idea for the guards. We can't slip in while they're changing shifts, so we might need to be a bit more direct."

Finch grinned. "Direct is good. Fireballs?"

"Maybe. It depends how many people are watching."

Half an hour later, we found ourselves back at the secret entrance to the Hexagon. After scanning the area to make sure nobody had followed us, Finch took us both through the same concrete-and-steel corridors. Only, this time, we didn't stop outside Katherine's office, nor did we head toward the war room. Instead, we took a right down one of the labyrinthine hallways and ended up outside a fairly innocuous black blast door with two guards standing in front of it. Finch gave me a pointed stare—it was time for me to do my thing.

This was clearly the Drake Shipton Library, although there was no sign to give the game away. It was more the presence of the guards than anything else, as no other door had any officers standing in front of it.

Now, the moment had come to snatch my mother's spirit and get the heck out of here. We had to strike now or lose the opportunity for good.

"Telekinesis," I whispered. "And we can't be seen."

Finch smiled. "Aye, aye, Captain."

"And don't kill anyone."

"I won't if you won't."

Ducking back behind the corner of the hallway, I raised my palms and let the Telekinesis come. Fortunately, there was nobody else in this part of the Hexagon right now. It had two doors and a dead-end to the right of us. Clearly, people only came here if they really needed to, and right now, nobody did.

With Finch beside me, urging Telekinesis into his palms, we sent out four lassoes of bristling energy. They lashed around the throats of the guards before they even knew what was happening, the two of us pulling tight until their faces started to turn red. They scrabbled at their throats to try and get rid of the lassoes, but we'd been too quick, and they weren't prepared. I sent out a wave of Empathy at the same time to gauge what state they were in. I felt panic and terror surging out of them, starting in a violent wave before it began to fade. Finch and I kept hold of the lassoes until that sensation of panic had faded away to almost nothing, and then I released my grip and motioned for Finch to do the same. The guards slumped to the ground immediately, their eyes closed, but their chests were still rising and falling.

Glancing around once more, I sprinted for the figures and checked their pulses. They were fine, just unconscious, which meant we only had a short time to get in and get out.

"What do we do with them?" Finch asked.

"Drag them inside. We can't leave them out here. Can you get the door open?"

He chuckled. "We've talked about this, Sis."

"Just do it, will you!" I hissed.

"It's not that simple. There'll be a ton of hexes to work through first. This is why we needed that key from Katherine's residence—that's the only direct way in. But it wasn't there. She must be keeping it on her."

Keeping an eye on the guards to make sure they didn't wake up, I stepped up to the door and watched as he drew his hand across the doorframe. Hexes lit up all over the place. This was going to be tougher than we'd thought. Then again, it was Katherine's library, with her most prized possessions inside.

"How do I break them?" I asked.

"Cover it with your palms and unpick it with your Chaos. Just give me a sec to make a time-lapse bubble and we'll be good to go." As promised, he forged one of the familiar bubbles around us and the door, giving us more time to get this done. Even so, I kept glancing at the guards, just to make sure they wouldn't suddenly sit up and fight back.

I covered the first hex with my palms and powered my Chaos energy into it. Like Finch had said, it was sort of like picking a really complicated lock or tugging at the right strings of a knot to get it to untie. The bronze tendrils of my Chaos slithered into the charm, seeking out the parts that needed breaking. Those spots pulsed, as if trying to push away my Chaos. I sent a thin stream of Fire through my hands and singed away the pressure points, making the entire hex collapse.

Finch gave a low whistle. "Not bad."

"Thanks." I moved on to the next one, the two of us rapidly making our way through the hexes, hoping to finish before the guards woke up or someone came past and spotted the bubble. A few of the charms were feistier than the others, some billowing out black smoke and one sending out a horde of silver spiders that tried to scuttle up my arms. I shuddered at that one, incinerating them all in a wash of Fire. There was one that sent up a hologram of Katherine, her face whooshing toward me like a ghoul. I closed my eyes and sent a mixture of Telekinesis and Fire toward it, picking it apart in the same way I'd done the rest of the charms, and watching with some satisfaction as Katherine dissipated. *If only it were that easy in real life.*

At last, we had all of the hexes out of the way, but there was still one hurdle to jump over. We needed the password to actually open the door, same as with Katherine's office.

"Tell me you know it?"

Finch smirked and put his hand on the handle of the library. "Of course I know it." He whispered something in Latin, and the handle lit up red. It sounded similar to the password he'd used on Katherine's office, with a slight change of words. It was likely something equally nauseating and self-indulgent. A wave of relief washed over me as the blast door slid to the side. Grabbing the female guard by the back of her shirt, I dragged her into the room beyond, with Finch dragging the guy in after me. He closed the door behind us, whispering the same spell that had unlocked it in the first place.

Once I had bundled the female guard into a nearby cupboard and Finch had stowed the guy away in a cabinet, I stood up and took in my surroundings for the first time. My eyes flew wide in awe. It had been styled in the same fashion as Katherine's office, with a cosmos swirling overhead, aquariums slotted into the wood-and-gold walls, and rows upon rows of bookcases lining every available space. There were glass display cases, too, holding rare and remarkable treasures. Everywhere I looked, I found something else to gawk at.

In the center stood a glass case with a gold gauntlet inside, and a small card stating that it had once belonged to Queen Nefertiti, the greatest witch in all of Ancient Egypt. Beside it, there were Esprits from a bunch of famous, and infamous, magicals: a blade belonging to Genghis Khan, a coin pendant from Mother Shipton, a staff from Aleister Crowley, a rough-cut chunk of onyx from Nostradamus, and even an ancient bracelet which had, apparently, belonged to Cassandra herself—the great Grecian prophetess.

I wondered if Wade knew his ancestor's Esprit had wound up in Katherine's private collection, the thought of him making my heart beat faster. The sooner we could get this done, the sooner I'd be back at the SDC with him.

"This place is insane," I whispered. Libraries had that effect on me.

Finch laughed. "It's pretty cool. It's just a shame nobody ever gets to see inside it."

"Well, we better hope my mother's spirit is in here somewhere. Shinsuke said to look for the statue of Eris... not that that helps much." There were statues of Eris everywhere. My heart lurched at the prospect of finding her in this place, especially with our one marker rendered useless. I'd been pushing my emotions surrounding her to the side, trying to keep my focus on the task at hand, but it was impossible not to feel a million and one things, now that we were getting closer.

I'd never actually met my mother. Katherine had taken that from me. And the idea of seeing her spirit was almost more than I could bear. Sadness and confusion and hope swirled in a vortex deep inside me, refusing to be ignored.

As we started our search, I called out to Finch. Talking to him was the only way I could keep my head in the game, without getting too sucked in by what I would say to my mother when we found her. Would she even be able to hear me? I wasn't sure which was more unnerving—the idea of being able to talk to her and have her reply, or her not being able to talk back.

"Why do you think Tess decided to become a mole for the National Council?" I asked, drawing my fingertip along a row of ancient-looking tomes.

Finch peered around a nearby bookcase and shrugged. "It might have something to do with her sister, Larissa. She died on a mission, and Katherine didn't care. Katherine said she'd gotten what was coming to her and refused to let Tess retrieve what was left of her sister in order to bury her. I doubt she'd have forgiven that in a hurry."

"I hadn't considered it might be a super personal grudge," I said softly.

"Don't forget, Katherine uses people. She used me. She used Shin-suke. She used Hiro. She uses whomever she can, for as long as they're useful to her. I guess she thought it proved Tess's loyalty, when she didn't try to argue. I can't wait to see the look on her face when she finds out."

"She can't find out, Finch. Not yet. We need Tess as much as she needs us." I didn't want Finch getting carried away with his vendetta. Tess could be useful to us here, even after we escaped with the spirit. Ratting her out served no immediate purpose... even if seeing the look on Katherine's face *would* be a brilliant thing. Plus, she was sort of on our side, if she was working against Katherine. That gave her the right to our silence, for now.

Finch chuckled. "Don't worry, I know what's at stake. In the end, when everyone figures out that she's only using them for her own gains, they'll all be ready to jump ship. One way or another. This ship is already sinking, and those rats will be out of here quicker than you can say 'Eris.' And I can't wait."

As I continued searching, book titles jumped out at me. The first one my hand rested on was called *Into the Otherworld* by a man named Sebastien Delacroix. Opening it up, I scanned the index for any interesting chapters. One leapt out of the page, and I flicked to the corresponding page and tore it out, stuffing it in my pocket for later. I didn't have time to read it now, but I'd take any useful information I could get.

I hurried to the next statue of Eris, looking behind it, and around it, for any sign of Hester's spirit, but all I found were more books and cases filled with artifacts. None of them gave any indication that they held my mom's spirit inside them.

"Got it!" Finch yelped a few minutes later. I sprinted from the book-case I was searching, to find him at the far end of the room, his hands grasping a small charmed jar that had been placed on a special altar. It was tucked behind a towering statue of a marble goddess. *Eris, again, I presume?* I looked at the statue, noting the golden apple held aloft. It was identical to the rest of the statues in the room. Man, Katherine really liked to show off. The statue even looked like her.

My eyes drifted toward the jar, which was very similar to the soul jars Papa Legba had used, only slightly bigger. A faint white mist swirled inside the glass, the charms lighting up as it held back the spirit within. I couldn't tear my gaze away. I found myself getting lost in the swirling mist, trying to pick out something more human. Something that let me know, beyond all doubt, that my mother was in there.

The hazy fog grew more agitated, the white mist thickening as it threw itself against the glass, dispersing instantly before coming back together again. *Can you see me, Mom?* Did she know I was here? Did she recognize me, even after so many years? Tears filled my eyes, and my heart gripped in my chest. I touched the glass, smoothing my fingertips across the surface as the charms that were carved into the glass started to glow. The mist slammed harder into the glass and paused where my fingertips rested, fine tendrils slithering up the inside, like they were trying to touch me.

"I'm here," I said softly, my voice choked with emotion. "Mom, I'm here. Just hold on, we're going to get you out of this place."

Finch stared at me strangely. "Big moment for you, huh?"

I nodded, unable to speak. The charms grew even brighter. She knew I was here, and she knew who I was, even after all this time. I guessed it was that unbreakable bond between mother and child, the one I'd never experienced, until now. I wanted to grab the jar from Finch's hands and smash it here and now, letting my mother out, but he tugged it away, as if he knew exactly what I was thinking.

"What the hell do you think you're playing at?" A familiar voice cut through the tense silence of the room, making us both turn in fright. Tess stood at the far end of the aisle, a few steps in front of the main door, her eyes narrowed in anger. "This is the second time I've caught you somewhere you're not supposed to be. Don't tell me, you were waiting for Katherine?" Sarcasm dripped from her words as she moved toward us.

Finch and I exchanged a worried look. How were we going to wriggle our way out of this one?

THIRTY-TWO

Finch

"One of you had better start talking," she warned. "What are you doing here?"

I smiled. "Don't suppose you'd believe us if we said we were just browsing?"

"No, I wouldn't."

Ah, Tess, don't you see? We're all on the same side here.

"How about—we just stumbled in by accident?" There was a pleasant irony to knowing what we knew, while Tess had no idea. But just how far was she willing to go with the ruse? I was eager to find out.

"Again, no," she spat. "What are you after, huh? Who sent you here? Are you working for the National Council? I knew there was something off about you, the moment I set eyes on you."

I should've been concerned, but I was just amused. This was a hilarious situation. Here we all were, working for the same team and trying to pretend otherwise. It was the best kind of car crash. And she was playing her part so very, very well.

I glanced toward the far left of the room. Another statue stood there, one of my mother's odes to herself—a statue of Eris, with the same golden apple in her hands. That emblem was getting old, and I hated the sight of it. Behind it, I saw the telltale shimmer of a hidden door. It was so subtle I almost missed it, but it was definitely there. A memory came rushing back. Katherine, telling me about a secret entrance into this place. She'd never given me the exact location, she'd just told me to "look for Lux" if the island was ever in trouble and I needed to come here without using the main entrance. Did that door have something to do with Lux? I racked my brain, but I couldn't think of how the two might be connected.

I looked back at Tess and wondered if I should just knock her out and run for the hidden door, with Hester's spirit in tow. *Too risky, even for you.* The moment Tess came to, she'd be sprinting to Katherine as if her life depended on it. Which, given the circumstances, it kind of did. If she could pin the mole label on someone else, she would. It was the spy's rule of thumb: cover your own ass first, worry about the consequences later.

So, instead, we entered a face-off. *The Good, the Bad, and the Ugly* music should've been playing. *Du-du-du-duuuu, du, du, duuuuu.* I gripped the jar tighter to my chest. No way she was getting her hands on this. I hadn't come all this way to hand it over. And if she thought otherwise, well… I'd break out the big guns.

"Tell me what you're doing here," she snapped, taking a step forward.

"That's close enough, Tess." I held her gaze, my breath ragged. Having an escape route so close made it all the more frustrating. I supposed I could kill her and hide the evidence. Then again, Goody Two-shoes Merlin wouldn't like that. But what else could we do? The tension stretched between us, none of us knowing what to do.

"You can pretend you didn't see this. We know you're not what you seem," Harley said. *Oh yeah, helpful.* Even if Tess *was* the mole, she wasn't going to out-and-out tell us. She might think we'd been sent to pick out the traitor. This girl was going to keep up the pretense until the bitter end, I could feel it.

"I want to know *what* I'm seeing," she shot back. "Who sent you?

And what are you doing with *that?*" She eyed the jar, and I knew the gig was up. She'd piece it together in no time, if she hadn't already.

Harley took a step forward. "Nobody sent us. Just forget what you've seen, and we'll go, unless there's something you want to tell us? You know, about who you are?"

Are you insane? I shot her a look that I hoped conveyed the sentiment.

"Hand that over, or I'll be forced to kill you. I've got nothing to say to you, other than you'll die for this." Tess took a step forward, mirroring Harley.

"I said that's close enough!" I barked.

"I mean it, both of you. I'll kill you where you stand if you don't tell me what I want to know."

I smirked. "Oh yeah? You and what army?" I knew Tess was strong, but not that strong. At least, that's what I was banking on. Electro powers were formidable and rare, but I had Harley. My secret weapon. Still, things were getting a little too hairy for my liking.

"Fine. You asked for it." Tess raised her palms.

I needed to play our wild card. Now. "We know who you are, Tess. We know you're the mole that's helping the National Council. Nice job, though, trying to pin it on us. Real nice."

She froze.

"I'll take your silence as confirmation?" I smirked. We had her.

She seemed to rally. "What? That's ridiculous! Who told you that? They're liars, whoever they are. I'm no mole, though I can't say the same about you."

I laughed. "Nope, not a lie. And you know it as well as we do. As soon as my contact knew we were joining the cult, he warned me about you. I guess he was right. You've shown your true colors." I gave a slow clap. "In fact, you were *so* convincing. I even had my doubts about his sources."

Silence stretched between us. Tess gave nothing away on her face. She was as calm and collected as ever. *What if this doesn't work?* I'd taken a page out of Harley's book in calling her out. But maybe Harley's book didn't always work. I started thinking of other ways out of this, in case Tess kept up the ploy. Right now, however, I couldn't see another route that wouldn't end with us dead.

"We could use an ally, and I'm guessing you could, too," Harley said at last.

Tess glowered. "An ally? Don't make me laugh. Why should I trust you?"

I hugged the jar tighter. "Is that an admission of guilt?"

"I sent all that information anonymously," Tess murmured. "No one should've known."

"Why, though? Why betray Katherine?" Harley asked. I figured she must be using her reverse Empathy, if Tess was crumbling so easily. *Sneaky. I like it.* The more time I spent around Harley, the more I realized we weren't too dissimilar. She was just better at hiding her devious streak.

"I joined the cult willingly," she protested.

"So what happened?" Harley replied.

"I joined with my sister, Rissa. We wanted the fame and the glory that Katherine promised. We didn't want to live ordinary, oppressed lives anymore, always hiding in the shadows. Especially being Electros, people looked down on us, and people were suspicious of our power, and we were tired of it. Plus, we wanted to see a change in the world. A change where we didn't have to hide anymore." The words were pouring out of her, like she had no control. "We knew there'd be some consequences. We knew it would start with death and fear, but then, once Katherine became a Child of Chaos, there'd be happiness and prosperity for the magicals who were true and worthy."

"And you thought you'd get to decide that?" Harley laughed bitterly. "You really thought Katherine would deliver that kind of utopia for magicals?"

Tess scowled. "We believed it for a while."

"What changed?" I asked.

"My sister was killed, and Katherine didn't care. I asked if I could bring her body back, but she denied me. She said that Rissa should rot where she was for disappointing her," Tess explained. "I knew, right then, that she wasn't doing this for anyone but herself. I also saw what she tried to do to her own son. She asked me to lead the mission to have him killed, but I didn't want to. And then Kenneth volunteered, and I said I didn't mind passing it to him so he could prove himself. She bought it, but it made things even clearer for me. She didn't give a damn about anyone but herself, not even her own flesh and blood. That hit a nerve with me, I guess."

"Do you still feel that way?" Harley pressed.

Tess held her face in her injured hands. "I do, but now I'm scared. I might be feeding intel to the National Council, hoping they'll dismantle this whole operation, but I can't see a way out of this place. Not a way where I get to live, anyway. The farther Katherine gets with this Child of Chaos thing, the more horrible it all seems. She killed children. *Children*. And she barely flinched."

That was my mother. If something wasn't up to par, it wasn't necessary. She had no emotional attachment whatsoever, not even to me. While Harley was busy focusing on Tess, I tucked the jar under my arm and put my hands behind my back. I didn't want them to see what I was doing. Not yet. I had a little trick up my sleeve, but I'd only use it if I had to.

"Even others in the cult are starting to doubt her. The vibe is bad here, seriously bad. They were promised protection and love, which, for a lot of them, was the first time they'd experienced anything like that. But now, all they're getting is abuse and threats and terror. They're just pawns in Katherine's game, and she's got no qualms about sacrificing them all if it gets her what she wants."

"What did you expect?" I shot back, my tone sour. It sickened me. Yeah, it was hypocritical, but so what? At least I'd entered this after years of indoctrination. I hadn't come willingly, per se. My mind had been battered into submission first. These saps had heard one proclamation of future fame and glory and given up their morals. They were greedy, and that was all there was to it.

"Not this! Not death and fear around every corner! Not being forced on missions that are getting more dangerous by the day. She's sent a team to break into The Hague! That's where the European Council of Magicals holds its meetings. Do you have any idea how guarded that place is? If even one member makes it back, I'll be shocked. And she won't care. She has Naima rounding up new magicals every day. When one falls, another takes their place. It's endless. And they're everywhere. She has people all over the globe, in setups like this. Secret pockets in every city. This isn't bringing about a new world order—this is world domination. Plain and simple."

I snorted. "Again, what else did you expect?"

Tess paused and leveled her gaze at me. "Peace."

"Then you're an idiot."

"That's easy for you to say. You've only just arrived. You've got no idea what she promised us, and no idea what she's using us for. We're not followers, we're an army. And her ranks are swelling by the day. I couldn't even begin to count how many people she has working for her."

"Does the Kool-Aid not taste so good anymore?" I smirked at her.

"What would you know?" she hissed. "I wouldn't expect you to understand. And if you're planning to turn me in to Katherine, then it's important that you know what you're up against. She's not what you think she is. She's a murdering psychopath who doesn't give a damn about any of us."

Oh, I understand perfectly. I was about to retort, when two figures sprinted down the aisle. The guards were awake. They eyed Tess before looking at Harley and me. I was really starting to wish I hadn't picked the jar up. I was standing in front of them, red-handed.

"You!" the first guard snapped, looking right at us. "Did you lock us in those cabinets? Did you strangle us?"

"None of you should be in here! You know the rules! Now, who did this to us? Which one of you was it? Start talking before we have to force it out of you!" The second guard looked at Tess, his eyes narrowing.

Tess's face morphed into a mask of innocence. "What happened to you? I just heard a commotion inside and came to investigate," she said. "I found Volla and Pieter in here, snooping around. They were the ones breaking the rules, not me. I was just trying to figure out what was going on."

I grinned at her. *So this is how you want to play it, huh?* "Oh, she's good."

Harley grimaced. "I guess she's playing hardball."

"Probably thinks she's got seniority over us," I whispered. "Nobody's going to believe the newbies over her, are they?"

"What are *we* going to do about this?" I heard the nerves in Harley's voice.

"I'm thinking."

"You haven't answered our question. Who did that to us? Which one of you broke in here and tried to kill us in the process? I've already triggered the alarm, so don't think you can get out of here without us getting to the bottom of this. One of you did this, maybe more of you, and I want to know who!" The first guard looked to us, while the door to the library flew open to reveal the arrival of more magicals, drawn by the noise and, presumably, the alarm. *Vultures.* I spied Shinsuke in the crowd. He was watching us intently.

"We didn't know this place was off limits. There was nobody guarding it, and there's no sign or anything," Harley replied to the guard. "We found Tess in here, so we figured it was okay. We just wanted to know what she was doing, that's all."

Two more figures joined the crowd—Katherine and Naima had shown up to the party. *Great, perfect, superb, let's make this a public execution.* Harley stiffened beside me. I wanted to tell her it was going to be okay, but I couldn't. I didn't know that it would be, and I wasn't prepared to see her burst into a fountain of blood and guts. Nor me, for that matter.

I thought about just smashing the jar right then and there, after all, since we'd been caught red-handed. But Harley shot me a sudden, desperate look as I shifted it in my hands. She clearly knew what I was thinking. And the timing was all wrong. If I broke the jar now, she wouldn't have the chance to say goodbye to her mother. Both of us knew how much was at stake. This was more than a farewell. But, I got it. I understood that desire in her, that longing to at least speak with the mother she'd never known. If I smashed this here, I was taking that away from her. And, frankly, I didn't have the heart. *You've lost your edge, Finch.*

Instead, I lifted my hand to the St. Christopher medallion, but Harley shook her head violently. *Not here,* she mouthed. I guessed it wasn't the brightest idea to call for the cavalry in a situation like this. If Isadora suddenly appeared in this room, she'd be surrounded before we could even get through her portal and back to the SDC. There were too many people to make it work. Katherine was right here. We'd all get ourselves captured. Plus, it'd be all the evidence Katherine needed to figure out who we really were. *Ugh...* It seemed like we were forever stuck between a rock and a really freaking hard place.

"What's going on here?" Katherine strode toward us. "Someone had better start talking, or this library is going to get redecorated. I don't like red for walls, but I'll stomach it if I have to." Her eyes fixed on Tess before moving to Harley and me. Yeah, I really could've done without holding this jar.

"I heard a sound coming from the library, Eris, and I was investigating." Tess jumped on the offensive. "I found these two snooping around. I tried to stop them."

That's quite enough from you, Crux. With the mission on the line, it was us or her, as much as I hated to be backed into a corner like this. She could've been an ally, after all.

"What a load of self-serving horsecrap!" I shouted back. "You were trying to steal this, and we stopped you. You want to stop Eris from completing the third ritual. Don't try to lie. You threatened to kill us if we didn't hand it over." I looked to my mother and swallowed the urge to throw her against the wall. "Tess is the snitch, Eris. She's your mole."

THIRTY-THREE

Harley

Are you out of your freaking mind?

I wanted to say it out loud, but that would have given us away as the traitors. Still, I couldn't believe what Finch had just done.

Tess was trying to help the magical world, and we'd just signed her death warrant. Well, if Katherine believed us, that was. Granted, Tess had no idea who we really were, and she'd been about to sell us out to Katherine, but that didn't mean we had the right to get her killed. This was so many shades of moral gray area that I had no idea what to think. Right and wrong had gotten so blurred since we came here.

One thing was for sure, everyone was out for themselves in this place. And, if we didn't jump on the selfish bandwagon, it'd be our necks on the line.

Greater good, greater good, greater good. I kept repeating the mantra, but it didn't make this any easier to handle.

"Explain, now. With details. And quickly, before my itchy trigger finger slips and I decide to deal with this in a more direct manner." Katherine was keeping her calm exterior, but I wondered what was going on beneath the surface. Regardless, I had no time to think about the morality of this. We had to act fast or risk being splattered.

Finch stepped forward. "I received word yesterday from my source in the National Council, but I couldn't find Tess to confront her. Regardless, they did identify her as the informant. She's been selling your secrets because she's bitter and angry about her sister's death, and the fact that you wouldn't permit her to bring her sister's body back to the island." He was going at this full-throttle, no remorse necessary. "She just told us that you only use people, that you don't care about your followers beyond what they can do for you. She told us, outright, how much she hates you now, and how much your vision has changed from the one you promised everyone. She wanted us to find a way to escape this place—she told us we had to get out before we got suckered in."

Oh... clever. Even if Tess didn't make it out of this alive, airing all of Katherine's dirty laundry would mean she didn't die in vain. Everyone was listening, rapt. They were hearing everything that Finch had to say and would undoubtedly make their own opinions from it. Perhaps they'd share in some of Tess's thoughts—thoughts they'd been too afraid to admit to themselves.

Even so, I couldn't find my voice. Finch was doing all the talking, and I just felt numb and scared. This could only end one way, with either Tess's head on the chopping block, or ours. Maybe both, if Katherine was pissed enough. All of this had taken me by surprise, and I honestly had no clue how to react. It was all happening way too fast, leaving my mind spinning.

"You liar!" Tess roared.

Finch smirked. "Oh, really? Then how come I have a recording of you, saying exactly what I've just said?"

"You don't. You can't." Tess wavered, as if she wasn't quite sure whether or not Finch was bluffing. Neither was I, in all honesty.

He opened out his palms and closed his eyes, a holographic bubble appearing in his hands. Tess's face wavered inside it. A moment later, her voice echoed through the now-silent library. *"Even others in the cult are starting to doubt her. The vibe is bad here, seriously bad..."*

I gaped at Finch. I had no idea he could do something like this, but then, I didn't know everything he'd learned in this place. It looked like he'd picked up a devious spell or two along the way. Now, everyone had heard what Tess said, and the whole congregation was reeling in shock. Even Tess looked stunned, her eyes wide and panicked. She'd underestimated Finch's cunning, and so had I.

A moment later, everyone turned to look at Katherine. All bets were off. The calm, calculating figure everyone was used to had morphed into something else—a fiery hell-demon who'd finally had her buttons pushed. Her eyes flashed with poison, her lips curling into a grimace of sheer fury.

"Get her out of my sight!" she bellowed. "Take her to my private quarters this minute! If it weren't for the third ritual, I'd deal with you right now, you venomous snake."

Tess was shaking, her eyes wide in desperation. "Eris, please, you know me. I would never—"

"While you're waiting for me, I want you to think about what you've done," Katherine interjected, her tone lowering to a hiss. "I want you to think really, really hard. And, once you've realized the stupidity of your actions, I want you to think about your death." She took a step closer to Tess, getting right up in her face. "It's going to be painful beyond your imagination. I'm going to sift through every dark and terrible spell I have and pick the worst one for you. *Just* for you. It will be so slow that you'll wish your mother had never squeezed you, wailing and screaming, into this world. You'll wish you'd died in your sister's place, you can count on that."

Even though she'd tried to throw us under the bus, I felt sorry for Tess, not to mention guilty. Nobody deserved what she was going to face, especially not somebody who was working on the same side as us. Katherine meant it, too. She didn't use words lightly. She was going to annihilate Tess in the most horrific way possible, and there was nothing we could do to stop it. I glanced at Finch, who'd gone pale. He wasn't the remorseful type, per se, but he looked pretty shaken up right now. He'd given Katherine the evidence she needed, and now Tess was going to die. I knew they'd been friends, once upon a time. This had to be hitting him hard. His body was stiff with tension, as though he didn't trust himself to move a muscle.

The guards surged forward and seized Tess before she had the chance to make a run for it.

"Katherine, please, you've got to listen to me!" she screamed, as the guards took her away.

"It's Eris to you, you traitorous wretch!" Katherine howled in her face. "And I've heard quite enough from you. One more word and I will make your insides your outsides, in front of everyone here."

With fear in her eyes, Tess unleashed a searing crackle of Electro energy, sending the guards around her into spasms. As if she'd been expecting the attack, Katherine immediately sent out a lasso of Telekinesis, wrapping it around Tess's neck and squeezing, in a horrible replay of what we'd done to the guards. A few moments later, she was limp on the ground, her cheeks purple. I quickly sent out a wave of Empathy to check whether she was still alive. The pulse of her frightened emotions was still there, deep inside her, though fainter than it had been before.

Fresh guards replaced those who were writhing in pain on the floor, hauling Tess up by her arms and dragging her out of the library and away to Katherine's private quarters. I got the feeling Katherine wasn't quite done yet. She turned to the rest of the cultists who'd gathered at the entrance.

"Don't you have work to get to? Do you all think this is a free ride? That I'll do all the hard stuff, so you don't have to? I suggest you all get on with your duties, before I decide to add a few more to my kill list." She glowered at them, and they scampered. Only the security detail remained, all of them trembling before the sight of a furious Katherine. I sensed that they hadn't seen her lose her cool, either. "I want double security on this room, do you understand? Nobody is to get in or out until midnight on All Hallows' Eve. I want a rotation, twenty-four hours a day. If even one of you takes so much as a toilet break, I'll have your bladders removed. As for the two of you who were supposed to be guarding this place, I'll be coming for you."

They bowed low, a ripple of assent vibrating through them. Those guards were a problem. They hadn't seen our faces, but they'd tell Katherine they were attacked, in order to save their skins. I guessed we could always tell Katherine that we'd heard a commotion inside and had found the guards knocked out by Tess. That might work. Still, panic was bristling through my body in a torrent. We would be relying a lot on her faith in us, and I doubted she had any, right about now.

"Now, you two." She shot a look at us. "I want you in my study in fifteen minutes, so I can make sure Tess is put away in a Bestiary box and doesn't try any of her shock tricks again. And give me that jar, or I'll have your hands for wall ornaments."

She breezed toward us and tore the jar out of Finch's hands, striding over to an empty case on the far side of the room. There, she slammed it into the case and closed her eyes, whispering a spell that made the box light up with fierce red light. With that done, she stormed out of the room, leaving us to wonder what we'd gotten ourselves into. Now, we risked losing my mother's spirit forever, unable to do a damned thing to stop Katherine before she used Hester to complete the third ritual.

"I hope you've got a clever way out of this, too," I hissed at Finch.

He shook his head. "Nope."

Great... That's just great.

THIRTY-FOUR

Harley

With the library closed, my mom's spirit safely inside the locked box, and the guards restored to their positions, Finch and I had been frog-marched to Katherine's office so we could await her return. The injured ones had gone to the infirmary to get their frazzled skin seen to, while others had taken their place, all along the hallway. Fortunately for us, however, the guards who'd escorted us here seemed preoccupied with what had just happened, the three of them clustered a short distance away, speaking in scared whispers.

"Do you think she'll really kill Henry and Jenna?" one asked.

Another shrugged. "Of course she will. They allowed themselves to be compromised."

Meanwhile, I gaped at Finch. "So you're telling me there might have been a way out of that library this whole time, and you didn't think to mention it the moment we had my mother's spirit?" He'd just told me about the secret door he'd caught sight of, though a little too late for it to be any use.

He shrugged. "I'm telling you now, aren't I?"

"And what good is that?"

"Well, now we have a way out, even with all this added security. We can use it to escape when we snatch your mom's spirit again. Anyway, it wasn't like I saw it as soon as we got in. It was a last-minute spot."

"Yeah, provided we make it out of this meeting in one piece. What do you think the chances of that are?"

He smiled. "Fifty-fifty?"

"You're an idiot."

"Oh, come on, what are you so worried about? We've got our alibis covered. Those guards will attest to what we say. I can't say the same for Tess. As soon as we leave this meeting, we can get back into the library *through* that secret door and take the jar. It's not just an exit, Sis —doors go both ways."

I paused. "I hadn't thought of that."

"Now who's the idiot? I just have to find out where the entrance is. Katherine once said something about 'looking for Lux' to find it, but I don't know what that means. Not that I won't figure it out." The smugness was radiating off him, no Empathy needed. Glancing at him, I had to smile. If what he said was true, and he really knew the way back into the library through that second door, then we were closer to victory than I'd thought. This was the break we needed, and with Katherine distracted by Tess, it might be the perfect timing, too. Not that I felt good about it. I didn't want Tess to suffer like this. If we'd had more time, I would've tried to save her, but I didn't know if that was even a possibility now.

"We haven't won yet," I reminded him. "And can we not just talk about Tess like that? She's going to die because of your trick with the replay thing. Like, really die. In a horrible, horrible way. This isn't a casual threat."

He shrugged, visibly chastened. "But we can see the finish line, right?"

"Come on, let's just get through this and try not to get ourselves killed. And remember what Tess is giving up for us... *because* of us. Okay?"

"Killjoy."

We put on solemn expressions as Katherine rounded the corner, sweeping past us into the office. The door slammed behind her, leaving us confused. Were we supposed to just go in? Finch made the first move, knocking and waiting for her to reply, the two of us sharing one last, conspiratorial look before we entered the lion's den.

"Come in," Katherine called.

Gathering every ounce of courage I had left, I pushed through the door and into Katherine's study. She sat behind the expansive desk, flipping casually through a stack of large books with covers made out of a material that resembled human skin.

"What do you think, Volla—death by flaying to the bone and making her eat what comes off, or death by cellular disintegration, killing her one cell at a time? They're both time consuming, but that is what I promised. I can't let Tess down now, can I?" She chuckled darkly. My stomach churned.

Every scrap of Katherine's former anger appeared to have dissipated, leaving the composed Katherine we were used to. Her left hand glowed as she scanned it over the pages, revealing hidden words and symbols.

"Whichever you prefer," I replied, forcing my voice to stay calm.

"You'll get splinters if you sit on the fence, Volla," she tutted, looking up. "But I can't knock your punctuality. Sit."

We did as she asked, looking like naughty schoolkids who'd been brought into the principal's office. Only, with much higher stakes.

"Now, tell me what you were doing in the library. I know you weren't just trying to apprehend Tess. Before she was locked away in one of my personal Bestiary boxes, she insisted that the two of you were up to no good. I'm inclined to believe her, given how desperate she was. Traitor or not, I sensed it was prudent to listen." She smiled. "Plus, you're new. I'm always suspicious of newbies. Call it an occupational quirk."

I didn't know what to say. My mouth had clammed up. Fortunately, Finch took the lead and leaned forward in his chair.

"I already knew that Tess was the traitor, Eris." At least he was sticking to the script on this one. We'd figured, before coming here, that it was best to stay as close to the truth as possible, without the obvious discrepancies. "We were passing the library on our way to the war room, when we heard a commotion inside. The door was open, so we went in, and we found two collapsed guards and Tess heading for the door with that jar in her hands. I took it from her and was trying to put it back, when she turned on us and told us all that stuff about you."

He was improvising, and I didn't know if I liked it.

"When we saw Tess with the jar, that was it. We knew what she was up to, and we had to stop her so she wouldn't have the chance to ruin your plans," Finch continued. "The rest is history."

Katherine smiled, but there was something deeply unsettling about it. "About that trick you pulled with the replay—very clever. Did they teach you that in Russia?"

Finch nodded. "Our parents were eager for us to learn how to defend ourselves. We learned from ex-Russian secret magical services."

She shrugged, apparently satisfied. "I suppose deception is in your nature."

"I only use those skills if I need to, Eris," Finch replied.

"Yes, I suppose you do." That smile crept onto her lips again, sending a shiver through me. "I happen to like spells like that. They're so much more satisfying than voice recorders or polygraph tests. I can get on board with most technology, but I find these modern cell phones fairly distasteful, making everyone into zombies. *'Pics or it didn't happen,'* that sort of vile thing. Once I've achieved my goal, I'll see them banned. Make people actually sit up and take notice of the world around them. Then, they might see what they've been missing while they've been staring at their screens. Maybe I'll post one picture, to let them know that it *did* happen, on the day their world ends."

Katherine on Instagram? There was a strange idea. I couldn't imagine her posting snaps of her dinner, and hashtagging: #endoftheworld #blessed #cultlife. It made me want to laugh suddenly, but I pushed the giggle down. That was a sure way to get myself blown up.

"I'm thankful you two were there to intervene. Otherwise, who knows what might have happened. Tess's treachery is not something I can forgive or forget." She sighed, as if the weight of the world were on her shoulders. "I view all the members here as my children. I suffer when one of them suffers. I feel their pain, as any mother would. Every word Tess said was like a barb in my heart. It's unjust and untrue. All I want is to give these people their fair shot at a majestic life, free from the shackles of banality and human-run power. And yet, I'm spurned for it."

Geez, you'd be the last on the list to win Mom of the Year.

"I mean to bring them peace and prosperity, but that comes at a price. It comes with blood and sweat and hard work. They would see it handed to them on a silver platter, but I'm not a believer in letting things come to me. I grab what I want by the balls and squeeze until I get it."

Nice image. I shuddered discreetly, and Finch did too.

"Your job can't come without its sacrifices, right?" he said, surprising me.

She nodded. "Exactly. I do what I have to do, in order to make this world a better place for my children."

Don't rise to it, Finch! I wanted to reach out and grab his hand, to forcibly pull him away from the trap he was edging toward. But if I'd done that, she would've known something was up. Instead, I had to sit there as the carrot dangled in front of him.

"What kind of sacrifices?" he pressed.

She shrugged. "All kinds. Sending teams into dangerous scenarios. Getting rid of people who've become weak. Severing ties to people who betray me. That sort of thing."

"Like putting your son on the front line? He's in Purgatory now, right?"

Oh, Finch...

Katherine sighed, and I could have sworn she'd managed to muster a tear. "Yes, he is, and not a day goes by that I don't worry about him. He did so much for me, and I can't get him out. I might take risks, but trying to break into Purgatory is too dangerous, even for me."

Funny, since you sent Kenneth in there to kill Finch. I held the words in, even though I was dying to scream them in her face. I glanced at Finch, praying he wasn't stupid enough to listen to her. He knew what she'd done. Surely, she didn't still have any kind of hold on him?

"Are you going to punish us for being in the library?" I cut in, eager to get this over with.

She shook her head. "You did me a favor. I've got no reason to punish you. But, I should warn you, if I find you in there again, I won't be so lenient. Two strikes are one more than I'm used to giving, though I can make an exception on this occasion."

"So we're free to go?" I almost heaved out a sigh of relief.

"You are."

"Thank you, Eris. We won't let you down." I scraped back my chair and made to leave, and Finch followed. He seemed quieter than normal, his expression confused. I needed to get him out of here, pronto, before Katherine could weave any of her motherly magic on him. With us being so close to the finish line, I wasn't about to take two steps back.

"Pieter?" Katherine's voice sliced through the room. *No...* We were almost out of here.

Finch turned. "Yes, Eris?"

"Could you stay behind a moment? I've got some tasks for you. With Tess locked up, I need someone to take over her duties, and I can't trust Kenneth to handle them. Would you mind? I'll need to run through them with you." She smiled sweetly, but I knew the devil lurked behind her innocent demeanor.

"Uh... sure."

"Do you want me to stay and help?" I couldn't leave here without Finch.

She shook her head. "That won't be necessary. It's a one-man job, and two would be overkill. You can go."

"Relax," Finch whispered. "Just do your thing and I'll meet you later. Look for the *light* and you'll work it out."

Look for the light? I remembered what he'd said about Lux and the secret entrance to the library, but he said he hadn't figured it out himself, so how was I supposed to?

I really didn't want to leave him here, but it wasn't like I could stomp my feet until she relented. Reluctantly, I stepped out of the room, hearing Katherine's words as the door closed behind me.

"You have a great future in this cult, for sure."

THIRTY-FIVE

Harley

The answer to Finch's riddle hit me as soon I stepped out of the Hexagon and into the bright daylight. A titan loomed over me, crafted in the image of Nyx, the goddess of Darkness. If I was thinking along the right lines, then I had to look for the stone giant that represented Lux.

Keeping my wits about me, I wandered around the outer perimeter of the Hexagon, looking for Lux. I found her, ten minutes later, towering over the rainforest with a torch in one hand and a golden apple in the other. It couldn't be a coincidence. The entrance to the library's secret door had to be around here somewhere, if I'd gotten it right. I scoured the surrounding area, but everything was tangled in thick vines and mossy undergrowth. It didn't look like anyone had come this way in a long time.

Remembering how overgrown the secret doorway into the Hexagon had been, I ventured toward the high wall and yanked at the creepers and vines growing there. Something in the plants irritated my skin, making me itch like nobody's business. Giving up on the normal way of doing things, I cast a look over my shoulder to make sure nobody was watching and launched a stream of Fire at the vines. They withered within seconds, revealing a hidden door in the wall, which lay in the shadow of Lux.

The rusty lock crumbled away in my hands as I tugged the door half off its hinges and slipped inside. Realizing that someone might see what I'd done, I peered back out and sent up a couple of shrubs with my Earth ability, covering the crooked doorway from any prying eyes. I hurried through the dark tunnel beyond, using a ball of Fire to light my way.

The labyrinth of secret tunnels seemed to go on forever, the walls slick with moisture and changing from claustrophobically narrow to wide and echoey. My footsteps ricocheted all around me, giving the impression that I was being followed. My heart hammered in my chest, getting worse each time I turned around to check, convinced that someone was going to jump out at me. Now and again, I caught the shimmering wisp of some moving creature sliding through the solid walls and drifting across the damp ground behind me.

I whirled around as I felt cold breath on my neck, but nobody was there. In the distance, faint whispers echoed, muffled and unclear. The voices were all around me, and yet nowhere near, all at once.

Okay, this is creepy. I'd like to get off this ghost train now.

I damn near crapped my pants when a face suddenly swept up in front of me, illuminated for a split second by the glow of the fireball. It sputtered out in my terror. That moment in the pitch darkness was the longest moment of my life, my hands shaking violently as I fought to make another fireball. The voices got louder as I struggled, the feeling of cold breath snaking across every part of my skin, setting the fine hairs on end.

Come on, come on, come on. With a burst of light, a new fireball rested in my palms. I'd expected to see a horde of ghoulish faces. Instead, there was nothing but empty tunnel, stretching away into the distance. Steeling myself, I hurried along.

As I rounded a corner, a glowing figure appeared in front of me. I staggered back from the phantom, clutching at my chest, my breath ragged. The spirit paused for a moment, staring at me with hollow eyes. It was hard to make the man out clearly, but he seemed to be wearing an old uniform, his hair swept back in an old fashion, his entire demeanor giving off some serious 1800s vibes.

With it being All Hallows' Eve tomorrow, it seemed like the spirits that died on the island were beginning to manifest. And not just the cult members who'd died here, but the spirits of the soldiers and criminals who'd taken their last breaths inside the walls of Fort Jefferson, too.

"Be wary where you tread," the ghost hissed. "A morsel like you. You might find yourself a corpse bride before the night is over."

"Not in the market for any underworld vacations right now, thanks," I whispered. All Hallows' Eve was the one night of the year when the dead could wander the earth. It didn't happen until midnight, but it looked like a few intrepid spirits had arrived early to the party.

"A morsel like you... a morsel like you... a morsel like you," the spirit repeated, as a wave of desire and regret hit me in the gut. The emotions were flooding off the spirit, overwhelming my senses.

The spirit floated straight through me, and my body shuddered with the cold. As I shook it off, I noticed that my arms weren't those of Volla Mazinov anymore. I grappled for my Ephemera and saw that the gem was fading fast. *Crap!* This wasn't the time for this thing to glitch.

Trying to keep my panic from overwhelming me, I focused on the internal pulse of the Shapeshifter energy and pushed it back through my body. To my relief, Volla's arms came back into view, covering mine. Praying it would last another couple of hours, I gritted my teeth and continued my trek through the bowels of the Hexagon. The island itself, I'd learned from Finch, was cursed, thanks to Drake Shipton's dealings with the darker side of magic. On All Hallows' Eve, the dead walked among the living, to the point where they could even take someone back with them if they were strong enough.

I jumped as another spirit drifted out of the walls, blocking my path, this one a young girl who stared at me with vacant eyes.

"Are you my mommy?" she murmured. The grief and loss coming

off this girl was agonizing. It stung me right in the heart, my eyes filling with tears.

"I'm sorry, I'm not," I replied.

"Would you like to be? I'm lonely." She swept up in my face, making me squeeze my eyes closed. Fear replaced her sorrow inside me. Could these things really drag me off to the other side? I really hoped not. I really, really hoped not.

"I'm not ready to be a mom. Sorry."

I opened my eyes a fraction, to find that she'd moved on, but it was enough to make me feel dizzy and breathless. These tunnels would have been scary enough without Casper and his pals slithering out at me. It was all I could do not to run back the way I came, leaving these spirits to it.

Pressing on, I focused on happier thoughts. Papa Legba might have tried to kill me, but he'd get to see Marie Laveau at midnight, too. All Hallows' Eve was their one night to be together, and it warmed my heart to think that the lovers would be reunited after a long year apart. It made me think of Wade, and all the things I would rather have been doing. One thing was for sure—if I managed to get out of this mess alive, he was going to need a whole bunch of new shirts.

After what felt like a lifetime, I arrived outside a door. It was locked, naturally, but that didn't bother me. The guards were standing outside the library; they wouldn't hear me break the lock, as long as I was very careful. Drawing a wisp of enhanced Telekinesis through my palm, I fed it into the lock, feeling out the mechanisms. A loud click followed. I pulled the lock off the bolt and slid it to one side, peering into the room beyond.

To my relief, I'd found the library.

Creeping out into the silent space, I walked up to the box where Katherine had locked Hester's spirit away. The power thrummed from whatever hex Katherine had put on it, but that wasn't going to stop me. *It's like picking a lock, remember?* I pushed my palms flat against the door of the box and felt for the hex. I almost flinched as it stung at my fingers, biting into my skin. Forcing my hands to stay where they were,

I started to feed my Chaos into the hex, just the way Finch had taught me. The pressure points pulsated beneath my fingertips, but it was way stronger than whatever Katherine had put on the door to the library.

Undeterred, I focused my mind and started to unpick the hex. I'd managed to break three of the four counterpoints, when a sudden rush of hot air made me open my eyes. I was staring right into the eyes of a gigantic wyvern, its dragon-like wings stretched out, casting a shadow over me. Its lungs heaved in a breath, its mouth opening as it unleashed a violent torrent of Fire. I instantly staggered back, sending up a shield of my own Fire to defend myself against the onslaught. The Fire bounced back against the glass box, snapping the last corner of the hex Katherine had put on it, while my hands throbbed from the heat of the box's hex.

Lifting my palms, I sent a huge spiral of Fire straight into the wyvern's mouth. The creature choked on the unexpected stream of liquid heat. With it distracted, I lunged for the box and yanked open the door, snatching the jar right out of the case and tucking it under my arm. The wyvern was bent over, retching a dark, sickly liquid onto the floor. *Sorry, pal.*

I'd just turned to head back to the tunnel, when I heard the library door open and footsteps enter. Glancing down the nearby aisle, I caught my reflection in one of the glass cases that were set up to display Katherine's treasures. I nearly screamed at the sight of my own face staring back. For the second time, my Shapeshifter ability had decided to glitch, and I didn't have the time to fix it. My real arms had already filtered through, my jacket all patchworked again, like it had been when I got pulled through the Strainer.

Crap, crap, crap! Running back to the doorway as silently as I could, I tried to feel for the strange pulse of the Shifter energy inside me, but it was gone. The clock had run out on my Ephemera-gifted ability.

Making it to the door, I closed it as quietly as possible behind me and took off down the tunnel, sending a shiver of Earth energy back. Rocks rumbled as they shot up from the ground, creating a barricade between me and the door, that choking wyvern, and whoever was wandering about inside the library. There'd been no time to look, not now that I had the jar.

Juggling the spirit jar, I reached up to my Krieger-morphed pendant and pressed down three times, as hard as I could, to signal to Wade and Isadora that I needed extracting. As soon as they came for me, I swore we'd go and find Finch and get him out of here, too. It'd have to wait until he was done with Katherine, but that was better than being caught with Hester's spirit in my hands.

I started to panic when nothing happened. I was pressing the pendant like a crazy person, but there were no portals, no Wade, no Isadora, no nothing. *Maybe I need to be out in the open?* It seemed like a valid reason, what with me being stuck in a tunnel, but the opposite end of this labyrinth was ages away. And the ghosts were getting louder, their voices rising to a howl as I ran for my life. They burst out of the walls, lunging at me, their phantom hands clawing at my skin and making my flesh turn to goosebumps. They blocked my view of the path ahead.

I stumbled as two ghostly palms shoved me in the chest, knocking me back.

"What the heck?" This shouldn't have been happening. It wasn't All Hallows' Eve yet. Fear pounded through my veins, riding a wave of terrified adrenaline.

Finding my feet again, I tried to push through the hordes of spirits crowding the tunnels. Up ahead, I noticed one ghost standing apart from the others. He glowered at me, as if he knew who I was and hated my guts. I didn't recognize him, but that didn't matter right now. The ghost had opened his mouth wide, preparing to scream, no doubt to reveal that I was here, in the tunnels.

With no cards left to play, my fingers scrabbled at the lid of my mother's jar and twisted it off, releasing her in a swirling mist. If these spooks had some extra energy, thanks to the island, then it stood to reason that my mother would, too.

"Help me, Mom! Help me!" I begged.

From the vapor, limbs formed, and then a head, so familiar and yet so totally new and strange to me. I'd only seen her in photographs, but those pictures hadn't done any justice to her beauty. However, I didn't have much chance to admire her, as she raised her hands and whispered something into the ether.

"*Et abiit, ex inferis spirituum. Quam tibi debitum reditus tempus enim. Sit legibus alligatus huius regni. Ne molestum nobis iterum!*"

In the space of a second, the ghosts withdrew, dissipating into the darkness like fog rolling away from a morning field. I almost collapsed with gratitude.

"Thank you," I whispered.

Slowly, my mother turned to face me, her eyes sad. "Oh, honey... I know this sounds awful, but I was hoping I wouldn't see you here."

THIRTY-SIX

Harley

"What do you mean?" Her words hit me like a freight train. Wasn't she happy to see me? I blinked hard, still shocked that I was actually *seeing* her and talking to her—the mom I'd never known.

She smiled. "You've put yourself in a world of danger to be here. I had a horrible feeling that you'd come, and I was helpless to stop it. I would rather have gone on for a thousand years, trapped in this existence, than have you risk your life to come to this place."

"I had to."

"I know you did, honey. It's in your nature. I've heard Katherine talking about you, and I knew you would have to follow your heart and do something like this, to stop her from achieving her goal. I just wish there might've been another way. One that didn't put my daughter's life on the line."

"Is it bad to say that it was worth it, just to see you?" Tears choked my throat as I looked up at my mom for the very first time since she gave birth to me. This moment had been nineteen years in the making, and I still wasn't ready. Love and grief radiated out of her like a furnace, overwhelming my own emotions.

"I'd say the same, if I knew that you'd be safe," she replied, with a sad chuckle. "I never envied Katherine for anything when I was alive, but I envy her for having the chance to see you all grown up. She stole my life, and she stole every second I might've had to watch you grow. I've been trapped here, neither living nor dead, unable to cross over. And every day, every minute, every second, I've thought of you. I've thought of the young woman you've become, and I've hoped, with all my heart, for you to be happy." She reached out a ghostly hand. I reached back, my fingertips drifting through hers.

Just let me touch her. Just let me hold her hand. Just let me hug her. Tears fell from my eyes as I tried again and again, unable to make contact of any kind. I'd never hold her; I'd never feel her arms around me, hugging me tight; I'd never get to do all those things that had been stolen from me, too.

"This isn't fair," I murmured, trying to brush my tears away. It was useless—more came, trickling down my cheeks in an endless stream. A painful sob racked my chest as I struggled to come to terms with this harsh reality. I wanted my mom. I wanted her to be alive and breathing, with solid arms and solid skin. I wanted everything I'd never had. If I could have found a spell to turn back this whole world nineteen years, I'd have done it in a heartbeat, just to be able to look into my mom's eyes and have her pull me close.

"I know, sweetheart."

"Why didn't he save you?" I was weeping properly now, unable to stop the tears and the sobs from rising up my throat.

"Who?"

"Dad. Why didn't he save you?" Bitterness lingered in my voice. "Why did he kill you instead of saving you? He fought the curse off when it came to me, so why not you? I don't understand how he could do that—how he could see you and not know that he had to stop."

Her wispy hands sailed right through my shoulders, leaving a chill. I'd never know how warm she was, in real life. This was all I got, and I had to remind myself to be grateful. I could have gone on for the rest of my life without even seeing her, but at least I had this moment.

"Don't blame your father, Harley. He did what he could to try and stop himself, but she was too strong. That curse she used on him was too powerful," she said, her tone desperately sad. "He managed to save you because Katherine wasn't there at the time. She didn't know anything about you, and Hiram used that opportunity to take you away while she was busy elsewhere."

"Was Katherine there when he… when he killed you?" I asked.

My mom nodded. "His proximity to her meant he couldn't fight off the curse. She was the source, and she was in the room when it happened. She trapped my spirit as soon as Hiram killed me, because she was hiding in the shadows."

"Why didn't she kill you herself? If she hated you so much, why didn't she—" My voice broke.

She gave me a sympathetic smile. "It was precisely because she hated me so much that she wanted to watch me die at the hands of the person I loved most. And she wanted to punish me, even after I was gone."

"I'll rip her freaking head off." I wanted to use much stronger language, but this was my mom. I didn't want to give her a bad impression of the woman I'd become.

She chuckled sadly. "You are strong, Harley, stronger than any of us who've gone before you. I suppose I knew you'd be extraordinary, even before you were born. I thought it was just a mother's pride, you know, thinking my child was better than everyone else's. But you are. You're strong and fierce and kind and good, and that's all I could've asked for."

"I've missed you so much." I choked on the words, my vision blurry. "Every day, I wondered what I'd done wrong, to get dropped at some orphanage. But, even then, I missed you. I didn't know who you were, but I missed you so much. It was like a huge hole in my heart that I couldn't fill up. And then, I found out who you were, and what had happened, and that hole got so much bigger. I knew I'd never be able to fill it up, because you'd been taken from me, and you were never coming back from that. What made it worse was the fact that I knew, after all that time, that I'd actually been loved. I'd spent so long thinking nobody loved me and nobody cared, but that wasn't the truth at all." I sank to the ground, struggling to breathe. It felt like I was having an all-out panic attack. My chest had seized up, my heart pounding, my throat narrow.

"Oh, Harley." Her voice made it all the more painful. I could feel the agony flowing away from her, wrapping around my heart, squeezing the air out of my lungs. This was so much harder than I'd ever imagined. "If I could have changed it all, I would've. If I could've killed Katherine, or stopped her in some way, I would've done everything in my power to do that. But know this: you've always been loved, even though it had to be from afar. You've always been right here, every day of your life." She pressed her wispy hand to her breast, her face so sad that it broke me all over again.

"Then why did you let him kill you? Why didn't you fight?" The tears kept flowing down my face.

"I didn't have the strength to fight him," she replied. "I'd given birth to you, and I'd hidden you away. I had nothing left to give. But, even when he killed me, I knew he didn't want to. I could see it in his eyes as he held my gaze, right up until the last moment. He was crying when it happened, and his hands were shaking, as if he was trying to fight back. If she hadn't been there, he would have defeated that curse. He loved me, and he loved you, and he loved the world we'd created together. He'd been so excited about meeting you, and he used to talk all the time about what we'd be like as a family. It was all he'd ever wanted."

"Then why did he leave me?" All of my insecurities were bubbling to the surface.

"To save you, sweetheart. You know that. He had to, so that you could live. If Katherine had ever found out about you while you were a child, she would've murdered you. He had no choice. He loved you so much. He used to press his ear to my belly while you were growing and sing to you, and tell you all the things he was going to buy you, and all the things you were going to do together as you grew up."

I held my head in my hands. "He could've found a way to break Katherine's spell."

"I know this is hard for you, but you can't blame him," she urged, her phantom hands drifting through me again. This time, I felt the cold echo of her touch on my cheek. "He loved you. We both loved you with all our hearts. I remember looking down at you when you were first born. Even then, you were a determined little thing. You had this scowl on your face, and it made me laugh so hard. I didn't get a long time with you, but I savored every moment. I kissed you all over your pudgy little face and munched your little hands and held you so tight. I remember you falling asleep on my chest, listening to my heartbeat. That's the memory I've kept the closest, all these years."

"I wish we'd had longer," I murmured.

"Me, too. More than anything."

"Did you know I'd be like this?" I looked up at her, my muscles relaxing slightly, at least enough to drag in a decent lungful of air.

"What do you mean?"

"Did you know I'd be powerful like this?"

She smiled. "We weren't sure. Given our heritage, I presumed you'd be special, but there was always the chance that my side and Hiram's would counteract each other and you'd end up either Mediocre or magicless."

"I'd still have come here, to find you."

"I know you would've, honey. That's the woman you've become." She paused for a moment. "There's just one thing that troubles me."

"What's that?"

She sighed. "I can sense the conflict in you, between Light and Dark. You've been having some problems with it, I'm guessing?"

"That's putting it mildly." I managed a wry chuckle.

"The thing is, when it comes to your Darkness, you'll always have trouble taming it. Even without the Light competing for power, you'd have had problems controlling it. That's always been the way with the Shipton family," she explained. "The secret to getting it to do what you want, when you want, is to feed it when it demands feeding."

"That explains all of the wild things I've been doing lately." Controlling Purge beasts, for one.

She nodded. "If you don't feed it, it'll fight to gain control. And if you're not careful, it can end up controlling you. My sister is the perfect example. Although, with her, it's more a case of overfeeding."

I was about to ask for more information when a portal tore open in front of me, blasting me with a rush of cold air. Isadora staggered through the hole a moment later, looking pale and exhausted. She barely acknowledged Hester's spirit as she stooped to catch her breath.

"Isadora, what's wrong?" I jumped up, hurrying toward her.

She looked up at me with worried eyes. "We've got a problem."

Too right we did. Finch was alone in an office with his mother, and there was every chance that he'd snap and reveal himself. Or worse, that Katherine would be able to get him back on the cultist train. She'd done it before, and despite the progress Finch had made, there was still that lost little boy in him who was just desperate to have a mother.

THIRTY-SEVEN

Finch

"So, you see the colossal mess Tess has left me in?" Katherine said. She'd been yakking on about Tess's responsibilities for the last half hour. Tess had had her hands full, that was for sure. The list of responsibilities was as long as my arm, and to be honest, I'd already forgotten half of them. I just had to make sure it looked like I was listening. Playing the role of Pieter Mazinov to Oscar-worthy perfection.

"Quite the stink, yeah."

Katherine nodded. "Now, let's get down to the important stuff. All these duties are secondary to the third ritual, which I need to get off the ground ASAP. Tartarus is going to be a bitch, I won't sugarcoat it. It's Erebus's domain, so it was never going to be a picnic. It's just irritating, because I was relying on Tess to get everything ready for our Bestiary snatch so we could get going with the fourth ritual as soon as this one's over. I need Echidna, and the Bestiary has Echidna, but now I've lost my way in, so to speak. Ergo, I'm in a bit of a fix, which is where you come in. I knew Electros were tricky, but this takes the cake."

The great and mighty Oz has no other solutions? You disappoint me, Mother.

"Don't you have a backup plan?"

She smiled. "Of course I've got other solutions. Not that I'm against advice, if you've got any pearls of wisdom to hurl my way?"

My blood was boiling. This was the longest I'd been alone in a room with Katherine since before I got shuffled off to Purgatory, so focus was proving difficult. All I could think about were a million ways to kill her and remove the evidence, before anyone even knew she was dead.

"I'm as stumped as you. I'd need to know more details," I replied.

"If you needed to break into a Bestiary, how would you do it?"

I shrugged. "I might use a Gemini device, if I had one. They can work pretty well, and you don't necessarily need to put them somewhere yourself. You can have someone else do it and trigger the other end from the outside." I figured it was a relatively innocent answer to give. Katherine would just assume someone in the cult had told me about it.

Her eyes widened suddenly. "A Gemini device?"

"Yeah, they're not too hard to get ahold of."

"You've used one before?"

"We were taught about them by the secret services. Same way I learned how to use that replay spell."

She paused. "But, you know, those replay spells aren't always accurate. They can be manipulated, if the user is skilled enough, right?"

What was she getting at?

"I wouldn't know. I've always thought they were dead on. Not much you can do to doctor them."

She smiled. "No, I suppose not. You must've been around a lot of great magicals in St. Petersburg?"

"A few."

"Name some for me," she said.

"Konstantin Rasputin, for one. Marina Skoptsy. Zlatan Selivanov. They all moved in our circles." I had to think fast on my feet.

"Noble company indeed. I've been trying to get Konstantin for years."

I chuckled. "He's evasive. Comes with the territory, I guess."

"So, humor me again for a moment—how would you do it?" she asked.

"Huh? You mean break into the Bestiary?"

She shook her head slowly. "No, I mean how would you kill me, if you had the chance?"

I froze. "What do you mean? I don't want to kill you." *There it is, boys and girls, the biggest lie I've ever told.*

She laughed wildly. "Oh, come on, how long are you going to keep up this charade, Finch? Don't get me wrong, you're doing an excellent job, but it's getting a little tiresome. You should have gone a bit more 'method' if you really wanted to convince me. You know, *really* embody Pieter Mazinov instead of making simple, Finch-like mistakes."

"I don't know what you're talking about. I am Pieter Mazinov."

"And I'm the Queen of England." She smirked at me, and I knew it was hopeless. She knew, beyond all doubt. "You know, I've been wondering if I should get myself a proper crown. What do you think? Too much?"

"It wouldn't fit on your fat head," I sniped back. It was childish, but I needed to say something while I fought to come up with the quickest exit plan ever. Trying to talk my way out wasn't an option. Sweat was already pouring down my face. My heart was racing wildly. *Come on, Finch—think!* My eyes glanced toward the door. There were guards lining the hallway outside, but I figured I had worse odds if I stayed in here, with her.

She chuckled. "Ah, Finch. Believe it or not, I've missed you."

"Yeah? I doubt that. You tried to have me killed, remember?" I peered over her shoulder at the aquariums and wondered if I could break them and distract Katherine. There were a bunch of amphibious monsters in there that wouldn't have minded a taste of her.

"Don't you want to know how I knew? I bet you're dying to."

I glowered at her. "Even if I don't, you're going to tell me anyway."

Moving away from the tanks, I fixed my eyes on a large plant pot on the back shelf. With my hands under the table, I sent out fine tendrils and lashed them around the base. One swift knock to the back of the head and I'd be able to buy myself some time.

"To see the look on your precious little face? Absolutely." She grinned like a maniac. "I figured out it was you the moment you mentioned the Gemini device. A silly move, even for you. It wasn't hard to put two and two together based on that. Only two people knew about that device, and they're harder to come by than you'd think. Plus, those two people were under strict instructions to keep that failure to themselves. They wouldn't have mentioned it to you, under any circumstances. It all started making sense. Coincidental, is it not, that you *happened* to stumble across Naima and grab her attention? And that all these doors *happened* to be open? I confess, I should've figured it out sooner. I guess I've gone soft."

I snorted. "You're about as soft as a block of granite." The plant pot edged forward.

"Anyway, I should've known it was you when you sold Tess out like that. You were merciless, just the way Momma taught you." She chuckled to herself. "And I know a lot more than you think. I knew Garrett Kyteler was feeding the SDC information from the National Council. So, if the SDC knew about Azarius, then so did Harley. That girl can't help herself. What can I say? She's obsessed with me." She took out her phone, her fingers dancing across the screen. I didn't know who she was messaging or what she was saying, but I knew it couldn't be good.

I didn't know whether to be shocked or disappointed. We'd come so far, only to end up like this. *Maybe I should've stayed in my cell.*

"You were born merciless. You killed Adley just to get back at me, because you thought she'd somehow bend my loyalty. If you'd left her alone, I probably wouldn't even be here. She had nothing to do with this! You murdered her, in cold blood, and for what? To prove you could? Because I loved her more than you? Which sick part of your Freudian brand of crazy is it, huh?" I brought the plant pot to the very lip of the shelf, trying to keep Katherine distracted before I struck. Not that I didn't mean what I was saying. I meant every word.

She rolled her eyes. "You're not still pouting over that, are you?"

"You were born cold. You were born without a heart. Funny thing is, you left me with one—I guess I got that from Daddy Merlin, right? Ironic, isn't it, that the man you hated the most in this world gave me the one thing you couldn't? A freaking conscience!" I snapped. "When you murdered her, you made me see how much I loved her. How much my heart had felt, and how much it wanted to feel. You tore it to shreds, Katherine. You brought me to this!" I dragged the pot off the shelf, aiming for her head.

She shot her hand back, the plant pot exploding. "What were you going to do, Finch? Brain me?" She chuckled. "You know how I hate being interrupted while I'm soliloquizing, and I was just coming up with something good. Now, where was I? Oh yes—Harley. Little Volla is going to have her head on the chopping block. Naturally, I'll make you watch. I've still got that Sal Vínna spell around here somewhere. I might make an obedient son out of you yet. Plus, it'll be so much easier this time. Two people to kill instead of… I don't even know, I lost count after the first few."

I stared at Katherine as if I could somehow melt her flesh from her body, just by glowering hard enough. "You leave her out of this." The words slipped out before I could stop them.

She sneered. "Ah, so you're the one who's really gone soft?"

"Shut up."

"Wow, snappy retort. I guess you didn't gain the gift of banter from me, either," she muttered, casually eyeing her phone for a moment. "Now, come on, take off that stupid disguise. I'd like to look my son in the eyes. My beloved boy. Apple of my eye. Fruit of my loins."

I shifted into my real body, not for her sake but for my own. With all this anger bubbling inside me, it was getting hard to manage the Pieter Mazinov disguise.

"There he is! How handsome!" She laughed coldly.

I smirked. "You might know who I am, but it doesn't matter now.

You're too late. That little mind of yours that you pride yourself on was too slow. Harley has Hester's spirit by now. She'll have escaped, and you'll never get that spirit back."

Katherine grinned. "Naima already knows about our runaway and has dispatched teams to intervene. Although, the spirits of All Hallows' Eve will probably be more useful right now. So, if you're talking about the tunnels, the ghosts know who their mistress is. They'll bring her here so I can kill her, and she'll be out of my hair for good. Wouldn't that be nice? I could do with some peace and quiet. Plus, this way, I'll never have to hear about a Merlin ever again. Bliss."

I balled my hands into fists. "I thought you needed Harley. You wouldn't kill her. You're all talk."

"I don't want her dead, per se, but there are plenty of things far worse than death, Finch. And I'll get to killing her, eventually. Just thinking about it gives me a buzz. I almost killed her the last time we met, which was a bit of an impulse on my part. But I've gone back to my original plan, now. There's so much power in that girl. It's tantalizing." She licked her lips. "She'll be perfect for me, when the time comes."

"Looks like you just want her dead to me. Another notch on your weird old bedpost of death."

She pulled a face. "Terrible metaphor, Finch. Come on, you can do better than that. Anyway, the fact of the matter is, I want you to come back to the cult. Yes, I tried to kill you. Yes, I had your sap of a girlfriend killed. And yes, you're probably a bit peeved. But focus on the bigger picture here. Whether you like it or not, I will win. It's up to you which side you want to be on when that happens."

"Are you out of your freaking mind?" I hissed. Of course she was. She always had been. My body was itching to hurl something at her, to inflict as much pain as possible on her. I didn't care if she thought she'd win. There was no way we'd let her. Even if I died here, Harley already had the spirit. I was certain of it. And, once it was released, Katherine would be laughing on the other side of her face.

"What if I could offer you something you couldn't refuse?"

I snorted. "Unlikely."

"How about Adley, back from the dead?"

I gaped at her. "Wh-What?"

"If you come back to my side and promise to be loyal, I'll bring Adley back from the dead. I'm in the process of recruiting a shiny new Necromancer—a good one, at that. Very powerful. If you come back to me, we can get Adley's body from the spot where she's buried and bring her right back. Given the way she died, they'll have put an anti-decomposition spell on her, in case they need to exhume her for any reason. She'll be fresh as a daisy, but she won't be pushing them up anymore. You can have her back. Promise I won't get jealous." She grinned. "All you have to do is say the word, and you don't have to hurt anymore. You can put that heart you're so proud of right back together again."

"You couldn't do it even if you wanted to," I replied, though I had to give her props for her approach. It'd come out of left field, and man, it was tempting.

If she could really do that... would it be worth switching sides for? Adley was the only person who'd ever cared about me. If I could just hold her in my arms again... Weren't you supposed to do everything for love, no matter what the cost?

"I could, and I can. I brought your great-grandfather back, didn't I? Yes, it got messed up, but I won't let that happen to Adley. Call it my way of making amends. But, in return, you have to come back to the fold. You and Adley both." She paused. "Look, I know you're annoyed with me about all of these murders and attempted murders, but the truth is, I wasn't comfortable with having you killed in the first place. Try and see things from my point of view—I didn't have a choice. You were a security threat, and I had to do whatever I thought was best. I didn't actually want you dead. Do you really think I'm that heartless?"

I was about to spit the answer in her face, but the old witch kept talking.

"And, before you answer with a snarky 'yes,' you should know that you were all I ever wanted. You were my prodigy and my legacy, and I loved you more than anything. I still do, in fact, which is why I'm willing to offer you Adley in return for your continued presence at my side. That's why you're still sitting here. I sent someone to kill you because I was a coward, and I couldn't do it myself. I wouldn't have been able to. But I only did that because *you* tried to betray *me* first. You were preparing to give up secrets. With so much at stake, tell me what else I could have done?" She looked at me with mournful eyes. All fake, of course. She didn't know what it meant to be mournful. She'd never shed a tear for anyone in her whole life.

"*Not* kill Adley. *Not* kill me. Leave me to rot in Purgatory. That's what you were going to do anyway, right? I didn't see any wrecking balls bringing down the walls of my cell."

"I regret doing it, if it makes you feel any better."

I gave her a deadpan look.

Katherine sighed. "Here's the heart of the matter: you made the first move, and I was forced to retaliate. I didn't want to, but you *made* me. If you'd kept your mouth shut, I would've come for you when all of this was over and put you back at my side. In fact, that's what I want to do now, since Harley sprang you out of Purgatory for me." She leaned over the desk, and I instinctively leaned farther back in the chair. "You know me, Finch. You know that I'll get Hester's spirit and consume it, and you know I'll complete the other trials, too. I'm always one step ahead. It took me, what, half an hour to sever your escape plans? And I'll keep doing it, until these rituals are complete. I won't be stopped. But that doesn't mean you have to lose. You can win, too. Just swap sides again. You can have everything you've ever wanted. Adley's right there for the taking, but you have to be bold enough to make the move."

I hesitated. I actually hesitated. She was offering up so much, and she was right—all I had to do was say the word.

But what about Harley? She wouldn't have understood. She still had her Wonderboy, alive and kicking. She was loved. She had friends. What did I have? Suspicion and doubt around every corner, from everyone I met. Adley would fix that. Adley would look at me again, with those eyes, and make everything better.

"Just say the word…" Katherine smiled, toying with the fountain pen on the desk. Was that what she'd make me use to sign this contract? Or would she ask for it in blood?

"You really think you've found a Necromancer who's powerful enough?" I hated myself for asking, but the thought of Adley, dead and alone in a tomb for all eternity, was worse.

"I have." Her eyes were bright. She knew she had me on some impossible ropes.

Have you completely lost it? The logical side of my mind was warring with the emotional side. If I did this, if I agreed to Katherine's terms, there'd be no going back. Harley would never forgive me. She'd never look at me the same way again. She'd hate me. They all would. Worse still, they'd all have been right about me.

"I'd rather see her die a thousand times than let you have what you want," I said, tears in my eyes. I tried to lurch forward in my chair, but she pushed me right back with a wave of Telekinesis. Behind the aquarium panels, the creatures were going crazy, drawn by Katherine's power.

Her body was almost crackling with the conviction of her words. Her promise that she could bring Adley back. She was manifesting it into the truth. And, the scary thing was, I believed her. She had such certainty in her voice that it was impossible not to.

But that didn't mean I was ready to turn tail, in spite of what she was offering. Harley had opened my eyes. She'd made me see that Katherine was vulnerable. And maybe, just maybe, that meant she wouldn't win—even if it meant losing my chance of getting Adley back. I didn't know if even I could be that selfish.

"Kenneth, can you bring the prisoner in?" Katherine called out.

I turned around in surprise, half expecting to see Harley in chains. Instead, I got the shock of my life: Wade Crowley. Kenneth was dragging Wade Crowley along in Atomic Cuffs. And, by the looks of it, Kenneth had gotten in a couple of good punches first. Although, knowing Kenneth, he'd done that *after* Wade had been clapped in irons.

"That's not possible." I almost choked on the words.

Katherine smiled. "You should never underestimate my determination, Finch. I've always got backup plans. Even my backup plans have backup plans. See, I always win, one way or another."

Harley wouldn't do a thing while Wade was here as Katherine's prisoner. My mother had gone straight for the jugular on this one. And I was utterly speechless. Harley didn't have my merciless streak. Even if it meant the world collapsed, Harley wouldn't leave here without Wade.

So, what are you going to do? I had two options: surrender, or do something insane. Right now, the pendulum was swinging to either side. How *could* I argue with Katherine's logic? She kept getting what she wanted. The evidence was irrefutable.

As I was about to make my decision, the door burst open and Naima rushed in. She was breathless, which was no mean feat for a supercharged Purge beast. "She has escaped, Eris. Harley has gone. We cannot find her."

I turned around in time to see Katherine's expression shift into one of shock as she got to her feet in a rush. "How could this happen? The spirits… they were loose! They should have restrained her by now!"

I grinned in spite of myself. *And you shouldn't underestimate the determination of Harley freaking Merlin!*

Naima bowed her head in shame. "Something occurred within the tunnels, Eris. The spirits were all hiding, and they were scared. They were cowering in the crevices."

"What's the matter, Katherine? Don't you have a backup for that?" I jeered.

Her face was a picture of fury. But then, just as swiftly, it morphed into something else. A smug grin that I wanted to swipe off. "It isn't over yet, Finch. Not by a long shot." She looked toward Kenneth as she hurried for the door. "Kenneth, cuff Finch and watch over him and Wade until I return. I've got something I need to take care of." Despite her urgency, she paused. "Oh, and Naima, I suggest you find a way to make up for this colossal screw-up. Otherwise, blood, guts, nasty spells, etcetera, etcetera."

Naima bowed even lower. "Yes, Eris. I will."

"You see, Finch? Your sister left you here. She got what she wanted, and she left you here. If anyone is using people, it's Harley Merlin. You and Wade were just the stooges." She sneered at me.

I smirked. "Go screw yourself, Mother. I'd rather die a stooge than be a vessel for your selfishness. I will *never* forgive you for what you did. Any of it."

Katherine shrugged. "Fine, suit yourself. You can rot here with Harley's Knight in Aluminum Foil."

Wade flashed me a desperate look as Kenneth tugged roughly on his Cuffs. What did he want me to do? Katherine swept out of the room without another word, and I found I didn't care. Ol' Kenneth might have managed to capture Wade, but there was no sign of Isadora. Which meant one thing: Harley had a way off the island.

THIRTY-EIGHT

Harley

I staggered out of Isadora's portal with my mother's jar clutched to
my chest. She'd gone back inside for now, as it wasn't safe for her
to be freed inside the tunnels where the weird pull of All Hallows' Eve
was at its strongest. I had to resist the urge to tear the lid right off, just
so I could see her again. Isadora hadn't told me what had gone wrong
yet, but I was surprised to find that we were still on the island. I'd
expected to end up at the SDC. Instead, we'd landed near the titan that
housed Naima's Bestiary, Isadora's portal crackling and snapping like it
was having a hard time holding. It evaporated a moment later with a
rush of air, leaving behind a worrying puff of black smoke.

"What's going on?" I asked her outright. "Is there something wrong
with your portals?"

Isadora shook her head. "It's this place. It's messing with my energy." She took a shaky breath. "As for what's going on... Katherine has
Wade."

"*What?*" I tried to stay calm. Katherine had Wade, but that was okay
—we could go back for him, right? We could get him out of this mess.
Finch, too. I wasn't leaving without them.

"Wade and I felt you press your end of the rescue button, and we headed straight through a portal to the location it gave. Only, it wasn't quite as precise as we'd hoped. We portaled in right beside this room with a bunch of guards outside. We were ambushed instantly. Wade got caught by Kenneth, but I managed to escape through another portal. I tried to grab him, but Kenneth had already hauled him off, and Wade shouted at me to find you."

"Wade sent you to find me?" That was Wade all over, putting my safety above his own.

"I managed to MacGyver the rescue button a little to get clearer coordinates, which is when I found you in that tunnel. It's this place, this compound, this island, Harley—it's tricky, and that's all I can say without swearing my head off. There's something wrong with this whole setup."

"It probably has something to do with all the curses and protection stuff Katherine's got hidden all around the island," I said, forcing myself to keep a level head. "She's probably got a few added tricks to throw a Portal Opener for a loop, too, just in case the island gets discovered."

Isadora nodded. "You could be right. My portals haven't acted like that since I was a teenager."

"It's this way back to the Hexagon. We can run there and take out the guards as we see them, since I don't have my disguise anymore." I moved to go, but Isadora grasped my wrist, pulling me back.

"You can't go and get him, Harley." She stared at me. "That's exactly what Katherine is counting on. I know you're worried, but you can't rush headlong into this. Katherine thinks she knows you, so you have to do everything in your power to do the opposite of what she's expecting."

I shook my head, gritting my teeth. "I'm not leaving him there, Isadora. Katherine will kill him out of spite, you know she will."

"I'm not saying leave him there—I'm just saying Katherine is probably waiting for you to come charging in so she can demand something in return for his safety. Your life, most likely. It's a trap."

"So what am I supposed to do?" I hung my head, completely torn.

The guy I loved was with Katherine right now, getting who knew what done to him, and I was here, unable to help him.

Isadora loosened her grip on my wrist and took my hand in hers. "I think you know what you have to do, Harley." She glanced down at the jar in the crook of my arm.

No... I knew this had been the goal all along, but now that the moment had come, I didn't know if I could do it. Even in spirit form, she was my mom. I didn't want to have to say goodbye to her. But what else was I going to do? Keep her in a jar like Katherine and whip her out whenever I felt sad? I shuddered, remembering the glass coffin with the shriveled raisin of Drake Shipton inside it. If I kept hold of my mom's spirit and didn't release her, I'd be no better.

Tears filled my eyes. We were supposed to be off this freaking island by now, but we were still here, and things were getting worse by the second. But freeing my mom... This was the one thing I had left in my power. The one thing that would make whatever happened to us worth it. *And hey, you might join her sooner than you think. Silver linings...*

With a painful sob racking my chest, I unscrewed the lid of the soul jar and threw it to the ground. My mother's spirit swirled out, stretching into the ghost I'd seen before, in the tunnel.

"You're so brave, honey," she said, her gauzy hands drifting through my face.

"I don't feel very brave right now." I noticed that Isadora had stood off to one side, to give my mom and me a moment.

"I know, sweetheart. I know this is hard for you, but it's not easy for me, either. I'd stay by your side if I could, but if I do that, then it means Katherine will always have a way of completing the third ritual."

I nodded slowly. "I know."

"You have to let me go now, honey."

"I know... but this is going to hurt like a bitch."

She chuckled. "Language."

"Sorry. It is, though."

"Merlins don't hide from a challenge, no matter how tough it might be," she whispered. "And if the legends about soulmates being together in the afterlife are true, then I've got a hunky slice of husband waiting for me on the other side."

I choked out a sad laugh. "Mom."

"This doesn't mean I'll be gone, Harley. I've always been with you, and you've always been with me. That won't change just because my spirit isn't tied to this world anymore. I'll be able to watch you properly, wherever I am. As long as you keep your father and me in your heart, we aren't going anywhere. We'll live on because you remember us."

"I just wish we had more time." Tears trickled down my cheeks, and my heart felt like it was about to shatter into a million pieces. Pieces I'd never be able to put back together again.

"So do I, sweetheart. So do I." Her eyes turned sad. "Just promise me you'll live a good life, okay? Promise me you'll be happy. As happy as you can possibly be. Take pleasure in every tiny thing, even if it's just Christmas lights, or fireworks on the Fourth of July, or the best damn pancakes you've ever eaten. And remember what I said about your Darkness. That way, I know you'll be okay."

"You really have to go, huh?" I dropped my chin to my chest.

"I really do, but only because it's the natural order of things. I died, and I should've crossed over, but Katherine stopped me. This is how it's supposed to be, as hard as it is. I'm just glad I got to see you, at last, and that I got to talk to you, even if it was just for a short time. That's a gift I never expected to get. I might not like the circumstances, but I can't deny that I'm grateful."

I nodded. "Me, too."

"I love you, Harley."

"I love you, too." I sobbed out the words, my body shaking violently.

"Be happy, sweetheart. Find love, find the best friends you can, find all the good stuff in this world and surround yourself with it. Don't be sad, and don't feel like you're on your own. I've been stuffed in a jar for nineteen years, but I've never moved from your side. I'll still be there, I promise. Look for all that good stuff, like I said, and you'll find me and your dad, too."

My heart felt like it'd been turned inside out. "I miss you."

"I miss you, sweetheart. So much."

"Be happy too, okay? Give Dad a kiss when you see him, but nothing too gross. And tell him... tell him I forgive him," I rasped out the words, fighting for breath.

"I will. And, Isadora, thank you for taking care of her." She began to disintegrate in front of my eyes, and it took every scrap of strength I had not to try and reach out with my Telekinesis and bind her to this world forever. I wouldn't do that, not to her. My Darkness wasn't getting fed this time.

"It was the least I could do," Isadora choked out, brushing tears from her eyes.

"I love you!" I ran toward what remained of my mom, reaching out to touch the last, faint tendrils of her spirit.

"I love you, more than you know." She evaporated, her voice whispering one last sentence on the breeze. "You were the best thing that ever happened to us."

I sank to the ground on all fours, dragging air into my lungs like I'd almost drowned. I had to get myself together, but how was I supposed to do that when it felt like I'd been torn apart? I closed my eyes and focused on Wade, using the Euphoria technique to shift my concentration. He needed my help now, or I'd be saying a gut-wrenching farewell to him, too.

I couldn't change what had happened to my mom. I couldn't bring her back to life. This was the way it had to be, and by letting her go, I'd wrecked Katherine's plans to complete the third ritual. We'd stopped her, my mom and I. Hester had been a badass to the end.

You're not getting the last laugh this time, Katherine.

Slowly, I hauled myself back up and dusted the grass from my jeans, before turning to a silent Isadora. "We need to get Wade and Finch out of there."

"Are you okay? Are you sure you don't need another minute?" There were tears in her eyes again, making me realize that couldn't have been easy for her, either. That had been her sister-in-law.

I shook my head. "I'll be fine. I need to focus on Wade and Finch right now. I can mourn my mom when we're back at the SDC and Katherine is dead. Then, and only then, will this make any sense."

Yeah, I'd stopped Katherine's ritual, but two of the most important men in my life were still trapped in the dragon's lair, and my Ephemera-given power was all out of juice. I had no idea what was going to happen next, but, until all of this was over, and I could retreat into my bedroom and cry my eyes out until I had nothing left, I wouldn't shed another tear. That wasn't what my mom would have wanted.

"Well, we need to think rationally before we do anything," Isadora said.

I nodded. "You're right. We need a plan. A good one."

THIRTY-NINE

Finch

"I bet you didn't think we'd catch you, did you?" Kenneth said smugly, pacing between the two chairs where Wade and I sat. I watched Wade closely as Kenneth brushed past him. He reached up discreetly, his wrists still locked together with Atomic Cuffs, dislodging something from Kenneth's belt and covering it with his palms.

"Wasn't exactly a fair fight," Wade muttered. An idea came to me. Kenneth was in peacock mode, and he was the only one in the room with us. The aquarium beasts had swum away, with nothing left to interest them, leaving just the three of us—Wade, Kenneth, and little old me. Two against one was a slightly fairer fight. Trouble was, I needed to get Wade on board without Kenneth catching on.

"Way to go, Crowley. No, really, this has got to be some of your best. Why didn't you just portal right into Katherine's bedroom, snuggle up real close?" I snarked. My leg jiggled as I sat in the chair, glaring at him in the one beside me.

Wade shot me a cold look. "People in glass houses, Finch."

"What, shouldn't wander around naked?"

"You know exactly what I mean."

I snorted. "You think I'm the one messing things up? Seriously? I'd be out of here by now if you hadn't flubbed it." I flashed him a discreet wink, but he missed it completely.

"Looked like you were getting backed into a corner to me."

"I'm good at wriggling out of things. You, of all people, should know that. I was dealing with it."

Wade laughed bitterly. "What, without your fancy disguise? Face it, Finch, Katherine figured you out, and you weren't getting out of here any more than I am now."

"Foolproof, you said. You said those button thingies were *foolproof*. Do you need a dictionary? Don't you know what that means?"

"Hey, you can't blame me because they didn't work the way we thought they would."

"A poor man blames his tools, Wade. And you're the biggest tool I've ever met!" I shot back.

"Shut it, both of you!" Kenneth snapped.

I grinned at him. "Why, don't you like what you're hearing? I take it back. *You* are the biggest tool I've ever met!"

"I'm warning you," Kenneth hissed.

Meanwhile, Wade was still focusing on me. "Who you trying to impress, Finch, huh? Mom isn't here anymore, pal. You don't need to act all big now that she's stormed off." He glowered at me. "Admit it, you were going to switch sides. Admit it!"

That stung, especially since the dimwit hadn't caught on that this was a ruse yet. "Were you not listening? She can go stuff herself."

"You won't speak of Eris like that!" Kenneth glared at us, but Wade ignored him.

"You think I bought that? I know you, Finch. Everything you do is just for show."

"Not everything, although *some* things are," I replied, with a roll of my eyes that screamed, "Get with the program, Wade." This time, he caught it. A small smirk turned up the corners of his lips. "As far as I'm concerned, Katherine can take a very long walk off a short cliff. Call me Captain, 'cause I'm going down with this Titanic mess, same as you. Cheers for that, by the way."

Wade huffed out a labored sigh. "Oh yeah, because it's all my fault?"

"You got caught by Kenneth freaking Willow, Wade! You might as well have been caught by a damned Jigglypuff."

Wade rolled his eyes. "Geek."

"Idiot."

"Nerd."

"Spineless!" This was gathering a bit of heat. Good. I landed a sharp kick to Wade's thigh. He glared back and kicked out his leg, landing a blow to my hip. I sensed there was a bit of actual frustration coming out of him, but what the hell. I kicked him again, trying to scoot my chair closer. He kicked back, his cheeks red.

Private Predictable rushed forward and dragged me out of my chair, just before it started to get interesting. Kenneth actually growled. I wanted to laugh in his face. Who did this kid think he was? Still, this was my shot. I lurched back and threw him off balance.

"You bastard!" Kenneth gasped, flailing wildly.

"Yeah, blame my mother." I swiped my foot at his ankle, and he went down like a sack of spuds. The thud he made when he landed was satisfying. The pathetic little yelp was pretty good, too. I stomped my foot down on his chest as he groaned, pinning him there.

"You won't escape. We've got you now!" Kenneth wheezed as he struggled to get up. I stomped down again, for good measure.

"You want to get on with those Cuffs, Flyboy?" I cast a look back at Wade.

He nodded and hurried to remove his Cuffs, with his hands behind his back. I'd seen him swipe the keys from Kenneth earlier. So I had to give him that nugget of skill. He clumsily slotted the keys into the lock and removed the Cuffs. They fell to the floor with a hefty clank.

"You won't defeat me!" Kenneth howled. I jabbed my foot against his throat, sick of his whining.

"Really? Looks like that's exactly what's happening to me."

"No! I refuse! You're unworthy!" Katherine's guard dog was trying to slip his hand into his pocket. *No colored puffs today, sunshine.* I tried to shift my weight and stamp on his hand, but it was too difficult. If I moved, I'd lose my balance, too. He had opened his mouth to call out a curse when a figure whizzed past me.

Wade knelt down and punched Kenneth right in the face. I heard the crack as it impacted. A second later, the kid's eyes rolled back. Wade had knocked his lights out.

"Nice one!" I whooped. "Now, get these things off me."

Wade grinned. "I've been dying to do that ever since I met the punk." He stood up and unlocked my Cuffs, then ducked back down to clap them on Kenneth's wrists.

"Is it wrong that I'm a bit jealous?" I asked, rubbing my wrists.

"Of what?"

"Of you knocking Kenneth clean out."

He chuckled. "No, I bet you're at the back of a pretty long line."

"Yeah, I bet even Katherine's standing in that line." I looked toward the door. "Right, we need to get out of here ASAP. I know a way."

Wade nodded. "I just need to make a call first."

"Now?"

"It's related," he shot back. *Ah, so there was some real bitterness back there?* He took out his phone and punched in a number before lifting it to his ear. "Isadora? Is Harley with you? Thank God! Should we come to you or do you want to come to us? Yeah, we got stuck in Katherine's office… no, she's not here. She's gone to find Harley."

I rolled my eyes. "Speed it up, this isn't a social call!"

"Okay, we'll stay here. But hurry, I don't know how long it'll be until she's back." He hung up and cast me a withering look. "That was important."

I grinned. "Oh yeah? You buckling up, Crowley, now that your girl is coming to pick us up? I want her back by eleven. And no funny business. If I see a hickey, I'll come 'round your house with a shotgun."

Wade spat out a laugh. "They're on their way, yeah."

"And Isadora said Harley is okay?"

"Seems like it."

I ran a hand through my hair. "That's good. That's really freaking good. I gave her some vague clue about getting into the library, and I had no idea if she'd figure it out. Then again, she's a Shipton. We always figure stuff out."

He smiled. "Sounds like you were worried about her."

"No, I was worried for myself—that we'd never get the hell out of here. I didn't *want* to count on her. I was worried about getting this nightmare of a mission finished. Never again, by the way. You people are all liabilities."

He smirked. "Correction: you were *very* worried about her."

"I'll die before agreeing with you, Crowley." A small smile crept onto my lips.

"Close enough."

Weirdly, the tension between us seemed to be dissipating. *Ooh, could this be the start of an oh so awkward friendship?* I had no idea. It didn't seem likely, but it had felt really friggin' good to stick it to Katherine in front of her precious cult members. And Wade had been my enabler. Maybe that's what he'd be—my enabler. Plus, it looked like we were both going to spend a decent chunk of our lives worrying about Harley. I guessed that gave us something in common. Although, I'd meant it about the shotgun. Now that I had a sister I gave half a damn about, I wasn't going to make it easy for Crowley. Mostly for my own amusement.

A few minutes later, a portal tore open a hole in Katherine's office. Papers and books went skittering everywhere. The aquariums cracked, fissures forming in the glass, but not breaking it enough for the water to gush out. *Oh, she's going to love that.* Isadora and Harley stumbled out. I was about to run forward to hug Harley, but Wade brushed past me and wrapped his arms around her. *That was probably a stupid idea anyway.* I had a reputation to uphold. And that didn't include hugging my sister. Even if I was glad to see her in one piece.

"What happened?" Wade asked as he held Harley close. He caught her lips in his and kissed her hard.

"We don't have time," I snapped, tapping my wrist. "We're still in Katherine's office, in case you forgot. And, seeing that you're back to your usual scruffy self, Harley, I'm guessing your Shapeshifter energy ran out of gas? Let's scoot!"

I guessed it was sort of sweet, but there was a time and a place for emotional PDAs. Plus, it served as an unwelcome reminder that I didn't have anyone waiting for me. Not anymore. She was dead. And I couldn't get her back... not after I'd shoved Katherine's offer right back in her face. It still stung a little, to know that I'd had one shot to have my own reunion, slurpy or otherwise, and I'd given it up through some new sense of morality. It didn't stop me wanting her, even though I knew I'd done the right thing. I couldn't even put her in a jar and keep her on my shelf.

Harley started speaking rapidly as we gathered around Isadora, bringing us up to speed in the span of a few sentences. She was obviously excluding a ton of details, but it was enough to give us the gist of what happened in the tunnels, with the ghosts, and her mom, and the eventual release. I felt sorry for her, after hearing that last bit. It couldn't have been easy to do that.

Wade mentioned what had happened in here and why Kenneth was blacked out on the floor, while Isadora lifted her hands to form another portal.

"We can celebrate once we're back at the SDC," Isadora said, sending bronzed tendrils swirling into the atmosphere.

Then the door burst open.

For the love of Grayskull, what now?!

Shinsuke stepped into the room with another magical at his side. My heart sank. I knew him well. Bakir Khan. Not the swiftest or strongest of magicals, but he had a sharp head on his shoulders, which might present a problem. Clearly, they'd been sent to bring Wade and me to Katherine's private quarters for another round of threats that'd cost me thousands in therapy.

"What the—" Shinsuke glanced at us, confused.

Bakir, however, was gearing up for a fight. And I was in the mood for a little exercise.

FORTY

Harley

The magical who had come along with Shinsuke lunged forward to strike. Wade ran at him, full pelt, knocking him flat. The poor guy had barely managed to get his Chaos together. It fizzled out in his palm as he lay still, unconscious.

"Wow… That was surprisingly short-lived," Finch said, lowering his hands.

Judging by the state of Kenneth, too, Wade had some frustrations he was working out. But I was so glad to see him again. I couldn't even put into words how happy I was to be able to hold him and kiss him.

Shinsuke looked like he had no idea what to do. He could fight and stay on Katherine's good side, or he could let us go. The only trouble was, his face was totally unreadable. His emotions were in turmoil, too, giving me little clue which way he was going to swing. But I couldn't risk letting him make the wrong choice.

"Shinsuke, don't fight us," I said, putting up my hands like I was a negotiator trying not to get shot. "Come back to the SDC with us. This might be your only chance to get out of here, and it'll definitely be your last chance to see your father before he gets taken to Purgatory. If you stay here, you'll wind up dead."

"Who are you?" He narrowed his eyes at us. *Ah, yeah, I'd forgotten about that.* I wasn't Volla anymore, and Finch wasn't Pieter. I mean, he definitely recognized Finch, but he had no idea who I was. Our paths had never crossed.

"I'm Harley Merlin. I'm from the San Diego Coven. Finch and I were disguised as the Mazinovs so we could try and stop Katherine from becoming a Child of Chaos," I explained at a rapid pace. "Finch, you want to give me a hand here?"

Finch stepped forward and morphed into Pieter for a moment, just to prove the point. "Not too shabby, right?"

"I was using some Shifter energy through an Ephemera, but it's stopped working. But I promise you I was Volla this whole time," I said urgently. "We've been fighting to bring Katherine down, and you can help us. But you have to come with us now. This is your only shot. If you won't do it for anyone else, just think about what she did to your dad. He's going to Purgatory because of her. Now, what do you say?" The clock was ticking, and we were leaving either way—with him or without him.

Shinsuke paused. "I don't know if that's a good idea. Katherine is very strong, and she doesn't take kindly to deserters. I would be putting myself in the line of fire if I went with you."

"You really want to stay here, with a psychopath?" I had to put it bluntly.

"No, but that doesn't mean your way is any better. At least here, from the inside, I might be able to help."

I shook my head. "You saw how well that worked out for Tess. If you stay and take up her position as the mole, then Katherine will sniff you out. She's looking for betrayers now. How long do you think you'll have before she comes for you?" I felt a fresh sense of guilt about what had happened to Tess, and I really didn't want that happening to Shinsuke too. Despite his blank face and mixed emotions, I knew he wanted to join us. At the very least, he didn't want to be here anymore, and that was good enough for me.

"I know this entire organization is wrong. I've sensed it. And I no longer wish to be a part of it, but—"

"No buts, Shinsuke. Either you stay here and you die, or you come with us and you help."

He dipped his head. "I would like to see my father again. And I would like to help you, but…"

"Shinsuke, get these off me!" I whirled around to see that Kenneth had woken up from his little snooze and was writhing frantically to get the Cuffs off. Not that wriggling would do him any good. He couldn't even cast a curse with those things on. *At least, I hope he can't.*

Figuring it was best not to risk it, I sent a pulse of reverse Empathy toward him, gathering up a bunch of sad emotions to feed into him. My specialty. He suddenly stopped wriggling, his face crumpling into a mask of misery. A moment later, tears were streaming out of his eyes, and his chest was heaving as he sobbed uncontrollably, like a little kid who'd had his favorite toys taken away. There was nothing he could do to stop it as he covered his face with his hands and wept like he'd never wept before, heaving out ugly, gigantic sobs that bellowed through the room.

"Hey, Finch, you were right," I said.

He frowned. "Huh?"

"Weeping Willow wasn't a bad nickname after all."

He grinned. "You doubted me?"

"Isadora, can you get us out of here now?" I shifted my glance to her. "Shinsuke, it's now or never. Are you coming with us or not?"

He still didn't seem sure.

Finch rolled his eyes. "We haven't got time for this. Do you want this kid back at the SDC?"

I nodded. "Yes."

"Great, then he's coming." Finch sent out a lasso of Telekinesis and wrapped it around Shinsuke, tugging him closer. With one swift punch to the side of the head, he knocked Shinsuke unconscious, the guy lolling in Finch's arms. "Happy?"

"Finch!" I frowned. "We need to have a talk about your tactics…"

"Sure, later. Let's get going," Finch said, with an anxious look toward the door.

Isadora nodded and set to work again, the bronze light twisting around her fingertips in an elegant coil. With her eyes closed, she pushed the energy outward, tearing a fresh hole in the fabric of space and time. It added a few more thread-veined cracks to the tanks, and more of Katherine's belongings flew against the walls. The more the merrier, as far as I was concerned. I wanted her to come back here and see what had happened, and I wanted it to burn her up inside. I wanted her to hurt the way I'd hurt when I'd let my mother go. She'd walk into this room and know she'd failed, and that was going to be so freaking sweet, even if I wasn't here to see it.

With air rushing out of the void, the edges crackling and sputtering in that worrying way, we sprinted into the portal one by one, Isadora bringing up the rear. Glancing over my shoulder, I noticed Finch snatching something off Katherine's desk before he darted in after me. I staggered out into the familiar, clinical surroundings of the infirmary of the SDC. Never had I been so happy to see strip lighting and hospital walls. In front of us, looking slightly alarmed, sat Krieger and Jacob. They'd evidently been waiting for us to return, but it took a lot of experience to get used to seeing a portal open.

"Thank goodness!" Krieger heaved a sigh of relief.

"We thought something bad must have happened," Jacob added, looking like he wanted to rush forward and hug us all.

As the portal snapped shut behind us, I looked around at Wade, Finch, the unconscious Shinsuke, and Isadora, and almost collapsed in hysterics. Instead, I just grinned like an idiot as a wave of relief washed over me.

"We did it. We freaking did it," I murmured. Glancing at the others, I could tell they shared my relief and awe that we'd actually managed to pull this off.

Wade nodded, with a grin. "We did. We freaking did!"

We'd stopped Katherine from completing the third ritual, and now she had no way of getting it done. All Hallows' Eve started in six hours, on the stroke of midnight, and we'd beaten her to the punch. We finally beat her. I had to pinch myself to make sure I wasn't in some weird simulator.

The only one who didn't look too happy was Finch. He seemed on edge, running a hand anxiously through his hair. He was acting like he had something to hide. Did it have to do with what he'd snatched from Katherine's desk? I doubted it. He'd probably just taken something to annoy her. But this wasn't the behavior of someone who'd taken some kind of petty revenge. This was the behavior of someone who felt very unsettled.

"What is it, Finch? You're sort of killing my buzz here," I said, as Wade and Isadora debriefed about what had gone on. Finch still had his arm around Shinsuke, who was coming around slowly, his eyes blinking open in a daze.

He frowned. "It's just… well, Katherine was pissed when she heard you'd got your hands on Hester, but I don't know if this is actually over. She wasn't quite angry enough, if that makes any sense?"

"No, it doesn't. What do you mean?"

Wade glanced up. "Something up?"

"She… She should have been livid, but she wasn't," Finch said. "And she kept saying she had backup plans for her backup plans. I'm starting to wonder if she had a backup plan for Hester's spirit. Like, she's got other options or something." Finch looked like he might be sick. "I should've known it was too easy."

Shinsuke raised a limp hand. "Finch may be right."

"Can you *explain*?" I pressed.

"Well, when Katherine gave the order for me to come and fetch Finch and Wade, she did mention something about other options. She was quite smug about it. She muttered something like, 'They think they've fooled me. Well, we'll see who gets a nasty shock when midnight rolls around.' That would suggest she has a backup plan, as Finch said."

I could have ripped my hair out. "And you're telling me this *now*?"

Shinsuke bowed his head. "I thought it was just Katherine being

Katherine. When I saw you all in her office, I presumed she didn't know how far along with the plan you were. I'm sorry." He paused. "I may have said something sooner, had Finch not decided to resort to brute force."

"It's not your fault," I said, trying to swallow the bile that was rising up my throat. He was right. If we hadn't knocked him out, he might have been able to say something about it.

"There is one more thing." He looked uneasy.

I leveled my gaze at him. "What?"

"I came from her private residence, when I was sent to collect Wade and Finch." He paused uncertainly. "Well, the thing is, she had just murdered Tess. It's one of the many reasons I'm glad I came with you."

My stomach sank. I knew Katherine was going to do it, but that didn't make it any easier to comprehend. One moment, Tess had been alive, and now she was dead. And we'd put her in that situation. That was never going to be easy to live with.

"What does that have to do with midnight?" Wade cut in.

"She may have said that a 'traitor's' ghost qualifies as a 'worst enemy's' ghost, in her book."

I slammed my fists into the nearby table and let out an ungodly scream. Everyone turned in shock, but I could tell they were reeling too. This was the last thing I wanted to hear. And what made it worse was the fact that we could've done something about it, five minutes ago. Now, we were royally screwed with no cards left to play.

"Why didn't you mention any of this before we left, Finch? Why didn't you say you were worried?" I asked. "Why didn't you bring up your suspicions in the office, where we could still have done something about them?"

He raised his hands. "Hey, I'm not the one who overheard what she said. Blame Shinsuke if you're going to blame anyone. This isn't my fault."

"Oh, God," I gasped. "If you'd said something, *anything*, back on the island, we could've fixed this. A whisper of doubt and we'd have listened. But now it's too late!"

Wade put his hand on my shoulder. "We still have six hours, Harley. We can still fix this."

I shook my head, my hands trembling. "No, we can't, Wade. Eris Island won't be there anymore, if we try to go back through the portal. Katherine will have moved it by now, you can bet anything on that."

She'd fooled us again. And what was worse, she'd made us believe we'd beaten her.

FORTY-ONE

Finch

I hated getting put in the spotlight. And I hated seeing Harley like this. She was pissed at me, for sure, and she probably had good reason to be. Yeah, I should've said something earlier. But could've, would've, should've wasn't going to help us right now.

Plus, how was I supposed to tell her the main reason I hadn't mentioned anything? Was I just supposed to come right out and say that I didn't want her getting hurt by chasing Katherine into some otherworld again? No chance. I didn't want her thinking I'd gone soft.

Besides, Shinsuke was more to blame than I was. He could've said something *before* I'd knocked him out. Staying behind wouldn't have done any of us any favors. I just hoped I could convince Harley of that.

"Look, I know you're upset, and I know this looks pretty bad right now, but Katherine was on to us. She knew who you were. She knew who I was. There was nothing we could've done, even if we'd known about Tess sooner," I said.

I mean, there was *one* thing I could've done. But it'd only have served me. *And Adley...* There was no point mentioning the offer Katherine had made to me. It wouldn't have scored me any brownie points. It'd only have made Harley more suspicious. She would have known I'd hesitated, even if it was just a slip in my newfound morality. Mostly because she would have slipped too, if it had been Wade's life offered up on a silver platter. But that didn't mean I wasn't sore about the choice I'd made. And I didn't appreciate all this blame, considering what I'd given up for them.

As I said Tess's name, it finally hit me that she was dead. Like, actually dead—and in no small part because of me. I'd called her out. I'd put her in Katherine's crosshairs. Now she was gone. Or trapped as a spirit, anyway. Not that there was much difference. Dead was dead.

Damn...

Harley glowered at me. She was getting good at that. "That was no reason to run, Finch. If you knew there was even the slightest chance we hadn't won, you should've *said* something."

"Hey, there was nothing we could've done at that point without getting our heads mounted on pikes. And I don't know about you, but I kind of like having my head attached to my body. At least, if we face her elsewhere, we've got bigger numbers now." I held her glare. "You'd have been just peachy, but she wouldn't have hesitated to kill the rest of us back there, just to piss you off."

Harley frowned. "What do you mean, *I'd* have been peachy?"

"Katherine's back on the I-want-Harley-alive train. My guess is, you don't want to find out what station she wants to pull that train into." I sighed. "Even so, we shouldn't test her limits. We can't afford for you to get captured for whatever she has planned." Jacob stifled a laugh. I shot him a cold stare. "What are you laughing at, Chuckles?"

He shrugged. "I think it's cute."

"What part of *that* sounded cute to you?"

"You love your sister."

I stared at him. "What did you just say?"

"I said, it's cute that you love your sister. It's obvious—you don't want her getting hurt." Jacob was clearly loving this. Me? Not so much. I was about to lunge toward him and rip those girlish giggles out of his throat when Wade stepped between us.

"Easy, Finch. It's nothing to be ashamed of."

I glared at him. "You want your face rearranged too?"

"Just calm down. There's no reason for this to come to blows. We've got enough on our plate without in-fighting, okay?"

"Someone needs to teach that kid to keep his trap shut," I grumbled, backing off.

"Are we done with the squabbling?" Harley chimed in. But she didn't look as angry anymore. There was a subtle change in her face as she glanced at me. And, maybe, a hint of a smile. *They're all going to think I'm a Care Bear now.* Although, if anyone tried to rub my tummy, they'd get a kick in the face.

I scowled. "I am if this dumbass is."

"Truth hurts," Jacob retorted with a smirk. Wade immediately put up his hands in case I tried to lunge for that twerp again. *Pfft, as if I'd give him the satisfaction.*

"We need solutions, and we need them now," Harley said. "We've got six hours until midnight."

I nodded. "This isn't over, by any means. Yeah, the island might've moved, but we've got one more option. One that probably suits us better anyway, since Katherine's minions won't be running about everywhere. Or, at least, not as many of them."

"Go on…" Harley had definitely softened up a little, but I wasn't off the hook yet. *Why aren't you breathing down Shinsuke's neck?* It didn't seem fair that I was getting all the flak, just because I was Harley's half-brother. Family, huh?

"Our only choice now is to go to Tartarus just before midnight tonight and face her there. She won't be expecting us." I took a breath. "The only problem is, Tartarus is a royal pain in the ass. It's the most dangerous of the otherworlds by a long shot. Read any book about these places, you'll hear the same thing. I've never been myself, but if the legends are true, we'd better be ready to face our worst nightmares."

Harley delved suddenly into her pockets and took out a crumpled ball of paper. "Speaking of books, I took this from the library." She unfurled it and began to read. "'In the Asphodel Meadows, we find the realm of Nyx, the night realm, in which perpetual darkness reigns over the land. In Greek mythology, this is said to be the place where those who led plain lives endure their afterlife.'"

"Huh?"

"It's information about the Children of Chaos," she replied. "'Tartarus belongs to Erebus and has long been tied to those who must be punished, eternally, for their mortal sins. The Garden of Hesperides is the land of Gaia. It is where the golden apples of Hera were said to grow. It is where Eris, the goddess of discord, was said to have obtained the very Apple of Discord that began the Trojan War. Lethe is the land belonging to Lux. Elysium, or, rather, the Elysian Fields, belong to all four Children of Chaos. It is neutral territory, where they may gather to discuss the mortal world. It belongs to no one Child and is said to be the resting place of great heroes and warriors, several of whom have fallen to the challenge of becoming a Child themselves. If philosophers are to be believed, there are many otherworldly dimensions beyond these, but no Child of Chaos rests there. There are but four, omniscient in our world.'"

Isadora frowned. "So, Katherine wants to be a new sort of Child, one of her own creation, designed after the goddess she feels the most kinship with—Eris, the goddess of discord?"

"And if the Apple of Discord came from Gaia's world, does that mean she's gearing up to face Gaia?" Wade chimed in.

I shrugged. "Who knows? But the book seems to suggest that the neutral ground is Elysium. Which means one thing: that's where Katherine will make her final challenge, if we can't stop her first."

"So, we call that the backup to our backup," Harley said. "Right now, we need to get everyone together, get as many weapons as we can find, and get to Tartarus. We have six hours until midnight. Katherine is going to be there, with Tess's spirit."

The backup to our backup? Sounds familiar. Harley and Katherine really were starting to look like two sides of the same coin. Trouble was, only heads or tails could win. And I didn't know which way the coin would land.

FORTY-TWO

Harley

The hours were ticking by until midnight, and my heart was in my mouth.

The whole Rag Team, minus the ever-absent Garrett, had gathered in the infirmary, preparing for what was to come. Alton was here, too, in order to keep Finch and Shinsuke's presence in the coven a secret. We were armed to the teeth, thanks to Astrid, to make sure we had a way to fight if our energy floundered or Katherine had another one of her special forcefields up. We had one thing still working in our favor —the element of surprise. Katherine thought we'd come back here, thinking we'd won. She wouldn't be anticipating us coming after her in Tartarus itself.

Still, it was a terrifying prospect, especially after Finch's warning.

I thought about what the page I'd torn from the Drake Shipton Library had said. In mythology, Tartarus was the place where tortured souls spent their eternity, paying penance for terrible things they'd done in their mortal life. Even Louella had supported that belief by explaining that it was mostly described as a literal hell. *So comforting.* Then again, I'd faced the devil enough times to not balk at the idea of facing her in a place more suited to her character.

"Does everyone know what they have to do?" I asked, checking the bandolier of knives across my chest. I also checked the clasp on my Esprit to make sure it was securely back where it was supposed to be. It felt so freaking good to have it back after so long without it. It'd almost been like missing a limb.

"We're taking this bitch down," Santana replied with a grin.

Raffe chuckled nervously. "What she said."

"Time for the touchdown!" Dylan whooped.

"We'll stop her," Tatyana added solemnly. "We have to."

"I've missed you guys," I said with a nervous smile. The Rag Team was back together, and that felt better than anything in the world, despite what we were about to face.

"I'm going to stay behind and help Alton keep Levi busy with an *urgent* coven matter." Astrid smiled secretly, as if she was already plotting the perfect emergency.

Louella nodded. "I'll stay with Krieger and prepare for when you get back."

"I'll also be waiting for your return," Isadora said, her tone anxious. She was letting me go into the unknown once again and couldn't risk coming with us. She'd tried to convince us that her skills were better served with us, but we'd voted in a majority for her to stay. It didn't rest any easier with me that Jacob was going to be heading into danger, but Isadora was still having some portal trouble after the island. And, frankly, we were going to need a Portal Opener who wasn't glitching, regardless of the risks.

"And I'll be your portal guy." Jacob smiled happily. After his recent otherworld screw-ups, he was clearly delighted to be allowed back into the action.

"Like everyone said, we're taking her down… tonight," Wade said, his arm around my waist.

"Yeah, yeah. We all know what's at stake here." Finch was trying his best to be blasé, but I could tell he was nervous about this.

"And you have my swords in your fight against Katherine. I must do this for my honor, and for that of my father." Shinsuke crossed his swords. We'd made the last-minute decision to let him come with us, even though it would be putting him in the direct line of Katherine's anger. She hated deserters more than anything, but we figured it might serve as a good example to her followers, to see someone like Shinsuke switching sides at the eleventh hour. Maybe, just maybe, it'd persuade a few more of them to jump ship.

Jacob raised his hand. "There's just one problem. I didn't want to mention it before, because everyone was getting pumped up and stuff."

"What's up?" I eyed him curiously.

"How are we actually getting to Tartarus? I know we got to the Asphodel Meadows and Gaia's place okay, but that was only because I had a scent to follow. I don't have one for Tartarus."

Finch smirked. "Ah, so the kid *doesn't* know everything."

"You want to share, Finch? We're kind of running out of time here." I gave him a warning look.

"Well, we need to find Katherine's exact location in Tartarus, right?"

"Stating the obvious there, Finch."

"I've got just the thing we need to find her," he replied, a mischievous glint in his eyes. He pulled a simple-looking fountain pen out of his pocket and handed it to Jacob with a smug flourish.

Jacob frowned. "What's this?"

"Call it our compass."

"I don't follow," Jacob replied. Even Isadora looked dubious.

Finch rolled his eyes. "Don't they teach you anything at portal school? If you have a personal item belonging to someone, you can use it to track their location anywhere. You can only use it once, though. It'll disintegrate as soon as the portal opens, but it'll lead us right to Katherine. I swiped this off her desk before we escaped from her office."

Isadora shook her head. "I've never heard of that before."

"Believe me, it'll work," Finch insisted. "With the right focus, the Portal Opener can open a portal close to the person an item belongs to in order to find them. I'm surprised nobody's ever told you about it. Then again, who were you going to ask? It's not like your kind are swarming about the place. Luckily, I had a whole library of rare books at my disposal, and I spent my time *very* wisely. You wouldn't believe what I've got up here." He tapped his temple pointedly, grinning.

"Yeah, we could do with a bit more of whatever you've learned. You know, just whenever you feel like sharing," I said. "All these last-minute admissions of yours are starting to give me gray hairs."

He chuckled. "What can I say? I like to keep folks on their toes. Always act a little bit stupider than you are. Then, nobody asks you for anything. It's foolproof." He glanced at Wade and Krieger. "You know, like, *actually* foolproof. Unlike that emergency button thingie you made."

Dr. Krieger paled. "There was very little time to test them, in my defense."

"Don't listen to him, Dr. Krieger. He's just trying to rile you up." I offered the good doctor a reassuring smile. He'd done so much for us already, at great risk to his career. Yeah, those buttons hadn't worked perfectly, but the island had messed up a lot of stuff, including Isadora's portal. *That reminds me, I need to get my St. Christopher back at some point.* I noticed it still hanging around Finch's neck and decided not to mention it. Weirdly, it felt comforting to see it on him.

"Can you make it work, Jacob?" Wade asked, his arm still firmly around my waist.

Jacob nodded. "I think so."

"Okay then, let's stop talking about it and get on with it. We've got a cult leader to get rid of." I locked eyes with everyone in the group, feeling the anticipation rise through my body, setting my Chaos alight. I wished I had a crystal ball to let me know what the outcome of this was going to be, if only so I could be sure that I'd see every single face in this room when we came back. There were no assurances, but I knew my people—I knew how tough they were and how determined they were to stop Katherine dead in her tracks. We were ready for this, readier than we'd ever been. We'd spent the time since the last ritual honing our abilities, and this time, she wouldn't get the better of us.

Jacob held the pen tightly in his hands and fed his energy into his palm, the bronzed light enveloping the object. He closed his eyes, a sheen of sweat glistening on his forehead. A moment later, a small blast of light forced his hand wide open, and the pen floated out on a wave of thrumming Chaos. It drifted up into the center of the room, hovering for a moment, before it exploded outward in a blinding blast of rushing air and vivid sparks. It disintegrated entirely, and the particles spread out, forming a weirdly uniform line. As Jacob pushed his Chaos energy toward the line of particles, a huge hole tore through the fabric of the atmosphere, creating a stable portal that, hopefully, would lead us straight to Katherine.

"Well, here goes nothing," I murmured, casting an anxious glance at Wade. It felt so good to be back beside him again, and I prayed we'd make it through this together. After all, we had a lot of catching up to do.

I walked toward the crackling portal and stepped through, bracing myself for what we would find on the other side. Taking my lead, the rest of the Rag Team followed, with Astrid, Alton, Isadora, Louella, and Dr. Krieger watching us go with anxious eyes.

FORTY-THREE

Harley

I stumbled out into pitch darkness. Had I somehow gotten stuck in the portal tunnel? *Gaia, this better not be you again. No time for side trips right now.* I couldn't see a single thing in front of me, but there were sounds all around me, getting closer.

"Guys?" I whispered.

"Yep, this is not a drill. It's pitch black in here." It was Santana's voice, coming from just behind me.

"Watch your step," Tatyana whispered. "I can sense something."

I frowned. "Spirits?"

"No, not spirits exactly. It's something else," she replied.

The sounds got louder as I took a tentative step forward. I heard the rumble of a growl, deep in the throat of an unseen creature, followed by the snap of jaws. An undercurrent of hisses and slavering tongues peppered the louder noises, though I wasn't sure which unnerved me the most. One thing was for sure: I'd seen this before. I'd been here before, in that dream I'd had back at the stone hut.

If Finch comes toward me with a knife, I'm going to scream.

A second later, I became aware of shapes shifting in the darkness, dangerously close to where we were standing. I couldn't see them, but I could feel their presence, and I didn't need any spiritual insight to know that wasn't good.

"Any sign of Katherine?" Jacob hissed.

"I think you might have dropped us a little too far," I replied. In the distance, I could see a barely discernible, glowing light, with figures standing in front of some kind of object—an altar.

"There are three of them," Raffe said, his voice weird and raspy. *Great, just what we need. A rabid djinn.*

"Can you see who they are?" I asked, praying Raffe could keep a lid on the djinn until we got closer to Katherine.

"Katherine, Naima, and Kenneth," he said, without a pause. I turned over my shoulder and saw two small, glowing red orbs in the darkness. The djinn was out in full force, no doubt sensing the presence of its leader, Erebus. *Well, this is creepy.* Combined with the unseen creatures all around us, this was getting more unnerving by the second.

"Raffe, hang on, okay?" Santana urged.

An eerie chuckle split the air. "Oh, he's not home right now. Call back later."

"Kadar, behave yourself." Santana sounded worried.

"What are you afraid of? A little darkness?" The djinn chuckled again, somewhere close to me. I could feel his hot breath on my neck. *Ugh.*

"We need to get closer," I said, ignoring the djinn. If this was the otherworld of his leader, then he might prove useful here. As long as he didn't try to eat us first.

"Anyone going to mention whatever's lurking in these shadows?" Jacob's voice squeaked.

"We need some light." I heard Wade's voice beside me, the tone calming my rapidly beating heart.

I heard a crackle of energy as a fireball burst into life in Wade's palms, his ten rings glowing. The moment it cast its light on our surroundings, the Chaos monsters in the darkness surged forward in a snarling, snapping horde of jaws and fangs and glinting eyes. For a split second, it revealed the mass of Chaos monsters that waited in the shadows. They stretched as far as the eye could see, freezing my blood in my veins with sudden terror. Evidently, the torn page that had spoken about this place had got it slightly wrong—there were no tortured souls, only a heap of these Chaos monsters.

I caught sight of a blur out of the corner of my eye as Finch lurched forward and sputtered out the glowing fireball with a wave of Telekinesis, pushing it into the darkness, where it dissipated into a star of sparks.

"Run!" Finch hissed. "We need to run!"

He brushed past me, his footsteps echoing in the black otherworld. With no other option, I raced after him, heading for the distant glow of doom. The footsteps thundering behind me let me know that the rest of the Rag Team was following suit.

I jumped in fright as a rush of air swept forward from behind me. I saw the telltale crackle of a portal and started to freak out. Had Jacob abandoned us? That wasn't his vibe at all. Another portal opened up ahead, closer to the altar and frazzling in an alarming way, with Jacob just visible in the faraway light. I realized he was using that dangerous initiative of his again, using his portal energy to analyze the situation closer up. He was way faster than these monsters, and they didn't stand a chance of catching him. I guessed, in this place, he could only hold the portals open for a short time, and in sharp bursts. Too quick and temperamental for all of us to pile through them.

We, on the other hand, had nothing but our legs to carry us through this nightmare world, and I could already feel the shadows pressing in on us. Unseen claws swiped at my ankles, just as they'd done in my dream, the snapping jaws way too close for comfort. I heard a yelp behind me, but I didn't know who it had come from. I wanted to yell back and find out whether everyone was all right, but the din of the creatures had grown to a deafening volume. There were growls and roars and howls everywhere I turned, with eyes flashing in the dark.

I stumbled and fell as something snagged my leg, dragging me to the ground. The creatures swept in, their breath foul and hot on my skin, their jaws gnashing. I dragged myself to my feet and kicked outward, smacking something in the face. It whined in pain, but I knew another creature would just take its place.

"Everyone alive?" I roared.

A smattering of voices responded. Doing a quick voice-count, it sounded like everyone was still with us. *Good... let's keep going.*

Meeting my mom had filled me with fresh determination and a renewed hatred for Katherine that would see me through any challenge. And this was probably going to be the hardest one I'd ever faced.

She'd locked my mom in a jar and kept her spirit bound to this earth. Nobody got away with that. Nobody. I could think about the bigger picture all I wanted, but there was something to be said for personal vendettas—and mine was ready to crush Katherine, for the sake of the big picture and the smaller snapshots of my life that she'd destroyed.

Powering through the Chaos monsters, we neared Katherine and her altar. A mass of bluish white light undulated on the altar's surface. My gaze flitted to a jar on the altar with a swirling mist inside. *Tess... I'm so sorry.* Even though she was a spirit, I could feel her terror and her grief. It flowed through the glass jar in painful waves that gripped my heart with ice-cold claws. Still, it meant Katherine hadn't completed the ritual yet.

Meanwhile, the Chaos monsters weren't letting up, flowing like a liquid tide toward us. The more we kicked them away and tried to batter them with the weapons Astrid had loaded us up with, the more they fought back. Right now, I had two knives on the ends of Telekinesis tendrils, slashing them aimlessly in front of me. Sometimes the blades made contact; sometimes they didn't. I just hoped I didn't accidentally injure one of the Rag Team in my blind fury to get at Katherine.

We were so close now. Barely ten yards stood between us and her, but there was still a swarm of monsters. It was becoming painfully obvious that we couldn't use our usual methods of attack to defeat Katherine. Not this time. Even if we got close, we'd have monsters at our back and Naima and Kenneth to deal with up front.

Katherine looked up, just as a tornado of fierce white light shot up into the sky.

"Well, well, well, here comes the Scooby Gang to fail to save the day, once again." She smirked. "You know, I was wondering if you would show up. Part of me was hoping you were all sitting around a table, toasting your success. Watching you die will be just as satisfying."

She raised her hands as if she were simply checking her nails and sent up a protective bubble of bronzed light. It stretched to encompass all of them—Katherine, Naima, and Kenneth, as well as Tess's spirit.

Don't you freaking dare!

I lashed out toward an oncoming creature, feeling something ooze over my hand as the blade of my knife bit into its face. It evaporated a moment later, and the beast dissipated into the atmosphere. Gritting my teeth in determination, I ploughed through the Chaos monsters, swiping my hands like a windmill as I fought to reach Katherine.

In the glow that dispersed from the eerie altar, I saw the rest of the Rag Team battling for their lives. Sparks of Chaos flew, and I could hear the swish of Shinsuke's swords as he took down a bunch of creatures. All around me, it looked like everyone was using a mixture of magic and brute force to get through. Jacob kept bursting in and out of scarily crackling portals, trying to find a way through the forcefield. So far, it didn't seem to be working. That thing was keeping him out, which I was almost grateful for. If he got inside, he'd have to be quick to break it down before Katherine retaliated. But I was getting closer, ready to help him if he managed to get through.

I kicked out my leg and knocked a salivating beast back into the shadows, giving me a direct path to Katherine and her bubble. Seizing the opportunity, I sprinted toward it, gathering a powerful ball of Fire in my palms as I ran. I hurled it at the bubble with every ounce of strength I had. It bounced back, exploding in a shower of sparking fragments.

I used Telekinesis next, pummeling a wave of it directly into the bubble, but the forcefield wouldn't budge. I tried to step through it, but that ended with my face being smushed against the shimmering shield, my nose stinging as I staggered back.

I expected some witty retort from Katherine, but she was entirely focused on the ritual. She reached for Tess's jar, and there was nothing I could do to stop her. That tornado of pure energy continued to surge upward, making the darkness spike and fork with Chaos-induced lightning. Trying to break through the bubble and simultaneously fight off the monsters was turning into a Sisyphean task. The monsters were drawn to the light of this central point, but they seemed wary about entering. Even so, there wasn't much space left to fight in the light, and we could barely see our own hands in front of our faces if we stayed in the darkness.

I hammered on the forcefield with every ability I had, trying to make a crack in Katherine's defenses. But it was no good. I couldn't break through. I couldn't even make a dent, and she freaking knew it. That made it even worse, knowing just how smug she was feeling right now.

With the sound of the ongoing battle clamoring behind me, I gaped in horror as Katherine unscrewed the lid of Tess's jar and let her spirit loose. Her figure became clear, the fine mist stretching out into limbs, and a body, and a face. She hovered in the air for a moment before the bluish light that writhed on the altar snaked upward, the tendrils wrapping around the spirit and dragging it down to the altar.

Come on, come on, COME ON! I slammed wave after wave of Telekinesis and Fire and Water and Earth and Air into the bubble, but nothing was working. Behind me, the monsters were starting to edge into the circle of light. Glaring over my shoulder, I peered at the rabid creatures.

"Leave me alone!" I snapped, my body overflowing with frustrated energy. My voice echoed across the beasts, carrying that weird, distant tone that didn't sound like it had come from me at all.

The beasts immediately backed off, looking confused by their own impulsive reactions. It was the same thing that had happened with the gargoyle in Katherine's second trial—only, on a much larger scale, my emotions amplified by my desperation.

Thinking fast, I turned to the sea of beasts that were in the middle of attacking my friends. "Leave them alone! Back off, now!" The words bellowed out of my lungs, my ribs searing with breathless pain.

The creatures looked at one another and backed away, melting into the darkness. It had worked. It had freaking worked! The Rag Team looked completely baffled, aside from Finch. As he stepped into the circle of light, he flashed me a grin.

"Way to go, Sis. Beast wrangler extraordinaire."

"Let's just hope it holds them," I muttered, turning back to the bubble. I'd seen flashes of crackling light exploding close to the bubble, letting me know that Jacob was trying to break through, but it didn't seem to be having any effect this time. Katherine had clearly added some extra juice to her forcefield, having learned from her previous mistakes.

Jacob stumbled out of a portal beside me, breathing heavily. All of this portal making was definitely taking its toll on him.

"Are you okay?" I rested my hand on his shoulder.

He nodded, panting. "I can't get through. She's got some sort of block on her portal."

Katherine laughed from inside the bubble. "What did you expect? I'm not too old to learn a lesson or two. And that portal ability was getting to be something of a thorn in my side." A sickening dread sank in the pit of my stomach as she took out a knife and turned to Kenneth, who was hopping like an excited puppy at her side. "Now it's your turn to prove yourself, Kenneth. Are you ready to participate in the ritual?"

"Of course, Eris." He grinned like a maniac.

"Come closer," she urged.

He did as he was told, practically licking his lips at the sight of Tess's spirit trapped by the strange, undulating light. "What do you need me to do?"

"Just stay where you are," she replied with a smirk. "This will be the easiest thing you've ever done."

"I'm ready, Eris."

She chuckled. "I'm so glad to hear that."

Katherine plunged the knife into his chest. A bloom of scarlet spread out across his shirt. He stared up at her with the confused eyes of someone who didn't realize he was about to die.

"I don't... understand." He choked, a splatter of blood spitting across his chin. His lungs would already be filling up, his life close to its end.

"Well, speaking of thorns in my side, you've been one from the very start," she replied, stroking her bloodied fingertip across his cheek, smearing a streak of scarlet across his skin. "You're beyond useless, really. And yet, I took pity on you. I gave you task after task, and you fumbled every single one. Even if you were standing in front of a target, you'd miss." Her voice was eerily calm. The steady serenity of a total, dyed-in-the-wool psychopath.

"Eris... I will... do better," he wheezed, his fingertips groping helplessly at the hilt of the blade in his chest.

"Do you need some help? Can you not even manage that by yourself?" She gripped the hilt and yanked it out of him, blood gushing everywhere. "At least I found one use for you. Otherwise, you'd have been dead a *long* time ago. You poor, stupid fool." She laughed coldly.

"I... don't... understand." He sagged against the altar, his hands slipping on the marble.

"Only the blood of an evil child can kill a spirit, Kenneth. Didn't your mother teach you anything?" She pushed him to one side, and his knees buckled as he collapsed to the ground. "Oh, that's right... you don't have one, do you?"

What? Now it made sense. That was the reason Katherine had been keeping Kenneth close, all this time, despite all of his failures. The evil bastard had had no idea. He'd genuinely thought that being part of a ritual was a promotion, instead of a death sentence. I'd have felt sorry for him, if I didn't hate him almost as much as Katherine.

This is what you get for killing kids, Kenneth. Those actions had filled him with the evil energy that Katherine needed to make this work, and she'd groomed him to perfection. She'd encouraged every bad impulse in him, knowing it would give her what she wanted. This woman wasn't just one step ahead of everyone—she was a million miles out in front, laughing at us the whole way.

The funny thing was, even Naima seemed shocked. *Nobody's safe, you idiot. Not even you.*

Wielding the dripping blade, Katherine brought it down with all the force she possessed and thrust it deep into Tess's spirit. For a moment, nothing happened, but Katherine's confident expression never wavered. And then, an almighty explosion went off. The rush of fierce energy pummeled out of Tess's spirit in violent waves. The forcefield splintered into a million pieces, and the altar imploded beneath Tess, leaving her soul hovering above the plinth. The blast powered out, smashing into all of us and taking out the endless rows of beasts that still lingered in the dark. It hit me right in the chest, pushing the air out of my lungs and sending me sprawling backward. Hot, fiery streams carrying tendrils of blue light in the center throbbed over the top of me.

A gut-wrenching scream went up from Katherine, who was holding her ground through sheer willpower and strength as the explosion pounded through her, blow after blow after blow. Her own body turned transparent for a moment as the flow of the tornado shifted. It began to power down instead of up, thrumming right into her and filling her with every particle of that spiraling blue-and-white energy. Naima was on the ground at her feet, covering her head with her hands, her amber eyes staring at Kenneth's limp, dead body.

As the initial explosion ebbed, I saw that Tess's spirit wasn't glowing anymore. It had turned a dull gray, though it still hovered in the center of this circle of light. Katherine, panting heavily with her eyes glowing a terrifying shade of silver, approached the dulled spirit.

"Et ex sanguine nati, et ad cinerem revertetur. Convertanturo-rationis humo munus ut consummare. Vos puero sanguis mala. Nunc te mea est," Katherine murmured, her hands pressing into Tess's altered spirit. Her ethereal figure fell apart, and what remained twisted into a spiral of dark gray mist. Katherine closed her eyes and inhaled deeply, drawing the particles of Tess's being deep into her lungs, like smoke.

I didn't know how much longer I had to stop this, nor did I know what steps were left in the ritual. I just knew that I couldn't let her finish this. There was only one option left, and I had to take it. I had to try the spell from my parents' Grimoire again—the one that would summon Erebus himself.

Everything comes at a price. But there was nothing else in this world that would stop Katherine. It was going to cost me a life, and I didn't know whose it might be, but this was our only chance. Our one, final shot at victory.

It hadn't gone well the last two times I'd tried this, with Astrid getting knocked into the altar and almost losing her life, and Santana Purging a serpent after stopping me, but then I'd never managed to complete the spell before. Erebus was a master of destruction. If we weren't completely desperate, I wouldn't have even been contemplating it. But the fact was, we *were* desperate.

Guilt and helplessness fought for the top spot in my head. Someone was going to die because of this, but there was the slightest chance that Erebus might ask for Katherine's life in return for being summoned, and I'd be only too happy to give him that.

We'd been backed into a corner. There really was no other way.

Forgive me. Please, forgive me.

FORTY-FOUR

Finch

I staggered back as black smoke billowed around Harley. *What the hell?* It had come out of nowhere. Was Katherine doing this? I looked toward the altar, but Katherine was in full demon mode, bleeding what was left of Tess's spirit dry.

I looked back at Harley. Was one of us supposed to stop her? Nobody else seemed to be moving. Then again, nobody else seemed able to move. They were all transfixed by Harley, who was muttering a spell under her breath. With every word, she drew the black mist out of thin air. It swirled like a thunderstorm, getting darker by the second. What little light we had from the altar's circle was soon in shade. Even the beasts looked like they wanted to get out of dodge real fast. They sensed something. Something bad.

Behind me, Raffe had covered his ears and was twisting and turning like he'd been possessed. Which, in a way, was his natural state. This was different, though. His eyes were flashing wildly—the djinn was winning. But why?

A deep rumble shot through the ground beneath us, and the last of the beasts went running. If they were scared, then something was coming. Something we probably didn't want to be around for. I couldn't even see Harley anymore—the black mist had shrouded her completely. But I could still hear her voice muttering in the eye of the storm.

It hit me like a bullet to the head: this kind of Chaos magic was dark and ancient. I could feel the power of it prickling my arms into gooseflesh. Even Harley's voice had changed. It was deeper, with an eerie echo that sent invisible ants racing up my spine. She was calling on something. No, not something... some*one*.

Erebus...

Yeah, one of us should really have been trying to stop her. And yet, it was like we were frozen to the ground. My legs had turned to logs. We were in his realm, and he was holding us prisoner. I knew the stakes when calling on Erebus. He'd want to have the biggest selection so he could handpick whose life he was going to take in return for being summoned. Sure, we were fresh out of options, but this was madness.

Still, that didn't make it any less impressive. *So she can summon Children of Chaos, too?* I'd had no idea. And I honestly had no clue how she was even doing this right now. Spells of this magnitude required a Grimoire at least. But she was flying solo, the words running out of her mouth as if they were an ingrained part of her. *You're starting to get annoying, Sis.* There was so much more to this girl than met the eye, even after spending a whole damned week with her. I knew when to give up, but defeat didn't seem to be in her vocabulary.

I hope you know what you're getting yourself into. It wasn't like she could read my mind, but I tried to will my thoughts into her head. This was pure insanity. There was no other way to describe it. Even Katherine had paused in shock. It should've been satisfying to see horror on her face, but her expression was mirrored on all our faces. And if Katherine thought it was mad, then it had to be beyond the realms of Whackville.

Wade looked just as horrified. "This isn't like the last time."

Santana shook her head. "She never got this far before."

"And you didn't think to stop her?" I stared at them in disbelief.

"How? Can you move?" Santana shot back.

"No, but that's not the point. Did you stop her before?"

"Well… yeah." Santana frowned.

"So why didn't you just do what you did last time?" I could hear the fear in my voice.

"I couldn't," Santana whispered. It looked like her Orishas were a no-go here. Even they had the sense to keep away from Erebus's freaking otherworld.

Come on, you clever girl. I turned back to Harley, equal parts terrified and curious.

I tried to push my foot forward, but it wouldn't budge. The swirling vortex of black fog had begun to grow limbs. Harley had already gone too far with the summoning spell. It was too late to stop her.

Erebus manifested from the depths of the stormy tornado, seeming to come from inside Harley herself. As he floated in midair, he sucked all the dark mist into himself, puffing himself up like one of those waggly men outside trashy car dealerships. He got bigger and bigger, until he was towering over us all in one massive, rippling shadow. Red eyes glowered out of a shapeless face like seething embers. *Ah, so that's why the djinn is freaking out.* These dudes were tied together in some way. Erebus, the fearless wrangler of the world's djinns. Spreading his disharmony across the globe, one demon at a time.

"Erebus, I have summoned you to your realm." Harley bowed her head, her body shining with sweat. I guessed summoning really took it out of a person, even a supercharged hero of a person. Her whole body was shaking, but her voice was strong, and it still carried that weird echo.

"I noticed." Erebus's sarcastic voice boomed from all around him. How else was he going to talk when he didn't have any visible lips? Still, the volume of it swept toward us in a wave of cold, powerful air.

"I know there's a price for performing this spell," Harley went on, struggling against the might of his voice. "I'd like to offer Katherine Shipton's life in exchange for summoning you."

Oh, you beauty! Now it made sense. She wasn't risking one of our lives, she was offering Katherine up to him on a silver platter. And, being a Child of Chaos, he'd be all too eager to gobble up the opportunity. This was a win-win. If he had a legitimate excuse to end Katherine, that took them all off the hook. No contest. No challenge. None of them having to give up their spot to a jumped-up mortal.

"Katherine Shipton?" Erebus's voice bellowed.

"Yes. Her life for summoning you," Harley replied.

It was so beautiful, I could've cried. And the look on Katherine's face was priceless. I wished I had a camera so I could have captured it. It'd definitely have helped me through a lot of sleepless nights. Katherine looked like she was trying to get away from the altar, but the same thing freezing us was freezing her, too. *Oh, this is just too freaking good!*

"You devious little—" Katherine started to speak, the sound silenced as a shiver of fiery light shot through Erebus's shadowy center. A boom like a thundercrack ricocheted through the otherworld. From his misty form, a black tendril shot out like an octopus arm. And it was heading straight for Katherine.

The shadowy end curved into a blade, the sharp, mystical point slashing right across Katherine's chest.

"A delicious specimen." A chuckle echoed from Erebus's throat. "I'll savor this one."

Blood sprayed out like a crimson fountain. It doused Naima, who was still curled on the ground, and spurted out so far and so fast that it splattered across Harley's startled face. The entire Rag Team flinched, myself included. In that moment, I felt some movement in my legs as Erebus's focus turned solely on his prize. However, the freezing thing seemed to have stopped working on Katherine and Naima, too. Naima leapt upward to try and stop Erebus from boring down on Katherine again.

Harley wiped the blood from her eyes and sprinted forward. She had her palms raised. I realized why, a second after she started running. Katherine had her palms raised, too. A surge of Telekinesis shot out of Katherine's hands, gripping the last of Tess's spirit and drawing it toward her like a chameleon snatching its prey. There was no way Harley could get there before Katherine swallowed her last bite. She was too late. We all were.

"You'll pay for that." Katherine smirked. The last of Tess's misted spirit entered her mouth. With her arms raised in triumph, she lit up like a lightbulb, from the inside out. The ragged gash across her chest disappeared, leaving smooth skin behind. Tess's spirit had boosted her already-powerful healing abilities to superhuman levels.

She'd done it. The bitch had done it. Even with Erebus slashing her chest, she'd done it.

"Oh, that feels good," she purred.

Naima let out a howling roar as Erebus's bladed tendril slashed across her back. She went sprawling to the ground, her claws gripping the shattered tiles around the altar.

"Naima!" Katherine gasped. Her arms were still raised in victory.

"I will not have my gift stolen!" Erebus, clearly annoyed now, sent out an infantry of tendrils. The misty fronds wrapped around Naima's body, pulling tight. They were crushing her. Her eyes were already bulging out of her sockets, and her claws dug deeper in an attempt to hold on.

Katherine immediately stopped her proverbial victory lap. As heartless as Katherine was, there was an unbreakable bond between Purge beasts and their creators. And it worked both ways. Right now, I could tell that Katherine was terrified for her lieutenant.

"Naima? Naima, fight him!" she urged.

But Erebus wasn't letting up. He squeezed his tendrils tighter. I grimaced as I heard bones crack. Blood sputtered out of Naima's mouth. He squeezed again, Naima's chest collapsing in on itself. More blood splashed out onto the tiles, and Naima's eyes stared vacantly forward. Katherine might have been glow central, but the light had gone out in Naima.

"NO!" Katherine screamed. With her palms up, she sent out a lasso of Telekinesis, combined with a flurry of Fire, to chase away the shadowed tendrils that held her mangled lieutenant. Erebus's fronds retreated for a second. It was long enough for Katherine to grip Naima and pull her to safety. Not that it mattered now. It didn't seem likely that Naima would pull through. Purge beast or not.

As Erebus rippled in the air, no doubt judging his next move, Katherine turned to look at me and Harley. Her eyes narrowed in brimming rage.

"I will rain down hell on the pair of you, until you realize that you chose so very, very wrong," Katherine spat. "As the death count rises, and you bury friend, after friend, after friend, you'll realize that it's all your fault. Look at them now, look at your friends, and remember their faces. Because you're going to watch them all die, one after the other, until there's only the two of you left."

"We'll keep coming after you, Katherine." Harley raised her palms, gathering a fireball between them. She unleashed hell, sending orb after orb of crackling flames, but Katherine swept the onslaught away. She was still glowing from Tess's spirit, her energy at its peak. Despite that, however, it looked like my mother was actually struggling. The fireballs were getting closer and closer to her face with every blast, her hands moving frantically to try and push the fireballs away. *Harley really is strong.* I'd never seen anyone break through Katherine's defenses before.

"Don't you get it? You can't beat me," Katherine replied, in between ducking Harley's energy blows. "You've tried everything, and you keep falling at the last hurdle. I wish you'd get it into your thick skulls. I tell you what, why don't I spell it out for you, nice and slow? I'm. Always. Going. To. Win."

"Throw everything you have at us, and we'll just keep coming. Why don't I spell it out for you, nice and slow? You. Won't. Win!" Harley roared back, firing a torrent of liquid Fire at Katherine. It narrowly missed her face, her eyes flying wide. She rallied, though, sending up a shield of bronzed energy.

"If you were my daughter, I'd have had you smothered in your sleep when you were a baby. Who knows? Maybe there's still time." Katherine chuckled coldly, before closing her eyes. Foreign words tumbled out of her mouth, but it took a moment for me to realize what she was saying. Understanding bombarded my head, but there was one bit I'd missed.

Oh, you've got to be kidding me! It was an Ancient Greek spell, older than any books. Katherine had told me about it once, after she'd torn it from the Librarian's lips. It meant, more or less: "I bind myself to you and spare my life in the act. I cannot be your reward. In return, I will do your bidding. As you wish. But another must fall so that I may rise. I offer you the soul of so-and-so in my stead."

I'd missed the name of the life she'd offered in return, but I wasn't taking any chances. It couldn't have been Naima. Even though she'd been crushed, her claws were still raking at the tiles. The beast wasn't dead yet.

"Harley, get away from there!" I bellowed at the top of my lungs. Katherine had said she wanted Harley alive, but on impulse, she'd have Harley killed. She'd always been a "consequences later" sort of psychopath.

"Not yet, Finch! Not until she's dead!" she snapped back, sending another torrent of Fire at Katherine. This time, it was Katherine's shield that wasn't strong enough to deflect Harley's power. The crackling blaze tore right through the forcefield, grazing Katherine's shoulder and prompting her to feint out of the way. The Rag Team weren't immobilized anymore and were joining in the fight. They sent wave after wave of their abilities at Katherine, with Tatyana and Santana hurling projectiles. Their spirits had abandoned them in this place, forcing them to turn to practical manpower. Well, womanpower. But it was hopeless. The idiots didn't realize the danger they were in. Mother dearest had left me with no other choice.

"Katherine made a deal, Harley. She's negated the one you made. I don't know who she's chosen instead to satisfy Erebus. If we stay here, one of us dies!" I yelled. Naima was still breathing, and there were no assurances that Katherine would sacrifice her lieutenant to Erebus. No matter how desperate she was. She'd rather have seen one of us fall first.

Harley stared at me, a stream of Fire sputtering out in her hands. "What?"

"Clever, Finch. Looks like you learned *something*, after all." Katherine smiled.

Harley's face changed. She knew I was telling the truth. Her eyes sought Jacob out in the gloom. "Jacob, NOW!" Harley sprinted toward the Rag Team as a portal tore open directly behind Jacob. Our ticket out of here.

"I accept your offer," Erebus boomed.

As Erebus's shadow swept toward us, I, Harley, and the rest of the team barreled toward the portal.

"Who is it, Finch? Who did she pick?" Harley screamed in my ear as we ran for our lives.

"Would you shut up and get through the portal! I'll explain later!" I shoved her with my full weight into the portal, watching the gaping mouth eat her up. Next, I turned to the Rag Team. "What are you all staring at? Get through the freaking portal!" While they were standing around, catching flies, Erebus was rushing toward us in a seething mass of darkness and Katherine was grinning like the maniac she was. She hadn't just won, she was making a clean sweep.

Jumping into action at last, the rest of the Rag Team raced toward the portal. Erebus had spiraled up into the air, forging a thunderstorm of deadly tendrils. They shot down like black lightning, jabbing at the others as they sprinted for their lives. One caught Raffe in the shoulder, but he managed to tear himself free. Behind them, in the shadows, the monsters were rallying to the cry of their master. They charged at the fleeing crew, roaring and snapping their jaws with excitement.

"FASTER!" I screamed. I had no idea why I was hanging around to make sure this bunch of fools were safe. They meant nothing to me. Trouble was, they meant something to Harley. If I abandoned them here, she'd never have forgiven me. *Yeah, we might want to rethink this whole emotion thing.* I was certain I'd been better off when I had no heart.

Shinsuke was the last to run up, fighting off the gathering creatures with his blades. As he lopped off the head of a dog-like beast that was about to leap toward us, something swiped at his leg and dragged him down. I lunged forward to help him, but Jacob grabbed me by the wrist. I tried to pull free of him, but his face was set with a determined look. Where Shinsuke had fallen, the beasts flooded around him. A moment later, I couldn't see him anymore. Just jaws and claws and spurting blood.

"You can't help him," Jacob shouted. With a surprisingly sharp tug, he pulled us both into the portal, the gaping hole snapping shut behind us. As I tumbled back through the darkness, the last things I saw were the glinting eyes of a thousand beasts and the slithering tendrils of Erebus, intent on a taste of blood.

I landed flat on my ass in the infirmary. Jacob lay sprawled beside me. Krieger and Isadora were staring at us, worried. Hauling myself up, I checked to make sure everyone was accounted for. *Yep, the Muppet Babies are all here... all but one.* His absence stood out, even though he hadn't been with us very long. You tended to miss the guy with swords on his back, but nobody else had realized it yet. Instead, Harley was glowering at me. Not exactly the thanks I'd expected after saving her.

"Is everyone o—" Isadora moved forward, but Harley interrupted her.

"What did you shove me for?" she barked at me.

"Like I said, Katherine made Erebus an offer. You'd have wasted time making sure everyone was through. I did the job for you." *Mostly.* I kept my tone curt. I wasn't going to be berated for doing the right thing.

"What offer did she make? How did she even do that?"

I gritted my teeth. "She saved herself by offering someone else up in return. It's an ancient spell. Nearly forgotten. It vetoes Erebus's killing power. And Katherine just put someone else in the guillotine, instead of her. Trouble is, I didn't hear who she said. She was talking too fast, and, what can I say, my Ancient Greek is a little rusty."

Harley and her Muppet Babies gaped at me like a bunch of owls. "She really did that?"

"You think I'm lying?"

"No... I just... I didn't think that was possible." Her hands were shaking.

"Well, it is. Like I said, old, dusty-ass spell. One from the Librarian's private stock."

Harley glanced at the others, stunned into silence.

"So it could be any of us?" Tatyana asked.

"Yep, that's about the crux of it." I shuddered at the word "Crux." It was too soon to even think about that. Tess had been gobbled up like misty soup. That memory wasn't going to go away anytime soon. "I think she might have sacrificed Shinsuke to Erebus." Shinsuke falling to the beasts would have been enough to satisfy the Child of Chaos. My throat constricted at the memory of Shinsuke getting dragged down by those creatures. It wouldn't leave me for a long time, even though I hadn't known him very well. Nobody deserved to go like that, unless it was Katherine.

"Shinsuke?" Harley looked around frantically. *Yeah, as if he's just going to pop up.* Humor was the only way I knew how to deal with something like this. It was horrible and awful, but I didn't know how to do anything other than joke.

"He didn't make it. He got pulled under by the monsters," I said, shooting Jacob a cold look. There might not have been time, but I knew we could have tried harder. Yeah, I hadn't known him too well, but that didn't mean I'd wanted to see him die. He'd have been a useful addition to the Rag Team. He was a Nomura, after all.

Harley's face crumpled. "What do you mean?"

"I mean exactly what I'm saying. He didn't make it back. He was fighting those creatures, and... well, he didn't make it to the portal in time." She didn't need the gory details from me. "Those beasts would've come pouring in after us if we hadn't left when we did. And, as far as I could tell, Shinsuke wasn't ever going to make it. They got him." I didn't want her blaming me, either.

Harley sank to her knees and held her head in her hands. "He's dead?"

"I think it's pretty likely, yeah." I wanted to say something to make her feel better, but what could make this better? Nothing. She'd wanted him to join the Rag Team for a reason, and now she was on the edge of tears because he was gone. I didn't like seeing her brought low, for any reason. Especially since I was the one who'd broken the news.

Her shoulders shook as the tears came. I wanted to comfort her, but I held back. Instead, Wade sank down beside her and put his arm around her. She leaned into his chest, bitter sobs racking her chest. She clung to him like he was the last life raft on a sinking ship. Everyone stared. It was impossible not to. But nobody could've understood what she was feeling. I did, to some extent. She felt responsible for this. She'd listened to Katherine's diatribe, and, despite herself, she'd bought into it. One ally buried. How many more would she have to see die? I wanted to tell her not to listen. I wanted to tell her that this wasn't on her. But the words stuck in my throat. Years of learning how to bottle up my feelings kept them there.

"We failed," she whispered. "We failed, and Katherine won. This was all for nothing. My mom, Shinsuke, Tess... they all died for nothing."

Come on, Finch. Grow some freaking balls! Don't just watch her heart break. I dug my nails into my palms. This wasn't going to be easy. Outpourings weren't exactly my strong suit.

"Pack it in, Harley." *Okay, not the best start.* "Pity isn't going to get us anywhere. This isn't a failed mission. It's a failed battle in a war that hasn't been won yet. And let me tell you something, we've got Katherine on the ropes. We made her crap her pants today. Do you know how often that happens? Never." I took a breath, realizing everyone was gaping at me. "I know you feel like hell, but this isn't over. And, if you want to make sure that Tess, Shinsuke, and your mother haven't died in vain, as well as every single person Katherine has killed, then you need to dust yourself off. Now. We can mourn when all of this is done. And if you dare listen to a word Katherine said back there, then you aren't the girl I thought you were. This is *all* her doing. Not yours. Not any of ours."

Harley looked up with red-rimmed eyes. "What if she was right?

What if she *is* going to win this? What if we can't fight her, no matter what we throw at her?"

"She's all talk, Harley," I replied. "So what if she's even more powerful? You've got more Chaos in your pinky finger than the rest of us combined. You broke through her Telekinesis *and* her forcefields. Do you know how many people I've seen do that? Zero. Well, one now. She's going to get cocky from all this energy she's sucked up. And that means she'll start making mistakes." I paused, steeling myself for the next truth bomb I was about to drop. A tough one for me. "Plus, this wasn't a completely failed mission."

"What do you mean? Of course it was."

I shook my head. "Not to me. I got you back. That matters to me... I guess."

Harley gave me a watery smile.

Wade smiled, too. "He's right, Harley. We've still got each other. We're still fighting. We're not going to give up, not when there are two rituals still to go. Why would we give that evil witch the satisfaction?"

Man, that's what I should've said.

"But where do we even go from here?" Harley murmured. I could see her rallying. That fighting spirit wasn't dead yet. She was a Merlin, after all, same as me. Finch Merlin sounded a hell of a lot cooler than Finch Shipton. Plus, it didn't come with all the added subtext of murderers and psychopaths.

"She'll be coming for Echidna next," Isadora said.

I shook my head. "Not if we can find Katherine first. Take the fight to her, so to speak."

"How?" Harley replied. Her voice was already getting stronger.

Picking up a cloth from one of the nearby tables, I walked over to Harley and sank down in front of her. With a gentle hand, I wiped the blood from her face. "Don't want you looking like an extra in a slasher movie," I said. "Wait... we can use this blood to trace Katherine. Right, Krieger?" I glanced at the anxious doctor, who'd been quiet this whole time.

He nodded and took a jar down from one of the shelves. "Yes, we can likely pick up Katherine's Chaos signature based on that sample and utilize the magical detector to find her, if the device becomes operational." He held the jar out, and I dropped the bloody piece of cloth inside.

"See, Harley, this isn't over. Not by a long shot."

She smiled. "You're right. It isn't. This won't be over until the psycho lady sings."

"My thoughts exactly." I held her gaze, grateful to have my sister back.

FORTY-FIVE

Harley

The following morning, after a restless night's sleep, we gathered again in the Luis Paoletti Room, using Alton's secret hallways to reach it undetected. Finch had spent the night in the storage cupboard of the infirmary, with Krieger keeping guard in case anyone came in unexpectedly. I remembered falling asleep in Wade's arms after trying to watch a movie to take our minds off things, but he'd been gone by the time I woke up. I'd been a little disappointed, wondering if I'd done something wrong, but he'd come to get me at seven on the dot, a smile on his face. I sat beside him now as we grouped around the main table.

Although Shinsuke hadn't been part of our group for very long, I still felt his absence. He'd died helping us, and the knowledge that he'd never get to see his father again stuck like a fishbone in my throat. We'd held a sort of vigil for him before heading to bed the previous night, lighting a candle in the infirmary chapel for him. It wouldn't bring him back, but it served as an honorable reminder of what he might have been.

Alton had joined us, his face a picture of anxiety as I relayed everything that had gone on in Erebus's otherworld, and in the last week during our time at the cult. I told him everything, even the stuff he'd already heard, just to make sure we were all on the same page. There was a whole lot of doom and gloom to get through, and none of us had even had breakfast yet.

"So, in a nutshell, Katherine completed the third ritual," I said. "We need to make sure she can't steal Echidna from the Bestiary. We have to let the National Council know what's going on, too."

We were in over our heads, at this point, and I wasn't too proud to admit that. We would've informed the National Council ourselves, but Garrett was AWOL and not answering his phone, and Alton had been otherwise engaged with Levi when we got back last night, his phone also going straight to voicemail.

"We thought we'd stopped Katherine when Harley released Hester's spirit, which would've meant Echidna was safe, but now... well, that didn't exactly go as planned," Wade added.

"But we *did* manage to gather some intel from the cult, and we freed... never mind." Finch sat back in his chair. The news of Shinsuke was still pretty raw for all of us. I hadn't been there in his last moments, but I knew Finch must have seen more than he was letting on. And if even he wasn't willing to go into details, I reasoned I didn't want to know what had actually happened to him.

Alton frowned. "You mentioned summoning Erebus... Since when have you been able to use summoning spells?"

"*That's* what you're focusing on?" Finch snorted. "Bigger fish, Alton. Bigger fish."

"It happened around the same time I learned I could read from unfinished Grimoires," I replied, as if it were no biggie.

Finch nearly fell off his chair. "You can do what now?"

"You heard me, Finch."

"Katherine would need a bib if she heard that; she'd be drooling all over herself." Finch chuckled, but I wasn't in the mood to laugh. Katherine had stolen any humor I had left.

"But how could you summon Erebus without a Grimoire, finished or unfinished?" Alton eyed me warily, like I was a curious animal in a zoo.

"It's from my parents' Grimoire. Somehow, I can read their spells, even without being near the book," I explained. Finch's eyes were practically bugging out of his head.

"You continue to surprise me, Harley." Alton smiled kindly. "Between that, this Purge beast control you have, and the rest of your abilities, it's no wonder that Katherine has decided she wants to use you. Not that she's going to have the opportunity, of course."

"We could really use your help on this," I said. "The National Council will listen to you, if you let them know what's happened. And, if they have any ideas, we'd like to know about them."

"We'll definitely have to notify the authorities, as you suggest," he replied. "The National Council, the local council, and the security services. And we'll have to let Tobe know that Katherine is coming for Echidna. We don't have to mention your involvement at all; we can just say that news of the third ritual's completion came from an internal source. As Shinsuke is no longer with us, we may be able to use him in that capacity. I don't want to make him the scapegoat, but if I can get the National Council to see that he was on our side, it might give him the honor he deserves, even after his passing."

I nodded. "I don't like the idea of it any more than you do, but that might be our best option. Say you intercepted a call that he was making to his father, and he revealed everything to you."

"That may work," Alton replied. "However, there is the problem of Finch to deal with, as well as informing the authorities. You need to get him back to Purgatory as soon as you can to reduce the risk of his duplicate failing."

Santana made a small, strained sound. "Yeah, about that—I've got no idea how much longer I can hold both at the same time. My concentration slipped a *lot* in Tartarus. I can still feel them, and they're doing their own thing, but it's only a matter of time before my Orishas can't keep it up anymore."

"I agree, it's getting way too risky," I said.

Finch cleared his throat. "No way. I'm not going back there."

I narrowed my eyes at him. "What?"

"I'm not going back to that place. I've gotten a taste for freedom, and I'm not giving that up for a glass box and a cold shower." He smirked. "Besides, I figure I've proved myself enough. I'm not jumping through a bazillion hoops to get out the 'official' way." He made bunny ears around the word, and the tension spiked in the room. This hadn't been part of the agreement. Now, everyone was staring at him.

"Finch, you *have* to go back," I said. "We agreed."

"Things change." He shrugged. "You can keep my copy there. If you really want to, you could sneak the Orisha out and make it look like I broke out. That'd give me some legend status. They'd have to add me to the handful of people who've escaped that hellhole. Not that I care what you do about it. I'm just telling you I'm not going back."

"Finch!"

"*Finch*," he mimicked, with a smile. "Listen, Katherine is still on the loose. I refuse to be in a cell while she's free and driving a bulldozer through everything."

I stared at him. "If Santana's Orisha fails, and you *aren't* where you're supposed to be, then we're all royally screwed. You'll put everything we've worked toward at risk. Come on, Finch, you know you have to do this."

He shrugged. "It's easy for you to just dictate what I should do—you haven't been there. You haven't lived in those glass cells. If you had, you'd be backing me right now."

"Yeah, well, I'm going to find out what it's like sooner than you think, if you don't do as you're told!" I snapped.

"Not my problem. Unless they drag me back themselves, I'm not going."

Santana slumped forward on the table, sweat glistening on her brow. She was breathing heavily, rasping in air. Raffe hurried to help her, shaking her by the shoulders until she blinked her eyes open again. She looked really pale, her expression dazed.

"Santana? Santana, what's the matter?" Raffe urged.

"My... Orishas. I felt something."

"What did you feel?" Wade jumped in.

"Someone... Someone killed the Orisha in Alaska," she gasped, pain etched on her face. No sooner had she spoken than a blinding flash exploded in front of her. As the sudden blast faded, I saw an orb of bluish light hover above the table for a moment, before it frantically dove inside Santana.

"What's going on?" I asked, my heart pounding in my chest.

Santana shook her head slowly. "I... I'm sorry. I don't know."

It became clear a moment later, when a second flash erupted in front of Santana and whizzed inside her. If the Orisha in Alaska was dead, then that meant only one thing—that second bluish orb was the Orisha from Purgatory, and Finch's duplicate was gone.

This was all going horribly wrong. And after the gigantic failure of the last week, I'd had just about enough of things taking a turn for the worst.

The door to the Luis Paoletti room burst open, and Leonidas Levi stormed in, flanked by armed security magicals and a sheepish O'Halloran. All of their Esprits were lit up, itching for a fight, with Atomic Cuffs poised and ready.

I stared at them all, wide-eyed. There was no way they could have known where to find us. But they had. And we weren't getting out of here without a serious fight.

"You are all a disgrace to the SDC! Look at you, you selfish, nasty, vile little wretches!" Levi bellowed, beyond furious. "I give you chance after chance, and you think you can pull the wool over my eyes? You appall me, every single one of you." He turned to me. "But *you!* You think you can just do whatever you like, with no consequences. Well, that's about to change. Not even I can overlook breaking a criminal out of Purgatory. Speaking of which, it looks like you've saved us the trouble of tracking this spiteful little creature down." He sneered at Finch.

"H-How?" I managed.

He snorted. "It looks like I'm not the only one you've made an enemy of with your dangerous games. I received an anonymous tip that the real Finch wasn't in Purgatory anymore, and I had the officers there look into it. I knew you had an evil streak in you, Harley Merlin—how could you not, considering where you came from?—but I didn't think you could stoop *this* low. Then again, what else should I have expected? You're just as bad as your half-brother, no doubt. And both of you were stupid enough to get caught in the act!"

"Katherine..." Finch muttered, his eyes flashing with anger. "Spiteful bitch."

"A nice trick, using those advanced duplicates. I wouldn't have been able to tell the difference, but then, I don't associate with criminals—I don't see the intricate details that those duplicates missed. But the officers did. Oh yes, they knew right away!" Levi spat. "When the officers confronted it, that Orisha had the decency to float away, which led us right here. The officers wanted to capture it, but I'm very glad they didn't. If they had, you might have had the chance to weasel your way out of here, and we wouldn't want that, now, would we?"

I glanced at Santana, who was slumped against Raffe, tears streaming down her face. I had no experience of it, personally, but I figured losing an Orisha had to be a painful ordeal. They were part of her, and she'd just had one torn away.

"I'm sorry," she whispered.

Levi glowered. "As well you might be, Ms. Catemaco. You are an accomplice in this, which makes you as culpable as these two, in my book." He jabbed a finger at Finch and me. "At any point, you might have said no or come to me with information. I would've protected you. But you chose them instead, and you'll be suitably punished for that."

I stood my ground. "You leave her out of this."

"You should learn when to shut your mouth," he snapped back. "You have nowhere to run to now. Anything you say will only make it worse for you. Not that I'm banking on a lenient sentence. In fact, I'd be inclined to insist on the harshest punishment they can offer. Then you might learn your lesson, Harley!"

"This isn't possible," I mumbled, more to myself than anyone else.

"Oh, I can assure you it is *very* possible." Levi snorted. "I bet you thought you had everything all tied up with a neat little bow, didn't you? This must be quite the shock, to find out you aren't nearly as clever as you think you are. Well, let me tell you how surprised *I* was when I received a call, a few minutes ago, telling me that someone had killed Harley Merlin in Alaska. Do you know, I almost shed a tear; I was so shocked and distraught that someone had done something awful to you, because I was foolish enough to believe you were trying to better yourself. And then, while the seminar leader was still on the phone, I heard him scream and tell me you'd disintegrated into thousands of bluish sparks and faded away."

Crap...

"It hit me then, what you'd been up to. I remembered how those last duplicates had disintegrated. It wasn't hard to put two and two together." He sneered at me. "Whoever gave me that anonymous tip should get a bottle of champagne, because that was the cherry on top. That was the moment of absolute certainty. Indeed, it gave me precisely what I needed to see you put away, for the rest of your life, where you can't harm anyone, ever again. You've finally proven yourself to be the real criminal that you've always been. I should've known you'd turn out exactly like your father."

Anger and confusion bubbled up inside me as I fought to speak. "You don't understand, Levi. You've got it all wrong. Yes, I broke Finch out of Purgatory, but it was only so that we could—"

Levi slammed his fists down on the nearby table. "I don't want to hear another word out of your mouth! You have said quite enough. Anything else you want to say, you can say at your trial, before they haul you away to prison." He shot a glance at O'Halloran, who still looked uneasy. "O'Halloran, have your men arrest everyone and take them to the cells. There will be an investigation as soon as the proper authorities arrive, and it will end with these disgusting Shiptons in Purgatory. I would stake my life on it. You have no cards left to play, no tricks left to pull, and nowhere left to run. Nowhere."

I glanced at the secret door we'd come through, knowing there was one place we could run to. But could we get there before the security personnel apprehended us? Even if they didn't, they'd chase us through the coven until they caught us. Levi had us cornered, and we were going to have to fight with everything we had to get out of this.

FORTY-SIX

Harley

W ade stepped in front of me, his arm across my chest. "You aren't taking her, or us, anywhere. Not until you hear us out. You might change your mind if you knew what we'd been through and why we did what we did."

"We deserve the right to speak. I assure you, you will want to hear what we have to say," Tatyana added. My heart swelled at the sight of my friends forming a line in front of me, even if I knew it was useless. Even Isadora had joined the line, though I noticed Krieger and Alton kept back. Their fate was less certain, but if Levi was involved, it didn't look too good for them, either.

"This is bull, Director Levi." Dylan put his Herculean might between the Rag Team and Levi.

"What harm is there in listening to what we have to say?" Astrid chimed in, already tapping away discreetly on her Smartie. I didn't know what she was doing, but I doubted any of the skills in her extensive armory could get us out of this fix.

"You don't need to do this, Father," Raffe spoke, his tone menacing. Santana was still leaning on him, utterly heartbroken, and I didn't know who was in charge anymore—Raffe or the djinn. It had been touch and go between them in Tartarus, and I got the feeling that Raffe had come back with the djinn nudging his way to one hand on the steering wheel.

Levi scowled. "The less I hear from you, the better. I might have expected such deeds from this unruly mob, but I thought you would have been sensible enough to stay out of it. I can see that your actions here are my failings as a father. I ought to have kept my eye on you at all times. With that *thing* inside you, I should have put you under lock and key years ago."

Raffe snarled. "You'd have liked that, wouldn't you?"

"Director Levi, we should talk about this privately." Alton stepped in before the djinn got any ideas. "Why don't we go to your office and discuss all of this in a less tense atmosphere? It will make sense to you, once you've heard the truth of the matter. Come now, we should be civil about this. There's no need for Atomic Cuffs and armed guards."

O'Halloran glanced at Levi. "Sir?"

"Arrest them now." His voice was eerily calm.

With a reluctant nod, O'Halloran and the security personnel advanced on the Rag Team. There was nothing I could do to stop them, not without getting us into even more trouble. I doubted "fighting a horde of security magicals and taking out the director of the SDC" would look good on my résumé. Still, that didn't lessen my desire to do *something*... anything, to get us out of this.

The Chaos in my veins pulsated with anticipation, begging to be used. *I can't feed you right now, Darkness.* I was pretty sure my mother hadn't meant for me to go all Rambo with my Dark side, despite her warning to feed it whenever it was hungry.

"Hey, get your hands off me!" I snapped, as the security personnel strode right up to me and slapped a pair of Atomic Cuffs on my wrists, doing the same to Finch. Levi wanted us first, by the looks of it. I expected to feel the sapping energy of the Cuffs at work, but they burned instead.

I gathered my Chaos into myself and fed the energy down my arms. It sputtered against the Cuffs, pressure gathering beneath them like a bubble. I pushed again, feeling the connectors crack, and the sapping power of the Cuffs drifted away harmlessly. It looked like I was wearing them, but I could still feel my energy brimming in my veins. It wasn't stopping me the way it should. *Good.*

On the other hand, it looked like the rest of the Rag Team were coming to a pretty grim conclusion, judging by the resignation coming off them in waves. The security personnel clapped Atomic Cuffs on Alton's wrists next, and then Isadora's. My aunt looked back at me with a reassuring smile. She'd definitely been in worse scrapes than this. I just hoped she could come up with some way to escape, now she had the Cuffs on. She wouldn't be able to use her Portal Opening abilities with those things sapping her. I didn't want anyone spending the rest of their life in Purgatory because of me, although that was probably a little self-centered. They hadn't gone to Tartarus and plotted the cult infiltration for me. They'd done it for the world, and the terrible things Katherine would do to it otherwise.

I almost lashed out at a guard as he yanked Santana out of Raffe's arms and slapped the Cuffs on her wrists. I noticed Raffe about to spring for the guy, when Wade shot out his arm and held him back, with a slow shake of his head. The red flash in Raffe's eyes subsided. Neither Raffe nor the djinn was stupid. They knew how dire the situation was, and punching security personnel would only add to our sentence. Whatever that might be.

One of the guards was just about to clamp a pair of Cuffs over Tatyana's wrists, when the ground shook violently. A few of the security personnel toppled over like tin soldiers, while the one who'd tried to cuff Tatyana staggered backward. I glanced at Wade in alarm. There was a very slim chance this was just a regular old earthquake, but I knew all too well that the interdimensional bubble wasn't affected by that sort of thing. Which left one horrifying possibility…

The SDC was under attack.

As soon as the thought crossed my mind, another shudder rippled through the Luis Paoletti Room, knocking me back into the table. Wade had his arm around my shoulders before I even knew what had happened. Another shock ricocheted through the floor and the walls, the savage vibrations shaking the beds. Jars and vials of spell ingredients tumbled from the surrounding shelves.

Alarms blared all around us, red lights flashing. The security magicals' radios crackled with terrified voices, an underscore of screams ripping through the speakers. I dodged a falling jar of sharp tools, a few jeweled knives thudding into the table where my torso had just been.

"What's happening?" I hissed at Wade.

"I think she's here," he replied, confirming my own guess.

A sickening rumble tore through the coven, a crack splintering across the floor. The inner windows of the Luis Paoletti Room shattered into a thousand jagged shards. Over the radios, desperate voices cried out for help.

"The Bestiary! It's the Bestiary!" One, solitary voice exploded through the speaker. Time seemed to freeze, all of us staring at the radio where the voice had come from.

Alton paled. "The Bestiary is failing."

Another gut-wrenching rumble shuddered through the room, the bronzed glow of the interdimensional bubble rippling in fractured waves, spitting and sparking like a frayed wire. It was similar to what I'd seen when Jacob accidentally broke the bubble in the training room, but far, far more terrifying. This was on a coven-wide scale, and the cracks were getting wider with each rumble. The walls thrummed with pent-up energy, and that energy had nowhere else to go but out.

I hit the deck as a massive explosion erupted from the far side of the Luis Paoletti Room, blowing right through the decimated door. All the windows and glass jars burst into a waterfall of glinting fragments that skittered across the floor. A huge crevasse opened in the hallway opposite, dragging chairs and tables down into the abyss, where the pressure of the bubble crushed them into nothing. It was like watching a black hole devour a planet, drawing everything around it into the gaping emptiness. Soon, it would reach us.

"We have to get out, now!" I yelled.

For the first time ever, Levi didn't argue with me. He took the lead, rushing out of the office and into the main body of the coven. We followed him, even those of us with Cuffed wrists, leaping over the fissure that was getting wider, dragging more and more things into it. One of the security magicals stumbled at the lip of the hole, teetering for a fleeting moment, before he fell headfirst into the darkness. The sound and sight that followed didn't bear repeating. It was like watching a can get crushed, only that can was made of flesh and bone and had been flattened to a pancake before it dissipated in a flurry of ashes that glinted bronze in the dark pit.

Cuffing us and taking us away didn't matter now, even though a few of the security magicals were keeping a suspicious eye on us as we ran. No doubt they thought we'd done this, too. But this was *all* Katherine's handiwork. It reeked of her.

The corridor beyond the Luis Paoletti Room was far worse. Enormous cracks spider-webbed across the bubble that was holding everything together, with blinding light bursting through them. Sparks jumped toward us in white-hot flecks, the forcefield around the SDC phasing in and out in a way that made my legs turn to jelly. If this thing collapsed, we'd all be crushed inside it, the dimensions colliding in the most horrific way. I could see Balboa Park through one of the sputtering fissures as everything inside the SDC spilled out into the human realm, the bubble trying to divert its energy wherever it could.

In the hallways, screaming people sprinted for their lives, trying desperately to jump the cracks that were opening in the floors. One got sucked out of a gap in the wall. His howl sent a chill up my spine. I had no idea whether he'd been squashed, or he'd simply been spat out into Balboa Park. I hoped it was the latter.

"The kids… oh my God, the kids!" I stared at a group of frightened children huddling together on the opposite side of one of the interdimensional ravines. If I could've leapt to them without being sucked in, I would've. Judging by the way the ravine was devouring the walls and the paintings and the chairs and the carpets, however, I knew I'd never have made it.

At that moment, Bellmore barreled out of the nearby corridor and grabbed the first child by the hand, leading them away in a terrified train. I prayed they'd find a way out of here. There had to be protocols for this type of thing. Glancing at Levi, I started to doubt it. He looked like a lost, scared little boy who'd been backed into a corner by a rabid dog, with no way out. Besides, the exit to the Fleet Science Center was on the opposite side of the coven, and there was an enormous crevasse between us and that exit.

I whirled around as someone grabbed me. It wasn't Wade—he was standing right in front of me, staring in silent shock as the SDC fell.

"There's no time," Finch hissed, his hand tight around my forearm. "We need to fix this before we're all burger patties."

"What do you—" Before I could finish my sentence, Jacob had torn open a portal, and Finch had dragged me through it, leaving the rest of the crew behind. I heard myself scream "Wade!" as the portal snapped shut again, separating us.

"What the hell, Finch?" I roared as we staggered out into the crumbling Bestiary.

He narrowed his eyes, breathing hard. "We need to fix this before this whole place collapses. You're the only one who can stop the Purge beasts from getting out."

I looked toward the towering atrium that shot up the center of the Bestiary. Tobe was curled up on the ground beside it, a trickle of blood meandering from his mouth. It looked like he'd tried to stop it with his bare hands and gotten a nasty shock. I could see his chest still rising and falling, which gave me hope. If Tobe had died trying to save this place, it would've broken me, there and then.

A mass of energy twisted up the wire veins of the atrium. It was going to blow, any minute. And when it did... it was game over, not just for us, but for the rest of the magical world. Covens would collapse all over the world, if they weren't already crumbling.

"Incoming!" Jacob yelled, knocking me to the ground as a gargoyle swooped low over my head.

As I looked up, my hands covering my head, I noticed that the gargoyle wasn't the only monster on the loose. They were all out, running wild in the Bestiary, snarling and snapping at each other in an attempt to gain supremacy.

I got to my feet and pulled off the useless Cuffs. Closing my eyes, I drew in a deep breath. This was going to hurt my ribs, but that was better than the alternative. But first, I had to find the right emotions. I had to get them to feel what I wanted them to feel. With all the terror pulsing through my veins, that wasn't going to be hard. Digging deep, I gathered up a ball of fear and the desire for them to stop and summoned my inner Chaos to boost it. I balled my hands into fists and opened my mouth.

"STOP! Stop, right now, and return to your boxes! Stay there until I say otherwise!" The words boomed out of my chest, my lungs burning as the strange voice erupted from my throat. It wasn't mine, and yet it was a part of me.

Cautiously, I opened my eyes, just in time to see most of the monsters cowering back into their boxes. They looked almost as confused by the surreal scene as I felt. They didn't know why they were doing it; they just knew they had to obey. With their heads bowed, they shuffled into their enclosures, many of them closing the door behind them. It had worked, right when I had needed it to.

"That's what I'm talking about!" Finch whooped.

"Wow..." Jacob stared at me in shock, his face a reflection of the security magicals', the ones who were still standing.

Cheers for that, Katherine. If I'd never gone to the cult, I'd never have learned this skill. Although, it wasn't a complete success. There were still countless boxes left empty, the monsters already gone from the Bestiary. My voice could only reach so far, and I doubted the missing monsters had been able to hear me.

"We need to get to Echidna," I said, already running for the back hall where her box was kept. Jacob and Finch hurried after me. *Please let her be there, please let her be there, please let her be there...* This was the sole reason Katherine was destroying the Bestiary. As I sprinted, I paused for a moment to shake Tobe by the shoulders. He jolted awake, startled.

"What happened?" he asked, rubbing his head.

"The Bestiary was attacked. I got most of the monsters back in their boxes, but you need to flip the switch to lock them."

He frowned. "How?"

"There's no time to explain."

He nodded and jumped to his feet. "I will ensure they remain confined."

Satisfied that those monsters wouldn't get out again, I charged on toward Echidna's private hall, with Jacob and Finch beside me. Behind me, I heard the echo of boots on the Bestiary floor, thudding through the air like the drums of war. Glancing back, I saw black figures running in. It would only be a matter of time before Levi, O'Halloran, and the security magicals got to Echidna's box, too. Everyone knew what was happening here, and everyone knew why. I took one scrap of solace from their militant arrival—if they were here, then that meant the members of the Rag Team were safe.

We powered through the doors to Echidna's hall and sprinted toward the box on the plinth. I got there first, leaping up the steps to the side of her box. I froze as my hand rested on the open door.

Echidna's box was empty.

"She's gone!" Finch barked, smashing his fist into the glass.

"Katherine did it," I whispered, overwhelmed with a million emotions. None of them good. "She got Echidna and let the Bestiary fall. And yet people think she has the magicals' best interests at heart. If they could see this..." I didn't have the energy to finish the sentence. It spoke for itself. Even here, jagged cracks webbed out, showing glimpses of the outside world, the edges fraying as the Bestiary's power ebbed.

I turned as the hall doors opened, and Levi and his men thundered in.

"Stop!" he yelled.

I glanced at Jacob. "He's not capturing us. Not at a time like this."

"Bigger fish, Sis. Am I right?" Finch flashed a worried smile at me.

"Exactly. Much bigger fish." I stared at Levi as he approached. He raised his palms to strike at me, sending a flurry of powerful Telekinesis at me. With anger burning up inside me, giving my Chaos an even sharper edge, I simply swiped it away with my own Telekinesis, which was far stronger than his. Meanwhile, Jacob worked on a portal.

"Don't you dare!" Levi roared, but he was too late.

With a grimace of contempt in Levi's direction, I stepped back into the portal and watched it snap shut on Levi's furious, ridiculous face. He'd forced me to do this. He was forcing me to abandon my team, and Wade. He was the one refusing to look at the bigger picture. The coven and the Bestiary were falling, and all he cared about was capturing me. He'd led me to desperation. Rage twisted like barbed wire in my stomach. If he'd just listened...

FORTY-SEVEN

Harley

I doubled over as I caught my breath, focusing on the wavering head of a daisy in the grass beneath my feet. My heart was still racing after what had just happened, and hatred burned in my chest. Katherine had managed to get her paws on Echidna, and she'd almost destroyed everything in the process. I had no words for just how much I wanted to end her.

For as long as I lived, I never wanted to see the Bestiary like that again. All those people running for their lives, trying to avoid getting crushed to death… I could still hear their shouts for help, could still see the terrified expressions on their faces. And then there was Wade and the rest of the Rag Team. They were still there, at the SDC, dealing with the fallout. While we were… I didn't know where, right now. I was still trying to get my breath back.

Finch and Jacob were beside me, also looking a little unsteady. As I dragged fresh air into my lungs, tinged with the unexpected, mouth-watering scent of barbeque, I took in our surroundings at last. My stomach sank at the sight before me. *Why did you bring us here, Jacob?*

Mr. Smith was manning the grill, while Mrs. Smith had been in the middle of carrying drinks out of the house. She looked as if she might drop them as she stared at us, blank-faced and stunned by our sudden arrival. Ryann was there too, a skull candy cookie halfway to her mouth, frozen in surprise. Plates of cookies covered a patio table, along with a huge cake decorated in bright colors, and flowers and skeleton masks were just about everywhere.

We'd ended up, quite literally, in the Smiths' backyard, slap bang in the middle of a Día de los Muertos celebration. The Smiths had no Mexican in them whatsoever, but they'd take any excuse for a good, old fashioned shindig.

I didn't know whether to sink to my knees in happiness or run for the hills. They'd clearly seen the portal we'd just tumbled out of, and they were going to have questions. Either that, or Mrs. Smith would think she'd put one too many shots of tequila into the punch. I doubted we'd get so lucky.

I had no words. I shot Jacob a hard glare.

He shrugged. "This was the only safe place I could think of!"

"Why, where are we?" Finch muttered. "Mexico?"

"Not quite," I replied. This could only spell trouble. Not just for us, but for the people who'd taken me in and cared for me when I had nobody else. Memories of the Ryder twins bombarded my brain, but I couldn't think about that now. I needed to get my crap together.

Focus, Merlin.

"Harley… is that you?" Mrs. Smith started to move toward us.

"Mrs. Smith, hey." I forced a smile onto my face.

"Harley!" Ryann cried, running over. *Did they see the portal or didn't they?* It was hard to gauge.

I nodded. "Sorry I haven't kept in touch lately. There's been a lot going on."

"But you're here now, and that's what matters," Ryann said, eyeing me suspiciously. I could see she wanted to say something about what she may, or may not, have seen, but she didn't. Was she saving it? Was she trying to figure out what had just happened, trying to make logical sense of it in her non-magical brain? "And who are your friends?" she asked, instead.

"This is Jacob, and this is Finch." I gestured to them, Finch hiding his Cuffed hands beneath his shirt.

Jacob smiled sadly. "Nice to meet you, Mrs. Smith."

"Have we met before...?" she replied, looking even more confused.

"Yo, are those burgers I smell?" Finch glanced at Mr. Smith, who was absently turning patties on the grill.

"You hungry? There's plenty to go around." Ryann was doing her best not to mention the portal. Perhaps they didn't believe their eyes enough to mention it. I just had to hope it stayed that way.

"Yes, help yourself to food and drinks." Mrs. Smith nodded, her eyes fixed on the spot in the air that we'd fallen through. I could see the cogs whirring, like she was still trying to make some sense of it. "Did you just come from—"

"Can I just head to the bathroom real quick?" I cut in. "I'm desperate."

"Of course, Harley. You know where it is," Mrs. Smith replied, her tone distant.

"I could use a trip to the little boys' room, too." Finch smiled tightly. He needed to get those Cuffs off before someone noticed.

"Yeah, me too," Jacob added, his eyes fixed on Mrs. Smith. *Poor guy.*

As a trio, we headed into the empty house. Halfway to the bathroom, I dragged them into the living room, my palms sweating. All around us were the memories of the two years I'd spent here. The comfortable, gray velour couch and the striped blue cushions with the yellow buttons. The TV on the wall, where I'd spent Sunday afternoons watching football with Mr. Smith and Ryann. And the photographs that filled every available space. Me in my high-school graduation gown, a scroll in my hands. Me with Ryann in the backyard, about a week after I first arrived here. Me with all the Smiths, lounging on the beach in the Bahamas. They were happy snapshots of simpler times.

"No offense, Harley, but this doesn't look like the bathroom to me," Finch said.

"Come here." I snatched at Finch's wrists and put my palms across them. I pushed crackling Chaos energy out of my hands and into the

Cuffs, fighting against the surge of their power. I pushed more and more into the metal, overwhelming the connectors until they broke with a satisfying *clink*. I opened my eyes to find Finch and Jacob staring at me. That seemed to be all anyone could do lately. I was like a circus performer.

"You can seriously break these things," Jacob gasped.

"We'd have been pretty screwed if I couldn't," I replied. "Now, Finch, take those off and hide them somewhere."

He did as he was told, sliding the broken Cuffs off and tucking them into his jacket. With a moment to breathe, I fought to gather my senses. "So, boys and girls, here's the pickle we're in. Katherine just completed the third ritual, and now she's dangerously close to completing the fourth, since she just waltzed in and stole friggin' Echidna. Shinsuke Nomura is dead. Thessaly Crux, the mole who was actually *helping* the National Council, is dead. Levi wants us all locked in a box. Tobe nearly died. The Bestiary is collapsing in on itself and taking everything with it. I watched a man get crushed to death like a pancake, and we have no idea where Katherine is. Oh, and my adoptive family is watching us right now, probably thinking I've lost my mind. Did I miss anything?"

Finch smiled. "You missed the part about setting your mom free."

"This is just another day at the office for you, huh?" I didn't know whether to smack him or hug him. He was taking everything so lightly that I couldn't help but feel irritated. Why wasn't he more upset? The covens were crumbling! The magical world was being razed to the ground, fragment by fragment. Unless this was his way of coping with high-pressure situations. Make a joke out of them, and they wouldn't seem so bad, that sort of thing.

Jacob peered nervously at us both as the silence stretched. "Hey, at least the three of us know we're definitely not going to Purgatory. That's got to be a silver lining, right?"

"A very, very thin one," I muttered.

Finch chuckled. "See, Sis? Your determination to get me back into

Purgatory got you a one-way ticket there, too. Either that, or you just couldn't bear to be without me. Is that what this is about?"

"One more word out of you, and I'll have Jacob portal you there myself." I narrowed my eyes at him, and he knew I wasn't kidding. I could see the flicker of concern in his eyes.

"At least we make a good team," he said, daring to say one more thing.

I sighed. "Let's hope so."

I wanted to scream so loud that it would bring the men in white coats. I wanted to pound my fists into the wall until I didn't hurt anymore. I wanted to portal right back to the crumbling SDC and bury myself in Wade's chest. But I couldn't do any of that, not now. I had to focus on the task at hand and take it step by step. As Finch kept saying, we had much bigger fish to deal with. Levi would get Wade and the others out, if only to save his own skin. It was just what happened to them after that, that worried me. Plus, Tobe was up and alert, which hopefully meant he could do something about the Bestiary. We wouldn't know for a while whether it had been totally secured, but I vowed to check all the news channels for any talk about something happening in Balboa Park.

If we went back now, we'd be captured. The three of us were wanted criminals now. That mark would be on our backs wherever we went, but that wasn't going to stop me. Katherine had threatened everything the magical world had built, and she'd tried to crush everything I held dear in one fell swoop. *Just the way she promised.*

But I'd made a promise, too. A promise to all those kids, and magicals, and innocents that Katherine had murdered. A promise to my mom and my dad. A promise to Tess, and Shinsuke. And a promise to the friends I had, whose lives were on the line.

I am coming for you, Katherine. And when I find you, my face will be the last thing you see before I kill you. She hadn't beaten me yet. I was going to keep fighting until I had nothing left to give.

I snapped out of my private thoughts as Ryann ran into the living room, looking worried. "I knew you weren't going to the bathroom."

"It's not what you think," I replied.

"So you didn't just fall out of the sky, then? Did I imagine that?" Ryann looked frantic, like she'd just learned that the laws of physics were a lie. Which was kind of true.

I burst into a fit of sudden hysterics, the laughter bubbling out of me in an unstoppable torrent. *Oh, where on earth do I begin?*

Ready for the next part of Harley's journey?

Dear Reader,

Thank you for reading *Harley Merlin and the Cult of Eris.* I hope you enjoyed it.

Book 7 - ***Harley Merlin and the Detector Fix*** - is available now!

We'll be getting into the head of one of my very favorite characters. Other than that, all I'll say for this book is… expect the unexpected. ;)

Visit www.bellaforrest.net to order your copy.

I'll see you there…

Love,

Bella x

P.S. Sign up to my VIP email list and you'll be the first to know when my next book releases: **www.morebellaforrest.com**

(Your email will be kept 100% private and you can unsubscribe at any time.)

P.P.S. I'd also love to hear from you. Come say hi on Facebook: Facebook.com/BellaForrestAuthor. Or Twitter: @ashadeofvampire. Or Instagram: @ashadeofvampire.

Read more by Bella Forrest

HARLEY MERLIN

Harley Merlin and the Secret Coven (Book 1)

Harley Merlin and the Mystery Twins (Book 2)

Harley Merlin and the Stolen Magicals (Book 3)

Harley Merlin and the First Ritual (Book 4)

Harley Merlin and the Broken Spell (Book 5)

Harley Merlin and the Cult of Eris (Book 6)

Harley Merlin and the Detector Fix (Book 7)

THE GENDER GAME

(Action-adventure/dystopian/romance. Completed series.)

The Gender Game (Book 1)

The Gender Secret (Book 2)

The Gender Lie (Book 3)

The Gender War (Book 4)

The Gender Fall (Book 5)

The Gender Plan (Book 6)

The Gender End (Book 7)

THE GIRL WHO DARED TO THINK

(Action-adventure/romance. Completed series.)

The Girl Who Dared to Think (Book 1)

The Girl Who Dared to Stand (Book 2)

The Girl Who Dared to Descend (Book 3)

The Girl Who Dared to Rise (Book 4)

The Girl Who Dared to Lead (Book 5)

A Blaze of Sun (Book 5)

A Gate of Night (Book 6)

A Break of Day (Book 7)

Series 2: Rose & Caleb's story

A Shade of Novak (Book 8)

A Bond of Blood (Book 9)

A Spell of Time (Book 10)

A Chase of Prey (Book 11)

A Shade of Doubt (Book 12)

A Turn of Tides (Book 13)

A Dawn of Strength (Book 14)

A Fall of Secrets (Book 15)

An End of Night (Book 16)

Series 3: The Shade continues with a new hero...

A Wind of Change (Book 17)

A Trail of Echoes (Book 18)

A Soldier of Shadows (Book 19)

A Hero of Realms (Book 20)

A Vial of Life (Book 21)

A Fork of Paths (Book 22)

A Flight of Souls (Book 23)

A Bridge of Stars (Book 24)

Series 4: A Clan of Novaks

A Clan of Novaks (Book 25)

A World of New (Book 26)

A Web of Lies (Book 27)

A Touch of Truth (Book 28)

An Hour of Need (Book 29)

A Game of Risk (Book 30)

THE SECRET OF SPELLSHADOW MANOR

(Supernatural/Magic YA. Completed series)

The Secret of Spellshadow Manor (Book 1)

The Breaker (Book 2)

The Chain (Book 3)

The Keep (Book 4)

The Test (Book 5)

The Spell (Book 6)

BEAUTIFUL MONSTER DUOLOGY

(Supernatural romance)

Beautiful Monster 1

Beautiful Monster 2

DETECTIVE ERIN BOND

(Adult thriller/mystery)

Lights, Camera, GONE

Write, Edit, KILL

For an updated list of Bella's books, please visit her website: www.
bellaforrest.net

Join Bella's VIP email list and she'll send you an email reminder as soon as her
next book is out. Visit: www.morebellaforrest.com

CPSIA information can be obtained
at www.ICGtesting.com
Printed in the USA
LVHW040804131120
671477LV00003B/11

9 781947 607705